Praise for *The Good Luck Girls*:

'Perfect for fans of Leigh Bardugo's *Six of Crows* and Margaret Atwood's *The Handmaid's Tale* . . . readers will devour this romp set in a fantastical Wild West-style world, filled with a diverse cast of strong female leads.'

– School Library Journal

'Davis creates institutions, systems, and power dynamics with real-world echoes, making the themes timely and resonant.'

– Publishers Weekly

'The gunslinging, hard-riding action of a classic Western is balanced against . . . effective commentary on class and gender to make a story that is by turns heart pounding and thought-provoking.'

– Bulletin of the Center for Children's Books

ALSO BY CHARLOTTE NICOLE DAVIS

The Good Luck Girls

THE
SISTERS
OF
RECKONING

Charlotte
Nicole Davis

First published in Great Britain in 2021 by
HOT KEY BOOKS
4th Floor, Victoria House
Bloomsbury Square, London WC1B 4DA
Owned by Bonnier Books
Sveavägen 56, Stockholm, Sweden
www.hotkeybooks.com

A CIP catalogue record for this book is available from the British Library.

ISBN: 978-1-4714-0931-8
also available as an ebook and audio

1

This book is typeset using Atomik ePublisher
Printed and bound in Great Britain by Clays Ltd, Elcograf S.p.A.

Hot Key Books is an imprint of Bonnier Books UK
www.bonnierbooks.co.uk

For Danielle and Theresa,
my own sisters in arms

CHAPTER ONE

There was a world outside Arketta, of course—but you never felt the full weight of that truth until you stood at its border yourself.

It looked no different to Aster on the other side. The same trees grew in Ferron, their spring green leaves shimmering in the wind, and the same road snaked between them like a wide, brown river. But here, in Arketta, there were dustblood debts, and raveners on hellhorses, and welcome houses full of children and vengeants to cry out at the cruelty of it all.

And there, in Ferron: freedom.

Aster shifted in the delivery wagon's driver's seat, gripping the reins tightly in her sweat-slicked hands. Raven, always a girl of few words, was even quieter than usual, her face set in a carefully neutral expression as they approached the border checkpoint. This wasn't the first time for either of them smuggling a girl into Ferron for the Lady Ghosts, but it hadn't gotten any easier with experience. Aster had never known the border agents to be lax in their duties.

The crates in the back jumped as Aster brought their wagon to a stop. There was one wagon ahead of them in the inspection line. Beyond it stood an armyman's guard tower, one of dozens lining the border and standing high as the tree line. Aster could just make out a gray-uniformed Arkettan soldier standing atop the nearest tower, a voltric rifle in his hands, pointed down at the line of wagons below. That was the arrangement the two nations had struck to protect their border—Arketta provided the men, and Ferron provided the weapons.

One shot from that gun would arc through a man like lightning.

"Do me a favor and double-check the guarants are still in your bag, will you?" Aster mumbled under her breath.

"You know damn well I just checked for them a mile back," Raven reminded her.

"Well, check again. I don't need us getting up there and finding out we lost them between there and here."

Raven's lips twitched up in a smirk, but she complied, sifting through her satchel with slender fingers to make sure that the government documents were there. Raven had always been a striking girl—tall, lithe, with russet brown skin that was dappled with patches of white. Her long black hair was twisted into sisterlocks, and her favor, a cascade of raven feathers that shimmered in the light, was only partially obscured by the high collar of her dress. She and Aster were dressed as merchants' fortunas, and the guarants were the official papers, signed in bewitched ink, that would prove their identity. It was illegal for a dustblood to cross the border into Ferron without one, and the Arkettan government usually only issued them to the few extraordinary dustbloods who had worked off their debt and earned their freedom. But there were rare exceptions to the rule, and one such was for Good Luck Girls who had been purchased outright by a brag as his personal consort—or fortuna—and who might need to cross the border with him.

Not that Aster belonged to anyone, not anymore. The guarants had been given to her by the Lady Ghosts, secured for them by one of their anonymous allies in the government. The papers were impossible to forge and had been incredibly expensive for the ally to obtain. If they didn't stand up to scrutiny, it wasn't just Aster and Raven's lives on the line—it was the whole network the Ladies had built.

"See? Right where we left them," Raven murmured, showing Aster the documents. Aster felt her expression relax ever so slightly. "Nothing to worry about, boss."

Boss. The word rang false in Aster's ears. At nineteen, Raven was a year older than Aster, and she had been with the Ladies longer, too. But Aster had been put in charge of their missions given her experience on the road—as if herding her half-feral friends across the Scab was anything like trying to lead organized rebels. She took pride in the respect the other Ladies paid her, but the expectations that came with it could be overwhelming. She couldn't afford to fail.

It had been near a year since Aster and the other Green Creek runaways found the Lady Ghosts. Since then, the public had been told that all of them were dead, captured and killed by the brave lawmen on their trail. Aster suspected that Jerrod McClennon, head of the wealthiest landmaster family in Arketta, had spun the lie to save his own reputation after they'd escaped his estate. In truth, Clementine, Tansy, and Mallow had all been borderjumped into Ferron.

The only exception, of course, was Violet, whom they'd had to leave behind.

But Aster, in her stubbornness, could not bring herself to believe that Violet was dead.

If McClennon was lying about the rest of them, then he was lying about her, too. He had to be. Violet would have survived that night. She would have survived whatever McClennon had put her through since. Maybe she would have even escaped on her own, somehow. And as soon as Aster got proof, she was going back for her. Her conscience would not let her rest until she did, no matter how many other Good Luck Girls she borderjumped to safety.

Focus on the task at hand, Aster thought roughly, before her guilt could sink its teeth in any deeper. The girl in the back of their wagon now was hardly *safe* yet.

The good news was that these border agents, along with most of the rest of the world, believed Aster was dead. Beyond that, she looked completely different now. She had shorn her hair into a military crop. She had changed her favor from an aster flower to a sunburst. And she was dressed like a high-end fortuna, not a bandit on the run. There was no reason for anyone to recognize her or suspect she was anyone other than who she said she was.

But still . . .

Two armymen waved the wagon ahead of them through. Aster snapped the reins and led the horse forward, tightening her mouth as one of the armymen approached. He was tall, clear-eyed, cut like canyon rock, with no shadow at his feet: a dustblood, like the majority of the rank and file of Arketta's armed forces—a lifetime of service would see his family's debts forgiven. The gold buttons on the man's immaculate slate gray uniform winked in the late afternoon sunlight. Like his companion in the guard tower, he was armed with voltric weapons: twin pistols that whined at the edge of Aster's hearing like the drone of flies.

"Papers," he said to Aster in a bored tone, holding out a hairy hand. Then his eyes widened as they fell on Aster's and Raven's favors. "You girls have guarants?" he asked more roughly.

"Yes, sir, right here," Aster answered evenly. "We're transporting goods for our keeper. Be meeting him right on the other side of the border." She handed the guarants over to the armyman, along with export documents for the cargo. He fixed a lens over his eye and scanned the papers slowly. If the guarants were legitimate, the bewitched ink, seen through the lens, would glow.

"'In the service of Anthony Wise,'" he read aloud slowly. He glanced up at Aster and Raven, a smirk tugging at the corner of his mouth. "Well, aren't you the lucky ones, finding that one special brag who's willing to make you his forever. Tell me, what's Mr. Wise doing sending his Luckers to do his business for him? Doesn't seem very *wise* to me."

Aster tensed, but Raven shook her head imperceptibly.

"It's strange country, Ferron. Mr. Wise gets lonely up there," Aster said, keeping her tone level. "We've made this run half a hundred times to visit him. Just so happens this time we're bringing some cargo with us. Why should he pay someone else to do it when we already know the way?"

Doubt passed over the armyman's face. Aster didn't break

her gaze, forcing her body to remain still even as her mind whipped itself into a frenzy. If he'd been at this post a long time, he might know they weren't the same Good Luck Girls sent for Anthony Wise in the past. The Ladies were careful to account for these things, but there were so many moving parts, so many places for this to go wrong—

At last, the armyman put his lens away and handed the guarants back. Aster let out a low breath.

"Says here you're carrying a shipment of tobacco chaw," he said, holding up the export documents now. "I'm going to need to take a look in the back."

"Of course, sir."

Aster flashed a reassuring smile at Raven before climbing down from the driver's seat. But behind her smile, her mouth had gone dry. They *were* carrying boxes of chaw—but of course that wasn't all.

Aster led the armyman around back, conscious of his gaze dragging along her like the slow drip of molasses. He was following her too closely, his breath damp on the back of her neck, the whine of his gun setting her teeth on edge. Aster swallowed her anger, swallowed the old fear churning in her gut and crawling up her throat. The armymen had been some of the worst back at the welcome house, desperate and frightened, or drunk on their limited power, looking for girls to break between their scarred hands. If this one didn't try anything, it was only because he respected the authority of her keeper.

"All right, let's have a look," he muttered, pushing impatiently past Aster to survey the boxes stacked in the back of the wagon. He looked down at the export documents again, then hopped up to begin his inspection. Aster held her breath as he took the crowbar from the sideboard and pried the nearest box open. She had expected this would happen—an inspection of the supplies. There was nothing criminal for him to find in this first box, but if he found the false bottom in the last box on the left . . .

He picked up a small pouch of chaw, turned it over in his hand, and put it back. Moved on to the next box. The Lady Ghosts grew and packaged the tobacco themselves. It was necessary to maintain the fiction of Anthony Wise. It was true that they would make valuable shine from selling it, but that wasn't the point. The point was getting across the border.

Eventually the armyman came to the final box. Pried it open, rummaged through its contents.

Aster tensed, mentally begging the girl inside to remain still, remain calm.

Then, satisfied, the armyman sighed and let the lid fall. "That'll do," he said, hopping down from the wagon. "Get on out of here."

Aster felt a rush of relief. She hurried back up to the driver's seat, where Raven was waiting for her.

"Well?" Raven asked under her breath.

"We're good," Aster murmured, taking up the reins. The armyman waved them forward, and she started down the road. But before they'd gone more than a few feet, his partner whispered something to him and he ran back to Aster's side, hand at his holster.

"Hold there," he said.

What the hell?

Aster exchanged a panicked look with Raven. For the briefest instant, she considered spurring the horses into a gallop and barreling through the checkpoint. They could be across the border and half a mile down the road by the time the armymen mounted up.

But the sniper in the guard tower—

No.

That wasn't the Lady Ghost way. Nothing about Aster's fight-or-flight instinct was the Lady Ghost way. It was only by keeping a low profile that they had lasted this long.

She had to stay calm.

"Sir?" she asked, meeting the armyman's eye.

"My partner tells me a girl about your age has been reported missing from the Firegulch welcome house. Let me see them favors again."

Aster turned down her collar to expose the rest of her favor, the rays of the sun stretching down the side of her neck. Raven did the same, showing the armyman the cascade of feathers on her neck.

The armyman narrowed his eyes, then nodded. He stepped back and waved them through.

"Tell Mr. Wise not to send his women to do his work next time, hear?" he hollered after them.

Aster didn't respond. *Stay calm,* she told herself. But she wasn't calm. She was tense, waiting for a sudden shout of recognition, for a shot of lightning to rip through the wagon. It wasn't until they had rounded the bend a mile down the road that her heart began to slow. She exhaled, looking at Raven, who pulled out a silver flask and took a short swig.

"You can relax," Raven told her, smiling a little. "The worst of it is over."

"It can *always* be worse. I'll relax when I'm damn well ready," Aster muttered. But she felt herself grinning back at Raven all the same. "Honest to the dead, for a second I thought I was going to gut that bastard back there."

"So did I," Raven said with a snort. "But you kept a cool head. You're getting better at this, you know."

The praise gave Aster a warm rush of pride. Raven had always reminded her of a cat—aloof to most, but fiercely loyal to those who earned her respect. If, after three of these missions, Aster was finally winning her over, that had to be a good sign.

They continued down the road, Aster again struck by the realization that she had entered a different world. Ferron was not a perfect place, she knew—far from it—but unlike Arketta, it had never been a prison colony for the old Empire, had never seen hundreds of thousands of people dragged to its shores from the Empire's countless other conquered lands. Generations later, dustbloods were *still* paying their debts, no longer to the fallen Empire but to the enterprising landmasters who had taken its place. The Reckoning: where every meal a dustblood ate, every stitch of clothing they wore, and every night they slept in a landmaster's tenant camp was added to a never-ending tally that no workingman's wages would ever satisfy. And for women, the only "escape" was a welcome house.

But somewhere in Ferron's capital, Steelway, Aster's sister and their friends were now living in a much truer freedom.

A sudden, unbearable ache of longing filled Aster's chest as she thought of Clementine again. She had never been apart from her sister for so long. She felt unbalanced without her. Perhaps this was how it had been for her ancestors when they'd had their shadows cut away. And then there were Tansy and Mallow, whose good humor Aster had missed more than she'd ever imagined, and Zee, whose steadfastness she had come to rely on so much that the ground felt unsteady beneath her feet without him now.

By the dead, how tempting it was to simply keep riding and disappear into a new life with them . . .

But you have work to do.

At last Aster and Raven came across two young dustblood men on the side of the road sitting in the back of an empty wagon. The boys both wore denim coveralls over thick, longsleeved flannels. Aster didn't recognize them, but they fit the description of the Ladies' contacts in Ferron. The one on the left hailed Aster with his hand held high. Then he vaulted over the side of the wagon and walked over to greet them as they pulled to a stop.

"Fine day for a stroll," the boy said neutrally.

"Looks like rain," Aster responded, completing the passphrase. As soon as she did so, he broke into a smile.

"You're late," he said. "Had us worried."

Aster climbed down from the driver's seat and clasped his hand. "We got held up at the checkpoint. Nothing serious."

"Well, I'm glad you made it." The boy and his partner began transferring the crates from Aster's wagon to the empty one. The last crate on the left was heavy enough that it took both of them to lift.

"Most valuable cargo in this one?" the second boy asked.

Aster nodded. "Take good care."

"Always do."

And true to their word, they handled the box gently, easing down from the back of Aster's wagon with it and climbing into the back of the next. When they opened it later, the girl inside would step out into a new life of her own.

"And if you could do one more thing for me," Aster said furtively as the boys made their way back around to the front of the wagon. She handed the first boy a small, folded piece of paper. Maybe she couldn't see her sister, but damned if she wasn't at least going to write to her. "When you get to Steelway, ask for the girl with the clementine favor and pass this along, please. Tell her it's from Dawn."

CHAPTER TWO

By nightfall Aster found herself back at the Lady Ghost headquarters, in the bedroom she shared with Raven and two other escaped Good Luck Girls, Hannah and Lucille. While the others had already gone down to the mess hall to eat supper with the rest of the Ladies, Aster and Raven changed out of their merchants' dresses from the mission. Warm, yellow lantern light spilled across the room from a single side table that stood between the two bunk beds, and rumpled clothes were scattered across the floor. There were no windows down here, of course—the abandoned mine the Lady Ghosts called home was a quarter mile underground—but Raven had put up some leadpoint drawings of Arketta to give themselves a taste of the outside world. The Scab descending into dusk, the Goldsea rippling in the wind, the city of Northrock twinkling beneath a sliver of a moon . . . there was a haunting beauty to her art, the deep shadows and heavy lines betraying something of the darkness that Raven and the other girls all shared.

As much as Aster enjoyed the landscape art, though, she liked Raven's self-portraits even better. Most of them were drawings of Raven now, that catlike imperiousness glinting in her eyes, with her locs piled high like a headdress or falling loose across her variegated face. But there were a few of her as a child, as well, when she'd still willed herself to try to live as a boy and gone by a name that was now dead to her. Her drawings were real to her in a way the world was not, Raven had explained, the only place she could imagine herself as the girl she'd never gotten to be or as a woman made of softness and curves. It was something Aster had always admired about her, and even envied—not just the ability to envision a different world, but to bring it life.

"So, are you gonna tell me?" Raven asked from her bed, where she had sat down to peel off her stockings.

Aster struggled to pull her own dress off over her head. "Tell you what?" she mumbled through the fabric.

"Tell me what message it is you're trying to get to Clementine."

"I have no idea what you're talking about."

"Come on, now," Raven said, raising a brow. She had an intuitiveness that sometimes reminded Aster of Clem—which only made it that much harder for Aster to lie to her. "I saw you slip something to the wagon driver. I know it wasn't for him."

Aster rolled her eyes as she tossed the merchant's dress aside. A rash of gooseflesh ran up the rich, deep brown of her bare arms, muscled from lifting weights and hitting the heavy bag. In the months since joining the Lady Ghosts, Aster had set about making herself stronger—never again did she want to feel as vulnerable as she had in those first days on the run, too weak to even sit up straight in her saddle.

"Listen, obviously it's not going to be me who peaches to Priscilla," Raven went on when Aster didn't rise to the bait.

"I'm just warning you, if she finds out, she's not going to be happy. You know the rules—no contact with the outside world without her say-so."

Priscilla was the leader of the Lady Ghosts, the kindly older woman who had first welcomed Aster and the other Green Creek girls a year ago.

Aster scowled as she dug through her trunk of clothes. Priscilla was in every way Mother Fleur's opposite—patient, generous, forgiving. Aster respected Priscilla. The last thing she wanted to do was disappoint her.

"There's nothing in the letter for her to worry about," Aster promised.

"So you admit to having written it."

Aster huffed. "Look, I just wanted to get in touch with Clem, make sure she's doing okay. Even back at the welcome house, I could . . . we've never been apart like this before. But I'm no fool, I wrote in code. Even if that letter falls into the wrong hands, nobody'll be able to trace it back to us."

Raven shook her head, sighing like a woman three times her age. "One of these days, Aster, you're going to push too hard. I only hope somebody's there to catch you when you get pushed back."

They finished changing. Raven slipped into her favorite skirt and blouse while Aster shrugged into a worn red homesteader's dress. Long-sleeved and ankle length, it was the sort of practical clothing that the Lady Ghosts typically wore when they weren't going in disguise. Once she tugged on her ankle boots, she followed Raven down to the mess hall so they could join the others for supper.

14

It had been unreal, the first few weeks with the Lady Ghosts, and sometimes it still was. Living with some fifty women and girls was, in many ways, like being thrown back to Green Creek—the friendships and friction that formed between age mates, the common complaints about pockmarks and split ends, the rumors and gossip that passed from mouth to ear. But every girl at Green Creek had been a prisoner, while every girl at the Graveyard was here by choice. The mines might not have had the luxuries of a welcome house, but neither did suffering hang heavy in its air—and that made all the difference. Even now, as Aster walked down the dimly lit underground passageway, she felt more grateful than she ever had walking along the ornately carpeted hallways of the Green Creek mansion.

Aster and Raven entered the mess hall, a low-ceilinged room filled with worn wooden tables topped with mining lanterns. Brown-yellow light bathed the faces of the former Good Luck Girls crowded together on the benches. They'd already started eating, bent over their plates or reaching for pitchers of water. The moment they saw Aster and Raven, though, the other Lady Ghosts erupted into cheers. Aster felt her cheeks warm as the applause washed over her.

"Congratulations on another successful borderjump, Ladies," Priscilla said once the noise died down. "That makes six so far this year. Those are some of our best numbers yet. Raven, Aster—fix yourselves a plate. You deserve it."

Aster's chest swelled with pride, a grin breaking through her carefully constructed calm. She dipped her chin deferentially and hurried off towards the serving table behind Raven. The girl behind the table smiled at them and heaped generous

15

spoonfuls of baked beans and mashed potatoes onto their plates. As always, memories of Eli tugged at the back of Aster's mind, and, as always, she pushed them away. Eli was still working in the kitchens for the Scorpions as far as she knew, and still softspoken and serious and bald as a cue ball. As many new allies as Aster had made among the Lady Ghosts, it was hard not to miss the friends she'd left behind—the ones who had seen her through the hardest time of her life.

"Thanks," Aster said, grabbing a slice of bread and taking her seat next to Hannah and Lucille. Raven slid in next to her and started in on her food without bothering to greet the table.

"So how'd it go?" Lucille asked them, raising a brow curiously. She was eighteen, like Aster, with light brown skin and straight black hair she wore in a single braid. Her favor was a cascade of rubies, but, like most of the Lady Ghosts, she went by her given name. Aster and Raven were rare exceptions—Raven had left her former name and identity behind, and Aster still preferred to share her true name only with those she trusted completely.

"Went about as well as could be expected," Aster said, looking sidelong at Raven. "Had a little hiccup—the border agent stopped us at the last minute and asked to see our favors—but nothing too serious."

"If it *had* been something serious, the dead only know what this one would've done," Raven said with a smirk, taking a bite of her pulled chicken sandwich.

Aster ducked the other girls' glances. "It's true—I damn near threw hands when I saw that armyman coming back for us,"

16

she admitted. "But what if he had found the false bottom? Or if he'd realized our guarants were ill got?"

"Hasn't happened yet," Hannah said with a shrug. She had frizzy blond hair she'd tried desperately to contain beneath a dustkerchief and a favor of a bird of paradise along her white skin.

"Well, it's bound to eventually," Aster said stubbornly, straightening in her seat. Most of these girls had never been on the run in the way Aster had. They had been bought out of the welcome houses by fairblood allies pretending to take them on as fortunas, allies who would then see the girls safely to the Graveyard. Only one in a hundred girls had broken themselves out by force like Aster had, and so only one in a hundred knew what it was to try to survive the road with raveners and lawmen on your tail.

You had to be prepared for anything.

"All I'm saying is, I'd feel better if we were allowed to carry weapons," Aster went on. "It doesn't even have to be a gun. I'm better with my knife anyway—"

"You know we can't jeopardize the operation like that," Lucille said.

"But shouldn't we at least have a *plan*?"

"We *do*," Lucille answered, matching Aster's tone. "If you get caught, you give yourself up *peacefully* and reveal nothing."

And the Lady Ghosts lose a valuable agent that we can't spare.

"It's just . . . it's hard enough trying to help these girls," Aster said with a tired exhale, sopping up some of the gravy on her plate with her bread. "I don't see why we're making it even harder on ourselves. I mean, six girls borderjumped for

17

the *year*? We're already halfway through summer. We could do so much more if we were willing to take a few more risks."

"This is the way we've done things for years, Aster," Hannah said, an edge creeping into her voice. "Slow and steady, working through the system. The second our fairblood allies get a whiff of trouble on our part, they're out. We're not going to risk that just because you're feeling a little restless. You did good today. Don't take away from that."

Aster didn't argue further, though she itched to. She was still finding her feet here at the Graveyard. This wasn't like being on the trail with girls she'd known half her life. There were rules here, strategies, a hierarchy—and Aster was no longer at the top.

She glanced at Raven, who gave her a small shrug. Aster knew she wasn't the only one who wanted to push the Lady Ghosts further. She and Raven had talked about it before. It cost thousands and thousands of eagles to buy a Good Luck Girl out of her welcome house, and thousands more to get the paperwork to sneak her across the border. The Ladies were entirely dependent on charity from a handful of trusted fairblood allies and what little shine they could raise themselves by selling the goods they made here at their base. To borderjump even one Good Luck Girl represented months of painstaking labor and careful, coded correspondence. And while there were girls who might escape from their welcome houses on their own, they still had to find the Lady Ghosts without getting caught, and the Ladies had no infrastructure to help them. How many had been lost to the Scab or recaptured by the law?

They had to do better. They couldn't keep being ruled by fear. Every day that passed was one day too late for some girl.

But it's not up to me, Aster thought. She was lucky to even be here. It wasn't her place to make demands.

At least, not yet.

The clear ringing of a triangle cut through Aster's thoughts. She looked up at the head table, where Priscilla sat with two other women at her side. To her right was Marjorie, her second in command, an older woman with a warm, round face, a button nose, and salt-and-pepper hair pulled back in a messy tail. She was a member of the northwestern tribe, one of the Nine Nations that had made up Arketta before it had been transformed into a prison colony. Aster knew that those who had resisted the Empire's advances had gone on to become its first dustbloods, and that many of their descendants lived in the Scab still. But despite that, Aster had never seen much of Nine's cultures before, forbidden as any such open allegiances to them were. And so Marjorie, with her collection of miniature whalebone figurines and her stories passed down from the time before the Empire, had always been one of Aster's favorite Ladies to learn from. Marjorie and Priscilla had been working together for decades now, though neither had been in the field themselves for several years. These days, Marjorie spent most of her time running correspondence with their allies.

Standing to Priscilla's left was Agatha—Aggie—the one ringing the triangle. Aggie was younger than the other two women, perhaps in her mid-twenties, with dark brown skin and thick hair drawn back in a bun. She had run the most girls into Ferron of any of them, and she oversaw the logistics of the border crossings. Aster could not help seeing herself in

Aggie, and imagining a future where she might be the one at the head of the Ladies' most dangerous missions.

"Thank you for your attention," Aggie said once the hall had fallen silent, and then she began running through the announcements for the day, as she did every evening at supper. The repairs on the western tunnels were underway. A new horse had been purchased for the stables. They'd added twelve more signatures to a petition to be sent to the government. Aster's mind began to wander back to her argument with Hannah and Lucille, her frustration still simmering. They just didn't understand—

"Finally," Aggie began to wrap up, "we've just received word that Jerrod McClennon is going to be making a big announcement of his own next week in Northrock. No action to be taken on our end, but let's brace ourselves all the same. That man can't sneeze without whipping up a windstorm."

Aster sat up at the mention of McClennon, her nails biting into the wood of the bench. The last time she'd seen Jerrod McClennon had been in his manor outside Northrock, where he had offered Aster and her friends up to his raveners like meat on a platter—where Violet still might be, even now.

Anger rose in her throat like a hot coal. According to the papers, McClennon had been spending the past few months campaigning in the Scab, where he was running for governor. So what was he doing back in the big city? What announcement was so important that he'd come home to make it?

Aster imagined herself stealing away into Northrock, blending into the crowd gathered to hear him speak. She couldn't try anything, of course. That wasn't the Lady Ghost way. But she could at least find out what he was planning. And if the opportunity to take more serious action presented itself . . .

She glanced at Hannah and Lucille. As much as she respected them both, neither of them would help her hurt McClennon, if it came to that. But Raven, staring up at the head table from behind her black locs, her knee bouncing beneath the table, her impatience near as palpable as Aster's own—Raven might just understand.

I can get the two of us permission to go to Northrock, I'm sure of it, Aster thought. They were in Priscilla's good graces after their successful mission, after all. And it was just reconnaissance. Nothing more.

Or at least, that was what Aster was going to tell them.

CHAPTER THREE

Northrock was a completely different world in daylight.

The last time Aster had been here, it had been the small hours of the morning, the city suspended in the dark in a bubble of the blue-white light crackling off its streetlamps. The streets had been crowded with drunks and gamblemen, and Aster had only just managed to disappear into the chaos before the law apprehended her. It'd been obvious then that she hadn't belonged: a mud-covered Scabber in denims and a dustkerchief, her eyes wide as she took in the sights around her.

Aster still couldn't help gawking like a fool, but at least she looked like she belonged here this time around. Once again she and Raven were dressed as Anthony Wise's fortunas, guarants on hand for when they'd inevitably be stopped by any lawmen who saw their favors. As busy as the streets had been Aster's first time in Northrock, the crowds were at least three times as thick today, drawn by McClennon's imminent appearance. Fairblood families pushed past one another as they bullied their way in and out of storefronts. Dustblood workers swept away the confetti and peanut shells that soiled the sidewalks. Horse-drawn coaches clattered down the brick streets, and vendors shouted from every corner, offering everything from newspapers to sunhats to bottles of root brew. Faces were flushed under the heat of the summer sun, and the air was thick with the sound of commerce and the smell of sweat.

"This ripping place," Raven swore, adjusting her hat. It was a garish thing, all bright flowers and feathers. Aster's was even more ridiculous, were that possible. If she made it to the end of the day without stuffing it in a trash bin, she would consider the mission a success.

"What, aren't you used to the city by now?" Aster asked. Raven had been with the Ladies for almost three years, and they made regular runs to Northrock for supplies.

"You never get used to Northrock," Raven groused. "It's the asshole of Arketta."

Aster hid a smirk. "Come on, now, it's better than the Scab, surely."

"Says who? At least in the Scab they don't charge an ear and an eye for every little thing. I figure so long as I'm suffering I might as well be able to afford a damn drink. Listen, how much farther until we get to City Hall? This heat is killing me." Raven fanned herself.

Aster drew the map of Northrock from her handbag. The Ladies had given it to her to help them find their way to City Hall, where McClennon would be giving his speech, but they almost didn't need the directions. The crowd seemed to move as one, herding itself towards the main event.

"Looks like we're about three blocks away—"

"*Filthy Luckers*," an old woman suddenly hissed in Aster's ear, and then she shoved Aster hard from behind. Aster stumbled into the fairblood couple in front of her before she could catch herself. The man whirled around, his face red beneath his derby hat. When he saw Aster's favor, he grew even redder.

"Keep your hands off me," he snarled, taking his wife by the arm and pulling her away from them.

Aster's cheeks warmed with a rush of anger. "I didn't—"

"You just stay back, or we'll have the law on you," the woman said, bristling.

A pocket of space had formed around Aster and Raven, the people on the streets giving them a wide berth. Some looked on with hungry curiosity, others with obvious disgust. Folks had been shooting them looks all afternoon, but this was the first time anyone had actually called attention to their presence. The crowd's whispers washed over Aster like dirty dishwater.

"What are they doing here?"

"I thought there were no welcome houses outside the Scab—"

"Are they with a brag? Where is he?"

Shame churned in Aster's gut, and she hurried to swallow it back.

"Come on," she muttered to Raven, grabbing her hand and pulling her down the next street. "Let's go before someone makes a scene."

Or more of one.

Aster didn't think she could ever get used to it—walking the streets with her favor laid bare. Covering her favor up had been painful in its own way, of course, but this pain . . . feeling the heat of people's scorn, her suffering exposed like an open wound for all to see . . . this was, in some ways, worse. It was bad enough trying to hold her chin high when dealing with a handful of

24

border agents. Northrock was a city of hundreds of thousands.

She had changed her favor. It was supposed to be a source of pride for her now, supposed to represent everything she'd survived, everything she'd fought for.

So why did she still feel so small when people stared at her?

She dropped Raven's hand. A beat of awkward silence passed between them.

"Hey, we made it fifteen minutes in this town before you picked a fight. That's got to be some kind of record for you, right?" Raven said after a moment, bumping into her playfully.

Aster could tell Raven was trying to make her feel better, but she wasn't in the mood. "I didn't even *start* that fight. Some . . . grandmotherly type did."

"Old bat."

"Mm," Aster agreed. Something about the old woman's voice had reminded Aster all too much of Mother Fleur. Aster felt her focus slipping. Suddenly the sun on her neck felt too hot, the chatter on the street too loud. She closed her eyes and slowed her breathing, trying not to think about the bodies pressing up against her. Marjorie, the Ladies' second-in-command, had counseled her before on how to pull back from the brink of fear.

That panic you feel, Aster . . . when a man raises his voice or looks at you the wrong way . . . when anything *happens that reminds you of the welcome house . . . just know that we've all felt it. Your body thinks you're back in danger, so you have to remind it that it's not. Count your breaths. Close your eyes. Ground yourself in the present moment.*

And what if the present moment is *a dangerous one?* Aster had asked darkly.

Then remember that you've survived danger before.

"There's City Hall," Raven said, breaking in on Aster's thoughts. She pointed ahead of them to a domed white building. The Arkettan flag flew high and proud from its perch, a crimson chevron against a gray field, and the Arkettan national motto was engraved below the roof: GLORY TO THE RECKONING.

In front of the building stood a large wooden stage strewn with streamers. A group of well-dressed fairblood men—politicians, Aster could only assume—were seated on risers behind an empty podium. The grassy courtyard in front of the stage was roped off and packed with people eager for McClennon to appear.

The entire quad was crawling with lawmen. Brandishing sidearms and long guns, patrolling on foot and horseback, sweeping the perimeter with panting hounds.

Raven scowled. "Ripping badges."

"It's fine. We expected them." But not this many—Aster had never seen this level of heightened security for a public event before. Their escape from the welcome house, and again from the McClennon estate, must have put the fear of the dead into the old man. Aster might have gotten some wry satisfaction out of it if it hadn't made things so impossible for her. She wouldn't get her shot at McClennon today—that much was clear. Aster sighed, pulling out her guarants and gesturing for Raven to do the same.

"Whoa, there!" the nearest lawman said as soon as he saw them approaching the courtyard. His meaty hand fell to the billy club at his belt. "Who are you girls with?"

"Ourselves!" Aster said brightly. She forced her grimace into a smile. By the *dead*, she was bad at this. Where was Violet when you needed her? "Mr. Wise was kind enough to let us have an afternoon in the city, and we figured we might as well see what all the fuss was about."

The lawman narrowed his eyes as he took Aster's papers from her and looked them over through his lens. He seemed almost disappointed to find them in order.

"And you?" he said gruffly, turning to Raven.

Raven didn't even pretend to smile, just handed her guarants over wordlessly.

"All right, go on in," the lawman conceded, handing their papers back. "But no trouble, understand? These are decent folk out here. I hear any complaints about you two, and Mr. Wise'll have to pick you up from the lawmaster's office. And that's a promise."

"Of course, sir, thank you, sir," Aster chirped. *Bastard*.

They joined the crowd.

"Keep close to me," Aster ordered, focusing on her breathing once again as they made their way toward the front. "We can't afford to lose each other in this crowd."

"Don't worry. It's not as if I want to get any closer to these rich assholes than I have to," Raven muttered.

They found a spot for themselves beside a trash bin. Thankfully, the people around them were focused too intently on the stage to pay much attention to the unattended Good Luck Girls in their presence. They just shifted subtly away from Aster and Raven, as if they were part of the rubbish and exuding a bad smell.

"It's like they're trying to pretend they can't see us," Raven said through her teeth. "Do you reckon this man here would even notice if I swiped his pocket watch right now—"

The crowd suddenly burst into applause around them, drowning out all other sound. Jerrod McClennon was jogging up the stage and striding towards the podium, his hand held up in greeting, his grin bent like a skinning knife. He wore a gunmetal gray suit with a bloodred dustkerchief tucked into his breast pocket. His top hat was angled rakishly atop his head, his long auburn hair spilling out from underneath it. Two armed raveners walked out behind him, their hawk-eyed gazes cutting across the cheering crowd.

Aster stiffened. Being in Northrock was hard enough, but seeing McClennon's face again, seeing those raveners—

Aster's hands balled to fists at her side. Her vision fell out of focus.

You're not in danger. He doesn't know you're here. He can't hurt you.

She counted her breaths again until she regained her composure. By the time she did, McClennon had begun speaking. His honeyed voice rang out over the murmuring crowd. Gooseflesh crept up Aster's arms at the sound of it.

"—Thank you all for joining me here this afternoon," McClennon was saying. "After all these long months of campaigning in the Scab, it's good to be back in Northrock— the city I was born and raised in, the city of a million souls, the greatest city in the world!"

More applause.

"And what makes this city so great is that it represents the very best of Arketta," McClennon went on, settling into his speech. "It was here, in this very valley, that our armies overwhelmed the last defenses of the Empire. And it was here, in this very building"—he gestured to City Hall—"that our nation's founders dreamed up a world built instead for the working man: where even the lowliest of us might toil our way to the top and where none of us get any less than what we deserve. The day their words became law was a mighty day of reckoning, and every year since we have celebrated Reckoning Day! Glory to the Reckoning!"

"GLORY TO THE RECKONING!" the audience roared back.

Aster felt a twinge of impatience. This was all pretty typical grandstanding so far. They hadn't traveled all this way just to hear McClennon talk about his warped view of Arketta—Aster had heard all these lies before in every newspaper and history book she'd ever read. Had she and Raven come all this way for nothing?

But then, after a few more minutes of waxing poetic, McClennon finally came around to the announcement they had all been waiting for.

". . . And that is why, today, I am proud to announce the grand opening of the first ever welcome house located outside the Scab, right here in Northrock."

Aster's chest tightened painfully. She threw a panicked glance at Raven to make sure she'd heard right. Raven's honey brown eyes were bright with alarm. The Ladies had been receiving updates for months on a major construction project underway in downtown Northrock. A gambling hall, maybe, or a highend hotel. But its true purpose had been kept secret from the public—even with their connections, the Ladies hadn't known the new building was meant to be a welcome house.

Aster tensed as McClennon continued over the applause. "The McClennons and many of the other landmaster families have been working a long time to bring this to you all," he said. "For the first time in our nation's history, you will no longer have to brave the dangers of the Scab to enjoy its most celebrated pleasures. We are bringing the backcountry to you. The doors will open in two weeks' time, and the housemistress has already taken up residence there. She's a fairblood, like all the best of us, and so she will ensure that the girls at the Northrock welcome house are the most well trained in the country. I have no doubt she'll bring a level of refinement to the establishment that is worthy of this great city. So sure am I, in fact, that I've brought her here with me today so you all may meet her yourselves." McClennon's grin widened in anticipation. "Ladies and gentlemen, please allow me to introduce . . . Violet Fleur!"

No . . . Aster's blood stilled in her veins. *It can't be* . . .

There was no way he was talking about *her* Violet. Her Violet was being held prisoner. Her Violet was presumed dead. Her Violet was . . .

. . . walking out onto the stage on the arm of an elegant young man Aster didn't recognize. A bright blue dress swept around her feet, shimmering as if cut from the sky itself. Her normally straight black hair had been curled and piled atop her head with a white ribbon. Even from this distance, Aster could tell Violet was fairly glowing with health, her white skin blushing in the sun. The last time Aster had seen her, Violet had been fading in and out of consciousness and collapsing into the mud as McClennon's raveners chased them down.

And now she was standing at McClennon's side, a free woman.

An accomplice.

Aster's stomach heaved. She braced herself against the trash bin, startling the pigeons perched there. Raven looked at her in alarm.

"Aster? What's wrong?" Raven asked under her breath, grabbing her by the elbow to help straighten her up. Then she followed Aster's gaze up to the stage. ". . . Hold on, that's *your* Violet?"

Not anymore.

How many times had Aster dreamed about seeing Violet alive and well again? But this—this was a nightmare.

"Good afternoon," Violet said, smiling out to the crowd. Her voice was cold and smooth as glass, ringing with that same imperious quality Aster had heard a thousand times back at Green Creek. "And thank you all for joining us today. As many of you may know, I was once pursued by the law for my association with the runaway Good Luck Girls from Green Creek. So let me tell you now what I told Mr. McClennon here once they were finally apprehended: I was never an accomplice to these girls, but their *captive*, forced to use my knowledge as head girl to help them escape. It was a seemingly never-ending nightmare that nearly killed me—and, indeed, were it not for Mr. McClennon's mercy in nursing me back to health these past months, I have no doubt I would be as dead as they are now. So consider my work for him now my way of saying thank you, and believe me when I tell you I am the best woman for the job. I know by now how the minds of degenerates work, and I know how to recognize

31

and root out dangerous thinking before it ever takes hold. *My girls will be loyal, obedient, and accommodating*—and that's a promise you can pocket." She turned her beaming smile to McClennon. "It's been the pride of my life helping you make this dream a reality, Mr. McClennon, and as long as I live I'll be grateful for the second chance you've given me."

Aster was shaking, struggling to remain upright. There was once a time when becoming a housemistress had been Violet's dream in life. But Aster refused to believe, after everything they'd been through together, that Violet still felt that way. That she would ever agree to this.

Violet had to be lying. She was just a good actor. She always had been.

"Thank you, Violet. I couldn't have put it any better myself," McClennon said, taking up his place behind the microphone once again to address the crowd. "And you all can also rest easy in knowing that my nephew Derrick has been overseeing Violet's work for me." Here he gestured to the well-dressed young man beside Violet. "It's a damn tall order we gave him, taking on his late brother's responsibilities, and Derrick's done a damn fine job of rising to the challenge. He's looking after this welcome house in Baxter's honor, and those doors won't open until they have the McClennon seal of approval."

Aster spared a glance for the lean-faced boy on Violet's arm—his red hair carefully coiffed, his blue eyes sweeping uneasily over the crowd as he smiled and waved at them. Aster should have known he was a ripping McClennon. She gritted her jaw. She'd known Baxter had a younger brother, but word was that he'd been abroad studying at some boarding school.

And now he'd been called home to take Baxter's place. By the dead, how many McClennons was Violet *working* with?

Jerrod went on: "Finally, I'm incredibly excited to announce that the Northrock welcome house will be the first in the nation where the girls' Lucky Nights will fall on their thirteenth birthdays, rather than their sixteenth."

Surprise rippled through the crowd, but it soon turned to applause. All of Aster's emotions then—the anger pooling in her belly, the hurt tugging at her heart—fell away at this final proclamation. She was struck numb as McClennon's words echoed in her mind.

The girls' Lucky Nights will fall on their thirteenth birthdays.
Their thirteenth birthdays.

And then, like a wave, her emotions came roaring back, her anger turned to wrath, her hurt to disgust. She looked at Violet—

—and saw her own horror reflected back at her. Violet's mouth fell open, her eyes shining with shock. She took a half step back from McClennon. An instant later, Violet recovered, and her expression smoothed over to her usual serene smile. But in that moment, Aster was certain of two things: first, that Violet hadn't known about this.

And second, that she had been wearing a mask this whole time.

"She doesn't want to work with them," Aster breathed, so relieved the words fell out unbidden. The tension in her shoulders loosened. "McClennon's making her do this."

Raven didn't seem to hear her. Her lip curled in a snarl. "*Ripping hell,*" she swore under her breath. "Thirteen? Your friend's a damned *traitor.*"

33

"No, she's not," Aster whispered back. "She's just playing a part. She's always been good at that. But did you see her face just now? This was a surprise to her."

"So what?" Raven hissed. "How can she work with them at *all*? I would have let them kill me before they paraded me out on that stage."

For a moment, Aster was tempted to agree. But then surety settled in her stomach. It had taken her a long time to understand Violet, and an even longer time to learn to trust her. Violet had earned Aster's faith in her by now.

"She wouldn't be doing this unless she had no other choice," Aster said, shaking her head slowly. "They must have some kind of leverage over her—maybe she's only cooperating to keep them from doing something even worse. She needs our help, Raven."

Raven crossed her arms. "*Our?*"

Aster scowled. If even Raven couldn't be convinced, how was Aster going to manage to persuade the rest of the Lady Ghosts?

But seeing Violet's forced smile as Derrick McClennon led her offstage, Aster knew she had no choice but to try.

"Lucky Nights at thirteen?" Marjorie echoed, her voice low with anger and disbelief. She and Aggie sat on either side of Priscilla, who, through the entirety of Aster and Raven's report so far, hadn't said a word. The five of them had gathered around a table in a room the Ladies affectionately called the captain's quarters, a storage space converted into an office that the three leaders shared. It was where Priscilla briefed new recruits, where Aggie prepped girls for borderjumps, where

Marjorie listened to and counseled anyone who needed to let out their anger and sorrow and fear.

And now, it was where Priscilla and the others would decide how best to respond to the devastating news Aster had brought them.

Priscilla leaned forward in her chair, the wood squeaking as her weight shifted. Her brow knitted with clear distress.

"When does this new welcome house open?" she asked quietly.

"In two weeks," Aster said. Her hackles raised just thinking about it. "It's not much time, but if we hurry we can come up with a plan to break in and get Violet out of there—"

"Steady now," Aggie said, holding her hand up. "I thought you said Violet was going to serve as the new housemistress? Sounds like she's chosen her side."

"No, that's just it—she hasn't," Aster said urgently. "You weren't there, you didn't see her face. She had no idea McClennon was planning this."

"It doesn't matter. She's still working with him," Marjorie objected. "I know you two were close, Aster. I know how much it must hurt to see she's betrayed you after all you went through together. But we can't let our emotions cloud our judgment, and the truth is that Violet does not deserve your trust. Not anymore."

Aster gripped the arms of her chair, nails digging into the wood. "You don't know anything," she murmured darkly. "You can't have any idea what McClennon put us through. What kind of torture he might be subjecting Violet to even now to get her to go along with this. She's not his partner. She's his *prisoner.*"

Finally Priscilla spoke, her voice gentle but firm. "Even if that were true, Aster, what you're suggesting—that we break into this welcome house and *rescue* Violet somehow—it's simply not possible. That's not how we operate. We work within the law. You know that."

"But there isn't time to do it the right way," Aster said, her frustration slipping through. "To raise the money for guarants, to get them made, to come up with a story that even Jerrod McClennon would believe . . ."

". . . is impossible," Priscilla repeated. "I'm sorry, but Violet's profile is simply too high. She's beyond our help now."

"Forgive me, ma'am, but I just can't accept that. And besides, if we get Violet out of there, it delays the opening of the welcome house. For all those girls' sakes, we have to do this—"

Priscilla stood then, the legs of her chair scraping against the stone. She braced her palms against the table.

"That's enough," she said quietly. "We want to do something, Aster. Don't for a moment insinuate that we don't. But part of being in this line of work is making hard decisions. I will not risk our entire operation for one girl who may not even want our help."

Making hard decisions.

That was what Violet had always encouraged her to do.

Aster looked at Raven, who remained silent, her face inscrutable behind her locs. She clearly wasn't going to get involved.

"We're going to make this new welcome house our priority, Aster," Marjorie reassured her, perhaps reading the dismay on Aster's face. "Thank you for your thorough report. We'll find a way to help these girls, I promise. It just takes time."

Time they didn't have.

"Of course," Aster said, standing stiffly. "Thank you." Some part of her wondered if she ought to have apologized for forcing an argument, but she couldn't bring herself to. Her anger was too strong. It wasn't Violet she felt betrayed by, but the Ladies. She'd followed them, trusted them, idolized them . . . but for all the good they had done, they weren't willing to take this level of risk, and girls were going to suffer for it.

Aster followed Raven back to their bunkroom, stewing in silence. Their other roommates were out, well into their work for the day. Sewing quilts to sell, or tinning tobacco, or some other painstaking task a hundred miles removed from the ultimate goal of freeing girls who were trapped. Aster and Raven would be expected to join in. To carry on as if nothing had happened. Aster kicked off her boots in frustration, then winced as they hit the wall, leaving a mark.

"Sorry," Aster mumbled to Raven.

"Don't worry about it," Raven said. She considered Aster, then unfurrowed her brow, sighing. "Listen, Aster . . . I should've been more help back there. With Priscilla. It's not in my nature to stick my nose in other folks' business, but . . . I agree with you. We have to do something."

"I don't blame you. There was no convincing her," Aster said. She sat down on her bunk and ran a hand over her short hair. "And I understand why she's so afraid. It took her a long time to build what they have here. She doesn't want to risk that. But if the Lady Ghosts aren't willing to help Violet, then I'll have to do it on my own."

Raven's eyes widened. "You're going back to Northrock alone? That's *suicide*."

"I know. But I can't just leave her," Aster said softly. When Aster had first seen Violet, any relief she'd felt had been completely overshadowed by her anger at the possibility that Violet was willingly working for McClennon. But now that Aster knew she wasn't . . .

It would've been better if she had betrayed us.

Now we're the ones who betrayed her by leaving her behind.

"There are just some things you wouldn't understand," Aster said finally.

"What's there to understand? McClennon has your friend. You want her back. But I still have to ask, is this girl really worth dying over?"

Aster furrowed her brow. "It's not just about Violet. It's about all those girls. The Northrock welcome house can't open if it doesn't have a housemistress."

But, quietly, in the back of her mind, Aster thought to herself: *Yes.*

"Well, going with your gut has gotten you this far. I don't reckon it's wrong now." Raven brushed her locs out of her face. "So? You want company?"

Aster shook her head. "I appreciate the offer, but I can't ask you to risk your life, too. But could you do me a favor and cover for me? Just . . . come up with some story Priscilla will believe when she realizes I'm gone."

"As long as you come back, Aster," Raven said, a rare note of earnestness creeping into her voice.

"I promise I will," Aster reassured her.

She only hoped she was telling the truth.

CHAPTER FOUR

Aster stole away the next morning on horseback. A familiar thrill hummed in her blood as she made her way towards Northrock through the snarl of the undergrowth, dressed in her old denims and a duster jacket, the warmth of the late afternoon sun painting the nape of her neck. Something about being back on the run settled the restlessness in her gut. No more suffocating in fancy clothes and holding her tongue and pretending to be someone she wasn't. No more waiting for permission to do what needed to be done. If she failed, she would have no one to blame but herself. But at least she could rest easy knowing she'd done everything she could for Violet.

Still, as much as Aster might have disagreed with Priscilla, the last thing she wanted was to blow the Lady Ghosts' cover—which meant she couldn't operate as a fortuna of Anthony Wise tonight. Once she got to Northrock, she would put on her dustkerchief, and, until then, she would stay off the road.

Aster ducked as her horse carried her beneath low-hanging branches, cursing when she rode through the clinging silk of a spiderweb. After months with the Ladies, where their guarants had allowed them to work out in the open, it was jarring to have to return to skulking through the woods. The lush green forests of northern Arketta weren't as treacherous as the wind-torn, dust-choked mountains of the Scab, but it was still tough enough going. Mosquitoes swarmed to the sweat on her skin, and the mud underfoot sucked at her horse's hooves. There were no vengeants this far north, but there were still coyotes and bears and white-mouth vipers. She wished Zee were there to help her, or any of her old friends. But she was only about a mile outside of Northrock now, and she'd be back in civilization soon.

Not that that will make things any easier, she thought grimly.

Covering her favor once she got to Northrock meant she'd be working within a very limited time frame there—no more than thirty minutes to locate the welcome house and find somewhere nearby to hide where she could scout out the situation. She'd have to figure out a way to break into the building and then escape with Violet, all without drawing attention to themselves. Aster didn't dare hope the welcome house wouldn't be guarded at all, but she *did* hope, given the building was still empty, that it wouldn't be guarded as heavily as Green Creek. But if it was . . . well, she had her knife with her, and a revolver, too. She'd trained regularly with firearms in the past several months, and she had gotten much better with a gun since her days on the road. But she still didn't like using it.

She hoped it wouldn't come to that tonight.

Aster fought her way through the last stretch of woods before she came to the top of the ridge that overlooked the city below and the farmland beyond. There she stopped, reaching for her satchel and searching through it for her dustkerchief. Aster had long since replaced the old dustkerchief she'd stolen out of Augie's stable all those months ago: this one she'd made herself, soft black cotton with a silver paisley pattern. She wrapped it around the lower half of her face, sighing into the light fabric. Then she slid her rangeman's hat over her head. Like the knife at her side, there was something thrilling about slipping into her old routine. Even the danger was almost welcome.

It felt good to be back.

Aster steered the horse out of the woods and onto the main road, where stagecoaches, delivery wagons, and travelers on horseback all jockeyed for room to maneuver. Her skin had already begun to tingle lightly beneath her dustkerchief—the first symptom of covering a favor. That tingling would eventually become burning, and the burning would become pain, and the pain would become unbearable, and the favor would glow so brightly that it shone through the fabric, the cursed ink shining like a brand.

The road grew more crowded as Aster entered the city from the east. The evening sun was sinking in the sky, and Northrock was a city in transition: shops shuttering closed, voltric streetlights flaring to life, workmen walking home in rowdy groups of three and four while the wealthy rode down the cluttered streets in their coaches.

It didn't take Aster long to disappear into the fray. She tied her horse to a post and continued forward on foot so as to draw less attention to herself. She scratched at the side of her neck as she pushed her way through the crowd. Her gaze landed on a dustblood paperboy standing at the corner.

"*THE RECKONER*, EVENING EDITION," he cried out hoarsely. "TWO COPPERS."

A sudden thought struck her. "I'll take one," she said, fishing out the coins hurriedly. Just as she'd suspected, McClennon's announcement had made the front page. She snapped the paper open and scanned the article. The welcome house address had to be in here somewhere.

Come on, come on—

There.

Aster stuffed the paper in her satchel and took off towards her destination at a quick clip. By now her favor had begun to burn—not enough to be painful, but enough to make it harder for her to focus. A faint red glow would have started up beneath her dustkerchief, too. She didn't have much time. She turned the corner on the next street and hurried down the block.

And there, silhouetted against the deepening sky, was the welcome house.

There was no mistaking it for another building. Unlike the utilitarian, square buildings that lined most of the streets of Northrock, this was an exercise in excess: a four-story manor home painted purple and cream, with wide bay windows, steep gables, and a wraparound porch. Aster couldn't tell from where she stood where Violet's room might be, but just knowing she was so close made the knot in Aster's chest loosen, just a bit.

She exhaled and began to look around for a way in. The surrounding green space took up a whole city block, a carefully groomed lawn dotted with saplings and topiary shrubs. A maze of scaffolding encased the building, which was clearly still receiving finishing touches. A high diamond-wire fence lined the whole estate. A few curious passersby peered through the chain links, but a pair of raveners guarding the perimeter moved along anyone who lingered too long.

"*Dammit*," Aster murmured. She'd expected armed guards, but not raveners. She shouldn't have been surprised, though, not after the display of strength she'd seen at McClennon's event. She needed to make herself scarce before they caught wind of her.

Aster ducked down the closest alley. Once she was safely in the dark, hidden behind a row of trash bins, she ripped her dustkerchief off, exhaling with relief. The bricks were cold and damp beneath her, leeching through her denims. The heavy, earthy smell of the garbage made her head spin. But given that the adjacent shops were already closed, it seemed safe to bet no one would be using the alley until morning.

Raveners, Aster thought, leaning back against the building in frustration. *How the rip am I supposed to take out a pair of raveners by myself?*

Aster wet her lips. A memory flashed across her mind's eye unbidden: the ravener she'd killed back in the Scab, her knife buried in his chest, his eyes, the color of dried blood, fading to lifelessness. His body was still like that somewhere, perfectly preserved by its black magic, a testament to her first—and only— kill. Aster swallowed thickly. She didn't regret what she'd done. There hadn't been any choice.

But she didn't want to kill again if she didn't have to.

I'll just wait for an opening . . . a distraction, or a lapse in attention, or something. I'll know it when I see it. It's still early in the night, Aster told herself.

Still, a worm of doubt had begun to chew its way into the back of her mind. The Lady Ghosts would never find themselves this unprepared for a mission. They were meticulous, methodical, deliberate. They would have waited until they had a watertight plan.

But their way took time Violet didn't have.

So Aster turned her mind back to her mission and, spotting the fire escape on the side of the building across from her, leapt up to grab the bottom rung of the rusted ladder. Then she climbed up to the third story so she could look out over the welcome house from the safety of the shadows. The pain in her favor slowly subsided as its glow faded from her skin. The last light began to fade from the sky, too, and soon it was blue-black and gauzy with gray clouds. A soft, murmuring rain began to fall over the city—one of those passing summer storms that descended almost every day in this part of Arketta. Aster shivered against the damp and the chill.

Perfect.

At least the rain would make it harder for the raveners to see and hear her when the time came.

Aster sighed impatiently, restlessness riling under her skin as she settled into her reconnaissance. The raveners' patrol had a definite pattern, but they showed no signs of breaking it, and Aster had been waiting here for at least forty minutes now. Maybe she'd have to—

Then, suddenly, two more raveners approached the welcome house from the street.

Aster ducked lower instinctively. She could tell they were

44

raveners from the massive steeds they rode—hellhorses, just as cursed and dangerous as their riders. The raveners dismounted and led their horses to the gates of the fence, which one of the raveners on the inside opened with a scraping sound. His partner joined him a moment later.

The mournful melody of the clock tower rang out then. The top of the hour. Nine o'clock.

A shift change, Aster realized.

This was her chance.

She clambered down the fire escape as fast as she could without making too much noise. She had to climb that fence before the new shift started patrolling. Once her feet hit the ground, she paused to tie the dustkerchief around her face once again, then took off at a run. The clock tower began to toll in the distance.

BONG . . . BONG . . . BONG . . . BONG . . .

She made her way around to the back of the house, opposite the entrance where the raveners were talking. This street was quieter, but there were still a few scattered people walking down the sidewalk, huddled under their umbrellas. Aster didn't have time to worry about them. She began scaling the fence without slowing down. The cold, wet metal bit into the palms of her hands and clinked with every stab of her boots.

Quiet, Aster pleaded.

BONG . . . BONG . . .

"Hey! Damn kids—" someone swore, spotting her.

Keep going, Aster ordered herself. They weren't going to do anything about her.

She hoped.

45

Because it was too late to turn back now.

BONG . . . BONG . . . BONG . . . The clock went silent just as Aster swung up over the top of the fence and jumped to the ground on the other side. She grunted as she landed, rolling the way Zee had taught her. The damp grass muffled the sound of her impact.

But the raveners would be coming around the back any second now.

From here Aster could see a single lit window on the second floor, yellow-orange light emanating dimly through the gauze of the sheers. Aster could reach it if she climbed the scaffolding. That was Violet's room, it had to be—no one else had moved in yet, according to McClennon.

Aster ran forward before she could second-guess herself. The scaffolding proved much more difficult to climb than the fence. To reach the wooden platform that surrounded the second story, Aster had to balance on the thin, slippery X of the metal bars supporting it and inch her way to the top. She wasn't at all confident they would hold her. Move too fast, and the whole structure would come crashing down. Move too slow, and one of the raveners would spot her.

Aster gripped the cold, wet metal as she worked her way up. The beam beneath her feet shuddered with every step she took. Aster could just make out the sound of one of the raveners approaching, his stride strong and purposeful.

Shit.

She reached the wooden platform. Hoisted herself up with an involuntary grunt, rolled over onto her back, and crawled into the shadows just as the approaching ravener rounded the corner. There she waited, frozen, silent, as the ravener walked towards her.

Don't look up, don't look up, Aster pleaded.

A normal guard would have a lantern. A ravener didn't need one. They saw clearly in the dark, like the predators they were. Aster could just make out the shape of him in the streetlight as he stalked along the inner perimeter of the fence, scanning back and forth between the darkened property and the half-lit street.

Don't look up . . .

It wasn't until he rounded the next bend that Aster let out her breath.

"Okay," she whispered to herself, standing carefully. If these raveners followed the same pattern as the last pair, she had only a moment to move before his partner showed up. Aster crept over to the lit window, half hunched to keep her balance. Then she crouched out of sight and peered over the sill.

Aster's heart leapt in her chest, and she let out a breath that was half laugh, half sigh of relief.

There, thank the dead, was Violet.

She was dressed in a voluminous, bloodred floor-length dress with a wide skirt and puffy sleeves—the kind of elegant affair befitting a housemistress. Violet paced around a bed that was equally magnificent, her face drawn in clear distress.

Aster reached for the window, then paused. If she startled Violet into shouting, it would bring the raveners down on them both. It would be better to wait to sneak in until Violet went into her washroom. She would probably be getting ready for bed soon. Violet had always liked her beauty sleep.

But Aster couldn't wait too long. The longer she was up here, the more likely the raveners were to spot her anyway.

Aster weighed the risks, chewing on the inside of her cheek. The night air was cool around her, but she was sweating beneath her duster jacket.

Then, just as Aster was about to give up and break in, she peered over the windowsill again and saw Violet striding towards the washroom. A moment later, Violet closed the door behind her.

Aster moved quickly. She had spent years fantasizing about breaking out of a welcome house—never had she imagined she'd be trying to break *into* one.

Only for you, Violet, Aster thought bitterly.

She carefully slid the window open. Unlike the forty-year-old windows at Green Creek, this one opened without a sound. The metal of the windowsill bit into her palms as she climbed through the small gap, closing the window back behind her so the raveners wouldn't notice.

Then she turned to face the master bedroom, looking, desperately, for a place to hide.

Aster's boots sank into the plush carpet below. The smell of perfume hit her like a solid thing. And as her gaze swept the room, falling on the oil paintings, on the towering wardrobe, and on the bed, with its heavy blankets and gilded headboard and silk pillows piled high, she found herself suddenly transported back to Green Creek. Memories she'd buried oozed to the surface like oil from the ground, dark and thick and churning. She stood rooted to the spot, her pulse beating heavy and hollow against her eardrums. Her breaths grew short and shallow, the suffocating scent of the perfume making her head spin and her stomach churn. Aster tried to take a step forward, but her knee buckled.

By the Veil, don't do this. Not now. Please—

But Aster's head grew lighter and lighter until it felt like she was floating away from herself entirely, leaving her body behind. Who would breathe for her now? Who would keep her heart beating? She would die in this room and her remnant would be trapped here forever. And that was how Violet would find her, crumpled on the floor like a forgotten doll . . .

Violet—

Violet would come back any moment. She had to hide.

Focus.

Aster felt like she was submerged twenty feet underwater. She forced herself to suck in a slow, deep, painful breath. She counted in her mind like the Lady Ghosts had taught her. And slowly, slowly, she rose out of the darkness, breaking through the surface of her mind, returning to herself. Aster's next exhale was a half-choked sob. She stifled it with a hand, staggering towards the empty corner beside the wardrobe.

It felt like an hour had passed, but in reality, it probably hadn't even been half a minute. Sudden shame flooded over Aster as she pressed her back against the wall. She was glad no one had been around to see her like that.

But just as she began to regain her breath, she heard the click of the washroom doorknob turning.

Violet stepped into view, now dressed in her nightgown, her face red and raw from being scrubbed, her long dark hair tied up in a messy bun. She stopped short as she spotted the wet boot prints on the rug. But before she could cry out, Aster leapt forward on silent feet and grabbed her from behind, wrapping her hand around her mouth. The last time Aster had attacked Violet like this, when Violet had discovered them with Baxter McClennon's body, it had been because Aster had been afraid *of* her. Now she was afraid for her. She had to get her out of this place.

"It's me. It's Aster," Aster whispered quickly. Her voice was thick, and she swallowed painfully. "I'm about to let you go. Are you going to behave?"

Aster couldn't see Violet's face, but Violet nodded, and Aster released her. Violet whirled around immediately, her face twisted up with indignation. Her eyes locked on Aster's, and the piercing blue of them was almost enough to make Aster flinch.

Almost.

"Violet—" Aster started. Violet gave her a hard shove.

"*Damn* you, Aster," she snarled in a low voice.

"*What the hell was that for?*"

"For scaring the hell out of me. They told me you were dead."

"And you believed them? You know you can't get rid of me that easily," Aster said with half a smile. But she still felt fragile, unsteady in her surroundings. The sight of a familiar face made her memories reach up for her again, threatening to pull her back down into the water.

Then Violet wrapped her in a fierce hug, bringing Aster firmly back to the present.

"You have no idea how much I missed you, Dawn."

50

The sound of her true name made Aster's skin prickle. She had not heard it in so long.

"I missed you, too," she admitted softly. In fact, she'd missed Violet far more than she'd ever expected to. The Lady Ghosts understood the horror of the welcome houses, of course, but none of them understood what Aster had experienced at Green Creek specifically. It was like seeing her own reflection again for the first time in a year.

Violet stepped back and looked her up and down with continued disbelief. "Almost didn't recognize you with the military haircut," she said with a laugh, wiping away the wetness at the corner of her eye.

Aster ran a hand over her short hair self-consciously. "It definitely took some getting used to. Everything has. A lot has changed, Violet. We found Lady Ghost. It's actually a whole network of runaway Good Luck Girls working together. They borderjumped Clem and the others into Ferron."

Violet scoffed, clearly thinking Aster was joking, then blinked in disbelief once she realized Aster wasn't.

"Wait, *Ferron*? Ripping hell! *How?*"

Aster shook her head. As much as she wanted to tell Violet everything, they didn't have time.

"I'll tell you the whole story later. Right now we just need to get you out of here. The Lady Ghosts thought it was too big a risk to rescue you, so I came out here on my own."

"Rescue?" Violet pulled away from her. "No, Aster. You don't understand. I don't want to leave."

Aster stared at her, struggling to make sense of Violet's words. A sickening feeling shot through her stomach. "But ... Violet ..."

By the Veil, was I wrong about her?

Did she really switch sides?

Violet opened her mouth to explain, but was interrupted by a quiet knock at the door. She looked at Aster in alarm.

"Aster, there's something I need to tell you—"

The door swung open on oiled hinges.

And behind it, his coat glittering with rain, stood Derrick McClennon.

CHAPTER FIVE

Derrick stopped short at the sight of Aster, his blue eyes widening with shock. His dress shoes squeaked against the floor as he took a step back.

"Who the hell—"

Aster drew her knife before she could think twice, her blood surging. Damned if she was going to let another McClennon get in her way. She would send Derrick to join his brother beyond the Veil if she had to. Aster bared her teeth, ran forward.

But before she could reach him, *Violet* grabbed *her,* her long fingers wrapping around Aster's wrist.

"Don't, Aster! He's with us," Violet hissed.

Aster spun around, ripping her wrist free. Her heart was still at the top of her throat, her vision swimming. Violet's words slowly sank in.

"*What?*" Aster finally managed.

"I said he's with us. Tell her, Derrick."

Derrick's narrow face had gone the color of milk, his freckles standing out against his pale skin. He seemed in every way his brother's opposite—short where Baxter had been tall, bony where Baxter had been broad-shouldered and muscular. And whereas Baxter, by all accounts, had carried himself with an easy, swaggering confidence, there was something almost fragile in Derrick's demeanor. His delicate-cut jaw clenched as if in anticipation of a blow, his summer blue eyes clouded with some unspoken grief. He seemed anxious, but Aster wasn't even sure it was because of her.

But still—he was a ripping McClennon. Aster wasn't going to let her guard down just because looked like a kicked puppy.

"Aster? Aster from—from Green Creek?" Derrick stammered. "I was told you were dead."

"No such luck," Aster said, raising the knife again warningly. "Now explain yourself."

Derrick swallowed, his throat bobbing. He used the dripping black umbrella in his hand to point to the seating area in the corner of the room.

"May we sit while we talk, at least? I've been on my feet all day."

Is this bastard serious?

Aster glanced at Violet, who nodded.

"Fine. Plant your ass in that chair, then," Aster said impatiently. "But make it quick. We don't have all night."

Derrick sat neatly in the straight-backed armchair while Violet sat across from him on the couch. She seemed much more relaxed than Aster felt, leaning easily against the armrest. Aster remained standing, pacing, on edge.

"Well?" she snapped.

"Where to begin?" Derrick said, raking the rain out of his ginger hair. "In order to understand the work I'm doing for you, I guess, first you have to understand a little more

54

about the position I hold among my family," he started, his voice smooth and his words carefully articulated. "Like all the great landmaster families, the McClennons have a long tradition of raising two male heirs every generation: one they groom to handle matters of business, the other to handle matters of state. And, like my uncle Jerrod, I was always meant to be the statesman. My father sent me abroad for school, expecting me to learn about government and politics and the history of the old Empire. And though I never had a choice in the matter, I was happy to be away from all of this. All of *them*." He smiled thinly. "But when my brother, Baxter . . . died . . . I had to come back home and take his place as heir to the mining business. I've only recently returned, and it has been—" He paused, seeming to choose his words carefully. "—challenging, to say the least, adjusting to the new reality. I can tell my family doesn't trust me, with either the business or their secrets. There's an inner circle they won't yet let me into—which is why I didn't know you were alive, Aster. But I have been doing my best these past few weeks to convince them all that I'm ready, in hopes that they'll feed me information I can in turn pass along to Violet. We're working together, you see, to sabotage my family's business."

Aster stopped her pacing. Stared.

"But . . . *why*?" she demanded.

He tilted his head, furrowing his brow curiously. "You all know better than most what they've done. Would you rather I let them continue?"

Aster curled her lip. She couldn't tell if this boy was being smart with her or if he was just naive, but either way, she'd had just about enough of it.

"You think this some kind of game, you little—"

"Wait, just calm down," Violet sighed to Aster. Then she turned to Derrick. "Listen, if you think it's been hard getting your family to trust you, Derrick, then I *guarantee* you you're going to have a rough time convincing Aster here. So let me help." She turned back to Aster. "Before Derrick came home, McClennon was still keeping me prisoner. I'd sworn up and down that you and the others had forced me to help you, that I was repentant for the part I'd played in our crimes—and I could tell he *wanted* to believe me, Aster. He wanted to believe the one fairblood girl in the group would have known better. The rest of you could be expected to behave criminally, but me? No, there had to be an explanation for it. But it wasn't until Derrick returned that he felt comfortable giving me my freedom—under Derrick's supervision. Derrick asked if he might be able to keep me as a kind of 'welcome home' present, you see. His very own fairblood fortuna."

Aster threw Derrick a venomous glare. "*This* is supposed to convince me you're on our side?"

Derrick opened his mouth to respond, but Violet beat him to it. "I'm not finished. It was all a ruse, Aster. In reality, when Derrick first came to visit me, he told me he wanted to help me in whatever way he could. At first I didn't believe him, but the more time we spent together, the clearer it became he was sincere. So, I took a risk—I told him the truth. Now, not only am I finally in McClennon's good graces, Derrick and I have had an excuse to meet in private and discuss strategies."

"That's why I came here tonight," Derrick said.

"Look, if it weren't for Derrick, I would still be rotting away in McClennon's cellar," Violet finished. "He's the one who got me out. He's the one who recommended me for housemistress here. He's the one who gave me a chance to make a difference now."

Well, he sounds like a ripping seraphant, Aster thought irritably.

Nobody was that generous. He had to want something from them. Aster just didn't know what.

She chewed the inside of her cheek as she searched for an answer. Was he trying to play both sides? And if he wasn't, why should Aster put her faith in someone who was willing to betray his own family? What did that say about him?

She took a steadying breath, trying to hold back her impatience. "I'm going to ask you one more time, and don't play the fool, Derrick. Why are you—*you*—helping us?"

A shadow fell over Derrick's expression. Again, he seemed to consider his words carefully before speaking. He steepled his fingers together. Aster bit her tongue against the urge to repeat her question.

"Let's just say you're not the only one with cause to hate my family," he said at last, his voice softer. "And we'll leave it at that."

Aster looked at Violet in surprise, but Violet seemed just as caught off guard as she was, concern flickering across her face.

This is like Zee all over again, Aster thought exhaustedly.

It had taken Aster nearly the entire journey through the Scab before she let herself put her faith in Zee. But that same journey had changed her—she knew now that you couldn't do this work alone. You had to let people help you.

And to do that, first, you had to trust them.

"Fine, then." Aster sighed, giving in. "What kind of strategies, exactly, have you two been discussing?"

Derrick's relief was unmistakable. Color flushed his cheeks. "Well, I've been running point on this new welcome house," Derrick explained. "My father's helping me, of course, but he's keeping his distance—he sees this as something of a trial run for me before I start the real work in the Scab."

"So I've heard," Aster said. "We were at your uncle's little announcement ceremony the other day."

Derrick's cheeks grew redder. "Then you know Violet will be answering to me, which gives us a bit of room to maneuver. We were planning first to spare the girls the Sweet Thistle so they would remain clearheaded. We weren't going to let the raveners break their minds in, either. But then Uncle Jerrod suggested we lower the age to thirteen, to generate excitement for his campaign, and, well . . ." He spread his hands in a helpless gesture. "That was going to be our point of discussion for tonight. I'm going to try to convince my uncle to reverse his decision. But if I can't . . ."

Aster's impatience reached a breaking point. She began pacing once again, fighting against the trapped feeling that threatened to overwhelm her.

"No. Enough is enough," she said. "We're not going to *ask* anyone to do anything. We're going to do what needs doing ourselves. This welcome house can't be allowed to open, and we're going to make sure it never does." Even more than the

Lady Ghosts, Derrick was trying to work within the system. But it was like folks said of gambling—*the house always wins.*

You couldn't play by its rules. You had to burn the whole thing down.

Burn the whole thing down . . .

Aster stopped midstep, looking at the others as a sudden solution came to her. "We're going to burn this place to the ground. Tonight."

Derrick's carefully set expression fell inward with alarm. Violet's eyes went wide as doorknobs.

"Aster—" Violet began.

Aster pointed an accusing finger at her. "Don't look at me like that. *You* ought to know better. How long was it going to take you two to free these girls? What was your plan if you couldn't convince McClennon to change his mind about the Lucky Nights? We can't let anyone go through what we went through—not when we have the power to stop it right here and now."

"I understand what you're saying," Derrick began, "but I think—"

"I'm sorry, did I ask for your opinion?"

"—*but,*" he pressed on, "I think taking such a drastic action would only create more problems than it solves."

"They'd know it was arson, Aster," Violet said softly.

"*Good,*" Aster said, struggling to keep her voice down. Everything was rising to the surface now—the dread she felt being back in a welcome house, the rage she felt towards McClennon, the joy she felt seeing Violet again, only to turn to frustration that Violet would not side with her on this. It was a hellish bile in her throat, bitter and burning. "I *want*

McClennon to know it wasn't an accident. Let him see that his cruelty won't go unchallenged."

"And it shouldn't—but if you're going to pick this fight, Aster, you have to be ready," Derrick urged. "An act of protest on this scale . . . there's going to be retaliation, and not just from my family. From *all* the landmasters, from *all* the people of Northrock, from *all* the fairblood families in Arketta who are afraid the dustbloods are coming for them next." For the first time Derrick seemed truly agitated. "I have lived my whole life with these people, I know how they think. They believe you to be monsters. You cannot prove them right."

Aster was beside herself. Her, the monster? When they were the ones who made their living off violence? Who took their pleasure from it?

But still, even through the haze of her anger, she could see that Derrick had a point. The Lady Ghosts had only survived as long as they had *because* they worked within the confines of the law. They knew they weren't ready to fight the likes of McClennon head on.

But Aster *was* ready. She hadn't broken out of Green Creek, crossed the Scab, and joined the Lady Ghosts just to give up now. She'd already gone against Priscilla and the others, women she trusted and respected, to be here—she certainly wasn't going to listen to some foppish fairblood boy.

"Let people think what they want," Aster said finally. "I can't sit here and do nothing. I already came all this way, and the dead only know when I'll get another chance at it. We're doing this—we're doing it now."

"Aster—" Derrick pleaded.

"You're both right," Violet said, standing. She looked between Aster and Derrick. "*She's* right that we can't let this welcome house open, and *he's* right that the two of us have to maintain our cover—there's still so much good work we can do from the inside. Before, we would have had to choose one or the other. But now that you're here, Aster, we can have it both ways."

"So what are you suggesting?" Aster asked slowly.

"You burn this place down—tonight, like you said. We won't stop you. But you have to wait for us to leave and establish an alibi first so we won't be suspected."

Aster looked back and forth between them warily. This just sounded to her like a convenient way to give Derrick time to slip off and snitch to the law. But judging from the look on his face, Derrick seemed equally uneasy with Violet's plan.

"This welcome house is my responsibility," he said quietly. "If anything happens to it, I'm going to lose what little respect I have."

"And that's more important than these girls' lives, is it?" Aster bit back.

"No, of course not, I'm just saying . . . I'm no good to you if my family strips me of my power."

The McClennons could demote Derrick to an errand boy, and he would still have more power than anyone else Aster had ever met. She was about to say as much, but Violet spoke first.

"Give me a little credit, Derrick," Violet said. "I can help you spin this in your favor. This will be an opportunity for you to show some real passion and initiative, for once—and when your uncle asks for solutions, we're going to make sure you have some that work for us."

Derrick and Aster shared a doubtful look. Aster sighed and beckoned Violet closer, away from the McClennon boy. They turned their backs to him.

"Look, Violet, I'm trusting you," Aster said, soft enough that Derrick wouldn't hear. "If you're wrong about him—"

"I'm not," she promised. "Derrick's not a coward, Aster, he's just cautious—and he has reason to be. Like he said, he knows his family better than anyone else. But we're going to use that to our advantage, so we can't let him be implicated in this, hear?" She gave Aster's shoulder a reassuring squeeze. "I've got this under control, I promise."

Well, if there was one thing Violet was good at, it was keeping people *under control*. Aster sighed.

"Fine," she conceded. "You two hurry up and get out of here, then. I'll wait until midnight to start the fire, but not a minute longer. I need to have plenty of time to get out of the city before daybreak."

"That'll work," Violet said to Derrick, who was pinching the bridge of his nose.

"If I may ask you just once more to reconsider—"

"You may not. Go on now," Aster said.

Violet hurried into the washroom to get changed back into her clothes, leaving Derrick and Aster alone. Aster prowled back and forth impatiently, refusing to look at him, though she could sense he had more to say. He even seemed to open his mouth to speak, but Aster fixed him with a glare, and he pressed his lips together so tightly they disappeared. The rain on the roof pattered against the tense silence. At last Violet returned, saving them both, and Derrick stood up hurriedly and helped her into her coat.

"I've written down instructions for how to reach us by voltragraph," Violet said, pressing a piece of paper into Aster's hand. "You'll have to use an alias of course—'Sunny,' I was thinking." She smiled, brushing her thumb against Aster's new favor, then drew Aster into another hug. "Promise you'll be in touch as soon as possible, hear? It's so good to have you back, Aster."

Aster felt a hitch in her chest as she hugged Violet back. "You, too, Vi. Wander well."

Then Aster and Derrick faced each other. Derrick said nothing more to try to dissuade her, only holding out his own hand in a peace offering. A thin theomite ring glinted on his third finger—one all too similar to his brother Baxter's. Aster narrowed her eyes before accepting his hand and shaking it slowly. His grip was surprisingly strong.

"Thank you, Aster," he said.

She furrowed her brow. "For what? Burning down your welcome house?"

He managed half a grin. "No—for giving me your trust. You won't regret it."

"See that I don't."

Shaking hands with a McClennon, she thought, letting go.

She couldn't believe it had come to this.

CHAPTER SIX

Once Violet and Derrick had gone and enough time had passed, Aster crept downstairs to the reception room, careful to keep quiet so as not to draw attention from the raveners still on patrol. The gentle summer rain outside had stopped—good for committing arson, but bad for hiding the sounds of footsteps. Once Aster started the fire, she was hoping the raveners would simply be too distracted to notice her stealing away.

But she couldn't afford to let them catch her before then.

Aster's feet cramped in her boots as she tiptoed down the hallway, sneaking past the empty bedrooms. She always carried matches in her satchel, but she still needed to find fuel for her fire—the batting inside the furniture, maybe, or painter's paper, if there was any left over. It was essential to control the burn, at least at first. She couldn't be reckless about this, or she was going to get herself killed.

Aster swallowed the fear creeping back up her throat. Without Violet at her side she was getting jumpy again, startling at a glint of gold in the dark and at her own shadowed reflection in a mirror. Everything about this place—the narrow hallways closing in around her, the carpet that swallowed up her footsteps, the hot, heavy air thick with the smells of polish and paint—made Aster feel as if she were trapped like a fly in honey.

One, two, three, four, five, six, seven . . .

She reached the reception room.

The furniture was still covered with white sheets, the perimeter of the floor lined with paint-spattered paper. A bar stood in the back of the room, glasses sparkling on the wall behind it. Had it already been stocked with alcohol? Enough to start a fire, maybe?

It was worth checking.

Aster ducked down low as she approached the bar, careful to keep below the sight line of the windows. Sure enough, once she was safely behind the counter, she spotted rows of gleaming bottles of beer and liquor. She silently thanked the dead as she surveyed her options. She needed the strong stuff—Zee had taught her that much when he'd first showed them all the ways to build a fire. Alcohol was something you only used in an emergency, he'd told them. It could be hard to put that kind of fire out. He wouldn't approve of this application of his advice, Aster suspected. But what he didn't know couldn't hurt him.

Finally Aster found what she was looking for—firetongue whiskey, made from grain from the Goldsea. Folks said it was strong enough to burn the skin off a baby's backside.

It would certainly do the trick tonight.

"Ah. Here we go," Aster said to herself, unable to help a grin as she took a jug in each hand.

Armed with the firetongue, she crept back out from behind the bar and built the heart of her fire: paper piled on top of wooden chairs. Then she doused it with firetongue and poured trails of the whiskey across the floor. She splashed the walls, soaked the rugs, doused the piano and the grandfather clock and the claw-footed pool table. When she ran out of alcohol, she went back behind the bar for more, helping herself to a shot for courage before setting out again. It set her head spinning.

Thanks for the drink, you bastard, Aster thought delightedly. She couldn't help picturing the look on McClennon's face when he saw that his million-eagle welcome house had been burned to the ground. Working undercover had denied Aster certain pleasures. There was a kind of rush that you could only get from taking a rich man's shine.

Finally the whole first floor smelled so strongly of whiskey that the inside of Aster's nose burned with every breath. Sweat dripped down the back of her neck. Excitement coursed through her blood. She was filled with such a heady rush that she might as well have been drunk on the firetongue beneath her feet.

But she wasn't out of this yet. She could celebrate once she was safe.

Aster backed towards the stairs. Her plan was to leave the same way she'd come in. She'd drop the match and race upstairs before the fire had a chance to reach the second floor, and then she'd sneak out through the window. But she'd have to be quick. She remembered the fire safety lessons back at Green Creek—it was the smoke that would kill you, not the flame, and the smoke took only moments to bloom.

Aster pulled the book of matches from her satchel. Peeled a single match free.

You better be sure about this, Lucker, Aster thought to herself.

She asked herself one last time if it was arrogance to think she knew better than the Lady Ghosts. But it wasn't that she thought the Ladies' way of doing things was wrong—no, of course not. Only that it wasn't *enough*. The landmasters were upping the ante. Aster had to do the same. Just as there was a time and a place for caution, there was a time and a place for risk.

And it was here, and it was now.

Heart hitching, Aster crouched on the bottom step and struck the match. It flared to life with the warning hiss of a snake in the grass. The acrid smell of smoke filled her nose. Aster leaned forward, wetting her lips. Dropped the hungry flame to the floor.

Whoosh!

The fire leapt up and forward with terrifying speed. Racing across the floor, licking up the walls, engulfing the furniture she'd soaked in firetongue. Aster stumbled backwards on the first step. The dry heat immediately scorched her exposed skin. Fear shot through her. She regained her footing and sprinted up the stairs, the black smoke chasing her.

Shit! Shit! Shit—

Aster tried to hold in a cough, but it forced its way out of her throat, and once she started, she couldn't stop. She fell to her hands and knees when she reached the second floor, desperate to keep her head below the swelling smoke. The roar of the fire beat against her ears, its heat closing around her like a fist. She could hear the raveners shouting outside, but she couldn't make out the words. It didn't matter. Nothing mattered beyond getting out of here.

For a brief, terrifying moment, Aster thought she'd forgotten which room was Violet's. It was impossible to tell the doors apart in the dark. But then she came across the door they'd left open, and she crawled into the bedroom, shutting the door behind her.

Aster didn't waste any time. She scrambled back up to her feet, ran for the window, and slid it open. Sucked in a grateful gulp of the cool, clear night air. Then she climbed out onto the scaffolding, shimmied down the side, and jumped down into the grass. In her hurry, she landed poorly, and her ankle rolled beneath her. She bit back a yelp of pain.

"It's no use, we have to send for help!" one of the raveners barked out to his partner, his voice frighteningly close. Aster froze. In her hurry to escape, she had damn near forgotten about them. But then she spotted their silhouettes, both running towards the front gate at unnatural speed. As soon as they were out of sight, Aster splashed the soot from her face with puddled rainwater, tied the dustkerchief over her nose and chin, and made for the back fence, her gait lopsided as she favored her right ankle.

Sure would've been nice to have another cart full of hay to land in, she thought ruefully, remembering the last time she'd jumped out a welcome house window. But even though her ankle was throbbing and her throat was raw, adrenaline surged through her body, making the pain seem to disappear. She climbed up and over the fence, hardly noticing the bite of the metal against her palms.

It wasn't until she was safely on the other side that Aster gave herself a moment to take it all in.

She turned and faced the burning welcome house, listening

to the timber buckle and pop in the heat, watching the thick column of smoke rise gray against the black sky. The building had gone up so much faster than she'd expected. It was now fully engulfed in flames that blazed hot and bright as the maw of a blacksmith's furnace. What change had she forged tonight? How many girls had they spared how much suffering? It was only one welcome house in a country with dozens, but still. Aster's chest swelled with sudden elation. A grin split her face. McClennon probably thought he had seen the last of her. He probably had been a little relieved, despite himself.

Well, now he would know better. They all would.

Then the peal of the firemen's bells rang out in the distance, and the spell was broken. Aster snapped into focus, knowing she needed to disappear.

But it sounded like the firemen were coming from the same direction as where she'd hitched her horse—and the law would be with them, too, no doubt. The horse would be safe, but she wouldn't be, if she went back that way. What would the law think when they saw her fleeing the area, a dustblood in the wrong part of town, her face covered like a criminal's?

Aster bit her lip, weighing the risks, then disappeared down the darkened alleyway as fast as she could manage.

The bells continued to ring as more firemen's carriages headed towards the burning welcome house. Aster's favor burned beneath her dustkerchief as if in sympathy. Once she'd put enough distance between herself and the welcome house she reemerged on a busy street, where people stopped on the sidewalk and turned their faces up towards the smoke rising over the skyline. If it distracted folks from her presence, so much the better. She had only a little farther before she reached one of the bridges that would take her out of Northrock, and as far as Aster was concerned, she couldn't get there soon enough. Her work here was done.

The bite in Aster's throat dulled as she slowly regained her breath. What would Priscilla say once Aster told her what she'd done? Would she cast her out of the Graveyard? Suddenly it seemed like a possibility Aster had to consider. Stealing Violet out from under McClennon's nose would have perhaps been forgivable, but burning down a welcome house—

I'll explain everything to her. She'll see that it had to be done. She'll come around. She has to.

But if she didn't?

Aster's excitement cooled, hardened, sank in her stomach. She swallowed, wiping away the sting of sweat from her eye. Her sister and their friends were all in Ferron, and Violet was with the McClennons. If the Ladies cast Aster out, she would have nowhere left to turn.

The bridge was in sight now. A crowd seemed to have gathered on the near side of it. A deepening sting ate away at Aster's favor as she pushed her way past people. Her favor would start to show through her dustkerchief any minute now. She didn't have time for whatever this was.

"Excuse me—pardon me—excuse—" Aster stopped short, her voice dying in her throat.

A line of lawmen stood across the bridge, barking at anyone who tried to cross or pushing them back with the butts of their rifles.

"What the rip is going on?" Aster asked under her breath.

"You didn't hear?" a woman next to her answered. "You didn't *see*? The new welcome house is on fire."

"But I—I don't understand," Aster stammered, struggling not to let panic slip into her voice. "What does that have to do with the barricade?"

"Well, they're saying it was arson. The city is on lockdown."

"Lockdown?"

"That's right. No one in or out until the perpetrators are caught."

CHAPTER SEVEN

Lockdown?

Aster's mind spun. It had been one thing for the little towns in the Scab to go on lockdown, setting up checkpoints along the Bone Road, but a place the size of Northrock? How long would it take the law to search the whole city? How long before they gave up?

Or before they found her?

At least one thing was for sure: she wasn't getting out this way. She had to get away from these lawmen, now.

Aster's favor twinged with pain, and she brought her hand up to the side of her neck as she ducked down the alleys again, limping on her stiffening ankle. Once she was hidden in the shadows, she crouched down and took a moment to regroup, removing her dustkerchief.

Now what?

Every road out of this place probably had a barricade up, but they couldn't keep a city this size shut down forever. She just had to outlast them.

But for how long? A day? A week? She didn't even have anywhere to sleep tonight.

Aster's gut sank at the realization. She had a few eagles on her, but certainly not enough to afford lodging at an inn where she could lay low until this lockdown lifted—and even if she could, the law would be going door to door, questioning everyone.

She should have prepared for this. She should have brought more shine, should have secured a hideout, should have—

Should have listened to the Lady Ghosts.

Aster ground her teeth. There'd be time for regret later. Right now she had to figure out where she could spend the night. If she tried to sleep rough on the streets, the law was sure to pick her up. She needed someplace they wouldn't think to look.

If this were the wilderness, Aster would have known what to do. Zee had taught them how to find shelter and cover their tracks in the mountains. But Northrock? Sneaking around the city was a hell of a lot different than sneaking around the Scab.

Wait a minute—

What had been the name of the dustblood girl who'd first told her that? The girl who'd helped her find Violet the night Violet had stolen away to her father's house?

Cora.

Would she remember Aster? And even if she did, would she be willing to help her again? It was one thing to escort a stranger across town, but to protect them from the law while the whole city was on lockdown . . .

But Aster was out of options.

She waited a little while longer for her favor to cool, then, wincing, covered her face once again and set out into the streets. The first time Aster had run into Cora she had been on the opposite end of town, near the warehouses, packing plants, and loading docks that lined the Mercy River: the industrial district, where the majority of Northrock's dustbloods lived. Cora had explained that she and her friends slept rough in an old mill nearby. Aster just had to find it.

It took her near an hour to reach the right neighborhood, ducking in and out of alleys along the way to dodge the law and let her favor rest. The cold and the damp sank into her skin, setting her shivering, the muscles in her legs cramping up as she limped block after block. The industrial district was like a totally different city. Unlike the well-kept parts of town where McClennon had held his rally and built his welcome house, here the broken-down buildings crowded together like too many teeth in a mouth. Uncollected garbage spilled out from the alleys, and burnt-out streetlights left whole city blocks in the shadows. The very air was heavy with the smell of river water and sewage. Smoke from the mills blotted out the stars above. And one name appeared again and again on the face of every factory: CAIN. The man, whoever he was, seemed to own this part of town.

Then, beneath the sounds of the city and the hush of the river and the hum of the voltric powerlines overhead, a low, mournful chorus of wails echoed from deep inside the bellies of the endless tenement buildings.

The hair on the back of Aster's neck stood on end, a chill shooting through her veins.

Vengeants?

Here?

Vengeants *could* be born anywhere, she knew, but outside the Scab they were extremely rare. This many in one neighborhood wasn't a coincidence—it meant enough people had lived out their lives here in such suffering that their spirits had been too angry to move on and had turned violent after death. Which meant, of course, folks here would only suffer that much more, living as they did in fear of their dead. Vengeants were a problem that grew in magnitudes. That was how the Scab had become overrun.

When had things gotten this bad in Northrock?

And now McClennon wants to start building welcome houses up here, too?

Aster's gut churned with slick, oily panic. She had not had to worry about vengeants in months. She didn't even have so much as an iron horseshoe on her for protection.

She had to find that mill.

Aster continued creeping through the shadows, weaving up and down the darkened streets, her favor aching. Breaking into the welcome house, escaping the fire, fleeing across the city . . . she struggled to remember the last time she had been this exhausted. If someone—or something—appeared and attacked her now, she doubted she would have the strength to fight back.

At last she came across a massive, burnt-out building crouching in the darkness, its smokestacks collapsing in on themselves, its windows gleaming with broken glass. She could just make out the words CAIN'S CLOTHIERS under the silvered light of the moon. Hope sprang in Aster's chest. Her gaze fell to the building's entrance.

And there, gliding towards her on translucent, batlike wings, its skeletal hands outstretched, its skull bristling with antlers and fangs . . .

Aster's heart fell to her stomach, a whimper escaping her lips as she stumbled backwards away from the vengeant. Her hands flew up to cover her face instinctively. Her eyes squeezed shut—

BANG!

A gunshot cracked through the night.

Aster opened her eyes. The vengeant was turning tail and flying away with a squeal, its gossamer form smoking where it'd been sprayed with iron shot. The silhouette of a young woman stood in the now-open doorway, holding a smoking shotgun. She swung the barrel of the weapon around to point it at Aster.

"Keep walking, stranger," she called out. "We don't want any trouble from the living, either."

"No trouble," Aster promised, her voice trembling. She swallowed and fought to overcome the terror that had seized her. "I—I'm looking for someone named Cora. She's a young woman, short, with straight, dark hair. Last we spoke she told me she lived in an old mill around here."

The girl lowered her gun, if only slightly. "Who's asking?"

Aster hesitated. She would not give her identity away to a stranger.

"The Scabber girl she helped last year, the one she took to Tom Wells's mansion," Aster said after a moment.

The girl swore under her breath. "Another ripping stray. Look, I'll tell her, but it's your ass if you're lying."

"Thank you—" Aster breathed, stepping towards her.

"Aht, aht." The girl jabbed the gun in her face. "You wait out here."

She disappeared into the mill. Aster wet her lips, looking

76

over her shoulder anxiously, the base of her neck humming with dread. If the vengeants came back, she was running inside, and damn the consequences.

The minutes ticked by. Then, movement. Someone was coming back. Aster squinted, her eyes straining in the dark—

Cora.

Aster felt a flood of relief. She ripped her dustkerchief down.

"Cora! It's me—it's Aster—the girl you helped last year. Do you remember me? Please . . ." She trailed off, exhausted. "I need your help again."

"Aster." Cora spread her hands in welcome, smiling bright against the dark. "Something told me I hadn't seen the last of you."

The inside of the mill was drafty and damp, with warped wooden floors, holes in the ceiling, and broken-down machinery hulking in the dark like the skeletons of mythic beasts. Cora and her friends had set up a kind of makeshift tent city on the abandoned work floor, lit by the cherry-red glow of fires burning at the bottom of rusted metal storage drums. Cora's friends, most of them dustbloods near Aster and Cora's age but some only half as old, slept uneasily on the ground, while the few still awake shot curious glances at the pair of them.

Under the circumstances, Aster felt like she'd just walked into a room at one of Northrock's finest inns.

"Really, Cora, I can't think you enough for this," Aster repeated, wrapping her shoulders with the blanket Cora had provided her and sipping a mug of tea. Aster had trusted her enough to tell her the truth about the welcome house fire and the lockdown—this was twice now that Cora had saved her, after all, and she had not gone to the law after the first time. Still, Aster left out any mention of the Lady Ghosts, Violet, or the wild alliance with Derrick McClennon. Those were not her secrets to tell.

"Anything for one of the Green Creek girls, especially now that you burned down that damned welcome house," Cora insisted. Her bobbed black hair framed her ivory face, her dark, upswept eyes glinting with admiration. She held a fistful of red licorice whips in her hand, short fingers poking out of fingerless leather gloves, and she offered one to Aster as if it were a cigar. Aster accepted it hesitantly. "McClennon said you were dead, but I knew better," Cora went on. "Any story a politician pushes that hard *has* to be a lie. But it wasn't until I started reading about it all in the papers, you know, that I put together who you were. If I'd've known when we met, I wouldn't have taken your shine."

"I don't have much to give you this time," Aster admitted.

"Keep it. You need it more than we do right now."

Aster nodded gratefully and took a bite of the licorice, the burst of sweetness making her mouth water. After the night she'd had, it was almost enough to bring tears to her eyes. Aster's mind flashed with the memory of the vengeant fleeing, its pained cries splitting the night, and she shivered.

"Your friend saved my ass back there," Aster said quietly, the weight of her gratitude turning to sudden weariness.

Cora's eyes met hers. "You say that like it's a bad thing."

"I just don't know how I can ever repay you all."

"Not every good thing need come at a cost, Aster. Put it out of your mind."

78

Aster sighed, taking another long swallow of tea. It soothed her throat, still raw from breathing in smoke. "What are vengeants even doing in Northrock? I thought I'd left all that behind in the Scab."

The grin slipped from Cora's face. "So did we. But things have been rough in the industrial district lately. The landmaster family that owns most of the businesses down here, the Cains, have been cutting wages now that there's so many folks desperate for work. So there's a lot of bad feeling between the poor fairblood folks who have always lived here and the freed dustbloods who've started moving in over the past generation. There was a law a while back, you see, that offered dustblood men forgiveness of their families' debts if they served in the army. So we're seeing those families settle in cities like Northrock now."

Aster grimaced. She knew the law. The Reckoning preyed on dustblood men just as ravenously as it did the women, and she'd met far too many of those men at the welcome house. She didn't understand them, didn't understand how they could take up arms for the same country that had stolen everything from their ancestors and now treated them like vermin. At least toiling away in the mines was honest work.

But if it really had bought their families freedom . . .

She was in no place to judge. She'd do anything for her family, too. She already had.

"With so many of our folks moving in, it's been harder for the fairbloods to find work, and they resent having to live in the same neighborhood as the likes of us, too," Cora continued. "There's been harsh words, there's been . . . violence. Turf wars and acts of terror. Especially in the past few months. You and your friends caused quite a stir when you ripped your way through the Scab, I won't lie. It's got all the fairbloods on edge. There was even a bombing in one of our churches last week. And we're starting to see the effects of it all beyond the Veil. This has never been an easy place to live, but now . . ."

Now there are vengeants, Aster thought.

She felt like she'd aged ten years in the last ten minutes. She set her cup down and rubbed her eyes. "Ripping hell. Things were supposed to be better here."

Cora scoffed. "They are. And what does that tell you?"

Aster hung her head. There was a part of her that wanted to blame herself for the role she'd played in making things worse, but she pushed the thought away roughly. Vengeants were made over the course of lifetimes, not a few bad months. This storm had been brewing since before she'd even been born. And it was the *landmasters'* fault. They were the ones who hoarded all the shine and left everyone else fighting for scraps. Why should the poor fairbloods take out their anger on their dustblood neighbors, who had *nothing*?

"I reckon they just want to make sure we remember our place," Cora answered when Aster asked her. "No one wants to be on the bottom. The rich kick down the poor, the men kick down the women, the fairbloods kick down the dustbloods . . . and so on. Nothing changes."

But Aster refused to accept that. McClennon *knew* they were capable of changing things. He was afraid of them. She had seen it in the increased security at his rally. She saw it now with the citywide lockdown. The landmasters couldn't afford to let a bunch of Good Luck Girls take what they were owed. They were at the very bottom of the pile—if they shifted, the whole thing came crashing down.

"Anyway, don't let it worry you too much. You'll be safe enough with us," Cora continued. "We protect each other here, from the living and the dead alike."

"But the law—" Aster began.

"Is the least of our worries. They'll almost certainly search this old mill, more than once, I reckon, but there are places we can hide you when the time comes. You're not the first we've had to protect from them. You stay here just as long as you need."

Aster sighed. "Thank you," she said, her chest suddenly tight. She blinked back tears.

Cora just smiled at her. "It's like I said—anything for a Green Creek girl. You all changed things for folks like us. It gave people courage, hearing about you standing up to all those rich bastards. McClennon was a fool to tell the world you were dead. He went and made a martyr of you. Now everyone and their brother's looking to pick up where you left off. And the way things are going up here, with the welcome house, and the vengeants, and the fairblood retaliation . . . that kind of inspiration is exactly what we need."

A flicker of warmth grew in Aster's chest at Cora's words, chasing away the chill that had seeped into her bones.

"But if you're so hell-bent on paying me back, Aster, there's one favor I'll ask of you."

"Anything," Aster promised.

"You send that son of a bitch to meet the dead."

CHAPTER EIGHT

The lockdown lasted for two weeks.

Even with help from Cora and the other dustbloods, it was a near thing. The law ambushed the mill three separate times, turning the tent city over in their search and threatening to rough up anyone who resisted. Aster hid in a crawl space above the old main office along with two hotfoots—dustblood runaways—who had no guarants and would have been sent back to the Scab if discovered. Anger ate away at her as she lay there in the cramped, cobwebbed darkness, her hot breath filling the space, splinters biting into the palms of her hands. She listened to the sounds of chaos below, utterly helpless. She still couldn't help feeling responsible, and she resented it. She'd only done what she'd had to by burning down that welcome house . . . hadn't she?

When the lockdown finally lifted, it was with overwhelming relief that Aster said her goodbyes to Cora and her friends, thanking them for having risked their lives to shelter her for so long. Cora gave Aster a horse and some licorice whips for the road, bidding her to wander well. Then Aster left the mill and fled the city.

After two weeks of living rough, Aster was weaker than she'd been in months, and it was all she could do to keep her eyes from crossing as she galloped down the road back to the Graveyard. She'd never imagined, when she set out to Northrock to find Violet, that it would take this long for her to return. The peace and solitude of the Lady Ghosts' hideout would be a welcome respite.

Assuming, of course, that Priscilla was still willing to take Aster back.

Aster reached the mines by nightfall, dismounting and leaving the horse tied up outside before descending underground. Her footsteps echoed down the length of the tunnel, splashing through shallow puddles, sending rocks clattering in the dark. Every little noise made her jump. She was on edge, dreading the upcoming confrontation with the Lady Ghosts.

She'd had more than enough time to think about this, and she still had no idea what she was going to do if they turned her away.

The slope leveled out as Aster came to the base of the mineshaft, where two Ladies stood guard with pistols at their hips. One of them was Raven, leaning against the wall with her arms crossed, a bored expression on her face. Her golden brown eyes flashed with surprise at the sight of Aster.

"Raven," Aster exhaled. It'd been so long since she'd seen her that she couldn't help letting slip an exhausted smile.

"By the *Veil*, Aster, you took your sweet time. Just where the hell have you been?" Raven demanded.

Aster furrowed her brow in confusion. Didn't they all know by now? Wouldn't it have been in the papers? She'd asked Raven to cover for her, true, but surely that lie would have fallen apart once they'd seen the news about the welcome house and the lockdown. They'd have all guessed what she'd done.

"It's . . . a long story, Ray," Aster dodged. "Look, I need to talk to Priscilla. Is she in?"

The other guard, an older redheaded woman named Dinah, answered for her, her own eyes lit up with excitement at Aster's return. "Priscilla's in some kind of meeting right now."

"Who with?" Aster's asked.

"Couldn't tell you," Raven answered. "She and the other captains were very hush-hush about it. Must be one of their government contacts."

"Oh, well, I wouldn't want to interrupt—"Aster said hastily. Anything to put this off.

"No, no! Go, she'll insist that you see her immediately, Aster," Dinah retorted. "We were all of us fearing the worst."

Aster hesitated, and Raven sighed, stepping off the wall. "You want me to come with you?"

"Please," Aster said, relieved she hadn't had to ask. She knew Priscilla was not Mother Fleur, knew Priscilla would not hurt her, no matter how upset she got. But still, it would be easier with a friend by her side.

If there was one thing Aster had learned in Northrock, it was that she couldn't do any of this alone.

Raven looked to Dinah for permission, and Dinah nodded. "Go on—I can handle the rest of the shift."

"Thank you," Aster and Raven said at the same time.

They made their way through the tunnels towards the captain's quarters in heavy silence, Raven glancing at Aster every few steps like she'd seen a ghost.

"What?" Aster asked finally.

"What do you mean, *what*? Did you ever find Violet? Why didn't she come back with you? What were you doing out there for two damn weeks? I told Priscilla you'd gone into town on a supply run. She thought we'd lost you." Raven looked away. "So did I."

Aster stopped. They'd reached the captain's quarters, and she could hear the muffled sound of voices coming from the other side of the door. It sounded like there were a lot of them. Who was Priscilla even meeting with?

"I'm sorry, Raven. I did a reckless thing, and I stand by it, but Priscilla may never forgive me when I tell her. But I hope she can, and I hope you can, too—I never meant to cause you all any heartache."

"So . . . you *are* going to tell her, then? Whatever it is?" Raven asked.

Aster swallowed and nodded. *I guess I am.*

It was time to get this over with. She opened the heavy wooden door, wincing at the low groan of its rusted hinges.

And there, standing on the other side, was Zee.

And Tansy. And Mallow. And—

"Clementine?" Aster's voice cracked as she spoke. Everything else seemed to fall away. She stood rooted to the spot as her friends—her family—turned to face her.

The last time Aster had seen Zee, he had been wearing his grubby rangeman's denims and a work shirt stiff with sweat, his brown skin chapped from the unrelenting wind and the sun of the Scab. Now he wore black slacks and a patterned vest over a crisp white dress shirt, his curly hair slicked back with pomade like a city boy's. His dark eyes crinkled up with a smile as his surprise turned to delight.

Mallow was dressed more casually, with new blue denims and a brown leather jacket. An intricately patterned headband wrapped around her forehead and her short black hair. Her sleeves were rolled up over her bronzed forearms, her face lit up with a mischievous expression. Tansy stood by her side in a sky blue dress, her long blond hair twisted into a single plait draped over her shoulder. Fewer freckles dusted her white skin now that she was living up north, and she carried herself confidently, her shoulders thrown back and her green eyes held level. She and Mallow seemed more at ease with each other than Aster had ever seen them.

And Clementine . . .

Clementine looked like a woman now. When had that happened? She was as tall as Aster, and her round face had narrowed while her thin hips had filled out. The sophisticated sage green dress she wore stood out beautifully against her deep brown skin. But that look in her eyes was the same as it had always been—one of unbroken hope. Her lips parted in surprise at the sight of Aster, then spread into the girlish grin Aster remembered so well. Aster's chest swelled with emotion.

"What . . . what are you all doing here?" Aster finally stammered into the stunned silence.

"Lucker, what are *you* doing here?" Mallow shot back, looking as shocked as Aster felt. "Priscilla sent word you were missing and we came back to help find you."

Aster tore her eyes away from them and looked at Priscilla.

86

"You were gone for so long, Aster—I really thought we'd lost you," she said, her voice brittle with emotion. "I felt I had no choice but to let the others know."

"And *we* felt we had no choice but to look for you ourselves, no matter what it took," Clementine finished. She ran across the room to wrap Aster in a hug, and as her arms closed around her, something inside Aster broke. Tears sprang to her eyes and slipped down her cheeks.

"All of you?" she asked, her voice cracking.

"Of course all of us," Zee answered, and the others joined the hug until Aster was cocooned in their love. It only made her cry that much harder. She had not been held in such a long time. When they let her go, she laughed self-consciously, wiping her eyes.

"Well, I'm sorry to have made you come all this way."

"Don't be a fool, we're just glad you're okay!" Tansy said.

"Yes, of course," Priscilla said, forcing a smile through her confused expression. "But by the Veil, Aster, where have you *been*?"

Aster took a final breath to steady herself, looking at her friends for courage before she spoke.

"I was in Northrock. I got caught in the lockdown. I . . . I was the one who burned the welcome house down. I went there to find Violet and I couldn't leave without making sure those doors never opened."

It fell so silent in the room that all Aster could hear was the ticking of Zee's pocket watch. Her friends' faces were a mix of confusion and disbelief, while Priscilla's had become utterly unreadable, her smile fading.

"But, Aster . . ." Tansy said into the quiet, "the newspapers reported that some vagrant started that fire—a former Good Luck Girl who aged out and had become unstable."

"Wait, what?"

"Yeah, they already arrested her and everything," Zee went on. "That's why the lockdown lifted."

". . . And that's why none of you guessed it was *me*," Aster said slowly, the realization settling in.

They nodded and murmured in agreement.

"Do you think the law really believes that woman did it?" Clementine asked.

"No," Aster said, a pit forming in her stomach. "They're probably lying to save face, like when we escaped McClennon's manor. 'That woman' probably doesn't even exist. They'll still be looking for me."

The room fell into silence again, until Priscilla stood up, the legs of her chair squealing against the stone floor as she pushed it back.

"Well," she said briskly, bracing her palms against her desk. "That was hardly the answer I was expecting you to give, Aster. But I suppose the important thing is that you're safe. You certainly had everyone here worried."

Disappointment laced through her voice, and Aster felt even sicker as she swallowed the words.

"Ma'am, I promise, I never meant to worry *any* of you—"

"No doubt. But your friends risked a journey back to Arketta for your sake all the same. I'll leave you now to catch up with them, dear, but you and I will talk more in the morning . . . and I expect we'll have a good deal to discuss."

Aster felt helpless as she watched Priscilla sweep out of the room. Her stomach sank heavily. This wasn't how she'd imagined her triumphant return. She hadn't even gotten a chance to explain herself.

"Well! She's pissed," Mallow said once the door swung shut. "But I need to hear more about how you pulled this whole thing off."

"You're not upset?" Aster asked desperately, turning back to face her friends. She could handle disappointment from Priscilla, just about, but if her friends couldn't accept what she'd done . . .

"Upset?" Clementine repeated. "Aster, you've been in hiding, so maybe you wouldn't know, but it's only the fairbloods who are *upset* about that fire. Most of the rest of us haven't been able to stop crowing about it."

Aster grabbed hold of this like a lifeline. "Really?"

Zee nodded. "Even some of the dustblood men who'd usually support the welcome houses were happy to see McClennon get made a fool of by one of their own."

"Yeah, and last week a group of tenant farmers burned down a Sweet Thistle plantation," Tansy added excitedly.

"They did *what*?"

"Why the rip should they keep toiling over some Sweet Thistle for a welcome house that isn't going to open? That's what they figured," Mallow explained with a grin. "If a Good Luck Girl could stand up to a landmaster, then so could they."

"McClennon and them will keep trying to spin this in their favor, but it's too late—people are on your side, even if they don't know who 'you' really are," Clementine said.

"Yeah, I reckon Ms. Priscilla's just hurt that you went behind her back," Tansy finished. "She'll come around, Aster. This was a good thing you did."

Aster found her smile again, letting out a loose breath. She turned and locked eyes with Raven, who had been hovering at the edge of the group, seeming like she wanted to disappear into the corner of the little room. Her arms were crossed guardedly.

"Well, I couldn't have done any of it without Raven," Aster admitted. "She's one of my bunkmates, and she's been a great friend to me. Come on, I want you all to meet each other."

Aster waved Raven over, but Raven's eyes went wide and she held her hands up.

"I'm just here to get the rest of the story," Raven said. "I don't need to—"

"Good to meet you!" Zee said brightly, stepping forward and shaking her hand with enthusiasm. The rest followed his lead, one after the other, wearing Raven down with their excitement until at last her expression softened a little. She tucked a stray loc behind her ear, a faint grin on her lips as she joined their circle.

"This all started when Raven and I went to Northrock together to hear McClennon speak," Aster explained—and then she told them the whole story from the beginning. The undercover mission to McClennon's rally, where she and Raven had learned about the new welcome house and its horrific Lucky Night policy; the plea to the Lady Ghosts to help Violet, who clearly wanted no part of the role she'd been forced into; the effort to rescue her against Priscilla's wishes, which had also led Aster to Derrick McClennon; and the burning of the

90

welcome house, which had left her trapped in Northrock for two weeks.

"I *knew* Violet wasn't really working with McClennon!" Clementine exclaimed once Aster was finished. "Didn't I tell you all when we saw the announcement in the papers? Just another one of that man's lies."

Mallow punched her fist into her hand excitedly. "We should've trusted you. We should've trusted *her*. No one else could take a situation like that and twist it to their advantage."

"Yeah, I'm just glad she's okay," Zee murmured, looking away. Aster knew he blamed himself for not being able to save Violet, as Aster had so often blamed herself.

"I'm just glad *you're* okay, Aster," Tansy added, leaning back against Priscilla's desk. "You're lucky you're even alive. The smoke inhalation alone—"

"It was reckless, I admit," Aster agreed. "I should have thought it through more, all of it. But I didn't have time. There's not enough *time*. The work the Ladies do here is lifesaving, and I've seen that firsthand. But borderjumping these girls one by one . . . we're never going to save them all that way. I see that now. We have to think bigger, and we have to move faster."

"So, what, you're going to keep burning down welcome houses?" Raven asked skeptically.

Aster began to pace as she thought aloud. "I had a lot of time to ask myself that during the lockdown, and, as much as I'd love to burn down every welcome house in the Scab . . . I don't think I can," she admitted. "I was only able to burn down *this* welcome house because it hadn't opened yet. There weren't any girls there. But a welcome house that's already operational . . . I can't risk the girls' lives with something like that. The whole point is to save them."

And besides, Aster had begun to realize, for every welcome house she tore down, the landmasters would use their endless shine to build two more. Seeing the dustbloods' suffering in Northrock had been a sobering reminder of how far the landmasters' reach extended, how endless their resources were. She had to go to the source of the problem. These men could, with a stroke of a pen, close every welcome house their families owned and free hundreds of girls overnight. She just had to convince them . . . *force* them . . . to do it.

Aster stopped her pacing. *She* had no idea what it would take to make men like Jerrod McClennon give in to such a demand.

But Derrick McClennon just might.

This is bold as hell, Lucker, a low voice in the back of her head warned. *Bad enough you robbed a bunch of brags. Now you want to go and blackmail the richest families alive?*

Her mouth went dry.

If she was going to do this, she couldn't do it alone.

Aster looked around the circle. Her Green Creek sisters had finally found a taste of freedom in Ferron. Raven had carved out a real home for herself here with the Ladies. And Zee had already risked so much for her and her friends. It didn't feel fair to ask any of them to leave their hard-earned happiness behind to join her in a fight that would likely get them all killed.

"It's okay, Dawn. You can tell us what you're thinking," Clem said quietly.

Aster felt a hitch in her chest. Clementine had always known her better than she knew herself.

"I'm thinking . . ." Aster began slowly, "I'm thinking I need to hit the landmasters directly. Hit them hard, starting with McClennon. And I'm thinking I can't do it without you all."

"Hit them hard *how*?" Mallow asked, her eyes lighting up with interest.

"That," Aster went on, "is going to be a question for Derrick. We bring him into this—him and Violet both. They tell us where his family's most vulnerable, and those are the targets we go after. You say there are folks burning down the fields? There's no reason we can't do the same. I figure if we raise enough hell, McClennon just might be desperate enough to do whatever we ask of him to get us to stop." She met each of their gazes in turn. "And we're going to ask him to shut down his family's welcome houses for good."

The room fell so silent Aster could hear her own heart beating.

"Aster . . . he would never," Zee said softly.

Aster warmed with a rush of anger. "*Never* isn't worth two coppers to me. We were never supposed to escape Green Creek. We were never supposed to survive the Scab. We were never supposed to find Lady Ghost or run away to Ferron. So don't stand there and tell me I'm being unrealistic. It's worse than ever out there. *Someone* has to try." Her voice was climbing in her throat, and she paused and took a breath to calm herself before she continued. "Listen . . . you all have every right to walk away. I would never hold it against any of you. Everybody in this room has already been through more than any one person ought to have to bear." She swallowed. "But *I'm* doing this, and I'm not too proud to admit I'm going to need help."

"And you'll have it," Clementine said without hesitation, stepping forward to clasp Aster's shoulder.

"Always, Aster," Mallow promised.

"It would be an honor," Tansy said.

Zee nodded. "Just tell me where to be."

They all looked at Raven, who blushed faintly underneath their gaze.

"I wouldn't expect you to come with us," Aster reassured her quickly. "You hardly know these four—"

Raven's response was soft but sure, a smile lifting the corners of her lips. "I wouldn't miss it."

That night, for the first time in a year, they all sat down to share a meal together.

The Lady Ghosts had prepared pot roast for supper, celebrating Aster's safe return. Priscilla didn't mention the burning of the welcome house in her brief speech, saying only that Aster had been caught in the Northrock lockdown while on a mission. Still, Aster could see from Marjorie's and Agatha's distraught expressions that Priscilla must have told her second- and third-in-command about Aster's insubordination.

"I don't reckon there's any point in asking them for help with our next move against McClennon," Clementine said, following Aster's gaze to the front of the room.

Aster sighed. "No, I reckon not." If Priscilla hadn't been willing to risk a trip to Northrock to save Violet, she certainly wasn't going to want to risk a trip to the Scab to burn down more of McClennon's property. But maybe, Aster realized, it was all for the best—as she looked around the dining hall, its tables filled with women talking and laughing freely, she understood why the Lady Ghost leadership would be so protective of what they'd built. This place had been home to her for the past year, the only home where she had always felt safe and never wanted for anything. It wasn't that she wanted to leave—it was only that she wanted to give every Good Luck Girl the chance to feel this way.

"You think you'll come back here when it's all over?" Tansy asked.

"Maybe . . . although I wouldn't blame them if they decide I've lost their trust. I only hope they'll help me borderjump to Ferron so I can come live with you all." Aster just didn't want to be alone.

"Yes, by the dead, *please* come to Ferron," Mallow begged. "We need one more to round out our batball team."

Aster blinked. "Your what now?"

"Mal, no one's joining your batball team," Tansy said patiently, placing a hand over hers.

"Hah! That's what you think. I already got a few friends from work to come in on this with me. Then we'll have Clem at first, me at shortstop, and Zee out in right field where he can't cock it up too much."

"Hey—" Zee interjected.

Mallow was waving her forkful of roasted potatoes around excitedly now. "We just need a pitcher—"

"Oh? And where do I fit into all this?" Tansy demanded.

"Well, you'll be the ump, of course," Mallow said, grinning. She leaned over and kissed Tansy's temple. "We need someone levelheaded for that."

Aster laughed through her nose. These two were like the tide, pushing and pulling with tireless delight, and she'd forgotten how easy it was to get swept up in it. "Back up a minute, Mal," she said. "'Friends from *work*'? Who was fool enough to hire you?"

Mallow beamed. "The loading docks. It's hard work, and the pay's shit, but my arms are more fit than ever. And Aster, you'll never believe this, but one of the guys I work with is actually a son of the Nine, and from the southern tribe—the same as my dad's side of the family. There's a whole network of Nations hotfoots up in Ferron, apparently. They've been teaching me so many of the traditions my family couldn't. This headband, I made it myself."

"*Really?*" Aster asked, eyebrows raised. Mallow's headband, intricately patterned with red, yellow, and black chevrons, hardly looked like it had been stitched by a beginner.

"Well," Mallow amended, "one of the aunties helped."

Tansy laughed. "Still counts, Mal. And Aster, I actually have some genuinely exciting news of my own. I'm at the hospital now, working as a nurse, and I've been developing a cream that can numb favors for several hours, so we'll be able to keep them covered for much longer."

"*What?*" Raven said. She'd been keeping to herself, as was her way with new folks, but even she hadn't been able to bite her tongue at this news. "Hold up, *what*? How the hell did you manage that?"

"There's this experimental, ghostweed-based drug for pain relief that's being developed right now—Ferron's on the cutting edge of this kind of thing. It's not meant *for* favors, but I've been toying with the recipe, and, well . . . I finally got a batch that works." She blushed, shrugging.

Excitement stirred in Aster's belly. *This* was the kind of advantage they would need to survive what was to come.

"Tansy, that's amazing," Aster said. "I can't even begin to imagine how much this is going to help people."

"Well, I still have to perfect it. But it's on the right track for sure. I only have one batch with me right now, but it should be enough for the few of us, so long as we're careful with it."

"And what do *you* have to say for yourself, Clem?" Aster asked her sister, raising a brow. "Are you out there saving lives, too?"

Clementine snorted. "Hardly! I play the piano at the dancing hall down the street. There's so much culture in the city, though, Aster. People from all over the world come through our bar. They tell the most interesting stories. I only wish I could share my own," she added with a laugh.

Aster smiled, warm with pride. It wasn't all good in Ferron, Aster knew—Good Luck Girls would face hatefulness no matter where the wind took them. But to see her sister thriving, in a way neither of them could have imagined a year ago, still felt as unreal as a dream from beyond the Veil.

"Zee's got the most exciting job, though," Clem continued. "He works at a weapons factory, assembling all these high-end voltric firearms."

"And you're able to support her doing that?" Aster asked pointedly.

"*Barely*," Clementine answered for him. "And I swear he spends half of it on hair grease."

"Maybe, but what do we need shine for?" Zee countered, putting his arm around Clementine and pulling her closer. "The sun gives us all the gold we could ever want, and the moon all the silver. We're richer than kings."

Clementine giggled, pushing him away playfully. "You're so corny."

Aster was less amused.

"Well," she said bracingly, turning to Raven. "There you have it—a one-woman batball team, a barroom pianist, a copperless cornball, and a medic who may actually be brilliant enough to get the rest of us through this. Are you sure you still want to join this circus?"

Raven offered half a smile. "Well, it sounds like you still have room for a brooding artist. I'd be happy to offer my services."

Zee grinned in return. "I like her."

"She's relieved, I'm sure," Tansy said sarcastically. "Raven, what kind of art do you do?"

Aster expected her to deflect, but Raven's eyes lit up with excitement at the question.

"Leadpoint, mostly," Raven said. "The Ladies have been kind enough to provide me with materials. But before, at the welcome house, I had to make do with whatever I could find. I used old charcoal for the lines and shading and old newspapers for the canvas."

"Oh, which welcome house did you grow up in?" Clementine asked.

Raven's expression shuttered again, her smile fading.

"Sorry, that's really not my business—" Clem amended.

"No, we're about to be spending a lot of time together. It's only natural you'd want to know more about me, right?" Raven said, leaning back and crossing her arms. "But my welcome house isn't one you all would've heard of. It was an off-books establishment, meant to cater to . . . 'illicit' tastes. There were a lot of girls like me there. My folks sold me off as soon as I was old enough—said if I wanted to be a girl so bad, I could go and make a living of it."

Aster had never heard this story before, and it hit her like a gut punch. Most girls got sold to welcome houses because their families were desperate for the shine or genuinely believed their daughter would be better off. But to be abandoned by your parents out of spite . . .

"By the dead, Ray, I had no idea. I'm so sorry."

"Me, too. To hell with them," Mallow said in a low voice. Her face was drawn. "My brother and I . . . we were always kind of different like that. Not in the same way as you, exactly . . . it was more like we were both caught in the middle somewhere, between whatever it means to be a boy or a girl, him just a little too gentle and me just a little too rough . . . and the other kids would give us shit for it, of course, but never our folks. They always seemed to understand."

Tansy took Mallow's hand and turned to Raven. "I know we're no replacement for the family you've lost, Raven, and we're not trying to be, but . . . we've all had to learn how to be there for each other when no one else was. No one's going to drive you away from *this* family."

Clementine nodded excitedly. "Hell, if you've been looking after Aster in my absence, you're already as good as a sister to me."

Raven's expression softened just for a moment, then she drew her guard up once again, clearing her throat and looking away. "That's real kind of you all to say. I'll hold you to it." Then she uncrossed her arms and caught Aster's eye. "I reckon this all is part of the reason I've always felt for you, Aster, and the way you get frustrated with how the Ladies do things. They try so hard to work within the law, but as far as the law's concerned, I shouldn't even exist. Why should I respect it when it doesn't respect me?"

"*Exactly*," Mallow said, raising her glass.

"And I won't pretend I'm not feeling some kind of way about this plan of yours—I mean, I've never had to live rough on the road like you all, and I'm sure as hell going to miss my bed," Raven went on with a nervous chuckle. "But if the law won't protect folks, then someone else has to." She lifted one shoulder in a shrug. "It might as well be us."

CHAPTER NINE

They set out from the Graveyard the next morning, the sun warm on their backs.

As Aster had expected, Priscilla had refused to help them in their new mission to blackmail McClennon—but neither did she make any effort to stop them from leaving, even going so far as to provide them with fresh horses and supplies and a little bit of shine to get them started. Her anger from the night before had been replaced by an old woman's resignation, regret ringing through her voice as she bid Aster farewell separate from the others.

I feel like I have failed you, Dawn, she said.

The words broke Aster's heart. *Never. You saved me—you saved all of us. It's just my turn to do the same for others, as best I know how.*

Priscilla sighed at that. *I forget how intoxicating the courage of youth can be, though I might call it folly . . . I would wish you all to wander well, but I fear there's only suffering down this path you've chosen. And so, just go with my love.*

Her last words to them were still ringing in Aster's ears as they picked their way through the woods. *Go with my love.*

Aster's own mother had been a distant woman, bitter as the pit of a fruit whose sweetness had long since been eaten away. She had loved Aster, in her way, but she never said the words. And Mother Fleur—Mother Fleur had only ever loved her girls in the way a spider loved its flies. So Aster had not known how to respond to Priscilla's love, so freely given, even in the face of their split. The whole thing had struck some fragile part of her, and even now, hours later, she was struggling to harden her heart once again for the fight ahead.

"Damn mosquitoes all over the damn place," Raven muttered from behind Aster. The two of them were sharing a horse, taking point, while Clementine rode with Zee behind them and Tansy and Mallow brought up the rear. Raven swatted at the whining insects all around them—she clearly, like Aster, had gotten used to the luxuries that working undercover for the Lady Ghosts had afforded them, such as being free to travel on the road, sometimes even in a coach. But from now on, unless they used some of Tansy's precious ghostweed salve that would allow them to cover their favors for extended periods of time, they would have to remain in hiding. "How much longer until we get where we're going, Aster?"

"Another six hours at least, so settle in," Aster said. They were on their way to Bullridge, a town a couple hours outside of Northrock. Aster had sent Violet a voltragraph last night to hash out the details of their meeting, Aster writing under the alias they had agreed upon earlier:

Mr. Derrick McClennon:
  Please accept my deepest sympathies for the loss of the

Northrock welcome house. I so enjoyed learning more about the project when last we met. Now, more than ever, I wish to continue working together to help you bring about your vision for a better Arketta. It's been my good luck that several of my associates have recently arrived from Ferron and would like to meet with you as soon as possible. When and where would be agreeable to all parties for a conference?

Sincerely, Ms. Sunny O'Brian

To which Violet had responded this morning:

Ms. Sunny O'Brian:

Thank you kindly for your condolences. Mr. McClennon is glad to hear you're well. He'd be delighted to meet with you and your associates this evening. Please join us in Bullridge at the Broken Wheel Saloon at 8:00. He has reserved the private room so you may talk at your leisure. We look forward to seeing you.

Sincerely,
Violet

After everything she'd already been through in Northrock, Aster wasn't in any particular hurry to go back to another town, even a smaller one. It would've been better if they could've met somewhere more remote. Why had Violet suggested this place? Did Derrick just not trust the rest of them yet?

Well, that can cut both ways, she thought. The farther they rode, the less sure Aster felt about involving the McClennon boy. The welcome house fire had been a success *despite* his involvement, not because of it. And he had hardly been happy to go along with it—who was to say he'd want to help them blackmail his uncle into closing *all* the welcome houses?

Let's just say you're not the only one with cause to hate my family, that was what he'd said to reassure her. But how could he have as much cause as someone like Clementine, who'd nearly been killed by his brother? It felt almost callous to make Clem sit in the same room as him.

If he so much as looked at her the wrong way, Aster was going to knock the taste out of his pretty mouth—and she didn't care who else was around to see it.

Raven, shrewd as ever, saw right through Aster's stony silence.

"And what happens when we ride all this way only for Baby McClennon to tell us he's *not* going to betray his family, actually?" she asked.

Aster shifted uneasily in the saddle, the humid air suddenly too warm in her throat. "You haven't met him. He's not forceful like that. He'll do whatever we ask of him just for the sake of avoiding an argument."

"All right, but Aster . . . this is a big ask."

Aster sighed, no longer able to keep up the pretense. "Look, you're right. But if there's one thing the Ladies got right, it's that having an inside man is priceless. I'm not going to pretend I trust this bastard—I don't—but Violet trusts this bastard, and I trust her."

"I reckon she's the real reason you're going to all this trouble anyway," Raven said slyly.

Aster threw a glance over her shoulder. "What the rip is that supposed to mean?"

Raven shrugged, cooling herself off with the paper fan that she had seen fit to pack along with the essentials. "I mean, you were so desperate to get Violet back that you went to Northrock *by yourself* to save her. And now your first instinct is to go to her again, not just risking your life this time, but theirs, too," Raven said, gesturing to the others riding behind them. "You've told me about how much you two leaned on each other when you were on the run . . . I just worry, sometimes, that you never learned how to stand straight without her."

Aster's cheeks heated. She'd let Raven draw a portrait of her once, Aster sitting still for an endless hour while Raven studied her with her piercing gaze. This felt much the same. "I don't *need* anybody, Raven, and I don't much appreciate you suggesting that I'm being reckless with you all's lives, either."

"Hey, hey, easy," Raven said. "I'm just trying to ask you the tough questions everyone else is afraid to. Seems like that used to be Violet's job, but until we catch up to her, I feel like it's on me. I'm the oldest, after all."

Aster didn't know what to say to that. Raven was right again, but Aster didn't want to admit it.

"So you're saying we shouldn't be making this stop, is that it?" Aster mumbled, chastened.

"No, I'm saying I think you're doing the right thing for the wrong reason. But what does it matter, as long as it gets us our inside man? And besides, as much as you all have been talking up this girl, now I feel like I have to meet her. I want to make a good impression."

Aster grinned a little at that. "Since when do you care what other folks think of you?" she asked.

"Hey, just because I don't need anyone's approval doesn't mean it's not nice to have," Raven cracked back.

Their group reached Bullridge by early evening, dismounting to cover their favors before venturing out of the woods and into town.

"All right, let's give this ghostweed salve a try," Aster said, turning to Tansy. Tansy nodded and dug a large jar out of her satchel.

"Just enough to thinly coat your favor—remember, we have to conserve our resources," Tansy instructed them, demonstrating first on herself. Then she passed the jar along to Aster. The salve inside had a faint lavenderlike scent, though whether that was natural to the ghostweed or something Tansy had added herself, Aster wasn't sure. Aster carefully spread the smooth white cream over her neck and jaw, her heart kicking with anticipation. It was cool on her skin, even after being exposed to the heat of the day, and its numbing relief was immediate. Aster had been doing her best to keep her expectations in check, but she couldn't help letting out a laugh of triumph. She passed the jar along to the others.

"I still hate having to wear the dustkerchief," Clementine muttered, tying the fabric around the bottom half of her face.

"It's not for long," Aster promised. "Violet said Derrick reserved a private room for us at this bar. We only have to keep our favors hidden until then."

"Why couldn't the two of them meet us out here?" Mallow asked. She had carefully covered her headband with the brim of her hat to avoid suspicion once they got into town, though Aster could tell it bothered her to do so. "Is pretty boy afraid to get his shoes dirty?"

"More like he's afraid of *us*," Clementine answered.

"Yeah, Aster, do we need to be ready for trouble?" Zee asked, his hand falling to the revolver at his hip. "I mean, you all killed his brother . . . maybe this whole thing is a setup."

Aster glanced at Raven, whose face was already covered, though her raised brow betrayed her *What did I tell you?* expression well enough.

"It's not Derrick I'm trusting—it's Violet," Aster said again, exasperated. "And I'm trusting you all, because I know we can handle whatever this little fool might throw at us. Now come on, let's not keep him waiting."

They mounted up and left for the road leading into Bullridge, their horses' long, lazy shadows trailing out behind them, even though they themselves had none. It was still half an hour at least until sunset, but the ember-flies had already come out for the night, flickering faintly in the fading light. The sounds of the town flickered in and out just as gently: a hammer hitting a horseshoe, a wagon rumbling around a sharp turn, a dog barking for attention and a delighted child laughing in response. Bullridge had a clean, crisp look to it, the buildings along Main Street packed neatly and beaming with fresh white paint. It was nothing like the towns in the Scab, dust-choked and neglected, crawling with lawmen to keep out the dustbloods and entombed in deadwalls to keep out the vengeants. No, this was the kind of "nice place" that McClennon had in mind whenever he waxed poetic about Arketta and its fine fairblood families.

Aster hated it already.

"Look, there's the Broken Wheel," Raven murmured.

Aster followed her gaze. The saloon was at the end of the street, on the corner. A broken wheel hung from beneath the sign.

"Good eye, Ray," Aster said, turning to point it out to the others. It was hard to tell behind their dustkerchiefs, but they looked just as uncomfortable as Aster felt. She'd been out of place in the nicer parts of Northrock, too, but at least there were so many people there you could disappear in the crowd. Here, it seemed like everyone was watching them pull up to the saloon and tie their horses to the post.

"Not to put too fine a point on it, but where the rip is Derrick?" Mallow whispered harshly.

It was true—he was nowhere in sight. Aster checked her pocket watch, cursing when she realized it was already five past eight. He was probably just running a few minutes late, but they could hardly hang around here long without him.

"Well, no need to make a scene," Zee said quietly. "Let me take the lead on this one. They can't kick us out. We're not breaking any laws."

"Yet," Mallow mumbled.

They filed inside through the saloon double doors, their boots squeaking over the polished wood floors. Golden gasoliers hung from a tin-tile ceiling, bathing the space in a warm, honeyed glow. The murmur of conversation quieted as folks took note of Aster and the others. Of their covered faces, their shadowless feet. The patrons shifted uneasily in their seats.

Zee cleared his throat and walked up to the crowded bar as if he hadn't noticed the sudden turn in the atmosphere.

"Evening, sir," he said to the bartender, a thickset man with thinning hair. His nametag read: Russ.

"Evening," Russ said back neutrally, setting down the glass he'd been drying. "You all look like you've come a long way."

Zee didn't miss a beat. "That we have. We're here to meet a business associate of mine. I'll thank you kindly for a cider while we wait." He reached into his pocket and slid a pair of eagles across the bar. Russ looked at the shine but didn't take it.

"You from the Scab, then?" he pressed. "You must be, covering your faces like that. There's no need for all that here, you know. Dust isn't a problem in these parts."

Zee hesitated, but Tansy jumped in and answered for him.

"You live in the Scab long enough, and your lungs become sensitive to even trace amounts of dust in the air. Better safe than sorry, sir, begging your pardon."

Aster and Zee exchanged glances. Tansy was clearly just making shit up, but maybe it would be enough to convince this man. Everything he knew from the Scab probably came from a sensationalist copper novel.

The muscles in the bartender's jaw worked, but he relented, turning to pour Zee's drink. Aster exhaled softly.

Then a man standing beside them spoke up.

"Russ. Come on now. You can't let them stay."

Aster tensed back up immediately. The man had spun around on his barstool to face them, scowling beneath his bristly blond moustache.

"You saw what happened down in Northrock," the man

went on. "That welcome house fire—it was one of them that did it."

A stab of fear pierced Aster's heart. How the hell did he know? Her hand fell to her knife—

"We had nothing to do with that, sir," Zee said calmly.

"It was a dustblood, though, wasn't it? You're all the same."

Oh. Aster loosened her grip on the hilt of her knife, but her scowl deepened as the man continued. "Bad genes. Corrupted souls. Like animals. You all can't help yourselves." The man turned back to Russ. "It's not safe having them here. There's a reason their ancestors were shipped off to the Scab."

A rush of heat warmed Aster's cheeks, anger and shame burning through her like a fever. She opened and shut her mouth, swallowing back the defensive words rising to her lips.

"You watch your mouth," Mallow growled, even as Aster struggled to keep her own calm.

"Mal," Tansy warned in a whisper.

The man drew himself up. "What'd you say to me?"

"Just watch it, is all. You don't speak ill of our dead."

"All right, that's enough," Russ said, placing his meaty hands on the counter. "I'm going to have to ask you all to leave—"

"Well, maybe your dead should've made an honest living for themselves instead of becoming cutthroats and traitors—"

Mallow's fist flew from her hip and landed squarely across the man's jaw. He fell from his stool and landed in a heap on the floor, the glass in his hand shattering beside him. Aster stood frozen in shock. If the room had been muted before, it was silent now.

Then, a split second later, it erupted into noise.

110

"What the hell?!"

"Get them out of here!"

"Get your gun, Russ!"

"*What* did I say? *What the hell did I just say?*" the first man bellowed over the chaos as he climbed to his feet and gave Mallow a forceful shove. "No-good ripping *criminals*!"

Mallow fell backwards into another patron, who cursed and threw a wild punch at her temple.

"*Hey!*" Tansy yipped. She ran forward and kicked the second man square between the legs. He howled and crumpled to the floor. But then a third man grabbed Tansy from behind, wrapping his arms around her middle and lifting her off the ground.

Rip it, Aster thought. The time for discretion was over. She grabbed the nearest chair and swung it at the third man. It broke across his back. Then somebody else grabbed Aster by her shoulders and yanked her to the ground. Panic shot through her as she landed hard, pain jarring her bones. For a moment the old fear seized her in its jaws, crushing her lungs, forcing bile to her throat. Then Zee jumped over her and landed an uppercut to the man's gut.

Aster scrambled back to her feet, giving Zee a grateful nod. Everybody was in it now, even Raven, who vaulted over tables and threw half-full pint glasses back at a wild-eyed man chasing her. The once-tidy saloon was being swiftly destroyed, the air filled with the sounds of wood splintering, beer bottles breaking, and fists hitting flesh. Aster quickly found Clementine and stood back-to-back with her, the months of self-defense training she'd learned from the Lady Ghosts clicking into place as she dodged haymakers and countered with precise straight punches to noses and throats.

Then, suddenly, just as a man twice Aster's size bore down on them, two earsplitting gunshots cut through the chaos.

Everyone stopped and turned. Russ stood behind the bar with a shotgun in his hand. He'd blown a hole through the ceiling with his warning shots, but he looked well past the point of caring.

"I SAID THAT'S ENOUGH!" he roared over them all. "YOU LOT!" He pointed a stubby finger at Zee. "OUT!"

Zee was disheveled and out of breath, his dustkerchief askew. They were lucky he was the only one, Aster realized. If anyone else had had their dustkerchief ripped off, they all would have been exposed.

"But sir, our business associate—" Zee began.

Russ stomped out from behind the bar, advancing on Zee. Zee stumbled backwards, hands held up. Russ grabbed him by his collar, dragged him over to the double doors, and threw him out onto the street.

"*OUT!*"

"Zee!" Clem cried. She and Aster ran out after him, the other girls behind them. They crowded around Zee and helped him up.

"I'm so sorry, I'm so sorry," Mallow was saying, over and over. "This is all my fault. I just got riled up—"

"Don't apologize. That bastard had it coming," Zee said, wiping blood away from his split lip.

Several people had stopped on the street to stare at them. Aster's cheeks burned, and she averted her eyes. And then, with

112

her gaze cast to the ground, she realized that she recognized the immaculate pair of patent leather shoes in front of her. She looked up, her embarrassment deepening.

And there, sure enough, stood Derrick McClennon, Violet stepping out of their coach behind him. The brim of his bowler shaded his eyes, but Aster could make out the downward turn of his mouth well enough.

"And what fresh hell is this?" He sighed.

"And of course I'll pay for the damage," Derrick was saying to Russ at the bar. Aster and the others stood behind him, Tansy carefully dabbing at a cut above Mallow's eyebrow while Zee poured whiskey over his bloodied knuckles with a wince.

Russ was still red in the face. "It's not just that. Your 'business associates' here—"

"Employees," Derrick corrected. Then, turning to glare at the group: "And rest assured, their unacceptable behavior tonight will be foremost among the many matters I have to discuss with them. But I've come a long way to meet them here, and I hope you'll still allow us to use the private room."

Russ ran a hand through his thinning hair. "Yes, Mr. McClennon, of course. My apologies," he said, sighing in defeat.

Aster released a breath of her own. If it were anyone else, the bartender probably would demand to know what exactly their business was that was so damned important. But folks weren't in the habit of questioning the McClennons.

Derrick pulled out his coin purse, flashing a charming smile. "A round for the house, while we're at it. And double for you. For your trouble."

"Yes, sir. Thank you, sir. I'll make sure you're not disturbed."

"Good man."

Derrick crooked a finger, inviting the others to follow him to the back room. Aster swallowed back the acid resentment rising in her throat. At his soft, measured voice, at the sheer ease of his power. They'd walked in here and within minutes the whole place had practically come down around them in revolt. He'd walked in here and commanded instant respect without even having to ask for it. What must it be like, going through life like that, vanishing all your problems with a wave of your hand?

But this is exactly why we need him, Aster reminded herself. Only someone this high up in the landmasters' world could tell her how best to blackmail them.

Derrick opened the door to the back room, where a semicircular leather booth wrapped around a polished cherry-wood table with a leftover ashtray at its center. A pair of windows faced out towards the street, but he drew the heavy velvet curtains so they could enjoy some privacy.

"Lights, please," he ordered, to no one in particular, and Zee reached over to twist the gasolier knob to full brightness. Then Tansy closed the door behind them, drawing the little curtain across its window as well. Only once she clicked the lock shut did everyone allow themselves to remove their dustkerchiefs, sliding into the plush booth one after the other.

"So," Violet said once they were all seated, crossing her arms as she glared at each of them. "Care to explain what all *that* was about?"

"What had happened was—" Clementine started.

"*Don't* worry about it," Aster interrupted. "We have way too much to talk about."

"Yeah, like how the hell have you been, Violet?" Mallow asked, grinning. "I really thought I'd never see your mug again."

"Likewise, Mallow," Violet answered. "When Aster said you all had made it to Ferron I hoped maybe that meant you'd settled down into a quiet life. But now that I see you're still scrapping like a bunch of stray cats—"

"It's not Mal's fault," Aster said tiredly. "These people . . . they don't want us here. They were spoiling for a fight. I don't know why you couldn't have us meet somewhere less public, Derrick."

Now that they were alone, Derrick had dropped the charming facade he'd used on Russ, and he looked more like Aster remembered him at the Northrock welcome house: tired, anxious, overwhelmed. He heaved a sigh, running a hand through his red hair.

"Maybe he foolishly assumed you all would be able to behave yourselves in public," Violet mumbled. The way they had arranged themselves in the booth, it had worked out that Violet and Derrick, the fairbloods, were on one side by themselves. Aster didn't like it, didn't like the way Violet seemed embarrassed by them rather than coming to their defense. It didn't matter if she had a shadow at her feet. Violet was a Good Luck Girl, too.

"Ripping hell, you have no idea what we risked to be here," she continued.

"Well, this wasn't exactly a stroll through the park for us, either, Vi," Aster said, more bitterly than she'd meant to, her hurt turning to venom. "We gave up the Lady Ghosts' protection to meet *you*. We came into this snake's den to meet *you*—"

Raven caught Aster's eye, shaking her head subtly. Right. This isn't about her. Aster swallowed the rest of her words.

Violet opened her mouth to bite back, but Derrick held up his hand before she could. "Aster's right," he murmured. "It's not their fault. It's as I predicted before . . . the welcome house fire has put fairblood folks on edge. I wanted to meet somewhere I regularly conduct business so as to reduce suspicion, but . . . I should have anticipated this."

"Yes, but we're here now, so let's get on with it," Tansy said, clearly trying to keep the peace.

They began with a series of stiff introductions, each of them greeting Derrick with forced formality while he thanked them and smiled unconvincingly in return. But it wasn't until Clementine introduced herself that the brittle tension threatened to snap entirely. Derrick's smile slipped.

"Clementine," he echoed. "So, then, you're the one who killed my brother."

A voltric current sizzled through the group. Violet threw Derrick a warning glare. Zee shifted subtly to protect Clementine. Aster drew herself up and leaned forward.

"We all played our part in that, McClennon," she said in a low voice. "If it's going to be a problem, we best go our separate ways now."

He laughed humorlessly. "A problem? Hardly. It's the reason I agreed to meet. My brother, he always seemed so . . . indestructible to me. Indestructible and inevitable, like a train roaring down the tracks. I have spent my whole life

116

running after him . . . or perhaps running from him. I'm not sure which."

He was avoiding their eyes now, picking at his cuff. "The changes I'd like to see made in our government are changes most would consider impossible, but any person who could kill my brother is a person who has already *achieved* the impossible, as far as I'm concerned." He laughed again. "I'm just surprised it's a little girl."

Clementine bristled. "I'm the same age as you."

Aster kicked her under the table. "*So*," she said to Derrick, still wary, "you're sure there are no hard feelings?"

"All feelings are hard. But no—that train needed to be stopped. I can recognize that, even if no one else in my family can. And I can apologize, too, for what it's worth—I'm sorry, truly, for the pain my brother caused you." He sighed and seemed to collect himself. "So, Aster, now that you've got us all in one room, what did you want to talk about?"

Aster considered Derrick with something she reluctantly recognized as respect. She had not expected him to be so honest with them. Maybe it was all an act, but somehow she didn't think so. There was a rawness to him, some unspoken sorrow seeping out like blood from an unhealed wound. Aster had seen it half a hundred times before—but never in a man.

"Let's start with the welcome house fire," Aster began, clearing her throat. "How did your family react?"

"An excellent question," Derrick said, seeming grateful for the change of subject. He pulled a notebook out of his satchel, flipping it open to the place he'd marked with a ribbon. The page was filled with neat script. "The leadership of the Landmasters'

117

Guild had a meeting in the wake of the fire to discuss our response. My father brought me along, and I took notes—"

"Wait—who, specifically, was there?" Aster interrupted.

He paused. "Does it matter?"

"It might."

He leaned back, closing his eyes as he remembered. "The Harkers and Sullivans, of course, the second and third most powerful Scab families—the Harkers own the majority of the tenant farms, while the Sullivans own the largest railroad, and some of the associated mines as well. Then there were the Cains—new blood from up north, with dustbloods working in the growing industrial sector. And lastly there was Boyle, whose family does business on the coastline south of the Scab, in the shipping industry. There are hundreds of other lower-level landmasters working in Arketta, of course, both inside and outside the Scab, but those five families, collectively, control eighty-five percent of all dustblood labor—including the welcome houses. And the heads of those families have traditionally made up the Landmasters' Guild's council. An attack on one of us is seen as an attack on all of us."

Aster couldn't help curling her lip as Derrick rattled off the names of the men whose ancestors had carved up Arketta like so much meat for the taking, and who fed on its peoples' suffering still. The name Sullivan had been on the lid of every crate and the handle of every pickaxe in Shade Hollow, the old mining town where she'd grown up, and stitched, too, on the uniform of every ravener who'd ever terrorized her family. As Aster looked around, she saw her disgust written on all her friends' faces. She tried to keep the accusation out of her voice as she spoke.

118

"And if you were at this great meeting of minds, does that mean your family's finally let you into their inner circle?" Aster asked tightly.

"Given the severity of the situation, I think they felt they had no choice but to bring me in." Derrick hesitated, lacing his fingers together thoughtfully. "Perhaps, in hindsight, the fire was worth it for that alone."

"Well, I'm glad it worked out so well for *you*," Tansy said sourly.

"Hey, easy," Violet shot back. "Derrick took a lot of heat from his family for letting this happen on his watch. Just because they need his help doesn't mean he's on their good side now."

His freckled cheeks turned pink. "I have never been on their good side," he muttered. "But suffice to say, this meeting complicates things for us. The landmasters *know* it was a revolutionary, not some 'unstable Good Luck Girl,' who started that fire—and *my* family suspects you in particular, Aster, though of course they'd never admit to the others that you're still alive. It doesn't help that there have been several smaller incidents since then, including the burning of one of the Harkers' Sweet Thistle fields. As such, they're taking every precaution to keep the dustblood dissention from spreading any further. They're putting a zero-tolerance policy in effect at their camps—anyone caught discussing or attempting mutiny will be executed. Meanwhile, our connections in the government will be pressuring the authoritant to give the lawmasters more resources to control the situation." The authoritant—the head of the Arkettan government. If he'd gotten involved, things really had gone farther than Aster had realized. "Authoritant Lockley's not a member of the Landmasters' Guild, understand," Derrick went on, "but he's been the Guild's paid puppet for years. And for *my* family's part—" Here Derrick looked Aster square in the eye. "They're redoubling their efforts to capture you. Before, my uncle thought you had gone into hiding or died on the trail, and he was willing to let it go. But now that he suspects you're still fighting, he plans to hit back harder than ever." Derrick finally closed his notebook and sat back. "You'll have my support no matter what you decide—as I've said before, I think we have many of the same goals. But, with all this in mind, I ask you to *carefully consider* whether it's really worth it to continue with your more . . . direct approach."

"Well, it's funny you should say that, because we're actually going to be approaching all this more directly than ever," Aster said. But then she hesitated, suddenly afraid to expose her fragile plan to the open air for Derrick to dissect with his surgical reasoning. And Violet—Violet would not go easy on her either. She never had.

But Raven was right . . . I need her, Aster thought, the truth of it cutting through her stubborn pride.

And she needed Derrick, too.

She took a breath. "We want to blackmail the landmasters into closing down their welcome houses." There, it was out. "We keep burning down their property, like the welcome house, like the Sweet Thistle fields, until they give in to our demands."

Derrick stared. The muscle in his jaw twitched. "You must be joking," he said slowly.

Aster's cheeks grew warm. "I'm serious as the dead. We need your help deciding which properties to target."

"Aster, what you're describing is the work of an army. There is no way you could do enough damage to—"

"You leave the logistics to me," Aster said. "Like I said, we just need you to point us in the right direction."

"All directions lead to disaster!" For the first time, Derrick raised his voice, and Violet was quick to quiet him before he was overheard by the patrons outside. He continued in a tight whisper. "You do not understand—you cannot comprehend—the amount of shine these families make off the welcome houses. It is a more lucrative business even than mining. The demand never falters. The supply is endless. Welcome houses are the jewels of any landmaster's empire—"

Aster stood and reached across the table to grab Derrick by his crisp white collar, her knuckles digging into his sharp collarbones. The wood creaked beneath him as she dragged him closer.

"Keep talking about my friends in terms of 'supply and demand' and see what happens," Aster said through her teeth.

"*Aster*," Violet hissed.

"Easy," Zee pleaded. "We can't afford another fight here."

But then Derrick flinched, closing his eyes against the coming punishment, and there was something so familiar in his fear that Aster let him go immediately, as if she'd touched something cold and wet. Derrick fell back into the plush booth.

"I'm sorry," he breathed, brushing away the hair that had fallen in his eyes. "I didn't mean it like that. I only wanted to help you understand."

The nerve of this boy. Aster was shocked to find her eyes stinging with the threat of tears. "I understand better than

121

you ever could," she murmured, and sat back down heavily.

"So, Derrick, you're saying that the welcome houses are so profitable that nothing would be worth giving them up, is that it?" Clementine asked, looking between the two of them, clearly pleading for peace.

"Not nothing," Derrick said, his voice still shaking slightly. "Eventually, yes, you could make it too costly for the landmasters to keep ignoring you. But like I said, it's the work of an army. For the people in this room to take them on, alone . . . it's impossible."

"Well, then, it's a good thing you've expressed such an interest in achieving the impossible," Aster said dryly. "Look, Derrick, from what you're telling us, the welcome houses aren't something the landmasters are ever going to give up willingly—so waging this kind of war against them is our only choice. We owe it to these girls at least to *try*." Her eyes began to burn again, and she blinked them angrily. "You know your own family best, so let's make it easy and start there—what do the McClennons value the most?"

At last he seemed to consider the question in earnest. He swallowed, his throat bobbing.

"Your mining operations, obviously," Tansy suggested after a moment. "That's how you all got your start. So, what's your most valuable mine?"

"It doesn't matter," Derrick said. "To destroy that mine—to destroy *any* mine—would be incredibly dangerous. You'd need explosives."

Well, that could certainly be arranged, but Aster didn't much like the idea, either. There were too many variables they couldn't control. A rockslide, a cave-in, a sinkhole opening up and swallowing them—they'd need the help of an expert if they were going to try to blow up a mountain, and Derrick, for all his insider knowledge, had probably never so much as swung a pickax.

"It's a good idea, but we'd need more time to prepare. What can we do *now*?" Aster asked, trying not to let her impatience get the better of her.

"What about another welcome house, then?" Derrick offered. "If that's the business you want to see changed, why not attack it directly, rather than burning down farms or blowing up mines? I can suggest a few locations that—"

Aster shook her head. "We've already decided we don't want to put the girls in danger. The five of us alone barely managed to get away and survive being on the run. A whole welcome house full of girls . . . the little ones, the older women dependent on Sweet Thistle . . . I'm willing to take risks, but not with their lives."

Derrick puffed out his cheeks in frustration.

"You're making it very difficult for him to help us," Violet said pointedly.

"Stop coddling him," Aster snapped back. "Come on, keep thinking."

They all fell into silence as they considered the problem before them. The muffled sounds of the barroom filtered in from beyond the door.

"What about *you*?" Raven asked suddenly, leaning forward and fixing her piercing stare on Derrick. It was the first time she'd spoken since they'd started the meeting, and Derrick seemed startled to find her addressing him.

"What about me?" he echoed.

"Aster asked what your family valued most," Raven went on. "And something tells me there's nothing they care about more than their last living son. If we pretended to take you hostage, I reckon they'd give in to our demands right away."

It was as if Raven had lobbed a bomb into the middle of the room.

"Holy *shit*, Raven. I mean this in the best way possible, but how the ripping hell does your mind work—" Mallow said, grinning.

"It's brilliant," Clementine agreed.

"But where's the best place to pull this off?" Zee asked.

"Should we do it right now?" Tansy suggested.

"*Wait*," Derrick interrupted, his eyes widening. "I haven't even agreed to this yet."

But Aster's mind was already racing as she considered the possibilities. She leaned forward. "Derrick, think about it—it's perfect. We stage a kidnapping, you come into hiding with us, and then you can continue to help us without worrying about raising suspicion from your family, who will only be thinking about getting you back."

And we'll be keeping you close, so you don't have the chance to betray us, Aster thought, though she didn't say so.

"It would definitely light a fire under their asses faster than anything else," Violet admitted, a slow half smile spreading over her face. "Aren't you always saying you want to get away from them anyway, Derrick? I know *I* certainly do."

"Yeah, Violet, we could get you back, too!" Clementine said excitedly.

Aster and Violet locked eyes, and, despite the friction

between them earlier, Aster felt a kick of genuine excitement at the thought of having her back for good.

"But I can't just—I can't just leave my whole life behind for the dead know how long," Derrick sputtered. "Where could we even go that my family's raveners wouldn't find us?"

Zee cleared his throat, looking at Aster meaningfully. "We have friends who'd be willing to take us in, for a price. Might even be able to outfit us with some military-grade voltric weapons from Ferron, too, to help us get the job done." Aster stared at him blankly. "Sam Daniels and them," he clarified.

The Scorpions. Zee was probably being vague for Derrick's sake, not wanting to give away too much information about the rebels and their underground sanctuary for hotfoots. But they'd remained hidden from raveners for years in their network of abandoned mines. There was nowhere Aster would feel safer within the Scab.

"Zee, that's fantastic," she said, pulling out a notebook from her satchel so she could begin writing down the details. "What's the nearest town to their base camp?"

"Well, there's Scarcliff, of course—but I'm guessing we don't want to show our faces around there again after the bank robbery. So our next best option is Rattlebank."

"All right, and Derrick, does your family have any operations in Rattlebank?" Aster barreled on. "They must, they're every-damn-where. Could you say you have some business in town, find an excuse to be there?"

"There's a . . . a gambling hall. Our largest, actually. It's where we keep some of our finest cuts of theomite, as winnings. The place has been in our family for generations, and a lot of unofficial business gets conducted there. But—"

"So we stage the kidnapping there, and we steal the theomite and burn down the gambling hall while we're at it. I still think it's important to hit them in the wallet, too. And then we just need to find a way to get our demands out, explaining that we'll return Derrick once they're met—"

"Stop," Derrick whispered. He had braced his dovelike hands against the table, eyes closed and breathing slowed, as if he were trying to steady his stomach while on the deck of a heaving ship. "This whole plan . . . *assumes* . . . that my family would go to any lengths to get me back, when, in point of fact, they will be glad to be rid of me. My father has made it clear he believes the wrong son died, and my uncle, for all his half-hearted efforts to mold me in his image, is far more interested in advancing his own career. I am nothing more to them than a burden and a disappointment. It's not that I'm unwilling to do this—I will do whatever you ask of me, Aster—but you came here for my advice, and so I am advising you: do not pin your hopes on this."

Aster looked at Violet, bewildered. *What the hell is this?* Perhaps Derrick expected her to feel sorry for him—he certainly seemed to feel sorry for himself—but she could only think again how removed he was from reality. The world kept turning when *dustblood* children went missing, sure. But a fairblood child? The son of a landmaster? The *heir* to the McClennon empire?

"Derrick, for the love of the dead—" Aster began, exasperated, but Violet cut her off with a cool blue look, shaking her head subtly.

"Don't sell yourself so short, Derrick," she told him. "You are the last living son of the McClennon bloodline, your family's sole hope for the future. You may have your differences, but none of them doubts your value or importance. That's *why* they're so hard on you."

"But—" he protested.

"Take it from an outsider who's been living with your family for months now," Violet insisted. "They would tear down the Veil to get you back."

Derrick still looked doubtful, but he swallowed and nodded. "All right," he said, seeming to steel himself. "All right, I'll agree to this. But it has to be on my terms—no unnecessary violence, and no killing under any circumstances—"

Mallow let out an impatient sigh. "Here we go."

"Why do you assume any violence we would resort to would be unnecessary?" Tansy asked pointedly. "As opposed to, what, the necessary violence of the welcome houses?"

"No, I don't mean—" Derrick said. "I just—I just don't want anyone hurt on my account."

"It wouldn't be on your account," Violet said quietly. "It wouldn't even be on ours. It would be for the girls we're trying to free."

She looked at Aster meaningfully as she spoke, and for the first time since the meeting had started, Aster felt like they were on the same side. Aster's chest filled with sudden warmth.

"All right, then, it's decided. Our next stop is Rattlebank," she said. She tapped Derrick's journal, indicating for him to start writing. "Now let's hash out the details."

CHAPTER TEN

The last time Aster had caught a train, she'd been practically dragged underneath its wheels while her friends pulled her up into the boxcar they'd chosen to stowaway in.

This time, thanks to Derrick, she actually had a ticket.

"Dustbloods to the last car, single file, keep it moving," the conductor was saying as Aster and Raven shuffled down the narrow aisle between seats. They'd separated their group to avoid suspicion while they traveled—Aster with Raven, Tansy and Mallow with Clementine, and Zee on his own. The train would take them as far as the edge of the Scab, where they'd pick up a coach and ride the rest of the way to Rattlebank. It was to be a different route than they'd traveled before: back then, they'd been on the Arkettan National Line, but now, they were taking Sullivan Rails.

"I've never ridden a train before," Raven whispered to Aster. "Are they all this high class? This shit looks like a welcome house on wheels."

It was true—Derrick had told them Sullivan Rails had the finest luxury cars of any rail company, and so it seemed to be. An aisle of polished cherrywood flooring ran between two carpeted rows of velvet-padded booths that stood on gaudy gold claw feet. Heavy valances swept along the top of the wide windows like frosting on a cake. The passengers, all well-dressed fairbloods, shot Aster and Raven dirty looks as they passed, and raveners guarded the entrance to every car. It was not a place where any dustbloods were welcome, let alone Good Luck Girls. They had all applied the ghostweed salve to their favors so they could cover them with makeup for the next several hours, but that didn't help the fact that they still didn't have shadows.

"Your guess is as good as mine," Aster muttered back to Raven. "But something tells me the dustblood car isn't going to look anything like this."

Finally they reached the car in question. Aster and Raven pushed their way into the crowded space—unlike the fairblood cars, there were no velvet-cushioned seats or carpeted floors here, just rough wooden benches and windowless walls. There weren't enough seats for everybody, and some folks were standing or sitting on the floor. The air was suddenly stifling, hot and sticky as the inside of a mouth. Air holes had been punched into the sides, sending spears of sunlight into the dark, but it was hardly enough. A pair of frustrated children cried ceaselessly, and Aster couldn't say that she blamed them.

"Well, this shit looks like . . . shit," Raven observed.

Aster scowled. The fairblood passengers would probably say they were lucky to have been allowed on the train at all. Some of them were no doubt complaining, at that very moment, that they had to share a ride with a bunch of degenerates. But for the love of the dead, could they not at least have given them enough room to breathe?

I was more comfortable as a ripping stowaway, Aster thought irritably as she and Raven slid down to the floor to sit between a sleeping, stooped-backed older man and a woman with a fidgety infant in her arms. The rest of their friends settled in opposite corners of the car, the girls several rows behind Aster, Zee directly across from her. The train let out a long whistle and started to roll. The floor jolted below them as the wheels gathered speed, bruising Aster's tailbone. She supposed she had Sullivan to thank for that, along with so much else she had suffered.

Eight hours to go.

There wasn't much Raven and Aster could talk about without giving themselves away, so they settled into silence. The scattered conversations around them washed over Aster meaninglessly until one of them caught her attention.

". . . first those Green Creek girls kill McClennon's boy, and now another Good Luck Girl burned down his welcome house . . ." one young woman was saying to another. Raven perked up, looking up at Aster, who didn't meet her eye but nodded to show that she'd heard, too. Aster leaned forward subtly so she could listen more closely.

"My brother-in-law wrote us saying there've been riots in the south—some of the miners got together and destroyed all their tools. And I saw in the papers that another tenant camp ganged up on one of the raveners on guard and trussed him up like a turkey."

"Yeah," her travel partner said, "and there have been lots of people clearing off in ones and twos as well, hotfoots making a run for Ferron. Most of them probably got caught, but the law's overwhelmed right now—they can't catch them all."

Hotfoots, like the ones the Scorpions sheltered in their underground hideouts. Would the Scorpions have recruited any of them to their cause? Aster wondered. Young men who might help even more dustblood families escape the Reckoning? The corner of her mouth twitched in a smile at the thought.

"All this trouble, and you really think there won't be consequences?" the first woman continued. "We need to slow this down, not speed it up."

"I'm starting to think it's like this train, though—no stopping it until it gets where it's going. But it can't be any worse than where we are. As far as I'm concerned, we can't get there fast enough."

And then, despite the stifling air, the sweat sticking to her skin, and the ache in her knees from sitting cross-legged for so long, Aster felt a sudden lift in her spirits. When they'd robbed the brags last year, they'd been acting out of survival instinct, in their own interests. What they were doing now was something bigger, greater. Not just for other Good Luck Girls, but for anyone who had been mistreated by the landmasters. It was giving folks the courage to fight back, and that was worth any risk. Derrick didn't see this side of Arketta; he couldn't understand.

The conversation died down as a ravener entered the car and scanned the crowd, his orange eyes flashing in the half-light. Every half hour or so one of them would do this, forcing a kind of syrupy sluggishness over them all to keep anyone from acting out despite the frustration everyone surely felt after half a day on this train. In combination with the heat and the stench, the ravenings that made Aster's head spin were enough to set her stomach churning. But once the guards left, Aster saw the defiance in folks' eyes return.

"Damned raveners," the woman who'd spoken first muttered. "I swear they have a sixth sense about this shit . . ."

"Aster," Raven whispered. She didn't seem nearly as bothered by the ravenings as Aster might have expected, and, if anything, looked a little bored. "How much farther do you reckon we have to go?"

"We're almost there, I think," Aster said. She peeked through one of the airholes in the side of the car, the heat making her eye sting.

Red desert. Gone were the fertile forests of the north or the rippling plains of the Goldsea, replaced by cracked earth under a harsh blue sky with little more than scrub brush to break up the horizon. Rock formations were scattered across the landscape like dice tossed from a giant's hand. They looked small from this distance, but they were massive, Aster knew, up close.

It wouldn't be much longer until the desert rose into the mountain range that made up the Scab, with its mean, twisted trees and the animals that struggled to live among them— panting coyotes, low-bellied rattletails, creeping tarantulas . . . and people, too, just as wind-stripped and dust-choked as the rest of it.

An unexpected surge of homesickness swelled in Aster's chest. Her breath hitched, and she swallowed the feeling back resentfully. She had wanted nothing her whole life but to escape this forsaken place. It had offered her nothing but suffering. It did not deserve her, did not deserve the longing she felt now to feel its sun on her skin or taste its dust on her tongue.

It doesn't matter how far you run. This place will always own you, a dark voice whispered in the back of her mind.

Aster set her jaw. If she could not run away from the Scab, she would tear it down to its foundations and rebuild it to be the home it always should have been for her.

Aster's tangled thoughts were interrupted by another ravener entering the car.

Something about this ravener's aura immediately felt different, more powerful. Aster gasped as a rash of chills rushed up her skin and a crushing wave of hopelessness washed over her mind.

Why? Aster thought, anger cutting through the sudden sorrow the ravener had forced on them. No one was misbehaving. They didn't deserve this. This ravener was just toying with them for the cruel fun of it.

She turned to face the ravener, her throat choking with tears.

And felt her heart kick in surprise.

This ravener was a woman.

A woman . . . and a dustblood. With warm brown skin and dark hair pulled into a low, severe bun underneath her railworker's cap. She surveyed the room with eyes the lurid orange of a rotting pumpkin. One hand rested on the gun at her belt, her nails filed near to claws. She was beautiful, but in the way a hawk was beautiful—deadly and sharp.

Everyone in the room tensed up, even as the ravener let her influence subside. Their shock and fear were their own. Aster risked a glance at the others in her group to see if they shared her trepidation. Tansy and Mallow were clinging to each other despite the danger of such an action. Clementine's usual smile was wiped clear off her face.

And then there was Zee, whose face had fallen into a mask of horror and disbelief, his jaw slack, his eyes round with fear. He shook his head, murmuring something to himself. Aster almost called out his name involuntarily before catching herself. She knew Zee had always been more afraid of raveners than the rest of them. He had reason to be. His father had been a ravener, had slowly devolved into a monster while Zee and his three younger sisters watched. The grisly work of hunting down escaped Good Luck Girls and other hotfoots might have been enough to get their family out of debt, but it had come at a terrible cost.

Aster had never known what, exactly, Zee's father had done to him once he'd lost himself to that dark power. She'd been subjected to enough ravenings herself to know better than to ask. But whatever it was, it had been bad enough to make Zee lose his laid-back, easy confidence whenever they encountered a ravener.

And yet, Aster had *never* seen him this undone.

"LAST STOP!" the conductor announced. The train began to lurch to a stop, and the ravener smirked at them before turning and heading back the way she'd come.

And Zee, standing up and pushing through the crowd, followed her.

"*Zee!*" Clem hissed.

What the hell is he thinking? Had the ravening made him lose his mind? He couldn't follow the ravener girl into a fairblood car; he'd be questioned or thrown out—or worse.

134

Aster and Clementine both started to go after him.

But when Aster caught his wrist, he fixed her with a desperate look before snatching his arm free. There was no madness in it, only need.

"Go on without me," he said, his voice hoarse, almost pleading.

"Zee, no—" Clem insisted.

"I'll catch up tomorrow. I promise. Go on without me."

"But—"

"That was Elizabeth," he choked out.

Aster released Zee's wrist in shock and watched, bewildered, as Zee left them. Clementine let out a wracking sob, already fragile from the ravening, and now broken by this sudden turn of events. Several people turned to stare.

"Hey, it's okay," Aster whispered, quickly grabbing her sister's hand to calm her. "He clearly knows what he's doing."

Aster was still not entirely convinced of this herself, but to follow Zee now would risk exposing all of them—they would just have to trust him.

"Wh-why would he just *leave*? Without even telling us the reason—"

By now the others had caught up to them. "You know Zee wouldn't take off like that unless it was important," Tansy said.

"Yeah, and if anyone can take care of themselves on their own, it's that boy," Mallow added.

"I guess . . . but . . ."

"But nothing," Aster interrupted. She didn't want to draw any more attention to themselves than they already had, and bring that terrible ravener back down on them. "He said we'll see him tomorrow, so we'll see him tomorrow. Now fix your face before we get off this train, hear? We're back in the Scab now. Time to show it we're not afraid."

CHAPTER ELEVEN

The Scab had changed in the months since they'd left it.

Not in ways that would be obvious to anyone who hadn't grown up there, but that were immediately obvious to Aster and her friends. Derrick had given them enough shine to take a coach the rest of the way to Rattlebank, and it was from there, while peering out through the thin curtains, that Aster took it all in—the stronger presence of the lawmen, many of them now with sleek shepherd dogs at their sides. The resentment in the eyes of the fairbloods as they saw to their business in town, huddling in groups rather than walking alone. And the hardness at the corner of every dustblood's mouth as they went about their work, exhaustion and anger and dread aging even young men by years. None of it was new, but all of it was heightened, filling Aster with a deepening unease.

But the true shock came later, on the Bone Road.

Gibbets.

Cages where unforgivably disobedient dustbloods were hung up high to starve and die. They had always been used as a gruesome warning in the Scab, but whereas before they had been a rare and shocking sight, now tree branches were heavy with them. Some bodies had been there longer than others, fabric and bloated flesh sloughing off sun-bleached bones. Others were so fresh that Aster wondered for a horrified moment if they might still be alive, too far gone to fight off the carrion birds that picked at their hands and faces. And more than a few showed the telltale signs of a vengeant's claws—long, deep furrows revealing where the life had been ripped out of them. Perhaps these had been the lucky ones: they had died quickly.

But there was one thing these dead all had in common— signs posted beneath them that simply read: THEY REBELLED.

If you're going to pick this fight, Aster, you have to be ready, Derrick had warned her. *There's going to be retaliation, and not just from my family. From* all *the landmasters, from* all *the people of Northrock, from* all *the fairblood families in Arketta who are afraid the dustbloods are coming for them next.*

Aster was seized by sudden, sickening fear, uncoiling in her belly like a snake waking up. She closed the curtains against the horrific display, leaning forward to still her queasiness as the coach swayed down the road. Earlier, on the train, she'd been thrilled by the realization that their actions had had such a farreaching effect. But why had she so foolishly assumed that effect would always be a good one?

These people died because of us, Aster thought. *We burned down that welcome house. We made the landmasters feel threatened. And now you want to kidnap Derrick McClennon—*

No, this wasn't their fault. It was the landmasters'—

Landmasters angered by our *actions.*

"By the Veil," Raven murmured, looking out the opposite

window. "I've heard stories about the Bone Road, but I never imagined it would be this bad."

"It didn't used to be," Tansy said quietly. "Folks perished from the natural dangers of traveling in the Scab all the time, but the gibbets . . . this is new."

"All these bodies left out like some kind of ripping warning," Mallow muttered. She turned to Aster. "We've only been gone a year. What's happened to this place?"

Aster didn't have an answer for that, and it was with a heavy sense of foreboding that they disembarked from the coach at Rattlebank. Despite the clear night sky above it felt as if a heavy storm were pressing down on them, and Aster was suddenly anxious to go to ground. The rise and fall of the vengeants' keening was making the hair on the nape of her neck stand up. They were safe inside the town's deadwalls now, but it was still another four miles through the wilderness to the Scorpions' camp, where they would need to beg shelter not just for themselves, but for the McClennon boy once they'd taken him hostage.

They went the rest of the way on foot, following Zee's carefully written instructions. No one commented on his absence, but Aster could sense it weighing on the group, the suddenness of it, the strangeness. Without his help, it took them two hours to hike through the woods. Derrick had not been able to give them his theomite ring for fear of his father noticing its absence, so they had to fend off the vengeants with only their iron-filled shotguns. They had all gotten better at handling firearms, and Clementine could see the vengeants even without the help of moonlight, but they still had more than a few close calls. The cold night air froze the sweat on Aster's skin, cutting through her lungs like a blade. Fear reduced her to an animal—jumping at every sound, tensed in anticipation of pain. And this, too, like the red earth or the heavy sun, felt like coming home.

At last they reached the ghost town outside the abandoned mines where the Scorpions were based. Aster led them down the mineshaft and greeted the two young men on guard, relieved that they remembered her from their previous visit. The last thing they needed, after the long journey they'd had, was to be turned away now.

"We need to talk to Sam as soon as possible—tonight if we can," Aster told the guard as he led them to the camp in a mine cart, its wheels squeaking noisily in the dark of the tunnel. The guard was young, perhaps only fourteen, and his mining hat was so big and loose on his head that the light atop it wobbled every time he moved.

"Well, I'm sure he'd be happy to see you," the boy said, his soft voice barely rising above the sound of the cart. "But he's been busy as of late. More hotfoots'n ever, and not enough of us to take care of them. It's near impossible now just to keep everyone fed."

"Well that doesn't sound good," Clementine muttered from behind Aster.

"It's good if it means folks are leaving their landmasters," Mallow said.

"Yeah, but only if there's somewhere better for them to go," Tansy replied. "Bad enough they have to live underground—but now there aren't enough beds? Isn't enough food?"

"I thought you said the goal was to move runaways along to Ferron," Raven said to Aster. "What are they still doing here?"

"We've been waiting for the tunnel system to be completed," the boy answered before Aster could speak. "It's almost done now, though—the tunnels are all connected-like, they just haven't been made safe to use."

"Now that *does* sound good," Clementine said, and though Aster couldn't see her face in the shadows she knew her sister was smiling.

They reached the end of the tunnel, climbing out of the mine cart, and the boy spread his arms as he welcomed them back to the underground city of Camp Red Claw.

"Sam'll be in the main hall," he said. "Do you need help getting there?"

"No, you go on back to your post. We know the way," Aster replied.

"Thank you," Clementine added, and the boy tipped his oversized hat before climbing back into his mine cart.

The camp was much livelier than Aster remembered it, the yawning cavern filled with the echoing noise of children as they ran between the little wood cabins the Scorpions and hotfoots called home. There were other buildings, too, all of them strung with mining lanterns that filled the camp with warm yellow light—stables for the horses, kennels for the dogs, a medical ward for the sick and injured, an armory full of guns and ammo. Largest of all the buildings, and in the center of town, was the meeting hall, which also served as dining hall and dancing hall as needed. In front of it, in the town square, stood a statue of a scorpion cut from theomite-streaked stone: it was this that protected the living from all the dead beneath the mountain.

141

Sam Daniels greeted them at the meeting hall. He hadn't changed much since Aster saw him last—he was still tall, dark, and dapper, with a confident smile and a crooked nose. He was missing the last two fingers on his left hand, which he held out to Aster in welcome. His black eyes lit up at the sight of them.

"Well *this* is a fine surprise," he said. "When I got word you girls were back I assumed it was just a rumor. We all heard you were dead."

"No such luck," Aster said, mirroring his grin and clasping his arm. Cutter strode in behind him, dressed in mining grubs, his shaggy black hair pulled back into a tail beneath his cap, his brown face, half-scarred from an old burn, smeared with grime.

"If it isn't my favorite outlaws," he greeted them.

"Cutter here cried for a week after he heard you'd been killed," Sam offered.

"I did *not*—"

"Where is my brother?" Sam demanded.

"He's on his way," Cutter promised. His eyes swept over them. "Where's Zee?"

Aster glanced at Clementine, whose breath caught behind her smile. Aster did not know how to tell the boys that Zee had run into his long-lost sister, and that that sister was now a ravener. The dead only knew where Zee and Elizabeth had disappeared to since then—Aster could only hope he kept his promise to rejoin them soon.

Aster gave her own sister's hand a reassuring squeeze.

"Zee's on his way, too," Aster said carefully. "He got held up back at the train station. But he knows where to find us, of course."

Sam's smile faltered. "Is he in trouble?"

"No more than usual," Aster said, hoping it was true. "But we picked up a new friend since you saw us last—Sam, Cutter, this is Raven."

The boys introduced themselves to Raven, whose face shone with sweat despite the chill of the mines. Aster watched her carefully, remembering all too well how overwhelmed she herself had been when she'd first come to Red Claw, surrounded by loud and rough young men. Aster had reassured her that the Scorpions were good people, but still—it was hard to unlearn the lessons the welcome house had taught.

"You all look like you could use a bite," Sam said, crossing his arms. "You just missed supper, but if you don't mind leftovers you can help yourself to a plate while you tell us how the hell it is you're still alive."

"Thanks, Sam," Aster said gratefully. "And sorry we invited ourselves over unannounced like this. We had no way to get in touch with you safely."

"Aster, please," Sam insisted. "You are always welcome at our table." He looked back towards the door. "If my fool brother would be so good as to set it, that is."

And then, as if summoned, Eli hurried through the door. He was short and stocky where his brother was long and lean, and like Cutter, he was dressed in mining gear, his dark skin shining with sweat. He pulled a rag out of his back pocket to dry his smooth-shaven head and smiled that warm, genuine smile Aster remembered so well. Her heart hitched at the sight of it.

"Sorry to keep you all waiting," he said softly.

"Don't apologize, get to work," Sam said. "Our guests are hungry."

"Oh—um—did you want me to prepare the ribs for tomorrow, then—?"

"No, there's no time for that. Just heat up the chicken from tonight."

Eli scuttled off before Aster could say hello to him, although he caught her gaze as he passed her, a question in his eyes.

So it's true? You're all really alive? they seemed to ask.

She smiled back at him in response, dipping her chin in a single nod.

"So go on then," Sam said, taking a seat at the nearest table. They all gathered around him. "If the papers lied about you being dead, are they lying about your girl Violet working with McClennon, too?"

Aster sucked in a breath. "That's actually what we came here to talk to you about . . ."

She told Sam and Cutter everything—about how they'd escaped McClennon's estate and found the Lady Ghosts, about her decision to stay in Arketta while the others were borderjumped into Ferron, about her attempt to save Violet from the Northrock welcome house and the decision to burn it down. She left out any mention of working with Derrick, however. She could only imagine how a bunch of former miners would react to that news.

Guilt tugged at Aster's chest as she spoke. Everyone who worked with the Lady Ghosts was sworn to secrecy about their existence. To talk about them openly now with people Priscilla would never work with—it felt, despite every rash

144

decision she'd made until now, like Aster's first true betrayal of the Lady Ghosts. After everything they'd done for her, it left a taste in her mouth sour as bile—especially since she was still keeping Derrick's involvement a secret.

But we don't have a choice, Aster thought. *We need the Scorpions' help to save these girls.*

And the Scorpions needed the Good Luck Girls' help, too. Aster wasn't just here holding out her hat. She would make Sam and the others see that.

Halfway through the story Eli returned, doling out plates of pulled chicken and mashed potatoes reheated on the stove. He took a seat next to Aster at the end of the table, the smell of the kitchen still clinging to his clothes. He rested his elbows on the scarred wood and folded his hands together as if to pray, but instead he just studied Aster with eyes dark as molasses—not just looking at her, as men usually did, but seeing her, asking more questions of her. *Are you safe, though, Aster? Are you happy? Are you well?* She felt her face heat under his gaze.

"It's good to see you, Aster," he said finally, his voice as surprisingly soft as she remembered.

"It's good to be back," she replied, swallowing.

Aster pulled her eyes away from his and continued telling her story. Last time, when she had told Eli about her vision of their two groups working together, he'd been supportive, even as he'd warned her it would be a tough sell to the other Scorpions. She hoped he would still be on her side now that it was all actually coming together.

"So, let me make sure I understand," Sam said slowly as Aster

145

finished. "You want to burn down the McClennons' gambling hall in Rattlebank and demand he close his welcome houses, but in order to get away with it, you'll have to hide out here afterward."

"Zee said something about getting our hands on some voltric weapons from Ferron, too. To give us an advantage against the law," Aster added hesitantly. She was not used to asking for help, and the words sat uneasily on her tongue.

Sam raised an eyebrow at that. "Did he now? Always promising heaven and earth, that one. We don't have any such weapons here, but Camp Deathstalker has a well-stocked armory. They lend out their supply to the other camps as needed. You could certainly plead your case. You'd have to be willing to make the trip yourself, though. I'm afraid I can't be spared—you see how it is here."

"Yes, of course. Of course," Aster said quickly. "And I know, us asking you to risk discovery on our behalf is . . . a lot. But we could get you the shine to make it worth your while. Help you keep everyone here fed."

"I don't know, have you seen how crowded this place has gotten?" Cutter cracked. "I doubt even you all could rob enough brags for that."

Aster glanced at the others. The shine would come from Derrick, but she didn't want to admit that.

"You ought to know better than to doubt us by now, Cutter," Clementine said, saving her, and Aster nodded at her gratefully, even as the guilt in her chest grew.

It's one thing to lie to the landmasters and the law, but now I'm lying to my allies.

It was necessary, she reminded herself.

Sam let out a breath. "If it was only up to me, I'd say I'm convinced," he said. "But something like this—we'll have to put it to the whole group. The law has gotten a lot more aggressive these past few months, and they will be turning over every rock looking for you all. It's going to put our whole operation at risk. For a good cause, no doubt—but still."

"I'll be honest, I don't reckon the boys will like it," Cutter admitted. "Sticking their necks out for some Good Luck Girls . . . there are some who are bound to see it as a kind of betrayal to our cause. They think of you all as sellouts . . . and they're wrong, of course, but they're also loud about it."

"Yeah, but think about it," Eli said quietly. "If Aster's right, and burning down the landmasters' property really does force them to change their ways, that could be good for all of us. This time, it's about the welcome houses . . . next time, who knows."

"Exactly," Aster said, meeting his eyes.

"Well, let's hope they see it that way, then," Sam said. "We'll hold the meeting first thing tomorrow."

CHAPTER TWELVE

Aster's mouth was dry as she took her place behind the podium at the front of the meeting hall the next morning. The room was full of boys as young as twelve and men old enough to be her father, though most were in their teens and twenties. Some looked excited to see her, whispering to one another and stealing glances to the front of the room, but plenty of others were unsmiling. And they all bore scars from the work they'd done in the mines before joining the Scorpions. How many of them would be happy to risk what they'd built for the sake of a bunch of girls who lived in mansions? The welcome house was as much a hell as any sunless, suffocating mine—but Cutter was right. Most of these men wouldn't see it that way.

"All right, quiet down now! Quiet!" Sam shouted. He stood up front next to Aster, along with Eli, Cutter, and the rest of her friends. It felt good to have them here with her, ready to lend weight to her words. But she felt Zee's absence as a physical ache—and as hard as Clementine seemed to be trying to hide her worry, it was clear that she wished he were there, too. He had been their connection to the Scorpions. These were his people. He would know better than any of them what to say.

Zee had said he would arrive sometime today, and it was early enough, but still . . .

Where was he?

"Don't be nervous, Aster," Eli said from beside her, his voice a low rumble that cut through the noise.

"Who said I was nervous?" she muttered back, bristling.

Eli chuckled. "No one. I'm just saying, *if* you are—don't be. We're not worth it. I guarantee you half these boys flip their drawers inside out rather than wash them."

Aster wrinkled her nose in disgust, but she couldn't help a short snicker. It loosened some of the tension in her chest, and she flashed Eli a grateful smile.

Sam continued to shout over the hubbub until it quieted. "I need you rabble to give Aster here your undivided attention! She has an important proposal for us to hear, and I want you to consider it carefully before we put it to a vote."

"Thanks, Sam," Aster said. She fought back the fear that clawed its way up her throat. Not fear of speaking in front of a crowd—Eli was right, she didn't give a damn what any of these people thought of her, outside of her friends—but there was a voice in the back of her mind warning her that she was outnumbered and in danger in this room full of men. Her thoughts began to waver as she scanned their faces, threatening to uncouple from her body entirely. Light-headedness filled her skull, nausea swirling in her stomach. She swallowed, wetting her lips.

Count your breaths.

But they were too short now, too fast. Getting away from her. It was all getting away from her. She gripped the podium with both hands, nails biting into the wood.

"Aster?" Tansy said quietly, touching her shoulder.

One—two—three—four—

Five—

Six—

Seven.

Aster felt the panic pass. She let out one last shuddery breath, smiling back at her friends gratefully, then turned to face the crowd, stood up straight, and began to speak.

"You all know me as Aster of Green Creek," she began. "And despite what the papers told you, I wasn't killed by McClennon's men . . ."

There were outbursts from the crowd, asking questions and demanding details, but Aster held up her hand to quiet them and settled into her story. It helped that she'd already told it to Sam just last night. She knew what to say now—what to leave out, when to lie. She tried to gauge the crowd's reaction to see how they were responding to her plea, but it was hard to read them.

"We're going to strike at the landmasters where they're most vulnerable, force them to close the welcome houses. And that's why we need your hospitality—because they're damn well going to come after us," Aster finished, no longer needing to coax the passion into her voice. "The work you've done here—what you've accomplished with these tunnels—it's one of the most amazing acts of resistance in the history of Arketta. So please, I beg you: let us stay here until our own work is done. Help us help those who need it the most."

The room remained silent except for a few scattered murmurs. Aster swallowed.

"Do you all have any questions before we put this to a vote?" Sam asked into the silence.

"Damn right I have some questions," a voice from the back spoke up. "You say you're doing all this to free the Good Luck Girls from McClennon's welcome houses? Well, who's to say those girls even want to be freed? They're living like royalty. I don't think they'll thank you for putting them out of a job, and I don't much look forward to the rest of us caught and killed in the process, either."

There were mutters of agreement. Aster held back her frustration.

"None of you know what it's like to live in a welcome house. *We* do," she said, gesturing to her friends. "So believe us when we tell you, these girls would be more grateful than you could ever imagine. Some of them may even join your cause once they're free."

"I mean, I suppose I could think of one or two ways they could thank us, then," another voice cracked, and scattered laughter filled the hall.

Heat suffused Aster's face. She bared her teeth against the anger threatening to overwhelm her. But before she could form a response, Sam stood and spoke up.

"Enough!" he roared. It was the first time she'd ever seen him look truly angry. "Have you no shame? You call yourselves men but cower and bully like children. These women have accomplished more in the past year than some of you can hope to achieve in your entire lives. And now they come here, of all the places in the world, to ask for our help, on behalf of your own aunties and cousins and sisters and friends, and you have the audacity to laugh at their expense. I will not have it, do you hear? I *will not have it*." He surveyed the shamed faces. "Now," he finished, tugging at his cuffs. "Does anyone else have something to say before we put this to a vote? Does anyone have a *legitimate* concern?"

Aster's eyes stung, and she could not bring herself to look at Sam, because she knew if she did, the tears would fall. She blinked hard, counting her breaths in her head once again. For a long time, no one said anything, and Aster wasn't sure whether the silence was a good thing. The mood of the room had soured, that was certain—she didn't want the Scorpions to vote while they were feeling resentful. But Sam's words must have moved at least a few of them, surely.

"All right, then, let's begin the vote—" Sam started.

"I have a question," an older man in the back said, standing so his voice would carry across the room.

By the dead, Aster thought.

"Mr. Weatherby. Please," Sam said, yielding the floor.

The man's brown skin was wrinkled as a walnut, his clothes worn white at the knees and elbows. There was no anger in his eyes, only weariness. Aster gritted her teeth, then nodded at him to continue.

"Thank you," Mr. Weatherby said. "I have nothing but respect for you, Aster. I agree with Sam that some of the nastiness you've been subjected to today has no place in the community we're trying to build here. But I have to ask, for the sake of that community—how is it you're going to provide us all the shine you've promised in return for our sheltering you? It's not that I doubt your integrity, only the details. If you're

152

getting yourself into some kind of trouble for it—something that could double back on all of us—well, we have a right to know. Your lives, and ours, depend on it."

Aster swallowed, looking to her friends.

"I completely understand your concerns, Mr. Weatherby. But I'm afraid that is . . . privileged information," she managed. "For your own safety, it's best you don't know all those details."

The uproar that followed was expected, but Aster still recoiled at it. She wasn't sure how much longer she could take this.

"Privileged for who?"

"Why does she get to decide?"

"What the hell are they hiding?"

"Gentlemen, gentlemen, please," Sam urged.

"Are you going to resort to highway robbery again?" someone asked. "Because I'm all for taking some bastards for everything they've got, but you have to admit, that's not going to be enough."

"Not with all the mouths we have to feed now," someone agreed.

"And how are you expecting to get away with it when the law's going to be tearing apart the whole Scab looking for you? You can't be lucky forever."

It's not luck, it's hard work and skill and working together that got us this far, Aster thought angrily.

But working together with Derrick was bound to be an unpopular confession.

"I'm sorry, I don't mean to cause any trouble," Mr. Weatherby finished, sitting down. "I just—I don't feel comfortable voting either way until I know more about this."

Sam leaned in. "I understand your resistance, Aster. And you know everyone up here trusts you. But a little bit of honesty will go a long way with the rest of them. It's a fair question he's asking."

Damn it. She looked at her friends. Eli gave her an encouraging nod. Aster took a breath and pressed on.

"All right, all right," she said, to quiet the room. "I can tell you where we're getting the shine, but the information *cannot* leave this camp," she said. "As I said, *everyone's* safety depends on this."

"Just tell us already!" someone shouted.

Aster looked down at the podium, at the swirl of the wood grain, as if the answer were written there. Hesitating. Stalling. She had already told them the Lady Ghosts' secrets. What was one more betrayal? She looked back up, wet her lips, and spoke.

"Derrick McClennon," she began. "I told you our friend Violet was working for him as a double agent—but the truth is that he is a double agent as well. He's been feeding her—us— information, secrets from the landmasters' inner circle. It was thanks to him that we could afford to travel back to the Scab as quickly and safely as we did. And now he's offered to help us again: when we attack the gambling hall, Derrick will be there, and we'll stage his kidnapping and bring him back to the camp with us. We'll pretend to hold him hostage as further pressure on his family to give in to our demands, and he'll continue to provide us with information—and shine—while he's here."

The uproar that rose up now made the previous backlash seem like a whisper.

"You're taking shine from Derrick *McClennon?*"

"You expect us to work with that snake?"

"And give him three meals a day?"

"See! What did I tell you? They are *literally* in bed with the landmasters—"

Aster looked to her friends for help, but even Eli looked at a loss for words, a crease wrinkling his brow. Aster's heart lurched with regret.

I should never have accepted Derrick's help.

Then a defensive part of her spoke up. *I did what I had to do. Why can't anyone ever see that?*

If there was one thing she'd learned, it was that she couldn't do any of this alone—and that went for all her fellow dustbloods. They needed all the help they could get right now. They weren't in a position to turn Derrick away.

Several of the Scorpions started to walk out of the meeting room.

"Gentlemen, please!" Sam urged. "We still have to put this to a vote."

"What for? As if we'll ever work with a ripping McClennon? As if we'll ever work with anyone who would?"

"His family tried to *kill* you! What kind of coward goes crawling back to them for scraps?"

"These girls have no honor. No loyalty. We've always known—"

"I wish you would have trusted us with this secret, Aster," Sam said softly as the room continued to rail against her. "We could have tried to help you convince them . . . but now . . ."

"They'll never go for it," Eli murmured darkly. "They feel betrayed . . . and maybe they should." There was hurt in his eyes when he looked at Aster, and that's what finally broke her. She stepped away from the podium.

"Who are you to judge? Any of you?" she shouted over the noise. She paced back and forth like a catamount on the prowl, frustration setting her on edge. "None of you turned your nose up at the landmasters' shine when it was time to collect your weekly pay. But now that they offer it to us freely you're too good to accept?"

"Nothing is free! What is this deal costing you?" someone shouted.

"Whatever the cost, *I* will pay it. *I* am willing to pay it, for the sake of these girls. What are *you* willing to do?" Aster said, jabbing her finger accusingly at the man who'd spoken. "Look, I don't care what you, or anyone else, thinks of me. My pride is not what matters here. These girls are what matter." Aster thought of all the friends at Green Creek who she'd left behind—girls who, in the months since, would have been left to the mercy of dozens of violent men, who were being made to suffer more, each night, than anyone should in a lifetime. Bile rose in her throat. "Derrick has power. None of us can deny that. And we need power if we are to even the odds in this fight." She started towards the man who'd spoken. "Maybe *you're* the coward . . ."

"Aster," Clementine whispered, grabbing her arm and pulling her back. "Aster, don't. It won't help."

Aster blinked, her mind clearing as she met her sister's gaze. She looked at Sam, who was trying in vain to regain control of the room; Cutter, who was running a hand through his shaggy hair in exasperation; and Eli, who still couldn't seem to meet Aster's eye.

"It's not enough to get them to do it for the shine—not when it's coming from Derrick McClennon," Clementine said.

Tansy, Mallow, and Raven had huddled closer to Aster's side now, too.

"There's got to be something else we can offer them to sweeten the deal," Raven murmured.

"We shouldn't have to," Aster said through her teeth.

"I know." Mallow sighed. "But we're asking a lot of them—even if they're being assholes about it, expecting them to trust a McClennon . . . it's asking a lot."

Aster scowled. But she herself hadn't been willing to trust Derrick at first, either. She sighed.

"Well, what else could we say to convince them? It's not as if they were sold before we brought him into this, but now . . ."

"I think I have an idea," Clementine said quietly. "Derrick said there was a stash of theomite at the gambling hall—some of the finest specimens from his family's mines. We could steal it, bring it back here. That would make it a whole hell of a lot safer for the boys to travel through their tunnels, which is bound to be worth the trouble of hosting Baby McClennon."

"But Clem, Derrick isn't even here," Aster said. "We have no idea how much theomite there is. How can we make a promise like that when we don't know—"

"There'll be enough!" Clementine insisted. "There'll be more than the likes of us can even imagine, probably! You've seen how his people live! Just—please, Aster—we can't have come all this way . . . we can't have left Zee behind . . . for nothing. Make the offer."

Aster looked into her sister's eyes, unwilling to doubt her confidence.

She's right. We can't have come all this way for nothing. We have to at least try.

"Sam," Aster said, waving him over. He'd finally managed to quiet the room. She quickly whispered the new plan to him, and he nodded slowly, seeming to think it over.

"That might just work," he said. "Do you want me to put it to them?"

"No," Aster muttered. She refused to be cowed by this group. "Let me finish this."

Aster spoke up again, detailing this new offer to the group. Some still refused to look at her, but others showed undeniable interest, even excitement, at the mention of the theomite stash, their eyes lighting up like young boys' at the prospect of a much-longed-after birthday present.

Once she finished speaking, Sam put it to a vote—and it passed, but only just.

Watching the Scorpions filter out of the room, Aster didn't feel like she could call this a victory. Even knowing what Eli had told her about the way most dustblood men thought of Good Luck Girls, she had never expected them to be this resistant to the idea of helping.

"That was pretty quick thinking with the theomite," Eli said. He smiled, but it hung uneasy on his face, a sickle moon lost behind the clouds. His dark eyes still looked uncertain. "I'm glad you got them to come around."

"It shouldn't have taken all that," Aster said, unable to hide her frustration. "They should've been willing to help because it was the right thing to do, not because they were getting a mountain of jewels out of it."

"Well, working with Derrick McClennon is an added risk. I understand why some of them may have had trouble getting used to the idea."

Aster shot him a glare.

"I'm just saying," he said defensively. "The McClennons aren't the kind of folks you trust. But I trust *you*, Aster. We all do."

"Well, you sure have a funny way of showing it," she mumbled.

"Maybe you could try trusting us, too, hear?" Eli suggested.

After today's display? Not likely. But Aster was too exhausted to argue further. It was no use. The Scorpions thought they were safe here, thought they were free, and they were loathe to risk that. But how was she supposed to make them see that their freedom wasn't real? Not if they were still skulking underground because of the landmasters' law. It was that law that was their enemy, not Aster or any other Good Luck Girl. It would do no good for dustbloods to fight among one another for the scraps. None of them was free until all of them were.

There's no time for all that, Aster thought to herself. It had been hard enough getting everyone to come together to burn down this one gambling hall, let alone the whole of the Scab.

She would take it one battle at a time.

CHAPTER THIRTEEN

Zee finally arrived late that night—and he wasn't alone.

Aster was on the edge of sleep when she heard a faint knock at the door of the cabin that she and Clem had been given to share. She found her knife under her pillow before going to answer. After the contentious meeting earlier that morning, she wasn't sure she didn't have enemies here in camp now.

"Clem . . . please, it's me . . ." a voice faint with exhaustion whispered.

Zee?

Aster dropped the knife and threw the door open. Zee stood before her in the little pool of candlelight pouring out of the cabin, his face drawn and shadowed with stubble, his eyes bloodshot with exhaustion. A small figure stood at his side, wrapped in his coat like it was a blanket. A girl, no older than six or seven, her brown skin dry and cracked, her hair braided into four fraying pigtails. Zee held her close.

His sister, Aster realized, shock rippling through her: not just because they had the same face, but because she would have recognized that protective look in Zee's eyes anywhere.

"Aster, by the dead, you have no idea how happy I am to see you," Zee said, relief making him sag. "Is Clem—?"

"Zee!" Clementine cried from behind Aster, leaping up to join them. Zee stumbled forward and drew Clementine into a hug.

"I'm sorry," he breathed. "I'm so sorry I left. I'm so sorry I took so long to come back to you—"

"Don't be, I'm just happy you're here," Clementine said, stepping back and wiping her eye with the heel of her hand. "Who . . . who is this?" she asked uncertainly. The little girl still hadn't said a word, shrinking deeper into Zee's side.

"Oh, well, this . . . this is my sister, Emily," he said haltingly.

Clementine looked back and forth between the two of them, her eyes widening as she saw the truth in their faces.

"Your—your sister?" Clementine stammered. "But where did you . . . how . . . ?"

Aster opened her mouth to ask the first of a thousand questions herself, but Zee gave them a pleading look with his eyes. *Not now*, it said. "It's . . . a long story. But she'll be staying with us, if that's all right. I already talked to Sam."

Aster and Clem glanced at each other, confusion and concern passing between them.

"Of course," Aster said after a beat. "It'll be a joy to have her." She kneeled down to Emily's level, hoping to bring a smile to the girl's face or coax a hello out of her, but Emily was either too tired or too shy to react. She seemed to fold in on herself, like a flower in the rain.

What the hell happened to her, Zee?

Judging from the haunted look in Emily's eyes, Aster wasn't sure she'd like the answer.

161

Aster and Clem helped Emily get settled in one of the empty upper bunks, whispering to Zee as they told him everything he'd missed. It was only once Emily fell asleep that Zee began to tell them where *he* had been.

"I'm sorry I wasn't able to help with the Scorpions," he began. They were all sitting on the opposite bed, the low candlelight making shadows flicker across their faces. Zee took a long swallow from his canteen, hands trembling with exhaustion, before he went on. "I never meant to abandon you. But when I saw that ravener on the train . . ." He looked at Clementine, his eyes like a wounded animal's. "When I saw my *sister* . . ."

Aster's heart sank with an aching heaviness. She had hoped Zee had been wrong when he'd said the ravener on the train was his oldest sister.

"The dead protect us," she murmured.

"S—So you mean Elizabeth . . . she . . . just like your father," Clementine stammered, her expression slowly breaking in devastation.

Zee nodded, looking at them both for strength. "You remember how I told you my sisters disappeared while I was out on a job, back when I first started working as a rangeman? Well, it turns out they went into town at some point, and when they were on their way home, they were captured by a pair of raveners transporting girls bound for a welcome house. No one saw it happen; no one was there to help. They just vanished like the dead come daylight. They never made it to their destination, though. Elizabeth managed to bust the lock and break out with the other two. Elena, my middle sister, was killed by the raveners as they tried to run away, but Lizzy was able to get away with Emily. Went into hiding. Luckily the raveners didn't spend much time searching for them, since they weren't a part of their bounty to begin with. But now Lizzy and Emily were halfway across the Scab, and Elena . . ." Zee's voice broke. He swallowed and continued. "So Lizzy turned to ravening to support them. Felt she had no other choice. Didn't ever want to be vulnerable like that again. She eventually got hired on as a steward for Sullivan Rails, which was where we crossed paths. I followed her back to the room she was sharing with Emily at an inn. That's where she told me all this. I promised her I could get them to safety, both of them, but . . ." He trailed off. "She doesn't trust me. Said I was free to take Emily if I wanted, said she'd be glad to be rid of the burden, but that she wasn't going anywhere with me. And I don't blame her for that. If I'd been a better brother, they never would've gotten kidnapped in the first place. And Elena never . . . never would've been . . ."

"Zee . . ." Aster said helplessly. "I—I don't even know how to tell you how sorry I am."

"It's not your fault," Clementine insisted, holding his hand. "It's the raveners'—"

"And now Lizzy is one of them!" Zee said. His voice broke with emotion, and he quickly swallowed it back. "She's not as far gone as my father was in the end, not yet, but the girl I grew up with . . . I barely recognize her. The way she just handed Emily over to me like she was a dead dog and not our baby sister—"

Emily stirred, and they all quieted until she went still again.

"Is there anything we can do for Elizabeth?" Aster asked. Zee had become like a brother to her, and she would not let him wrestle with this loss alone.

Zee shook his head, his eyes glassy. "I've never heard of anyone coming back after becoming a ravener. She knows what this does to a person. She watched our father—I just can't believe she'd do this—"

But she'd done it for the same reason parents shipped their daughters off to welcome houses. For the same reason dustblood boys sold themselves to the Arkettan army. For the same reason Clementine had killed Baxter McClennon.

When you were desperate enough, you were capable of anything.

We can't keep putting people in these positions, Aster thought. It was tearing them apart, all of them.

"Zee, you still saved Emily, and that's what matters," Aster said. "And we're not going to let anything happen to her, hear?"

Zee nodded gratefully, and Aster took his other hand, and they held him until his silent tears were spent.

Aster met Violet the next evening outside the Rattlebank gambling hall. It was their job to scout the outside of the location while Derrick scouted the inside. Rattlebank seemed to be much like most of the dust-covered towns in the Scab, little more than two neat rows of rundown wooden buildings, their paint peeling from too much sun. Horse droppings and broken beer bottles littered the ground, while the air was thick with grit and biting flies. The gambling hall was by far the most impressive establishment here, three stories high and meticulously maintained, the anchor that kept the rest of the town from blowing away. It cast a long shadow over Main Street.

Aster and Violet sat on the porch outside the saloon across the road, dressed in oversized miners' grubs, dustkerchiefs pulled up to cover their favors. Meanwhile Raven subtly patrolled the perimeter, drawing the layout of the building in her sketchbook, while Tansy went to the drugstore to get more supplies for her ghostweed salve and Mallow went to the gunsmith's to buy ammunition. Aster's eyes darted up and down the street constantly for any sign that the lawmen on patrol were on to them. Thanks to the ghostweed salve, their favors wouldn't give them away, but the law was on high alert these days—Aster couldn't give them any reason to look twice at her.

It didn't help that Aster was on edge with Violet, too. Perhaps her mind had magnified the whole thing, as it so often did, but Aster felt like there'd been friction between them last time: Derrick had gotten in the middle of them like a stringy piece of meat caught between two teeth. And as grateful as Aster was to have the chance to talk to Violet alone now, her chest clenched at the thought of driving Violet further away.

Still, despite everything, it felt good to be near to her again, their legs just touching as they huddled together against the chill of the night.

". . . and now his youngest sister is staying with us at Camp Red Claw for the dead knows how long," Aster muttered under her breath as she finished catching Violet up on everything.

"By the Veil," Violet swore. She was idly passing a bent bottlecap between her slender fingers, worrying at it like a lucky copper. "I remember that ravener was on patrol in our car, too. Couldn't help noticing her—I'd never seen a lady ravener before. I thought something about her looked familiar, but I never in a hundred years would've guessed . . ." She trailed off, shaking her head and tossing the bottlecap away. "Damn."

"I hope it went better for you and Derrick?" Aster asked carefully. Violet's hair, usually brushed until it shone like a raven's wing, frayed out from beneath her canvas cap now, and dark circles lay under her bloodshot eyes like bruises. Even her shadow looked tired, stretched out before them in the light spilling from the saloon. Violet never let herself look vulnerable to the outside world, no matter how she felt. So why was she slipping now?

"We did all right for ourselves," Violet said with a sigh. "Got us a room in the inn down the way last night. Neither of us got much sleep, though."

"I don't doubt that. All due respect, you look like hell, Vi."

"It's this place." She sighed heavily. "This ripping place. It drains the life out of me."

"What, the Scab?" Aster asked, and Violet nodded.

"You don't realize how bad it is until you get out. Eighteen years I spent, listening to the dead keen every night, and after just a few months on the outside suddenly it's unbearable to me. Everything, all of it—just, unbearable. I don't understand. I lived here my whole life, and I slept just fine before. So what changed?"

Aster didn't have an answer for that, as much as she wished she did. It reminded her so much of her own conflicted feelings. Her hatred for "this place" was more complicated than Violet's seemed to be—although she almost wished it weren't.

"Anyway, Derrick has always been a poor sleeper, he tells

me, so I reckon he was just happy to have the company."

Aster found her mind straying to a dark place then, and it was not the first time it had gone there. "Derrick . . ." she whispered. "He hasn't . . . you know . . . tried anything with you, has he? Because if he has—"

"No, no," Violet said tiredly, leaning back with her palms braced against the porch floor. "He's a perfect gentleman. He slept on the floor."

"Where he belongs."

Aster couldn't help the barb, but to her relief, she sensed Violet smiling behind her dustkerchief for the first time that night. "You might take your boot off his neck for ten minutes."

Aster returned the smile, the fabric of her own dustkerchief scratching her cheeks. "Why should I? I've only just eased up on *you*, and I've known you for years."

"Mm, I almost miss it," Violet mused.

"But still, I wonder—"

There was a *crack* of a bottle breaking behind them, followed by a roar of male laughter, and it made them both jump. Violet gasped and clutched Aster's knee, fingers digging into the denim. The contact sent another jolt of voltricity down Aster's spine.

"Sorry," Violet breathed, withdrawing her hand quickly. "What were you going to say?"

Aster swallowed, trying to regain her focus. "I was just going to say that even if Derrick is being a gentleman about it, I . . . I can't help thinking he's sweet on you." And that bothered Aster somehow, though she couldn't quite understand why.

Violet raised a single brow. "*Really?* Because if I didn't know better, I would've said he was sweet on *you*."

"What?" Aster choked, forgetting, for a moment, to lower her voice. She quickly brought it back down to a whisper as a lawman passed them on his way into the saloon. "*What?*"

"It's true!" Violet insisted, laughing at Aster's expression. "He hasn't been able to stop talking about you since our last meeting, and getting all nervous when he does. I think you've made quite the impression on him. And who could blame him?"

"Look, it's fine if Derrick . . . respects me, but if he actually *fancies* me—"

"Would that be so terrible? He's not bad looking."

"He's just so . . . skinny . . ."

"The better to appreciate his bone structure."

Enough.

"Derrick and I have nothing at all in common," Aster said shortly.

"Ah, I wouldn't be so sure. You're both some of the most passionate people I've ever met, you're both hungry to see justice done. You both take on way too much responsibility for your own good. And you're both smart as hell, always thinking half a dozen moves ahead. You may disagree about strategy, but you're playing the same game."

Aster scoffed. That was all surface-level bullshit. It didn't change the fact that he was the son of the richest family in the country and she had been sold like livestock to avoid a lifetime of poverty.

"As for me and Derrick," Violet went on, laughing through

her nose, "I sure as hell respect him—to be honest, he may be the only man I ever have, except for Zee—but I don't want him. Not like that." She met Aster's gaze then, and her voice grew softer. "Is that why it's felt different between us since I came back, Dawn? You're afraid I chose that boy over you? You're afraid I, what, forgot who I am?"

Aster felt a lump roll in her throat at the sound of her true name, and she swallowed around it painfully. "I'm just afraid of losing you. I can't go through that. Not again."

Violet's hand slid over Aster's knee, and this time it lingered there. "Well, don't worry about that. I'm not going anywhere."

Aster let out a shaky breath. "Thanks, Vi. I just . . . can't wait to have you back with the rest of us."

"And how much longer will that be?"

Aster ran through the next steps in her head. "We still have to get the voltric weapons from that other Scorpion camp. Sam said it's a two-day journey underground. So accounting for the trip back, and a full day afterwards to recover and prepare . . . and then add another forty-eight hours to give us some room for error . . . we should stage the attack in seven days' time," she concluded. If her voice had been low before, now it was little more than breath. It would be bad enough to be overheard talking about suitors, but to be heard talking about treason would see them both in gibbets.

"That detour for the weapons—is it really necessary?" Violet asked. "Derrick wants this done as soon as possible. The longer we wait, the more lies he has to concoct to justify his being here."

Aster nodded. "We barely made it out of Scarcliff after we

hit that bank, and there have to be twice as many badges on patrol here tonight. We need every advantage we can get—not just for this fight, but for the fights ahead, too."

"All right then." Violet sighed. "I'll let him know. Seven more days, and then we strike."

More lawmen were coming up to the saloon from the lawmaster's office. It was time to leave before they were exposed entirely. Aster and Violet said their goodbyes reluctantly. Aster looked at the gambling hall one final time before she left, its silhouette sharp against the deepening blue of the sky. Then she turned back to Violet, allowing herself to speak above a whisper at last, forcing courage into her voice.

"I'll see you on the other side."

CHAPTER FOURTEEN

It was to be Aster, Tansy, Mallow, and Eli making the trip to Camp Deathstalker: Tansy to help them in case someone got hurt in the tunnels, Mallow to provide backup support against the vengeants they were sure to encounter, and Eli to serve as the liaison from Camp Red Claw. They woke up at five o'clock in the morning to make sure they could get a full day of travel in, Cutter offering to outfit them for the underground journey.

"Aster! Look alive. Today you become a Scorpion proper," Cutter said with relish. He was the only one who seemed fully awake, eyes bright with excitement and voice at full volume while the rest of them grumbled and squinted in the low-burning lantern light of the equipment shed.

"How much longer is this going to take?" Aster groused.

"Not long. Don't worry, we'll have you trudging through the bowels of the mountain in no time," Cutter promised as he pulled items for her off the shelves. "The captain over at Deathstalker is a friend of mine, as it happens—Sidney Miller. We're both central tribe. He grew up in a rebels' camp and went on to be a soldier in the War for the Nations, but the Arkettan army hunted his war party down. Sid got away, fell in with the Scorpions, and he's been with us ever since. He's a prickly bastard, I'll warn you . . . but then, I reckon he has the right to be."

War for the Nations? Aster struggled blearily to remember what she could from her schooling. It certainly had never mentioned anything about a war with the Nine Nations. None of the Ladies had mentioned it either, though, not even Marjorie, who had must have lived through it and who had been happy to share her history with the younger women.

Maybe her tribe wasn't involved, Aster thought.

Or maybe it had been something she hadn't *wanted* to remember.

Aster thought of asking Mallow if she'd learned anything about it in Ferron, but Aster didn't want to take away from the spirit of adventure that seemed to have seized the others. Everyone else had already been geared up. Tansy stood in a mining coat that seemed to swallow her while Eli helped her buckle it up, and Mallow took comically large steps as she practiced walking in the heavy layers. They were barely recognizable beneath the getup: a mining helmet made of hammered metal with a lantern on top, a thick canvas coat, slick rubber waders, and steel-toed boots. The coat was adorned with iron links that reminded Aster of chain mail from stories about the old Empire.

She was not overly eager for her own transformation.

"Aster," Eli said softly, coming to her side once he'd finished helping Tansy. Despite herself, Aster felt her stomach flip at the sound of his voice.

"It's my turn, apparently. Care to explain why Cutter here has us wearing our own body weight in mining gear?" Aster asked.

Eli chuckled a little at that. "The iron overcoat is to protect

172

us from vengeants," he explained. "And the rest is to protect us from the mountain. It's hard going through these tunnels, lots of uneven ground and low ceilings and long stretches half submerged in water. Not to mention the fact that it's bone cold and dark as the shadow of the Veil. The camps have been working on a cart system, but it's not completed yet. We'll be on foot for this."

"It's not going to make the going any easier, but I won't have you all exposed to the elements down here," Cutter said firmly, checking the others' lanterns.

"Here, the waders go on first. I'll help you out," Eli offered, holding them open.

Aster hesitated. The mining gear went over the clothes they were already wearing, and yet, still, there was something inherently intimate about letting someone dress you. Mallow and Tansy hadn't seemed uncomfortable accepting the boys' help . . . but then, they had not been through what Aster had been through.

I wish Violet were here, she thought. Or Raven. They would understand. Maybe—

"Left foot," Eli said. And then, so as not to show her fear, Aster did as she was told, stepping into the left leg of the waders, gripping Eli's broad shoulder for balance. Then they did the right. She and Eli stood flush against each other, their foreheads almost touching as he brought the braces over her shoulders and snapped them into place at her waist with gentle hands. His breath smelled faintly of the coffee he'd downed in three swallows to wake himself up.

Aster wondered if he could hear her heart racing as he helped her into the jacket next. A rush of shame raced up the back of her neck at the thought. She was not some blushing schoolgirl to swoon over a boy. It felt offensive, almost perverse, that she could react this way at all, an insult to the endless hardships she'd suffered. Never, in all her nights at the welcome house, had she welcomed a man's touch. So why the hell should she now?

Unease churned inside her belly. Discomfort gnawed at her skin. She wanted to shrink away, and she wanted to lean into his touch. She hated herself for wanting to enjoy this. She hated that she couldn't.

Finally Eli found a helmet for her, placing it on her head like a crown. He stepped back, smiling at his handiwork, teeth bright white against his dark gums. Aster was sweltering underneath all the gear, and every breath felt as if her chest were being pressed by a stone.

"Well? How do I look?" Aster asked, trying to keep her voice from shaking. Her face was hot, but it had nothing to do with the extra layers she was now wearing.

Eli looked her up and down slowly, nodding in approval. "Like a Scorpion," he said.

"Like a fool," she corrected. She looked to Tansy and Mallow, smiling unevenly, desperate to put this confusing moment behind her. "Come on, then, you all. Let's get this circus into town."

Eli had been right: this was hard going.

Aster could scarcely catch her breath as they hiked through the endless underground labyrinth. There were inclines so steep that they had to crawl forward on all fours, and the declines were dangerously sharp and slippery. In some places the ceiling

174

sank so low they had to crouch for hundreds of feet at a time; in others the walls pressed in so close together that they had to turn sideways to squeeze through the narrow gaps. Pools of standing water filled the tunnels with a damp, earthy scent that made Aster's stomach heave. Even during the dry, level stretches with room enough to stand and turn around, the ground was pitted with potholes and littered with stones the size of a man's skull. They were all of them one misstep away from a broken ankle. The mining gear was difficult enough to maneuver in as it was, but now, with mud caked onto Aster's boots and her coat soaked to the waist, every step was a mammoth effort.

And all of this in impenetrable dark and graveyard quiet. At least in the camp there had been light and life to distract them from the fact that they were a hundred feet underground. Here they had only their feeble headlamps and the chorus of their labored breathing. Aster could not remember when she had ever felt so small, so insignificant. It was folly, to think they could cut through this eons-old mountain. She felt its crushing weight above her like the judgment of the dead.

And to think, there were landmasters, mortal men, who thought they owned these mountains, who had put a price on every pebble. They would not last two ticks down here.

"By—the ripping—Veil," Mallow panted as they faced another incline. It was the first words anyone had spoken in at least an hour. Eli, who was taking point, turned to face them, the yellow-brown light from his headlamp making Aster squint.

"Go ahead and take a breather," he said, though he himself scarcely seemed short of breath at all. "The camp is at the top of the hill. We'll stop there for the night."

"Is it nighttime already?" Tansy asked, her voice faint. Like all of them, her face was painted with mud.

Eli nodded. "Almost. I know it's impossible to tell down here, but the vengeants still know when the sun's gone down. We made good time today. Usually, when one of us makes these runs with a group of hotfoots, it's a struggle to get to the base camp before the dead attack."

Aster could not even begin to imagine trying to shepherd a family of runaways through these tunnels. It was a miracle the Scorpions managed to get anyone out of the Scab.

This is why the Lady Ghosts do things the way they do, Aster thought. This *is the alternative*. What the Ladies had built was just as enormous and complex, just as dangerous, but in an entirely different way. They were fighting against men, not nature.

A sudden dark thought occurred to Aster, and when she spoke, her voice was so small it didn't even echo.

"Eli . . . the vengeants down here, are they from folks who died trying to make these tunnels? Trying to travel through them?"

Eli, who had stopped to take a drink, lowered his canteen and looked at Aster levelly. "Where did you think they came from?"

Aster shook her head. She guessed she didn't know. It was so much easier to pretend that vengeants didn't *come from* anywhere, to think of them as some natural disaster rather than the restless spirits of the wronged dead.

"So . . . how many people have you lost down here?" she asked.

"Too many," Eli said brusquely, turning back to face the incline, and he started up it without another word.

176

Aster exchanged glances with Tansy and Mallow. Maybe she'd touched on a tender subject.

They followed Eli up the hill, panting as they dug their heels into the clinging clay. The muscles in Aster's legs seized up in protest. The arches of her feet knifed with pain at each step. Aster was sweating so much beneath her getup that she didn't feel the cold leaching into the air around them. She wanted to catch up to Eli, wanted to apologize, but it was all she could do to keep upright.

Thank the dead we're stopping for the night, she thought. She could not take much more of this.

Finally the slope evened out, and at the top was a wide, open space with a sparse campsite—two large canvas tents and scattered crates of supplies. Eli was already striking up a fire.

"Hey, brother, let us help," Mallow said, wiping at the mud on her cheek with her rough gloves.

"Don't worry about it," he muttered. "This won't take long. Just—go on and get some food out of the crates. It should all be labeled."

They set to it, cracking open the crates and fishing out salted pork, dried bread, and canned beans. Then they got out the tin plates and cutlery. By the time they were done, the little fire had flickered to life, Eli squatting on his haunches next to it as he stoked it with the poker and added a fistful of grayleaf to keep the vengeants at bay. He stood when he saw them with their hands full.

"Here, I'll fix you all's plates—" he began, but Aster held up her hand and shook her head.

177

"No," she insisted. "Let someone else fix your plate for a change . . . but *don't* get used to it," she added pointedly when she handed the plate over.

Eli smiled a little as he took it, his fingers brushing hers. She looked away quickly, turning to serve Tansy and Mallow, and finally herself, and then they all sat wearily on the ground around the campfire. They shucked their gloves and headgear and dug into the tasteless meal.

It was then that the vengeants started, their keening echoing in the dark like the howls of a shot dog.

"Here we ripping go," Mallow muttered, taking a swig from her canteen as if she wished it were something stronger. Eli closed his eyes, a pained expression descending over his face. Aster looked at the others in concern. They were used to Zee and his acute fear of raveners, but Eli's sorrow in the presence of vengeants was unexpected.

"Eli . . . are you doing all right?" Tansy asked. "I mean, I know that probably seems like a foolish question down here, but . . . are you?"

"These mountains are a grave," he muttered, setting his half-eaten plate of food down. "I hate it down here. I always have." His dark eyes met Aster's then, and Aster felt a drop in her stomach as she remembered her first conversation with him, when he'd told her how much he missed the sun. Dustbloods deserved better than to creep around underground like vermin, that was what he'd said. What the Scorpions had built was nothing short of a miracle—and yet it still wasn't enough. "Up there, you can't know who the vengeants were," he went on. "But down here, they have names. Every one of them was someone we failed."

Aster set her own plate down. "Eli," she said urgently, "you can't blame yourself. You all gave these people a chance at freedom—that was more than they ever had working for the landmasters."

"And if you lost one of these two, would you be able to shift the blame so easily?" Eli asked, jerking his chin at Tansy and Mallow. "If it was their cries echoing down these tunnels, would you be able to sleep soundly here?"

Aster's blood froze at the thought as she was suddenly thrown back to the memory of when she'd had to leave Violet behind. It didn't matter that Violet had survived; the guilt was still sharp enough to leave Aster gutted. When Eli saw her struggling for a response, he seemed to relent, his expression softening.

"Sorry, I shouldn't have . . . Sometimes I get . . . It's like I said—I just hate it down here."

"Then why did you agree to come?" Aster asked pointedly. She didn't mean to make it seem like an accusation, but she couldn't help it. The vengeants' wails grew louder still, though it was difficult, with the way sound traveled down here, to gauge how much closer they might be.

Eli took a breath to steady himself. "Because after the way that meeting went, I didn't trust anyone else to do right by you," he said softly, barely audible above the rising din. "Sam and Cutter are family, of course, but they're too busy to run this errand, and the rest of the boys . . . I've never seen them that angry before. At first I thought it was just that they hated McClennon too much to ever want to play host to his son—that's what it was for me, Aster, and I won't pretend I don't still feel some type of way about that. But for the rest of them, it's more than that . . . it's you all, too. For suggesting that they ought to risk their lives or take up arms on behalf of a bunch of fallen women. I reckon it's easier for them to believe that Good Luck Girls are traitors than to admit they can't protect the women in their lives from the landmasters . . . that they can barely even protect themselves. I think it wounded their pride, seeing you call them out for that—but you're giving them a chance to get it back, too. They'll see that soon enough." He shook his head, picking his plate back up to finish the last of his supper. "But until then . . . I just think you're safest with me."

Aster felt her hackles rise at that. She didn't need Eli's protection; she'd done just fine without it for eighteen years. She almost said as much. But something about the worry lines cut into the stone of his face held her back. Perhaps he was the one in need of protection—from himself. From the shame that ate away at him though he'd done nothing to deserve it.

And that was something Aster understood.

Another piercing shriek from the dead. The temperature dropped even further, freezing the sweat on Aster's brow. Mallow threw a worried glance at Tansy and reached for the sawed-off shotgun at her hip.

"Eli, these bastards are getting closer," she said. "Are you sure we're safe here?"

He reached for the poker to stoke the fire again. "As long as we keep the grayleaf burning, they won't come too close—"

And then an unseen something passed overhead with a keening cry, the wind in its wake snuffing the campfire and plunging them all into darkness.

CHAPTER FIFTEEN

When the fire went out, Aster's courage went with it, her heart plummeting to her stomach. She scrabbled for her gun. She might just have been able to keep a level head down here as long as she could see where she was going, but to be trapped in utter darkness—

There was a roar of noise and a flash of light as Mallow let fly from her shotgun.

"No!" Eli cried. "We can't risk hitting each other. Everybody back to back first."

Eli reached for Aster in the dark, his hand brushing against her forearm. Aster jumped instinctively at his touch, then found his wrist and held it tight. She reached out with her other hand for Tansy and Mallow, grabbing blindly in the dark. Her fingers caught on the cold, greasy mail of someone's iron overcoat. Tansy yelped.

"It's only me!" Aster shouted over the growing roar of the vengeants. "Quick, where's Mallow?"

"I'm right next to her!" Mallow yelled back. They formed up in a circle, linked at the elbows. The air around them buffeted even more violently as the howling vengeants swirled closer.

The iron on their coats was the only thing keeping the dead at bay, but the vengeants were sure to test that strength against that of their invisible teeth and claws any minute now.

Eli's arm flexed against Aster's as he reached for his own shotgun.

"Okay, Mallow—" he began.

"We still can't see shit!" she protested.

"We wouldn't be able to see them if we had light anyway! Just fire straight ahead and I'll do the same. We'll rotate our circle around until we've cleared the area. That should give us enough time to get the fire going—"

Sudden, numbing cold as invisible claws raked across Aster's calf, unprotected by iron. Pain exploded in the twitching muscle, and blood soaked her denims. She buckled at the knee, letting out a cry she didn't even recognize as her own.

"Aster!" Eli roared. He fired off two rapid shots from the hip. The muzzle of his gun flashed like lightning. Mallow answered him with two shots of her own, driving back the vengeants approaching from the other direction. Aster struggled to stay balanced on her good leg as the four of them spun around, Eli and Mallow firing continuously until they ran out of rounds. The vengeants' cries grew scattered as they seemed to retreat, but Aster knew they'd be back in a second.

Aster heard the *snick* of Eli holstering his gun. "We don't have long. I'm going to get the fire going," he said.

The fire couldn't be more than a few feet away, but still, the thought of him leaving them filled Aster with sudden dread. "Eli, wait—"

But he was already gone, his absence a vacuum as he

182

disappeared into the dark. Aster shivered, half from fear, half from the cold still radiating out from where the vengeant had attacked her. She sensed the others turning to face her.

"Aster, where did it get you?" Tansy asked urgently.

"My left leg," she said through her teeth.

"Are you losing much blood?"

"No—I don't know—I can't tell. It's going numb."

"You're going to be all right," Mallow said, her gun cracking as she opened it and reloaded it with iron shot. "I survived these bastards, and so will you."

By now Eli had managed to fumble the matches out of his pocket. He set it to the kindling, guarding the little flame desperately as he tried to breathe life into it. Weak, thready light flickered up around them, casting exaggerated shadows over their frightened faces.

"By the Veil, they're coming back," Aster said sickly. She couldn't see the dead, but she could hear them gathering their strength, could feel the wind licking at her skin as they circled once again.

"It's all right, the fire's almost ready—"

Eli was suddenly thrown against the side of the tunnel, tackled by a screeching vengeant. He let out a grunt of pain as he slid to the ground, and again as the vengeant's claws raked his chest, sending up a flash of unearthly sparks as they met iron. Tansy shrieked. Aster took a lurching step towards him.

"NO!" he gasped, his face concentrated in anguish as the vengeant attacked him again. "The fire—don't let them put it out again—"

Tansy hesitated, then dashed to the fire, feeding it with more

183

wood and grayleaf until it burned so brightly that Aster had to squint. Mallow ran up beside her, firing with her shotgun just above Eli until the terrible force pinning him to the ground finally fled. The other vengeants were retreating now, too, their wails growing fainter and fainter as they were repelled by the stench of the grayleaf. Aster finally let herself fall to the ground beside the campfire, stretching her injured leg out before her and clutching her calf. Tansy and Mallow ran over to Eli and helped him over next to her. Not a moment after they dragged him away from the side of the tunnel, the wall fell in with a sound like thunder. Aster's heart jumped and she feared a collapse of the whole tunnel, but after a breathless moment, the earth seemed to settle.

"Ripping hell!" Mallow swore. "What was that about?"

Eli winced, his breathing labored. "All our shooting must've disturbed the tunnel. We're lucky it was only a partial collapse."

"Save your breath," Tansy ordered, concern wrinkling her brow. "Mal, can you fetch the med kit? I saw it in one of the crates over there."

As Mallow hurried off, Aster wincingly removed her mud-caked boots and rolled up the left leg of her waders and denims. The cuts on her calf were long but shallow, the blood already congealing on her skin. There was still a deathly cold to the injury, though, as if she'd been frostbitten.

"Aster, I'll be with you in just a second," Tansy promised, sounding harried.

"Don't worry about it, I'm fine," Aster said with a groan. Eli was the one who'd been attacked head-on. If it hadn't been for Tansy and Mallow's quick acting . . .

Aster didn't want to think about that. Instead she used her canteen to pour water over her wound and wash it clean. She watched Tansy work from the corner of her eye. Tansy was removing Eli's coat and shirt so she could tend to the injury underneath, his thickset chest striped with the same ragged cuts that tore down Aster's leg—but his looked deeper, the blood almost black in the half shadows of the firelight. Aster looked away immediately, queasy and, absurdly, ashamed. She felt as she had when Eli had been helping to outfit her, as if she'd crossed some line of intimacy by seeing him like this. To Tansy, an undressed man was just a body to be tended to. But to Aster, there could be nothing so innocent about it.

"Here, let me help," Mallow muttered, crouching next to Aster with bandages in hand. "I'm not so useless that I can't take care of this wound for you."

"Thanks, Mal," Aster said weakly. "I'm glad you're here."

"Well, where the hell else do you think I'd be?"

Mallow finished cleaning the wound, rubbed it with whiskey, and wrapped it with clean white cloth. The dressing of the wound almost hurt as much as the wound itself. Aster wriggled the whole time like a fish on a line. The pain finally subsided, but the chill remained. Meanwhile, Tansy stitched up Eli, who set his jaw against the pain but never said a word. What a fine pair they made, she thought grimly, neither of them willing to admit just how hurt they were.

Finally Tansy finished, helping Eli sit up.

"Thank you," he murmured, looking at Aster to see if she was okay. His dark eyes shone with apology. "I'm sorry I got you all into this."

"More like *we* got *you* into this," Mallow said with a snort. "Don't worry, we've been through worse, and I reckon you have, too."

Eli let out a thin chuckle. "Well, we should try to get some sleep now all the same. Tomorrow's hard going, too." There were audible groans all around, and Eli turned his cautious smile to Aster. "So . . . um . . . how do we want to split up in the tents?"

Uneasiness crept back up Aster's neck in a flush of heat. From any other boy, she would have interpreted this as an unwelcome proposition. But she could see the childlike fear behind Eli's forced indifference. He was distraught by what had happened, terrified to be alone down here. Perhaps there was even some part of him that thought he'd gotten what he deserved, being savaged by the hungry ghosts of people he felt like he'd failed. He would want to talk about these things with someone he hoped would understand, take comfort in the nearness of a living person who cared about him. Aster wanted to give him this. She wanted to be able to rest next to a man without her chest seizing up or her mind shattering like fragile glass. She hated being this way.

And yet, still, she put on her own fake smile and said, "I reckon I'll bunk in with Tansy and Mallow. They're used to my snoring by now."

Eli's eyes dropped, but he swallowed and nodded.

"Of course," he said roughly. "I'll take the first watch."

They reached Camp Deathstalker early the next afternoon, washing up like mud-covered earthworms after a rain. Aster was able to walk well enough on her injured leg, though it caused her much discomfort, but Eli was much worse off, having to stop every few minutes to catch his breath. He didn't talk much to Aster, though whether that was because he was feeling awkward around her after she'd avoided him last night or because he simply didn't have the energy, Aster couldn't tell.

Sam had sent them with a letter explaining their business, and it was this that they showed to the guards to be taken to see Sidney Miller, the captain of Camp Deathstalker. Unlike Camp Red Claw, this was built more like the Lady Ghosts' headquarters—since there was no natural cavern in which to build an underground city, Deathstalker was made up of several large rooms branching off from a main corridor lit with mining lanterns. But, much like Camp Red Claw, it was clear that this place was overcrowded with hotfoots being shepherded towards Ferron. People slept fitfully in hallways under threadbare blankets. The sound of ragged coughing echoed down the passageways, and the smell of sweat and unwashed skin hung thick and heavy in the air.

What must they have been through to get here? Aster wondered, still rattled from her own journey through the tunnels. *And how much farther do they have to go?*

At last they reached the end of the main corridor.

"Sid'll be in there," their guard said, nodding at the unlabeled door that stood before them. "That's his office—and he don't much care for unexpected guests, I'll warn you."

"Well, I don't much care about his feelings on the matter," Aster muttered. They'd come too far to be denied now. The guard shrugged and left them to it. Aster exhaled, raised her fist, and knocked on the door.

Sidney answered almost immediately.

He was taller than Sam Daniels, and he looked older, too, with rosy brown skin, black hair shaved close to the skull, and a sharp, narrow face. Her wore a bright red stripe of paint across his dark eyes, but otherwise was simply dressed. While Sam was fastidiously formal, wearing fine clothes even when he got his hands dirty, Sidney wore the grubby work clothes of a man who had no patience for pretense. He considered the four of them, his gaze lingering on Aster's, Tansy's, and Mallow's favors.

"And just who the hell are you?" he said, with a voice that slid over its words like gravel.

Aster exchanged a glance with Eli, who hesitated and handed him Sam's letter. Sidney muttered an indecipherable curse as he snatched the half-folded piece of paper, opened it, and scanned its first few lines.

"Come in," he said with a heavy sigh, motioning for them to follow him as he walked behind his desk and took a seat. Behind him hung the flag of the Nine, a black wheel with nine spokes against a sky-blue field. And on the desk's surface, along with a mess of ledgers, calendars, and newspapers, was a real-life deathstalker scorpion in a jar. Mallow leaned forward to tap the glass, eyes wide, but Tansy stopped her.

"So," Sidney said, looking up at them. "You want our voltric weapons, is that it? Think I'll just hand them over because you asked nicely?"

Aster curled her lip, already tired of his dismissive attitude.

They'd been through hell to get here. She opened her mouth to speak, but Eli touched her wrist gently.

"Those weapons belong to all of us," he said in a low voice.

"They belong to the *Scorpions*," Sidney corrected him. "I won't have you leaving our own people defenseless for the sake of this—this farce," he said, tossing the letter away.

Aster was not doing this again. "This isn't a farce," she snapped. "These are my friends' lives we're talking about. These girls—"

Sidney held up a hand. "Let me stop you right there, because I promise you I've heard this all before. The rousing speech, the call to action. I have been on the front lines of a revolution, and I watched it crumble. I thank the dead every day for the cooler tempers that kept me from throwing my life away for a lost cause. I'll be that person for you."

If there was one thing Aster could not abide, it was being talked down to. She let out a hissing breath through her teeth, lacing her fingers behind her head and staring up at the low ceiling as she tried to swallow back her anger.

"Hold up—you say you've been on the front lines of a revolution before," Mallow said, stepping forward. She gestured at the flag behind the desk. "You're talking about the War for the Nations, right? Cutter told us you were in the fighting."

Sidney narrowed his eyes. "What of it?"

"I'm a descendant of the Nine, too, on my dad's side," Mallow continued.

Sidney glanced up at her headband, seeming to hesitate, but then he crossed his arms. "And why should that make a difference to me? That doesn't make us kin," he said. "Look,

189

everyone's ancestors intermarried. Most Arkettans have blood of the Nine running through their veins. But this obsession with 'blood,' it's old Empire rot. The rich use it as an excuse to say they have a right to the lands they've stolen. To speak for us, over us. That logic won't work here. Your countrymen aren't the ones you share blood with, they're the ones you share tradition with."

"Well, I've been *learning* the traditions," Mallow insisted. "Or trying to, at least. It's not my dad's fault he couldn't teach me, or my grandparents' fault they couldn't teach him. Not all of us grew up in rebels' camps."

Sidney's face flickered with regret, and he sat up straight, his gaze sliding away from Mallow's. "My apologies, sister, for assuming. It's rare I meet anyone who makes that argument in good faith. But I'm afraid it doesn't change anything—in fact, I feel that much more responsible for keeping you all safe."

Aster, Eli, and Mallow looked at Tansy. It was her turn. She sighed, taking a seat on the edge of the desk.

"Well, I don't know anything about this war, so would you be willing to tell me more about it? What happened that made you so reluctant to fight again?" she asked.

"What happened?" Sidney laughed humorlessly. "What *didn't* happen? You all are too young to remember, clearly, but for a full year there were bloody battles erupting all over the Scab, rebels of the Nine trying to seize forts from the Arkettan army. This is occupied land, all of it, and we wanted to attack those occupying forces directly. But there simply were not enough of us to see it through. For every fort we seized—and we seized many—the others sent reinforcements to drive us back out. Finally, we felt we had no choice but to surrender, and we invited the commanding officer of the operation to our base camp to negotiate. We turned over our weapons, signed the treaty . . . and then he and his troops opened fire. On our unarmed men, on their wives, on their children—" Sid stopped short, his throat bobbing as he swallowed hard. He took a steadying breath before he continued. "Most of our soldiers were killed in the massacre, and those of us who survived ended up scattered all across the country. My cousin escaped to Ferron, and he's the one who smuggles us voltric weapons, when he can. I consider myself fortunate to have landed here, where I can still do some good. But it's with open eyes. I know now that the enemy does not play fair."

Aster felt her anger drain away, leaving behind the sickening kind of sympathy that can only be shared between those who have suffered the unimaginable. Her hands had balled up into fists at her side, but they now relaxed. "I'm so sorry. I . . . I never knew about any of that," she said quietly.

"Well, it's not a part of history they like to teach. Wouldn't want to give anyone any ideas," Sidney said with a heavy sigh. He stood, smoothing his shirt as if it weren't already wrinkled beyond salvation. "Anyway, to further prevent a revolt like ours from ever happening again, the government started their military recruiting program after the war, offering young dustbloods forgiveness of their debts if they joined up. So now they have more soldiers among their ranks than ever before . . . some of them even children of the Nine themselves. If we couldn't beat them then, you certainly can't beat them now."

"But Sidney—Mr. Miller—" Aster said quickly, standing in

his way so he couldn't leave. "We're not trying to go up against the army. We're going up against the landmasters. This is an entirely different fight—one we can win."

"No, it's the same fight, and if you can't see that, then you're not ready for it."

Aster stood her ground. He had felt the same passion she did now, once. "Those guns deserve to be put to good use again. Please. If nothing else, consider the shine we're offering for them. From the looks of things around here, you could use it."

Sidney scowled. He crossed his arms again.

"'From the looks of things around here'? Do you really think it helps your case to insult the people under my care?"

"Not the people. The conditions they're living in. And I don't blame you for that. Camp Red Claw's suffering, too—hell, the whole damn Scab is suffering—but don't you have a responsibility to try to make things better for them? What do your people need more: those guns, or food and blankets?"

His mouth twitched, but he said nothing.

"And you saw the part about the theomite we'll be collecting on this job?" Eli added, stepping to Aster's side. "We're about to make travel between camps much safer. It'll be worth it for that alone."

Sidney fixed his gaze on Eli.

"Cutter told you that, too, did he?" Sidney asked.

"He didn't have to," Eli answered. "But, yeah, he's the one who's been escorting most of the hotfoots underground. And personally, I'd feel much better about it if he had some theomite in his pocket."

Sidney closed his eyes for patience. "That boy would love

192

nothing more than to fight and die for the central tribe. I finally manage to convince him not to, and now he throws himself into the tunnels instead? I swear he is determined to see what's beyond the Veil. Is it too much to ask for all you youngbloods to just . . . sit *still* . . ."

"It might be," Mallow said, with no trace of her usual humor. "Please, Mr. Miller. I can understand if you're ready to lay down your weapons, but some of us haven't even had the chance to fight for our people. Some of us didn't even know we *had* people, not until we met them. And we—*I*—deserve to decide for myself when I'm done fighting for us."

Sidney was quiet for a long time. Then, at last, he opened his eyes and nodded once.

"Very well, then," he said softly. "I'll take you to the armory."

CHAPTER SIXTEEN

The return trip to Red Claw proved even more arduous. Aster's injured leg was still tender and forced a limp, while Eli still struggled to breathe with his ravaged chest. They were also now dragging several crates of voltric weapons along with them—long guns, handguns, and even something called a crank cannon. It was no small effort to pull the wheeled crates along the uneven ground, and whenever the passage grew too small, Eli had to dig out more space for them. Sidney had at least sent them with a small pouch of theomite dust, on the promise that they were stealing more soon, so they were able to keep the vengeants away. Still—it ended up taking them three and a half days to get back. Aster was glad now she had told Violet to wait a week before staging the attack on the gambling hall. She would need an extra day to recover, physically and mentally.

Aster retreated to her cabin for the next twenty-four hours as the bloody scratches on her calf healed to a muddy crust. The others came to visit to congratulate her on the successful supply run and to share their excitement for the job ahead. Robbing a gambling hall was challenge enough, but "kidnapping" Derrick in the process—it would take all their skill. Raven went over her sketch of the building with Aster so they could discuss exit strategies. Tansy helped her stretch and strengthen her injured leg to speed its recovery. Mallow updated her on the progress being made with the new voltric weapons. And Clementine and Zee kept her steadfast company, the three of them doing their best to keep themselves—and Zee's young sister—in good spirits. The little girl was still shy around strangers, but she seemed to have made herself at home here in their cabin, playing makebelieve with the little dolls Raven had crafted for her out of hay and twine.

Eli alone did not come to visit, too busy nursing wounds of his own. Or at least, that was what Aster told herself. Ever since she'd rejected Eli's offer to share a tent, he'd seemed hesitant and uncertain around her, as if she were a snake that had rattled its tail. But Aster could not bring herself to apologize—and what was there to apologize for, anyway? She did not owe him physical comfort, even if it was something that a part of her wanted to give. But perhaps he was just giving her the space he now thought she wanted . . . and perhaps she ought to be grateful for that. She had a kidnapping and a robbery to plan and no time to worry about this kind of thing.

At last, though, it was the day of the raid, and time for everyone to come together.

The group met at the camp's shooting range, where Sam and Mallow would show the rest of them how to use the voltric guns. Aster still preferred her knife to any firearm, but after everything she'd been through to get these, she couldn't help being excited to see their potential.

195

"All right, so what have we got?" Zee asked eagerly, clapping his hands together.

"Where to even begin?" Sam said with an eager grin. He brought them over to the first open crate. "I have a little bit of experience with voltric weapons, and I've been working with Mal here nonstop to show her what I know. I don't think you all should have any trouble using these, but just in case, you'll want to get the feel for them before you set out tonight."

He pulled out what looked like a revolver and broke it open. In place of the spinning chamber was a thick coil. The metal whined with energy, making Aster wince instinctively. She remembered all too well hearing that sound from the armymen at the border of Ferron.

"This is your standard voltric pistol," Sam explained. "The coil here holds the charge. It's what serves for ammo for weapons like these—once its energy is depleted, you remove it and insert it into a voltric source to give it a fresh charge."

"A voltric source?" Eli asked his brother doubtfully. He wasn't actually going with them tonight, not with his more serious injury, but curiosity had brought him out this morning anyway.

"Yes, like this!" Mallow chimed in. She ran over to another crate and fished out a boxy black contraption bristling with wires. "You use steam to generate power to this box, which then transfers that power to the coils over the course of several hours. Then—"

"We don't need to know the details," Aster interrupted, holding up her hand. "We just need to know how many shots that pistol can fire before the coil needs to be recharged, since, clearly, we're not going to be able to recharge it once we're out there."

Sam and Mallow looked at her like little kids who'd been told to put their toys away. Sam sighed in disappointment.

"Right, well, it's not an *exact* science—it depends on environmental circumstances such as humidity and altitude," he said. "But, on average, you should expect between ten to twelve voltric bolts from each fully charged coil."

"Wait—ten to twelve? That's *it*?" Raven asked incredulously. "You all went halfway to hell and paid a small fortune for us to get ten to twelve shots each?"

"Ten to twelve *voltric* shots," Sam said quickly. "A bolt of voltricity is much more useful than a bullet; one shot anywhere on the body is enough to incapacitate a man. Your aim won't have to be nearly as precise, and a ravener who would normally be immune to the pain of a bullet will still seize up from the shock long enough for you to tie him up or get away. All of this is assuming you're using nonlethal charges, of course—if you flip this switch here, to give your weapon a lethal charge, each shot will be powerful enough to stop a man's heart, but you'll only have half as many. Five or six."

"This is horrifying," Tansy volunteered.

"Listen, it's actually *less* horrifying than the alternative, Tanz," Mal reassured her. "You can't kill someone, or even seriously hurt them, unless you really mean to."

"Well, that's good to hear," Aster muttered, taking one of the pistols from the crate for herself. She didn't want to kill anyone tonight, not if she could help it. But if it came down to it, she wasn't going to hesitate. They would not hesitate to kill her.

197

Derrick's words echoed in her mind. *These people believe you to be monsters. You cannot prove them right.*

She gritted her teeth. He didn't understand.

Aster walked over to the row of targets, trying to hold the gun steady in her hand. She practiced with firearms regularly now, but it still took her a moment to conquer her fear every time. She couldn't afford to freeze up when the time came tonight.

She counted to seven and back, steadying her breathing, looking down the sights, feeling the warm hum of energy between her hands. She squeezed the trigger.

CRACK! A jagged bolt of blue-white light thundered toward the target at the end of the room. Aster leapt back in surprise, letting the gun drop from her hand.

"Well? What do you think?" Mallow said excitedly.

"I think that'll do just fine," Aster muttered, a grin slowly spreading across her face.

They all took turns with the sidearms, then moved on to the long guns, then the crank cannon, an enormous beast on wheels that let out a continuous stream of lightning. As Sam had predicted, it didn't take long for them to get the hang of how these new weapons were handled, but Aster could tell they were all surprised by the difference in power. Zee and Raven seemed delighted, while Clementine and Tansy seemed frightened. Eli just looked unhappy to be left out. As much as Aster would have appreciated his reassuring, steady presence, a part of her was relieved he wasn't coming. Eli was becoming a . . . distraction. And this job would require focus.

"All right, so we all know how to shoot the damn things,"

Aster said as they took out all the coils to recharge them before nightfall. "But Mal, are you *sure* they're going to be enough for tonight?" She turned to Raven, who was helping Sam unstrap a rifle from his back. "Raven, you got the closest look at the place. What exactly are we dealing with?"

Raven pulled out her journal from her satchel and spread it open to the two-page drawing she'd made of the gambling hall. Her portraits had a certain softness to them, the corners carefully sanded down by the pad of her thumb, but this was the sharp, clear work of a technical draftsman. Aster had not even known, until Raven had first showed it to her, that she was capable of such precise work.

"Right, so the gambling hall has three points of entry, with two raveners guarding each one. There's the main entrance in the front, a back door that leads to a veranda, and a service entrance on the side for the staff." Raven pointed these each out. "There are also raveners inside, of course, to watch out for foul play. Derrick tells us there're six of those, as well—three on each floor." She looked up, arching her eyebrow at Aster. "So . . . twelve raveners versus the six of us."

"And, not to be the bearer of bad news, but we have to consider the human lawmen, too," Tansy pointed out. "How long do you reckon we'll have before *they* show up?"

Aster remembered their bank robbery, when a whole town of lawmen had come after them. She scowled. How were they supposed to do that again, *and* get away from a dozen raveners?

"And don't forget the patrons of the gambling hall will likely be armed to the teeth as well," Eli said with a low chuckle. "This is the Scab, after all."

199

"We're not to engage with the regular folk," Aster said to that. "Derrick was clear on that matter. If we do, he walks."

Eli said nothing, though Aster could see his jaw working. An awkward silence fell over the room.

"Well, obviously we wouldn't want to do anything to upset Derrick McClennon. We have to do exactly as he says, after all," Sam said lightly.

"It's not like that," Aster insisted. "He just—he says we need to show the world that we're not looking to start mindless violence here. That regular fairblood families have nothing to fear from us. We'll need them on our side before the end."

But even as she spoke, the words felt false in Aster's mouth. Did she really believe that? Or was she just afraid to do what needed doing?

We're long past the point of trying to convince anyone. They've had hundreds of years to do the right thing and done nothing. I shouldn't be made to feel guilty for forcing them into action now—

She shook her head. There wasn't time for philosophical debates, not when they were about to start this job.

"Look," she said, looking around the room. "I'm not saying lie down and die if one of these gamblemen takes a shot at you. I'm just saying not to start anything with them, hear? We're going after the raveners and the lawmen because they're the ones enforcing the violence we want to change. We have to keep our story straight."

Clementine raised a hand. "I thought our story was that we were robbers?"

Aster sighed. "Yes, that's how we'll play it off in the moment.

But *after* the fact, once the gambling hall is burned down and Derrick is safely in our clutches, we're going to make our demands to the government, and they need to know we weren't targeting civilians."

They all looked at each other uncertainly.

"Anyone else? Any questions?" Aster asked. "No? Then let's continue."

CHAPTER SEVENTEEN

They rode out to Rattlebank on horseback, slipping down the darkened Bone Road like coyotes on the hunt. The cool night air whispered deliciously over Aster's skin, her first taste of fresh air since descending into the Scorpions' underground hideout. The bright eye of the moon hung in a cloudless blue-black sky, spilling light between the skeletal fingers of the branches above. Vengeants flickered in and out of sight in the corner of Aster's eye as they passed through the curtains of silver, wailing sorrowfully. Her arms rippled with gooseflesh, and her stomach was in a free fall of fear she tried not to let the others see. Iron wardants lined the Bone Road to keep the dead at bay, but she wouldn't feel completely safe until they had secured the theomite from the gambling hall.

Of course, by then, we'll have the living to worry about, she thought, wetting her cracked lips. Violet was already at the gambling hall with Derrick, surrounded by raveners. They couldn't risk blowing their cover, of course, and so wouldn't be able to help during the firefight. Aster doubted Violet was even armed. The thought of her getting injured, or even killed, in the cross fire filled Aster with a dread greater than any the hungry dead could press upon her. And then of course there was Zee, who now had his little sister to look after; and Raven, who had never been in a firefight before; and Tansy and Mallow, who had sacrificed their freedom to be here; and Clementine, Aster's only family and best friend . . .

"You know, I've always wanted to go to a gambling hall," Zee said idly, perhaps to cut through the tense silence they had all fallen into. He and Clem were at the back of the line, driving a wagon in which they'd hidden their spare weapons. "It's a shame we can't have a few hands before we hold the place up."

"Zee, how the hell did you ever manage to convince anyone your father was a professional gambleman if you've never even seen the inside of one of these places?" Mallow cracked.

Aster couldn't see Zee's face from her position at the front of the line, but she could imagine it reddening beneath his brown skin.

"Guess I was just lucky I was only ever trying to convince fools," he retorted.

"Well, if trusting you to be a halfway decent person makes me a fool, then paint my nose red and send me to the circus—"

Aster tuned them out as they continued bickering in low tones. She rode with Raven, who, like all the girls, wore a dustkerchief and ghostweed salve to cover her favor. They did not yet want to reveal their identities to the rest of the world—being presumed dead had given Aster freedom, and she had little enough of that to spare.

"You seem nervous," Raven said quietly, though she herself was grinning with excitement—Aster could practically feel it on the nape of her neck.

"Of course I am," she muttered. "We're about to raise hell in this town. I've raised enough hell in my time to know what that means."

"Well, I haven't raised hardly *any* hell in my time, so believe me when I tell you I'm ready for tonight." She raised her voltric pistol and made mocking zapping noises. "*Zztt, zztt!* These bastards are about to feel the wrath of the ancestors."

Aster was too tense to join in on her laughter. She glanced over her shoulder. "Ray, I need you to take this seriously."

"What, like those two?" she asked sarcastically, gesturing at Mallow and Zee, who were still trading insults.

Aster's face grew hot. "I need them to take this seriously, too! Look, this kind of thing sounds great when you're telling the story later, but you have no idea how many times we almost got someone killed out here. Hell, we all thought Violet *had* been killed. There's about a thousand things that can go wrong tonight. And if we're not careful, if we're not *focused*—"

"Hey, easy, it's going to be okay, Aster," Clementine promised her. "Don't get in your own head, hear? Raven's right—the dead are with us."

Aster said nothing, wishing she had her sister's faith that the seraphants beyond the Veil were watching them, guiding them. But if that were true, then where had they been the day she'd been sold to the welcome house? Or on her Lucky Night?

No, Aster thought—they were on their own.

It wasn't much longer before they reached town, its deadwall rising up before them, the theomite dust in its mortar glittering in the moonlight. There were lawmen guarding the entrance, as always, but now that Aster and the rest of the Green Creek runaways had allegedly been executed, the law wasn't checking travelers' identities the way they had been before.

There are still more of them than ever, though, Aster thought grimly.

Rattlebank was busier tonight than it had been a week ago, which would only serve to make the job ahead more difficult. They rode single file between the groups of drunken men and the badges trying to corral them, Aster lowering the brim of her hat to avoid meeting anyone's eye. Once they reached the gambling hall she dismounted and tied her horse to a post, motioning for the others to do the same. Several men were drinking or smoking outside the hall, the ends of their cigars glowing cherry red. And, as expected, two raveners guarded the door—one thin and twisted as scrub brush, the other built like a slab of stone. Their orange eyes flashed like a cat's.

"All right," Aster murmured, looking around at her friends. Noise and light spilled from the gambling hall, threatening to drown out her words and bathing their half-covered faces in a yellow-orange glow. Aster's heart kicked in her chest and her head swam with adrenaline, but she forced her voice to remain steady for the others. "Just like we planned, understand? Watch each other's backs and meet back at Red Claw if anything goes wrong."

They all nodded, and, with one last breath to prepare herself, Aster led them towards the main entrance.

"Evening," Zee said, nodding to strangers as they passed. One of the strangers spat his chaw, but the others just suspiciously watched them walk by. Everyone in their group had hidden their weapons under their long duster coats, but even so, they cut intimidating figures. The skinny ravener held his hand up to stop them at the entrance.

"Going to have to ask you to remove your dustkerchiefs before you enter the building. Boss's orders."

Aster glanced tightly over to Zee. Derrick hadn't warned them about this.

"Since when?" Tansy asked calmly.

"Since we ripping said so, dustblood," he said roughly. "Folks feel too confident starting trouble when their faces are covered. We don't want that here. This is a fine establishment—too fine for the likes of you, seems to me."

Aster thought quickly. They needed to be seen kidnapping Derrick, for the sake of his story, but on the way out, not in. Their plan had been to get as close to Derrick as possible before holding up the gambling hall so they wouldn't have to fight their way towards him. He'd warned them they wouldn't be allowed in his private room, but to be stopped right here at the front door . . .

The other ravener drew himself up, hitting them with a wave of fear. Aster's insides loosened and her pulse quickened, panic shooting through her veins.

"He said remove your kerchiefs. If that's going to be a problem—"

Maybe it was the sudden surge of fear in her blood. Maybe it was the impatience of weeks spent leading up to this moment. Maybe it was just her anger at the way the ravener addressed them. But before she realized what she was doing, the voltric pistol was in her hand. She pointed it at his chest.

"I'm afraid it is," she said.

He reacted more quickly than she'd expected, even though she knew how supernaturally fast raveners could be. He grabbed her wrist with frightening strength, flipped her over to the ground. Aster's fear then was entirely her own, a helpless cry escaping her lips. She scrambled backwards, looking up into the barrel of the gun the ravener was now pointing at her. His partner drew his own weapon and pointed it at the rest of the group. The other men loitering on the porch let out cries of surprise or whoops of delight at the promise of a brawl.

"You better clear out now, hear?" the second ravener roared. "All of you—"

CRACK!

Lightning ripped through the air. Hit the ravener square in the ribs. The ravener standing over Aster snarled and swung his gun around, only to be struck in the shoulder with another ribbon of blue-white light. On the other end of it stood Mallow, her voltric pistol humming with power.

"Sorry," she said, breathing heavily. "I didn't know what the new plan was, so I figured it was time to improvise."

The ravener let out a cry as he fell to the ground, twitching. The men on the porch scattered and ran away. Raven helped Aster back to her feet.

"Thanks, you all," Aster said shakily.

"Of course," Zee said, drawing his own weapon.

No turning back now, Aster thought. She kicked the doors open.

"WE'RE HERE FOR DERRICK MCCLENNON! EVERYBODY ELSE OUT!" Aster roared from behind her dustkerchief, raising her gun and firing once into the air.

Screams rose up from the crowded gambling hall at the sudden thunder. The piano player stopped abruptly. It was normal, in the Scab, to hear brawling on the streets, but not for it to spill into a fine establishment such as this. The whole interior of the gambling hall sparkled like the inside of a jewelry box, from the gold-tiled ceiling and the glittering crystal gasoliers to the polished redwood furniture and gleaming marble floors. The patrons, too, dripped with wealth: gleaming pocket watches and theomite thumb rings for the men, pearl necklaces and chains of precious gems for the women. They clung to each other in confusion and fear.

"I SAID OUT!" Aster shouted again when they all remained frozen, and she stepped to the side to leave the doorway clear, using her gun to point. "DON'T MAKE ME MAKE YOU GO."

Finally, movement. A stampede. People pushing past them, cursing as they went.

"Shit," Mallow murmured.

The raveners were muscling their way through the crowd. Three of them, with more coming from upstairs and outside. The group would have to take them out before they found Derrick. Aster scanned the room quickly. The bar would serve as perfect cover.

If they could get there in time.

"On me!" she said to the others, sprinting for the bar. The room was almost cleared of bystanders, and the raveners' first bullets whizzed past them. Aster crouched low as she ran, her leg twinging with pain. Then she dove behind the bar, scrambling on hands and knees over the sticky floor. The others tumbled after her. Shots rang out above them, shattering the glasses on the back wall and cracking the marble siding.

"Stay low!" Aster ordered desperately, looking back to make sure they had all made it. Mallow, Clementine, Raven, Zee—

"Tansy!" Mallow shouted. Tansy had tripped ducking the bullets and was still out on the main floor, exposed. She rolled over onto her back, whipping out her pistol and firing wildly. It shook in her hands.

"Tansy—" Mallow started to crawl towards her, but Aster grabbed her shoulder.

"No, don't expose yourself. We'll cover her from here."

Aster peered over the bar. There were eight raveners on the floor now, two of them cornering Tansy, unable to return her fire under the barrage but nimbly avoiding her every shot as they moved in. Aster leveled her gun and fired at the nearest one. Missed.

"*Dammit*. They're too ripping fast," Aster cursed as she ducked back down.

"Not for me," Mallow said darkly. She surfaced and fired off a shot in one smooth motion, and Aster heard the heavy *thump* of one of the raveners falling to the floor in convulsions. But now Tansy's own pistol was clicking emptily. She was out of voltage. The second ravener sneered and drew his revolver. Aster rose from her crouch—

—and took the ravener down with a shot to the stomach, the man doubling over and seizing as he hit the ground. Tansy scrambled behind the bar to join the rest of them before the other raveners could close in on her. But bullets still flew above them, threatening to hit anyone who surfaced to take a shot of their own.

"Thank you," Tansy said shakily, her eyes glassy as Mallow embraced her.

"As if we were going to leave you out there as bait," Clementine scoffed.

Mallow checked the charge on her weapon. "By my count that's four raveners down, eight to go," she said.

"Seven," Zee said, ducking back into cover, his voltric pistol humming. "But there's only five left down here. Where the hell are the other two?"

"Probably guarding Derrick's private room upstairs," Aster said grimly. They wouldn't abandon him, least of all during a fight. "We have to get him before the law surrounds this place, or we'll never escape. And the vault—we have to steal the theomite out of the vault for the Scorpions, too." She swallowed the slick fear in her throat. "We're gonna have to split up."

Clementine's eyes widened. "Aster, no—"

A bullet hit the cash register, cutting her off with the sound of coppers raining down on them.

"We don't have time to argue," Aster said through gritted teeth. "Tansy, I want you and Clem to get the theomite—and leave our list of demands behind in the safe, where they won't be damaged when we burn this place down. That's crucial, hear? Raven, you're going to come with me to get Derrick and Violet. And Zee, you're going to stay back here with Mallow and cover us—"

Sudden dread washed over Aster then, filling her belly with ice. Lethargy leached into her limbs. A sob escaped her lips as she struggled to keep from collapsing.

No . . .

The raveners must have gotten close enough to exert their power, poisoning her mind. She'd had more than her fair share of practice resisting their assaults from her time at the welcome house, but she'd never been forced to deal with this many at once before. Self-loathing, exhaustion, despair, and regret tore at her from the inside. Her vision blurred and doubled. Her breathing grew ragged and uneven. She felt as if her brain were being pushed through a meat grinder.

"We—we just need to—" Aster stammered.

She should never have brought them here.

They had been free, all of them. And she had dragged them back into danger for her own selfish need to be the hero. Her ambition would get everyone killed. Even now they all had the same glazed-eyed, slack-jawed look that Aster was surely wearing herself, waiting for the raveners to swarm them—

"Aster—*Aster*! Look at me," Raven said urgently, snapping her fingers in front of Aster's face. "Come on, they're almost on us."

Raven was the only one who didn't seem affected. She alone was keeping the raveners at bay, loosing shot after shot over the bar—though judging from the tense look on her face, she didn't have many left.

"How . . . how are you resisting them . . ." Aster said weakly.

"It's gonna take more than these bastards to knock me out of step," she muttered in reply. She flipped the switch on her pistol to the more powerful setting with shaking fingers.

"Don't, it'll use up the rest of your voltage," Zee warned, his face twisted up in pain.

"Then I'll just have to make it count," Raven said, her jaw set.

She rose up over the bar, clutching the gun with both hands, and let loose a flash of lightning so bright it left Aster momentarily blinded. A crack of thunder followed an instant later, along with the sudden explosive sound of splitting wood.

The raveners released their hold.

Aster clutched her head as her mind suddenly cleared. She climbed to her feet and peered over the lip of the bar.

Fire—engulfing the table Raven had blasted, swelling with smoke, sending the raveners scattering back.

"You said we had to burn the place down anyway," Raven said with a shrug.

For the first time since the night had begun, Aster felt a grin tug at her face. "Quick thinking, Ray." She looked at the others, who were also coming to their senses. It wouldn't be long before the raveners reasserted themselves. "All right, look sharp. There's no more time to discuss this. We're splitting up. Meet back at the wagon before this place comes down around us, hear?"

They nodded, Zee and Mallow taking up their positions while Clementine and Tansy bolted in one direction and Aster and Raven bolted in the other. Aster darted from table to table for cover as she led Raven towards the grand staircase, staying low to avoid both the thickening smoke and the raveners' bullets. Zee and Mallow's steady covering fire filled the room with crackling thunder and a lingering voltric charge that raised the hair on the nape of Aster's neck.

"So when the hell were you going to let me know you aren't affected by raveners?" Aster hissed as they reached the foot of the stairs.

Raven laughed harshly, and it turned into a cough as the smoke threatened to choke them. "If we survive this shit, I promise I'll tell you everything."

They went up the stairs back-to-back, Aster returning fire to a ravener leaping over a billiards table in pursuit of them, while Raven faced forward to confront the two raveners who would no doubt be guarding the second floor. Her gun was dead, but they had no way of knowing that.

"*Hell yes*," Aster whispered to herself as she finally landed a hit on the ravener. The lightning hit him square in the shoulder, sending him almost head over heels. She tried to count how many raveners were left, but she couldn't see through the smoke. There was no sign of her sister and Tansy, either. Her brief flash of triumph went dark. Did that mean they'd made it to the vault? Or had they been—

"Duck!" Raven said suddenly, grabbing Aster from behind and throwing her to the ground. Aster let out a grunt, hitting the landing of the second floor just as the blast of a shotgun roared overhead. Her gun tumbled out of her hands. Skittered across the floor. She crawled towards it.

"That's far enough, you little snake," a low voice growled, and the pointed toe of a boot came down on the back of her wrist. Aster winced, looking up at the ravener crushing her hand. His shotgun was aimed squarely at her face. Behind him, the other ravener had tackled Raven to the ground. She clawed at his face as he seemed to struggle to subdue her with his mind, his expression dark with concentration.

"End of the line, dustblood," Aster's ravener said, his salt-and-pepper-stubbled face splitting with a grin. His orange eyes flashed as he jabbed the muzzle of his gun between her eyes. "Now on your feet, nice and slow."

Aster swallowed. Desperately searched for any way out of this. She looked down the marbled hallway. To the gilded door opening at the end of it. And stepping out from behind that door—

Violet?

They locked gazes, the startled blue of Violet's widening eyes sending a jolt through Aster's chest. Her black hair was piled high in ringlets on her head, her midnight blue dress sweeping around her ankles. Derrick stood behind her in a three-piece suit, his hair slicked back, his freckled face even paler than usual. Time seemed to move at half speed then: Violet's gaze darting from Aster to her gun on the floor, Violet gathering her skirts and running for the abandoned weapon, Violet picking it up in her ringed fingers and firing on Aster's ravener just as he turned to face her. Thunder filled the hallway. The ravener's body seized with voltricity as he crumpled to the ground, Aster rolling out of the way to avoid him. The second ravener let out a roar as he abandoned Raven and swung around to attack Violet, reaching for his sidearm. Violet flinched back, firing again but missing. Raven regained her feet with shocking speed, grabbing the ravener from behind and reaching her arm around his throat to strangle him. His white face grew fiery with shock and anger.

"Quick, Vi! I can't hold him—" Raven urged.

The ravener broke free.

Violet seemed to steady herself and shot him again, and this time the lightning hit him square in the chest. The hallway fell silent but for the sound of their uneven breathing and the crackling of the spreading fire below. Aster climbed to her feet, shaking as if she'd been the one hit with voltricity herself.

"I thought *you* were coming to save *me*," Violet said at last, tossing the gun back to Aster, who barely caught it.

"You're alive, aren't you?" Aster said with a loose laugh, and, despite the peril of the moment—or perhaps because of it—they embraced.

"Where's the little orange rat boy?" Raven demanded as they separated. She was hurriedly collecting the raveners' weapons now that her own was spent.

"Present," Derrick said weakly, emerging from the shadows to join them, looking ill as he considered the raveners at their feet. "And begging your pardon, but I think we're going to need to find another way out of here."

He gestured to the stairway, which was swiftly succumbing to the flames that had spread throughout the first floor. The smoke was growing so thick they could barely see each other, and the ceiling blackened as it burned, the wood cracking and popping ominously. Aster sweated beneath her layers, fear sending a spear of frost through the heat in her chest. There was no sign of any of the others downstairs. What if they were passed out, or trapped, or too turned around to find the exit? Instinct urged her to dive into the inferno and find them, drag them out into the open air herself if she had to. She could not risk leaving them behind—

"*I said*—" Derrick tried again, his voice strained.

"I heard you," Aster barked, turning her back. There was no choice but to see this through, or none of them would survive.

"There's a row of bushes beneath the windows in the room

215

we just came from," Violet offered. "It's not the softest landing, but—"

Aster nodded gratefully. "It'll do. We'll jump. Follow me."

She didn't wait for any of them to argue, sprinting down the hallway, coughing through her dustkerchief. The heat peeled at her exposed skin and made her eyes run. By the time she made it to Derrick's private room, she had fallen to her hands and knees to avoid the worst of the smoke. The others crawled behind her. The large bay windows had already been opened to let in the breeze, the dark promise of the cool night air beckoning Aster closer. She peered over the sill, cursing quietly.

The law had surrounded the building.

There were at least a dozen men back here, and no doubt more out front. It wasn't unexpected, but it did complicate things. She turned back to the others, who crowded next to her.

"They're gonna be on us as soon as we hit the ground," she said, her voice low and urgent. "Remember, this is a hostage situation—that's the only way we get through all of them and back to the wagon, where, the dead willing, the others are waiting for us. Raven, I'll take the man of the hour here, and you take Violet, hear? We have to make it look convincing. Everyone just follow my lead."

Derrick locked eyes with Aster. "You mean—ah—you and me—?"

"You and me." Aster grabbed his hand before he could lose his nerve, and they stood, climbed through the window, and jumped. Aster's stomach rose to her throat as she fell to the earth, the cool air around her sucking the clinging heat away. Derrick squeezed her hand so hard it hurt, releasing at the last

216

instant so they could land properly. Branches scratched at them as they crashed through the bushes, a shudder running through Aster's bones when her feet hit the ground. She curled into a ball and rolled clear of the shrubbery. The lawmen shouted at the sudden sight of her, a chorus of clicks rising up as they released the safeties on their weapons.

"THEY'RE OVER HERE—"

"I HAVE EYES ON THEM—"

"ENOUGH!" Aster shouted back at them, jumping to her feet and yanking Derrick along with her. She pressed the muzzle of her voltric pistol to Derrick's throat, holding Derrick so tight against her she could feel the beat of his heart. She heard the *thud* of Raven and Violet landing behind her, and they emerged from the darkness to stand next to her.

"We have Derrick McClennon here, and his Lucker, too. Drop your weapons or we kill them both," Aster ordered.

"*Please!*" Violet wailed for good measure, throwing a crack into her voice.

The lawmen hesitated, neither dropping their weapons nor coming any closer.

"Unless you bastards want the death of McClennon's boy on your heads, you'll let us be on our way," Raven added, her voice hoarse from coughing.

"Do as they say! My uncle will sort this out," Derrick commanded then, and even with soot smeared across his face, leaves tangled in his hair, and the muzzle of a gun kissing the underside of his chin, the authority in his tone was undeniable.

"Orders?" one of the lawmen demanded.

"Let them through," another said, holding his hand up, and

the remaining lawmen lowered their weapons. Aster pushed Derrick forward roughly.

"*Easy,*" Derrick whispered. "If I didn't know better, I'd say you were enjoying this."

"Just trying to sell it," Aster whispered grimly. She still couldn't celebrate yet, not until she knew the others had made it out of that building alive.

She and Raven led Derrick and Violet around to the front of the building, the lawmen following them, their gazes hot with hate on Aster's back. One misstep, she knew, and they would bury a bullet in her skull.

Their getaway wagon was still waiting in the street, though more lawmen surrounded it, in a shootout with—

There they are.

Relief flooded Aster's blood. Tansy, Mallow, Clementine, and Zee had all escaped the burning building and managed to take shelter in the wagon, where their spare weapons had been waiting for them. They fired bolts of voltricity in all directions, ducking the bullets that flew back in return.

"You tell your men to back down," Aster growled to the lawman nearest to her. "*Now,*" she added when he hesitated.

He ran forward and gave the order, waving his hands frantically as he warned the other lawmen of the situation. Her friends cheered at the sight of her.

"That's right, back the hell up!" Aster yelled out to the law. "We're almost done here! Nobody else need get hurt!"

"Do as they say," Derrick repeated calmly.

The law stood down. They lowered their weapons. And at last, at last, Aster reached the wagon. She shoved Derrick in the back, keeping her gun trained on him the whole time as she climbed in after him. Then Raven and Violet piled in. Zee hurried over the top and took up the reins. Snapped them once, set the horses galloping.

"Make sure we're not followed," Aster ordered Mallow, collapsing in exhaustion on the splintered wood.

Mallow nodded once, snatching the covers off the last remaining weapon in their arsenal: the crank cannon. She began to turn its handle. A hum rose up around them, blue light building in the heart of the cannon, voltricity tugging at the small hairs on Aster's arms. Then a continuous stream of lightning lashed out, Mallow swinging the cannon back and forth on its axis as she churned the crank to keep the power going. The lawmen yelped and ducked out of the way. Wood splintered as it was struck, earth was singed black, and men fell stunned to the ground as they tried to give chase. The too-bright light cast everything in an unreal blue-white wash, and thunder rolled out in a continuous roar.

"Well, I reckon this will get my uncle's attention," Derrick said mildly.

The voltricity had set Aster's bones humming, and she could only nod in agreement, exhilarated by the power of the storm they had conjured.

CHAPTER EIGHTEEN

By the time they reached the Scorpions' camp it was the small hours of the morning. They'd had to leave the wagon and the crank cannon hidden in the woods and continue the rest of the way on foot, covering their tracks as they went. They'd bought themselves some time by stunning anyone who might have pursued them, but it was inevitable that the law and McClennon's raveners would pick up their trail come morning. Aster could not risk leading them back to Red Claw—the Scorpions had only agreed to shelter her on the promise that she wouldn't compromise their safety.

Still, it was a hero's welcome she and the others received when they finally returned home, Sam Daniels himself waiting to greet them at the base of the mineshaft. They caught him with his flask halfway up to his lips, his bright brown eyes widening at the sight of them as his grin lit up the dark.

"By the dead! I was just about to strike out myself to try to find you fools," he said, standing to clasp their arms each in turn. "Did everyone make it back? Violet, good to see you again! Raven, thank the dead you're all right. And you . . . you must be Derrick." Sam paused in his warm welcome, considering the

McClennon boy. Derrick looked about ready to drop—he was not used to hiking through the woods, let alone in the dark, and Aster had practically had to drag him the last mile as he jumped at every sudden noise or glimpse of the vengeants. His fine suit was quite ruined, his face soiled with soot and mud, his eyelids drooping with exhaustion.

"Evening," Derrick said wearily, holding out his hand. "Or morning. Whichever."

Sam clasped the proffered arm uncertainly, glancing at Aster. "Are you, ah, sure you got the right man? This one looks consumptive."

"Oh, don't worry, he always looks like that—" Clementine piped up, before Aster jabbed her in the side with an elbow.

"Derrick here's had a hard time," Aster said, clearing her throat. "We all have, actually. Can we be taken to the medical ward?"

"Of course," Sam said, turning and waving for them to follow him.

The rest of the camp was dark and sleeping, but lantern light still spilled out from the windows of the medical building like a lighthouse on the midnight sea. The place was run by self-taught volunteers—Tansy was the closest thing it had ever had to an actual doctor. There was only one volunteer working the graveyard shift tonight, and he ushered them in with a look of silent surprise.

"Yes, yes, the girls have made it back all in one piece, more or less," Sam told him brightly. "But they'll still need to stay here tonight to recover. Do we have enough beds?"

Inside, there were a dozen beds lined up in two rows, and three of them were occupied. One with an old man, one with a child, and one with—

"Eli," Aster said with an exhale of relief. He was propped up in his bed by a stack of pillows, his chest wrapped with fresh bandages. He winced as he sat up straight.

"Aster," he said, though it clearly pained him to speak. "Thank the dead. What'd I miss?"

And so Aster and the others recounted everything to Sam and Eli while their injuries were seen to: minor burns; cuts, scrapes, and bruises; ragged coughs from breathing in too much smoke. The worst injuries belonged to Zee, who had gotten his nose broken by the butt of a lawman's gun, and Derrick, who had twisted his ankle jumping from the window. Tansy gave him some whiskey for the pain, and, in his exhaustion, he fell asleep almost immediately.

"We were able to get into the vault, take the theomite, and leave the list of demands behind without too much trouble," Clementine explained from her own bed. "It was getting back out that was the hard part. By then, Zee and Mal had run out of voltage to give us cover fire, and there were still two raveners left we had to deal with."

"Plus the fire had spread throughout most of the first floor by then," Tansy said. "So we had to stay low to avoid the smoke."

"And as soon as we made it out of the building, we had to face the swarm of lawmen that had surrounded the place. It was a near thing," Zee admitted, wincing as he gingerly touched his swollen face. "If it weren't for Mal, we never would have made it—she had brought her revolver along for backup, just in case."

"Never leave home without it," Mal said with a hoarse laugh.

"Wait, so were the voltric weapons even worth it?" Eli asked, sounding upset.

"Oh, absolutely," Aster said immediately—and not just to reassure him. It was true. They never would have made it out of Rattlebank alive if not for the voltric weapons' ability to subdue a ravener in one shot. That, and . . .

"Raven," Aster went on. Raven was lying in the bed directly across from her and, as usual, had spent more time listening than talking. "You promised to tell me how you managed to resist the raveners. We wouldn't've lasted five minutes if it weren't for you."

"Yeah, that was a hell of a magic trick," Zee said, turning to her. "It's not something you could teach us, is it?"

Aster could hear well enough what he left unspoken—he wanted to know if there was a way he and his baby sister, Emily, could learn to live with their ravener sister, Elizabeth. Maybe he still held out hope that their family could be reunited again after all this. Aster felt her heart pang in sympathy.

Raven glanced around the room, seemingly uneasy at the sudden attention. Aster gave her an encouraging nod, hoping that, after everything they'd just been through together, she'd feel safe enough to let her guard down around the others.

"Well, I don't know for sure," Raven muttered. "I just have my suspicions."

"That'll do," Violet said wearily. She was lying down with a cold compress on her forehead, an aggrieved expression on her face as if she'd been shot rather than mildly scuffed up.

Raven laughed a little, sitting up straighter. "It's not something I was always able to do. When I was really young—five, six—they could break me with ease. But then, so could everybody else. Children, neighbors, landmasters.

My parents. I was always 'the piebald,' because of my skin, or 'uppity,' because of my art, or a 'nance,' because of . . . everything else. Even when I got to the welcome house, the other girls . . ." She trailed off, flicking her gaze back to Aster. "But by then I had long since learned how to lock myself, my feelings, away, so they couldn't be manipulated by others. So I couldn't be hurt."

"Not even by raveners?" Tansy asked skeptically.

Raven shook her head. "Not even by raveners." Her fingers went up to the raven feathers tattooed on the side of her face. "It's funny, you know, that word—*raveners*—it comes from *raven*, did you know that? Folks say it's because they're omens of death, servants of death, so loyal their own bodies don't even decay. But it's simpler than that, if you ask me—they're carrion birds. They attack the weakest among us, the most vulnerable. This favor was supposed to mark me as easy prey. But instead, it's become a reminder to me of how strong I've become."

Zee furrowed his brow. "That can't be all it is. All you girls have had to grow thick skins. Aster damn near has armor."

"And a blade to go with it, so watch your tongue," Aster warned.

Raven chuckled and shrugged. "Well, like I said, it's just a working theory. But if I had to guess what's different between us . . . I'd say it was that you all had family and friends before the welcome house, and each other while you were there. Your armor has weak points. But I've never had anyone like that. So my armor . . ."

"That sounds like a lonely way to live," Violet said into the silence, and Aster heard the pain in her voice. Violet had never

224

known her family, had rejected friendship at the welcome house for the sake of power. It was not the same as what Raven had been through, but if anyone were to understand what it was like to be alone, even if half by choice, it would be her.

"It was," Raven admitted, looking down.

"Was?" Clementine echoed in a hopeful tone.

Raven half smiled as she looked around the room. "Well, I admit, you Luckers are wearing me down."

The next day began their wait for McClennon's response. They'd kidnapped his nephew, burned down his gambling hall, and demanded his family close all their welcome houses. Even for a man as important as Jerrod McClennon, that wasn't the kind of provocation he could ignore for long. The mood of the camp was taut with excitement. Sam had doubled the guards to keep watch for raveners, and scouts rode into Scarcliff to get copies of the papers to see how the incident—and, more importantly, their demands—were being reported. Aster's skin itched with impatience for answers. All the time and resources she'd spent preparing for this, the bridges she'd burned, the lives she'd risked . . .

She needed this to work.

But rather than spend the day pacing alone in her room, she decided to distract herself by helping Derrick get settled in. She was less concerned about his own comfort than the possibility that he was going to get in the Scorpions' way. He would have no servants here; he'd have to figure out how to wash his own clothes and wipe his own ass. She would see to it that he was a burden to no one but herself.

Fortunately—or perhaps unfortunately, Aster couldn't tell yet—Eli decided to join her.

"This space is beyond anything I could have imagined," Derrick was saying as they toured him through the underground city. He'd shucked his tailored dress suit in favor of a dirty pair of denims and a comically overlarge flannel he'd borrowed from Eli. "Truly, a modern marvel of manpower and mining technology."

Eli, who was walking in step with him, threw an aggrieved look over his shoulder at Aster, as he did every time Derrick started talking like a politician. Eli was moving a little more slowly than normal, favoring his injury, but he still carried himself with that quiet pride Aster had come to know so well. He'd saved his best flannel for himself and had even seemed to iron it, the deep red of the fabric bringing out the rich brown of his skin, the sleeves rolled up around his thick forearms. He was not much taller than Derrick, but he *was* much broader-built, and Derrick hovered nervously beside him like a sparrow beside a sleeping catamount.

As for Aster, she held back from both of them. She still wasn't at ease around either of these two—the bass of their voices, the musk of their skin—but she refused to let them see that. She wished, desperately, that Violet were here. She always felt stronger with Violet at her side.

"I'm curious, how many souls live here?" Derrick went on with forced brightness.

"That depends—do you mean just the living, or the dead as well?" Eli asked.

"Oh! Are the dead—ah—are they a persistent problem here?" Derrick threw his own nervous look back at Aster. There were bruised circles under his eyes from staying up so late, and though he had splashed some water on his face, there was still plenty of grime on his neck and under his nails. Violet was right, though, Aster realized—Derrick was not bad looking, here in the half-light, if you squinted. The shapes of his shoulder blades rose up like folded wings beneath his loose shirt, and when he was excited about something, as he was now seeing the camp, the boyish light in his eyes was bright enough to thaw some of the frost Aster felt towards all men.

"The dead are not a 'problem,'" Eli said slowly. "The dead are our responsibility. They remain in the world of the living because it failed them, and here they'll stay until justice is done."

"That's an . . . ah, fascinating perspective. I've never thought of it that way. My father sees them more as pests to be driven out. We have hallowers cleanse our properties of any new remnants once a month. And the vengeants—well—if I never get that close to them again, it'll be too soon," Derrick said with a forced laugh.

Eli's jaw worked, and his walk slowed to a stop.

"Tell me, Derrick, do you fear the dead?" Eli asked, facing him squarely.

Derrick's throat bobbed. "Do I—do I fear—I don't understand—"

Ripping hell, Aster thought. It was time to intervene. She quickly stepped between the two of them, pushing Eli back gently.

"Leave him be, Eli," Aster said with a sigh. "You know just as well as I do that the rich aren't religious."

Eli's liquid dark eyes flickered over to her. "Neither are you, as far as I can tell, so why do you care?"

Aster's face grew hot at the accusation. That was different. She didn't trust the dead to save her. The rich simply didn't need them.

"Well—"

"We're actually incredibly pious," Derrick argued with a light scoff. "I never missed a service growing up; my uncle made sure of it."

"Yes, you can tell he's a righteous man."

Derrick laughed emptily, throwing a hand up in surrender and looking at Aster as if dealing with a difficult child. "Aster—please, I have no idea how we got on this. I meant no harm. Tell him. I just want to continue this thrilling tour. We were on our way to the kennels, I think—"

"You *should* fear the dead," Eli interrupted, stepping closer. "Their blood is on your hands."

Derrick's smile slipped. A line formed between his brows. "I'm well aware of that, Eli. I'm here, aren't I?"

"Yes, and what suffering you're being subjected to—"

"I hardly asked for this royal treatment! You *volunteered*. And I'll have you know I've suffered plenty. Last night I could have been killed a dozen different ways—an adventure *you* were conveniently absent for, I might add—"

Eli curled his lip. "You want to run that by me again, Red? Because I know I didn't just hear you say—"

"*Enough*, both of you," Aster snapped, pushing them apart. "What the hell is wrong with you? We're on the same side."

"Yes, thank you," Derrick said, red-faced.

"Shut up," Aster said wearily. "And you—" She turned to Eli. "Why don't you just let me take it from here? Go on home and rest up."

"What, and leave you alone with him?" Eli asked incredulously.

Aster raised a brow. "I can take care of myself just fine, thanks."

Eli looked down at the ground, clearly biting back his words. Then he turned on his heel and left them, striding off towards the cabin he shared with Sam. Aster sighed.

"Wait here," she ordered Derrick. She couldn't let Eli leave like this. She ran after him, grabbing him by the shoulder. It tensed under her grasp.

"Eli," she whispered. "Come on, just talk to me, please."

He shook her grip off and turned to face her. He hurried to hide the hurt on his face, but Aster still caught it.

"You couldn't bear to be alone with me for more than a minute back in the tunnels, but then when a nice little fairblood boy comes along, suddenly you can take care of yourself?" Eli asked, his voice low.

Aster took a step back, startled by his words—and, despite herself, frightened by his anger. She knew Eli would never hurt her, but her instincts ran too deep. She tried to still her heart before it could set her head spinning. Nausea swirled in her stomach.

"Eli . . . what the hell are you getting at?" she asked evenly.

"I'm here for *you*, Aster. Because I've seen how uncomfortable you are around men, and I didn't want you to have to deal with Derrick by yourself. But maybe it was actually just *me* you were uncomfortable with all along. Why? What is it that's so scary about me? Please? Because I swear it feels like the whole damn world thinks dustblood boys like me are just some kind of . . . *animals*. And I'm used to it from

229

them, I can take it from them, but you . . ." He gestured at her desperately. "Look, you can't even bear to meet my eyes right now. You're afraid of me. I can tell. *What* do I have to do to make it better?"

Shame warmed Aster's skin like dry heat. She hated that Eli could see her discomfort, hated that it hurt him. It was not fair to either of them. She forced herself to look up at him, setting her jaw as she searched for the words to fix this.

"I just . . . I need you to be patient with me, Eli," she said finally, so softly it was scarcely above a whisper. "You know what I've been through. You know how many 'nice little fairblood boys' were coming in and out of that welcome house. So you know, too, that I don't for a second believe the lie that they're somehow better people. It's not about that."

Eli couldn't seem to help himself, the words spilling out. "But then, why is it, with Derrick—"

"If I seem more at ease around Derrick, it is only because I don't care for him the way I care for you. And feeling that way . . . that *does* scare me," Aster admitted. She reached out to hold Eli's rough hand, her thumb sliding over the calluses of his palm, her pulse slowing as she steadied her breath. Eli's gaze flickered down to their hands, surprise lighting up his eyes. "I know I can be a frustrating person to care about," she said with a self-conscious half laugh. "My sister's made that clear enough to me plenty of times before. Hell, I get exhausted just trying to love myself—"

"I didn't say all that," Eli said quickly.

"—*but*," she continued, swallowing, "I'm asking you to try, hear? Just . . . give me a little more time to figure this out. It's . . . *this* . . . is new to me."

She withdrew her hand, smiling, relieved when Eli smiled back, crinkling up the corners of his eyes.

"All right," he conceded. "But I still don't like Derrick."

Aster glanced over her shoulder to where he was still waiting several yards away, swinging an old piece of wood around like a bo staff in his boredom, slashing at unseen assailants. Aster rolled her eyes, even as a certain affection for him rose up in her. It was not the same as what she felt for Eli, but the strength of it surprised her.

"No," she allowed with a sigh. "But we need him."

The next day, one of the Scorpion scouts returned with a copy of the morning newspaper. In it was the list of demands they had left for the law to find. Aster and her friends gathered around excitedly to see their words written large.

TO MR. JERROD MCCLENNON:

WE SPEAK FOR THE WOMEN AND GIRLS YOU HAVE SILENCED. WE BURNED DOWN YOUR WELCOME HOUSE. WE BURNED DOWN YOUR GAMBLING HALL. AND NOW WE HAVE TAKEN YOUR LAST LIVING HEIR CAPTIVE. IF YOU WISH TO SEE DERRICK MCCLENNON AGAIN, LISTEN WELL TO OUR DEMANDS AND LET THEM BE KNOWN TO THE PEOPLE:
1. YOU WILL CEASE BUSINESS AT ALL WELCOME HOUSES IMMEDIATELY
2. YOU WILL PAY ALL GOOD LUCK GIRLS FOR THEIR STOLEN LABOR

3. YOU WILL FORGIVE ALL OUTSTANDING
DUSTBLOOD DEBTS
    YOU HAVE ONE WEEK TO ISSUE A PUBLIC
RESPONSE. THE TIME HAS COME AT LAST FOR
THE PEOPLE IN POWER TO PAY WHAT THEY OWE.
                    SIGNED, THE RECKONERS

"Do you think they'll cave?" Tansy asked, clutching her collar anxiously as she scanned the page.

"I sure as hell hope so," Aster muttered. She had thought it would make her feel better, seeing it all in ink, but instead, it just made the pit of anxiety in her stomach grow heavier.

There was no turning back now.

"It's a good sign they published this—that means they've already done one thing we asked," Zee pointed out.

Derrick shook his head once, gnawing at his thumbnail. "If they've published this it's because they think it'll be advantageous to them somehow. They'll want the public to know so that they may turn them against you, offer rewards for information and such."

Derrick always seemed so certain things were going to get worse before they got better. Aster refused to believe that. She had to have hope.

"So . . . what are we supposed to do if they *don't* cave, then?" Mallow asked, looking around the circle. "Send them one of Derrick's fingers? Or?"

Derrick blanched.

"No, they'll give in," Aster insisted. "We just have to wait."

And so wait they did. The week passed at a crawl, Aster and

the others checking the papers every day for McClennon's response. As tense as things had been with the Scorpions when Aster had first asked them for help, she could sense a shift in the air among them now. They seemed to take pride in the part they'd played in bringing the landmasters down a peg, in embarrassing a man like McClennon on such a large scale. There was a feeling that they were all in this together now. Every day the scouts would let them know what the folks in town were saying, tripping over their own words in their excitement.

"I heard it was a bunch of escaped convicts from the Scorchbrush mines—that's where they keep the worst criminals. The animals—"

"No, it's the Nine Nations. They've been planning this for years. Another war to undo what the Empire did—"

"McClennon and them need to do something, even if that means negotiating with these bastards. I got family in one of his mining camps. I don't want them getting hit, too."

"Attacking our hardworking lawmen who put their life on the line? For the sake of a bunch of Luckers? What kind of morally depraved—"

And on and on. Aster didn't know how to feel about what she was hearing.

"The wrong people are scared," she said in frustration to Violet halfway through the week over a distracted game of cards. "I'm not out to hurt regular folks. We were so careful about that. It's only the lawmen and raveners and brags I have an issue with."

In the back of her mind was the fear that Derrick had been right about this whole thing after all, and they had already ruined any chance of success by turning the masses against them.

"Look, Aster, lawmen *are* regular folks," Violet said with

a sigh. "So are most brags. And so were the raveners, before they became what they are. And even if the landmasters aren't, a lot of regular folks look up to them. They see an attack on a landmaster as an attack on their own dreams for themselves. So of course they're going to take it personally when you threaten to take that dream away."

Aster scowled. "So what are you saying we do?"

"I'm not saying we *do* anything," Violet said. "I'm just saying— it's impossible to try to change things like this without making some 'regular folks' upset. And that's okay. It's not as if *they* cared when *we* were the ones suffering."

Aster was silent, chewing her lip as she looked over her hand. It seemed like every move she made would be a losing one.

"I just don't want to lose myself, Vi," she said quietly. "Sometimes I feel like I am. Everyone's counting on me, but . . . what if they shouldn't?"

Violet's smile faded. "Of course they should. I can't think of anyone better equipped to lead a group like this. You're the only one who could've gotten all of us to Lady Ghost—and that's just the truth."

"I didn't save all of us. I couldn't save you," Aster said quietly.

"Don't start. You did the right thing in leaving me behind. It's what I wanted. And I know you don't believe in this shit, but maybe it was meant to be. How else would we have ever gotten to work with Derrick?"

Aster tried to take the words to heart, but she still couldn't.

"You're not the only one I've let down, though," she said. "I betrayed the Lady Ghosts' trust when I left them. I almost lost the alliance with the Scorpions—"

234

"So you've made some mistakes. We all do. The dead know *I* have. At least you were acting on others' behalf. Most of us are just out for ourselves," Violet said dryly. "Look, at the end of the day, no leader is ever going to be able to please everyone. You just do the best you can with the circumstances you're given. Sometimes there are no easy choices, Aster."

Sometimes there are no easy choices . . . if that wasn't a summary of her life so far, Aster didn't know what was.

Aster sighed. "I reckon you're right."

"I always am. You just don't listen, is your problem," Violet said, in that maddening tone she sometimes took. "And now I'm telling you to listen to me again: you have nothing to feel guilty about, Aster. The laws of this land are *evil*. The welcome houses, the raveners, the Reckoning—evil. But your fighting against all that isn't. It's self-defense. Someone hits you, you have a right to hit them back."

Aster sighed again, setting her cards down. "All right, all right, I'll let it go."

"You just trust me: McClennon's going to make a deal with us before the sun sets tomorrow. I can feel it."

In the end, though, it wasn't until the very last day of the week that they received the McClennons' response.

Aster and her friends had gotten into a routine of waiting for the scout in the meeting hall every evening after supper, and with each passing day, more and more curious Scorpions and hotfoots waited with them. Aster felt the weight of their expectation like a stone on her chest, growing heavier every time the scout greeted them with an apologetic shake of his head as he handed her another evening edition without an official response. By the last day, the pressure was so immense that she could scarcely breathe. The meeting hall was filled with raucous, excited chatter, but it felt so distant Aster might as well have been underwater. What would she say to these people if McClennon hadn't given them a response by this deadline? Or if, the dead forbid, his response was *no*? What the hell was their next move supposed to be? How could she possibly—

"Here he comes," Clementine said excitedly, grabbing Aster's arm. The doors to the main hall swung open, and everyone turned as one to stare at the triumphant figure in the doorway.

"Front page!" the scout cried breathlessly. "Jerrod McClennon's response. It's right here."

"Well don't keep us waiting, you fool! What did he say?" Sam demanded.

"I didn't read it yet. I wanted to let you all be the first." The scout ran towards them, avoiding the eager hands that grabbed for the rolled-up newspaper in his grip. By now the noise in the room was deafening, and for the first time that day, Aster allowed herself to hope, the excitement sweeping up through her stomach and pulling a smile to her face. It was with a shaking hand that she grabbed the newspaper from the messenger.

"Go on, read it out loud!" someone demanded.

"Yes, let's hear it!"

"We all have a right to know!"

"Only if you all shut up first!" Sam ordered, holding his hands up for quiet, and within moments the roar fell to a murmur. Aster nodded at him in thanks, that loose smile still hanging uncertainly on her face, and took a moment to meet the eyes of the rest of her friends, too. Not just the Good Luck Girls.

Sam and Eli, Cutter and Zee, Derrick . . . everyone had risked their lives to bring them to this moment. All of them looked back at Aster with excitement and encouragement. Feeling steadied, she unfolded the newspaper and considered the bold, black headline, reading the words aloud for all to hear.

TO THE GOOD PEOPLE OF ARKETTA:

AS A BUSINESS MAN, AS A FAMILY MAN, AND AS A REPRESENTATIVE OF THE ARKETTAN STATE AND A CANDIDATE FOR ITS GOVERNANCY, I, JERROD MCCLENNON, DECLARE THAT MY ANSWER TO THE DEMANDS OF THESE "RECKONERS" IS NO.

Aster swallowed, cold dread sinking into her stomach at the words, but forced herself to continue in a strong, clear voice.

OURS IS A NATION OF MEN BORN OF STEEL AND STONE. NOT KINGS, NOT EMPERORS, BUT COMMON MEN WHO BUILT ARKETTA FROM THE GROUND UP THROUGH THEIR HONEST WORK ALONE.

BUT THE DUSTBLOODS KNOW NOTHING OF HONEST WORK. IT IS IN THEIR VERY NATURE TO LIE, TO STEAL, TO KILL FOR THEIR FORTUNE. THEY MUST BE KEPT IN LINE BY A FIRM HAND, AND WHEN MET INSTEAD WITH A SOFT HEART, THEY WILL NOT HESITATE TO STOP IT WITH A BLADE OR BULLET.

AND SO IT SHOULD COME AS NO SURPRISE THAT A NUMBER OF THEM HAVE RISEN UP AGAINST US NOW: THEY HAVE BEEN IN A STATE OF UNREST FOR MONTHS, REBELLING AGAINST THE REDEMPTION OFFERED BY THEIR WORK, AND RATHER THAN MEET THIS CHALLENGE WITH THE BRUTALITY THEY UNDERSTAND, WE HAVE SHOWN THEM A TOLERANCE THEY DO NOT DESERVE.

SO, NO, I WILL NOT BOW TO THE WILL OF COWARDS WHO WOULD USE VIOLENCE AND TERROR TO CONTROL US. I WILL NOT SHUT DOWN OUR FAMILY'S WELCOME HOUSES, WHICH KEEP THE DUSTBLOOD POPULATION UNDER CONTROL AND PROVIDE THEIR WOMEN WITH NECESSARY WORK.

I WILL NOT PAY THESE WOMEN, WHO ALREADY ENJOY MORE WEALTH AND COMFORT THAN MANY HARDWORKING FAIRBLOOD FAMILIES.

AND I WILL NOT FORGIVE THESE WOMEN THEIR DEBTS TO SOCIETY, AS THEY MUST EARN THEIR FREEDOM JUST AS THE REST OF US HAVE.

THESE RECKONERS THREATEN MY NEPHEW'S LIFE, BUT IT IS FOR LOVE OF HIM THAT I DO THIS: HE WILL NOT BE FREE—NONE OF US WILL EVER BE FREE—UNTIL THE DUSTBLOOD THREAT IS DEALT WITH.

THE LANDMASTERS' GUILD IS UNITED

IN THIS. AND SINCE THE RECKONERS
HAVE FOCUSED THEIR ATTENTION ON
OUR WELCOME HOUSES, OUR RESPONSE
TO THEM IS THIS: THE PROPOSED LAW
LOWERING THE AGE OF SUNDOWN GIRLS
TO THIRTEEN IN NORTHROCK WILL NOW BE
TAKEN NATIONWIDE. FURTHERMORE, EVERY
DUSTBLOOD FAMILY WILL NOW BE REQUIRED
TO SEND THEIR FIRSTBORN DAUGHTER
TO A WELCOME HOUSE. NEVER HAS THE
STRUCTURE AND CONTROL THESE SPACES
PROVIDE, OR OUR COMBINED EFFORTS TO
PROTECT THEM, BEEN MORE NECESSARY.

AND AS FOR THE RECKONERS THEMSELVES:
DO NOT WORRY, FELLOW CITIZENS. WE WILL
FIND THEM, WE WILL CAPTURE THEM, AND WE
WILL SEE THEM EXECUTED. FOR WE ARE MEN
BORN OF STONE AND STEEL—AND WE DO NOT
YIELD.

SIGNED,
THE LANDMASTERS' GUILD COUNCIL:
JERROD MCCLENNON
DENNIS BOYLE
LEONARD SULLIVAN
SYLAS CAIN
ANTHONY HARKER
COLIN HARKER

CHAPTER NINETEEN

Aster knew she needed to remain strong for the others, but in those wretched moments after she finished reading McClennon's response, it was all she could do to keep the tears from falling from her eyes.

Clementine did cry, curling into Zee's arms and stifling her sobs in his neck. Mallow's jaw was tight with fury, Tansy's face pale with shock. Raven swore, a dark expression descending over her eyes as she turned away from them all, Sam reaching for her shoulder to comfort her. And Derrick and Eli both turned to Aster, desperate and helpless, like lost children. Violet reached for her, Aster's name forming on her lips, but Aster could not bring herself to face any of them. She threw the newspaper down and ran from the meeting hall, closing herself in her cabin and crumpling onto the bed.

How could he . . .

Aster could scarcely control her growing anger at McClennon's words. His hypocrisy. *He* was the coward who had built his fortune off of blood and deceit. *He* was the animal who used violence and fear to control others. *They* had just been trying to stop him.

And now, as a reward for their efforts, he was going to pass a law that—

Aster coughed around a sob. She had felt this before, this pure, white hatred that would drive her to madness if she let it. She had always been careful, for her own sake, not to give in to it. She knew such uncontrolled anger would only make it that much harder to focus on the work that needed to be done.

But how the hell was anyone supposed to remain calm in the face of something like this?

Clementine entered the cabin then, with Zee and his little sister Emily behind her. Aster wiped away her tears, struggling to mask her emotions before the others could see her.

"Dawn, please—you don't have to pretend for me. By the Veil, I'm so sorry," Clementine cried, hurrying to Aster's side and wrapping her in a hug. Her own face was still wet with streaks of tears. "I don't understand how this happened. I really thought he was going to back down."

"He was never going to back down," Aster muttered darkly. "I was a fool to think he would."

"You weren't a fool, Aster. You had hope. Can't any of us get anything done without hope," Zee said, helping Emily into her bunk.

"Why is she crying?" Emily asked, worry crinkling a line between her brows.

"She just got some sad news, is all," Zee explained gently.

Emily's expression smoothed with understanding. "Like when you told me about Papa."

"Yes."

Aster felt her anger melt into a sorrow so cold and heavy it almost made her sick. What kind of world were they leaving for Emily? For all the little girls who would now grow up in a country where every family had to sacrifice a daughter to the welcome houses, and every welcome house started sundown work at thirteen?

All Aster had wanted to do was help them, and instead she had made things worse than she ever could have imagined.

No, she thought desperately.

I do not accept this.

Aster swallowed, holding Clementine tighter as she forced herself to find her resolve. They could not give up now. They could not let this stand. McClennon had escalated this conflict beyond all recognition—they would simply have to do the same.

If he wanted to blame and punish the entire dustblood population, then it was the entire dustblood population he would have to answer to. They outnumbered him, and he knew it. Why else would he be so desperate to destroy them?

Aster pulled away from Clementine, standing, pacing the room as her plan gathered speed. "We need to call on our allies," she said quietly.

Zee looked up from tucking in his sister. "Which allies?" he asked.

"All of them."

The next day Aster gathered her friends in the meeting hall, steeled by cold calm. She sat at the head of the table, reading their faces as best she could. It didn't seem as if any of them had slept any better than she had last night, but neither did they look defeated, not yet. They were too angry for that.

Good.

Violet sat at Aster's right hand, Derrick just beyond her. He leaned across her to whisper to Aster as the others took their seats.

"Aster, I've been up all night with this. I don't even know where to begin. I'm so sorry—"

Aster met his eyes and shook her head once. She knew he meant well, but if she acknowledged him, then she would only feel the need to soothe his guilt, and she did not have the time or energy for that. Jerrod McClennon was more evil than even she had thought, and that wasn't Derrick's fault, but still . . . even just seeing the resemblance in his face was difficult today.

Sam sat at Aster's left side, with Eli next to him. The glare Eli shot across the table at Derrick could have cut steel, but Derrick seemed too wretched to notice.

"So, what now, boss?" Raven asked Aster with a heavy sigh once everyone had settled in. "Do we strike back? Or do we retreat?"

"We strike back, obviously," Eli said, leaning forward. He looked to his brother for support. "It's bad enough they kidnapped our ancestors and dragged them over to these cursed mountains. Now they want to kidnap a bunch of little girls, too? No."

Aster scowled. The welcome house system had *always* been a form of kidnapping, as far as she was concerned. It didn't matter that the families were paid, or that they'd been given a "choice"—girls were still taken away, locked up, and never seen again. The problem was not that a just thing had been made unjust, the problem was that the unjust thing was now going to affect everyone else.

"I wouldn't be too hasty," Derrick cautioned. "Something

has to be done, of course, but maybe we ought to consider our strategy."

"*Our?*" Eli scoffed. "What have you done, exactly, besides sit on your ass and eat up all our food?"

Derrick flushed but ignored him. "I'm only saying—our actions so far have led the landmasters to this. We have to assume if we *keep* on this course, they'll come back with something even worse. I'm not sure we're equipped to deal with it."

"Just say 'I told you so' and get it out of your system," Mallow said acidly.

"That's not what I mean—"

"No, what you mean is that you don't want us messing with your dear old uncle or his friends," Eli muttered under his breath.

Derrick reddened even more. "You don't get to question my loyalty, Elijah. I have funded this entire operation. I've told you when and where to be. I've—"

"This bastard sounds like every ripping landmaster I've ever heard. Thinks now that he's paid for us he gets to order us around—"

"It's not like that! You think it doesn't upset me, hearing that my uncle has done this thing? I want more than *any* of you to see him stopped. All of them—"

"I sincerely doubt that—" Clementine broke in.

"*Enough,*" Aster said. Her head was pounding, and her heart was sick. "We can't fight among ourselves." That was what *they* wanted, that was how they maintained their control. "Eli, Derrick, you're both right. We can't back down, not after this. It's a ripping declaration of war. But we're also not ready to take on the whole Landmasters' Guild . . . they've come together for this. We have to do the same. We have to get help."

"Who else is there, though, Aster?" Violet asked gently.

Aster swallowed. "Well, there are the Lady Ghosts, for one, and the rest of the Scorpions. And there are other dustbloods outside the Scab, working against the landmasters' expansion in the north. And then there's the Nine, who have been fighting longer than any of us. This affects all of them. We need to bring them together."

"They're scattered all over the country, though," Sam said. "*How* would we bring them together, exactly?"

Aster was ready for this. "Raven and I can deal with the Lady Ghosts, and I have a contact in Northrock who's organized some of the dustbloods there—Cora, the girl who sheltered me after we burned down the welcome house. I've also talked to Sid back at Camp Deathstalker, and he might be able to get in touch with some of the old rebels of the Nine."

"All right, but you've met Sid," Cutter broke in. "What makes you think he'll go along with this? Him, or any of these people?"

Aster hesitated. It had taken endless bargaining just to get this one camp of Scorpions to help her with the gambling hall; she had no doubt that getting a larger group of people to agree to further retaliation would take nothing short of a miracle. The Lady Ghosts had not even approved of the rescue mission in Northrock. What she had in mind now went against everything Priscilla believed in.

But Aster had no choice but to try.

"It's like I said—these new laws affect everyone," Aster began. "They'll be angry, desperate, looking for ways to fight back. We just need to give them the means to do so. Which we can do, because now we have the one advantage no one else has: an inside man." She looked at Derrick. "Derrick, I can see you're afraid that no one listens to you, no one takes you seriously. But I'm here to tell you that I do. So tell me, then—what, exactly, are we up against?"

There was a red spot on his temple from where he had rested his head in his hand in his exhaustion. He sat up straighter, looking self-consciously up and down the table.

"Well," he said, "I only know what I was told before I was 'kidnapped.' There's every reason to think my uncle's plans have evolved since then . . ."

Sam cut him off with an impatient wave of his hand. "Yes, of course, just tell us what you can, Red."

". . . *But*, I think it's safe to assume that he at least intends to make good on his public threat to track you down and capture you as soon as possible," Derrick went on. "After everything that happened last year, he doubled down on his efforts to hire a new head ravener to lead his bounty hunters in future pursuits. And after the Northrock job, that search became a top priority. He found his bloodhound shortly before I left for Rattlebank: a woman who is a particularly powerful ravener and highly motivated to track you all down. How she even knew you were still alive, when it's such a closely kept secret, I don't know—let alone why she so dearly wants you dead. But I promise you that's who's searching for us, even now, as we speak." He had gone twitchy at the thought.

Aster stiffened, glancing over at Zee, who had tensed and reached for Clementine's hand.

"Did you say a . . . a lady ravener?" Zee asked levelly.

"Yes, it was unusual, to say the least—"

"What did she look like?" Aster interrupted.

Derrick looked between them. "Brown-skinned, average build, with her hair pulled back in a low knot and these upsettingly filed nails . . ."

"Lizzy," Zee concluded. Aster could see the anguish threatening to tear him apart.

"No, it's not possible," Clementine murmured. "You said she wasn't completely gone. Why would she—how could she—"

"She blames me for what happened, remember," Zee said, swallowing. "Whatever feelings she has left for me . . . they aren't good ones."

"Ripping hell, Zee," Sam murmured.

"Zee, I'm—I'm so sorry," Tansy said haltingly.

"Wait, what have I missed here?" Derrick asked, bewildered.

"That ravener is Zee's sister," Violet explained. "They've been in contact—that's how she knows about us. But Derrick, how does *McClennon* know about *her*?"

Derrick looked horrified. "I—I have no idea. My uncle never even learned your name, Zee. He certainly didn't know you had a ravener sister."

"Maybe *she* went to *him*," Raven said darkly. "After Zee showed up on her doorstep and told her all about his adventures, she probably saw an opportunity to take that information to the McClennons. Raveners are coldly calculating like that."

They all fell silent at the thought. Aster felt instinctively that it was true, and it filled her with despair.

"We can deal with Elizabeth when the time comes," she said

with forced calm, for the sake of the others. "We faced down a dozen raveners in Rattlebank. What's one more? Derrick . . . please . . . is there anything else you can tell us? Anything at all?"

Derrick was still silent, looking down at his hands, a dark scowl drawn onto the pale canvas of his face. His brows furrowed further as he seemed to come to a decision. Aster watched it flicker across the blue of his eyes, like light on water.

"You haven't said yet what your plan is, but I can imagine well enough: you and your friends are going to want to take another prisoner or two. Real ones, this time. Landmasters with considerable power. Men these laws can't be passed without. Losses devastating enough to convince Authoritant Lockley to listen to you, and not the Guild."

Aster opened her mouth—not to deny it, because it was true, but to reason with Derrick before he inevitably tried to talk her out of it. They had to take this all the way to the top of the government—nothing less would do now.

"Derrick—" she began.

He looked up at Aster and held her gaze. "I can tell you where to find them."

They spent the next day writing the messages to their allies, to be carried through the Scorpions' tunnels. Now that they had a fresh supply of theomite, the runners could deliver the messages and escort everyone back with considerably less danger . . . assuming, of course, that there would be anyone to escort back. But Aster had to hope that what she'd told her friends was true—that people would be too desperate and too angry to ignore her call to action.

The other Scorpion captains were the first to arrive.

There were some two dozen all told, their closest neighbors arriving within two days' time, the others straggling in throughout the week. Not every camp had answered Aster's call, but Sam seemed impressed by the turnout, greeting many of his fellow captains as old friends. As desperate as their situation was, Aster could tell he was still excited to host what was going to be, in his own words, a giant party. And so she left the planning of it to him, letting him find rooms for everyone to sleep in in the already-crowded camp and confine Eli to the kitchen to prepare feasts every night.

The Northrock dustbloods were the next to arrive—Cora and a handful of her crew. Aster greeted her with an arm clasp that turned into an embrace, eager to introduce her at last to her friends. It filled Aster with some much-needed confidence to see Cora's excitement and enthusiasm, and she felt sure that, whatever else happened, she'd have at least one faction's support.

Then, coming all the way from the Graveyard: the Lady Ghosts. Priscilla herself had not made the grueling trip through the tunnels, having sent Aggie in her stead, along with a few of the younger Ladies. Aster's chest tightened with a mix of emotions as she welcomed them—joy to see her sisters again, and regret for the way she'd left things. She knew Priscilla would not approve of any violence or law-breaking. What if these Ladies had only been sent to stop her?

And then, at last, trickling in from every corner of Arketta, came the rebels of the Nine Nations. Aster was most anxious about these allies, since they were the ones she had the least history with. And so, before it came time for the big meeting with everyone, Aster held a smaller welcoming party just for them. There were men and women of every age and from every nation. They all sat together in the meeting hall, passing around the platter of pork chops that Eli had made special.

"This is a clever thing you Scorpions have done, using the old mines for a hideout," an older woman was saying to Aster. She had introduced herself as one of the leaders of the southeastern tribe, her dress adorned with beadwork. "Our rebel camps are aboveground, so we have to constantly be on the move. But our ancestors were nomads anyway—we were ready for this."

Mallow was practically humming beside them. She was not usually one for shyness, but she had been uncharacteristically quiet throughout the meal, as if afraid to say the wrong thing. Finally, though, she couldn't seem to hold in her excitement.

"Our nations were neighbors, right?" she asked the older woman. "I'm southern tribe."

The older woman smiled with her eyes. "Yes, I can see that. You made your headband yourself?"

"Well . . . I had help . . ." Mallow admitted.

"Still counts!" Tansy reminded her.

"I'm from the northern tribe," a young man said. "So this is probably the first time in a generation your people and mine have been under the same roof. That's something to celebrate, no matter what comes of this larger meeting."

"About that—" Aster jumped in, hoping to settle into her pitch.

"Wait a minute," Derrick said, interrupting her. He had that gleam in his eyes he got whenever he sensed an opportunity for learning. "You mean you aren't all working together, all the time? The way my uncle described it—"

"Please, Derrick, don't ruin my appetite by mentioning that man," Cutter interjected.

"We're the *Nine*, not the One, McClennon," Sid added with a dry laugh—he seemed to have softened up at the sight of so much family. "We may work together, but we're all still separate, sovereign nations."

"So . . . we have to convince *all* of you?" Derrick asked slowly.

This was met with more laughter, though, privately, Aster was thinking the same thing. Her stomach churned with anxiety despite the sweet aroma of seasoning filling the air. She felt wildly out of her depth. The more time she spent with the Nine, the clearer it became that she had entered in the middle of a story, one that had begun long before she had been born and would continue long after the last landmaster had died. Who was she to tell anyone here how to write the next chapter? Most of the Nine were dustbloods, yes, but unlike the rest of them, they had a history here.

Aster's anxiety only deepened as the night drew to a close, and by the next morning, it had settled in her chest like an illness. It had been an agony, waiting to see which allies would arrive, but now that it was time for Aster to address them, it suddenly felt as if everything was moving too quickly. Convincing everyone to come and hear her out had only been half the battle—now she had to convince them to stay and fight. She doubled back over every detail as she readied herself in her cabin, stalling for more time. She had asked Violet to help her make herself presentable—partially because Violet was the best at these things, but mostly because Aster just wanted the reassuring comfort of her presence.

". . . and not that Raven ever tells anybody anything about anything, but, being the gentle soul I am, I finally got her to admit she had a drink with Sam the other night . . . Aster . . . Aster! Are you even listening?"

Aster looked up sharply from her mirror, to where Violet was watching her from her bunk, already—effortlessly—glamoured up in the evening dress she'd been wearing the night they'd kidnapped her.

"Sorry, I—I—" Aster stammered.

Violet stood and glided up behind her, close enough that Aster could feel the heat of her breath on her neck, her knowing smile fading as she met Aster's eye in the mirror. Aster's cheeks grew warm, and she quickly looked back at her own reflection, eyes drifting over the favor on her neck and the scar on her cheek and the line between her eyebrows that had settled there after years of wearing this exact scowl. She'd spent longer at the mirror this morning than she ever had at the welcome house, when it was actually expected of her. Combing through her growing hair, smoothing every wrinkle on her dress shirt, rubbing grease over her face until it gleamed. She needed to look like a leader today.

If only she actually felt like one.

"You know, if you're not careful about that grimace, your face is going to get stuck like that," Violet said lightly.

"Vi, this is serious," Aster muttered, turning away from the mirror.

"I know it is. But you always look good, Aster. Where's all this sudden self-doubt coming from?"

Aster refused to meet her gaze. "I just . . . how the hell am I supposed to convince them, Violet? Every time I've tried to fix this mess, I've only made it worse. It's like I said before. They shouldn't be following me. But now, if I do nothing—" Her voice cracked, and she shut her mouth, swallowing painfully.

"Hey, hey," Violet said softly, taking Aster's face in her hands. Aster's breath hitched at the sudden contact, but something stilled her normal instinct to flinch away, Violet's cool touch soothing her. She leaned into it, pressing their foreheads together. "Everyone here believes in you, Dawn. They wouldn't have come all this way if they didn't. You're the leader of the Green Creek girls. You're the martyr McClennon never meant to make. Hell, half these people still believed you *dead*, only to hear from you, personally, that you're still alive and fighting and that you want their help. They'll listen to whatever you have to say. So just be honest with them, hear? It's okay to let them see that you're angry and scared and confused. We're all angry and scared and confused. But by bringing everyone together, you're giving us a chance to do something about it. You're reminding us we're not powerless. And there's nothing more important than that right now."

Aster exhaled, reaching up for Violet's hands and pulling them down gently, their fingers intertwined. "You think so?"

"I *know* so. Have a little faith in yourself. Have a little faith in the rest of us. It worked out for me, yeah?"

Aster snorted a little and pushed Violet away. She felt lighter now, but stronger, too. Herself again.

"I guess," she admitted.

CHAPTER TWENTY

Aster had never seen the meeting hall so full.

For every familiar face there were a dozen Aster didn't recognize. The hall echoed with the sound of conversation and arguments and laughter. Rigid Northrock accents clashed with the lazy drawls of the Scab. The clink of cutlery scattered throughout the background like rain. Music floated above the cacophony, a frenzied jig played on banjo, harmonica, and drums. Eli stood behind the serving table, elbows deep in a pot of chili. The serving line snaked out the door. Sam breezed from table to table with easy confidence, introducing himself and welcoming the guests, flashing his charming smile at friends and strangers alike. The rest of Aster's friends sat at the head table. Zee tried to coax his little sister to eat her vegetables. Tansy and Mallow were playing a card game with Clementine and Raven. And Violet sat somewhat protectively beside Derrick, who looked so nervous that he might vomit.

Sam was right, Aster thought from the corner where she watched it all. This was a party. Not because they had anything to celebrate—no, quite the opposite—but because this was probably the first time in Arketta's history that so many dustbloods from so many different backgrounds had been able to gather out from under the eye of the landmasters. They could be themselves here, they were *safe*. There were more of them here than most of them had probably seen in their lives. And so there was a thrilling energy to every interaction, and even Aster, in all her trepidation, couldn't help being buoyed by it.

Sam sidled up to her, his face gleaming with sweat from all the running around he'd been doing. "There have to be over three hundred people here, Aster," he said with breathless excitement. "I've never seen anything like this. No matter what comes of today, you've done something great here."

Aster looked up at him. "You sure you don't want to be the one to take the reins, Sam? This is your home. None of us could be here if it weren't for you."

Sam sucked his teeth. "Not in a thousand years. I can wrangle a bunch of runaway miners into something halfway resembling a respectable community, but I never would have had the vision for something like *this*. You dared to imagine what the rest of us accepted as impossible. I'm just honored to bear witness."

Aster's cheeks warmed. Usually she rolled her eyes at Sam's ridiculous showmanship, but it was exactly what she needed to hear right now.

"The food line is almost finished," Sam said. "They'll be ready to hear you speak soon."

Aster clenched and unclenched her fists, trying to let out some of the tension that had built up inside her.

"All right, thanks, Sam," she said, exhaling. She made her way to the podium, looking out over the crowd. The last few people were taking their plates back to their tables, and Eli himself was returning to sit with the rest of her friends. Aster swallowed, ringing the bell to bring the room to attention. The babble slowly quieted as everyone turned their faces towards her.

This is it, she thought, and offered up a rare prayer to the dead.

"Evening, friends, and thank you all for being here," she began. "I wish we were gathering under better circumstances. But now that we're all here, I can't help noticing what a fine thing it is to see so many of us like this—talking freely, eating well, and ready to fight for our future."

There were murmurs of agreement and a few scattered cheers. Aster gripped the edges of the podium to steady herself and continued.

"At the start of all this, all I wanted was to see an end to McClennon's empire. There's no such thing as a 'good' landmaster, but the McClennons have always been the worst of them, and as far as I was concerned, that new welcome house proved it. My friends and I were willing to do anything to bring Jerrod down."

"You sold out!" someone shouted then. One of the Northrock dustbloods. "You claimed you kidnapped his nephew, but you're actually working with him! And now you expect us to as well?"

Aster set her jaw. She wasn't doing this again. "Derrick McClennon can no longer be called a landmaster. He gave up his position to be with us and has been using his wealth and knowledge to help us. This meeting never could have happened without him."

"This meeting wouldn't have even been *necessary* if you hadn't kidnapped him!" shouted someone from the Nine's table. "Now the landmasters are all riled up and coming to take our daughters. You should've left well enough alone. Things are worse than ever."

Aster flushed, guilt stabbing her. But then Sam stood to defend her.

"You speak as if things were somehow acceptable before," he said, "but they weren't. You know that—all of us know that. All of us were working, in our own way, to change that. And *any* significant change *any* one of us would have made would have resulted in a backlash like this—remember how the War of the Nations led to the recruitment of dustbloods into the military? The landmasters' response is just proof that these women have managed to do some real damage."

Aster nodded at him gratefully. "And I won't deny that I've made mistakes. I've hurt people I love, disappointed people I admire . . . but that's why I've brought you all here. I want to make it right. The decisions my friends and I have been making affect all of you—and so all of you should have a say in what, if anything, we do next."

"Well, obviously we have to do *something*," Aggie shouted out from the Lady Ghosts' table. "We can't let this new policy go unanswered."

"I agree," Cora said. "The landmasters have to know they can't get away with this. What do you need from us, Aster?"

Aster felt a warm rush of gratitude. Maybe this would be all right after all. She wet her lips, excitedly beginning to lay out her plans.

"Well, Derrick was a relatively small target—he's important to powerful people, but he's not that powerful himself." She glanced at Derrick. "No offense, McClennon."

"None taken," he chirped.

"So, I think it's time to start going after some bigger fish," Aster continued. "These landmasters—both the ones in government and the ones in industry—they're *criminals*. The wealth they've stolen from us, the violence they use to keep us in line . . . So it's time we treat them like the criminals they are. Let's take *them* prisoner."

There was scattered applause, but also murmurs of doubt.

"Who?" someone called out.

And then, from further back: "*How?*"

Aster had been ready for this, though. "Derrick will provide us the 'who.' He knows the names of the most powerful men in the Landmasters' Guild. Take out half a dozen of the right people, and we could bring the whole government to its knees in a matter of weeks." She looked around. "The 'how' is more of a challenge, though. These men are scattered all over the Scab, and after the stunt we pulled with Derrick, they're on higher alert than ever. No one's going to be out in the open unless they have to be, and when they are, they're all going to have extra security on them." She thought of McClennon hiring Zee's sister and swallowed back her regret. "It's the riskiest part of this plan, which is why my friends and I will be handling it ourselves. We have some experience in hunting down rich men. But we'll also need your help to make sure the remaining members of government feel the pressure to give in to our demands. We *have* to make it impossible for the landmasters to keep running their businesses until they make changes to the way things are done. I heard word of some dustbloods burning a Sweet Thistle field a couple weeks back—that's exactly the kind of action we need. Imagine something like that on a grand scale. With their leaders taken prisoner and their businesses in shambles, they'll have no choice but to listen to us."

Excitement rippled through the room—but uncertainty, too, Aster could tell. And not just from the Lady Ghosts, whose uneasy looks Aster had expected. One of the Scorpion captains crossed his meaty arms in defiance. The Northrock dustblood who had accused her of being a sellout still looked unconvinced.

Sam spoke up over the rising noise. "Listen, we all know that if we're going to do this, we have to be ready for the backlash. They're going to send out raveners to keep the peace, and those raveners won't bother making a distinction between the people in this room and the people we're trying to protect," Sam said. "So I think our first order of business *has* to be arming those people so they can defend themselves. The dustblood families who work the fields we burn are going to be extremely vulnerable. The Scorpions can assist with this—we have a connection to a Ferronite smuggler, and he can get advanced voltric weapons to us here in the Scab." He glanced at Derrick. "Now that we finally have the shine for it."

"We'll want to provide them food and clothing, too," Eli said, his soft voice still carrying clearly. "A landmaster provides folks with everything they need—we have to expect they aren't going to want to do it anymore. They'll try to starve out the common folks. We can't let them."

Sam nodded. "I'll hold a separate meeting with the other Scorpion captains to see what assistance, if any, their camps can provide. These have been thin times, for all of us, but as I said, we have McClennon's shine now. If we all combine our efforts, we can drive the raveners from the farms and mines, destroy the fields and tunnels, and prepare dustblood families to survive the days ahead."

There were shouts of agreement and scattered cheers. The apprehension in the room seemed to be easing.

Cora stood next. "It's a different game up north," she said. "We work in factories, not fields. But my crew and I have been talking about organizing strikes for some time now, and it sounds like there's no better time for it. We can look into tearing up a railway or two, as well. If the trains aren't running, it'll be that much harder for the landmasters to flee the Scab—or to call in reinforcements."

"That's good thinking," Aster said, embarrassed that she hadn't thought of it herself. But then, that had been the whole reason for bringing everyone together. "The landmasters won't be expecting any resistance outside of the Scab, either. They'll be overwhelmed. Anything you need, Cora—we'll make sure you have it."

The crowd cheered again. They were with her now, and Aster's spirits soared at the sound of them.

But then, from the Lady Ghosts' table, Aggie spoke up: "This is all well and good, Aster," she said, "but Priscilla'll still have questions for us—not the least of which is how the hell we're going to coordinate all this. An operation this big, all these people all over the country . . . we're going to have to be in constant communication. It's only a matter of time before that communication gets intercepted. How are we supposed to avoid our plans falling into the wrong hands?"

"The tunnels—" Sam began.

"Aren't going to be fast enough, not for this," Aggie interrupted, fixing him with a stare. "It takes your runners a couple days just to reach the nearest Scorpion camp underground, and we're way the hell up by the border of Ferron. That's going to take time we won't have."

"I may have a solution for that," Sid rumbled, standing and looking back at the allies he'd summoned. "When the old Empire invaded Arketta, they made it illegal to speak any of the languages of the Nine Nations, but we have kept them alive in secret—if we can provide ciphers to translate them for you all, you can use those languages to communicate. Send your messages aboveground, and even if the law intercepts one, they'll never know what we're saying. We can help keep everyone fed, as well. We all have family in agriculture—the fairbloods depend on us for that, still, all these centuries later. We control who eats, and what."

Aster looked at Sid in surprise. She had not been sure of the Nine's support at all, especially after the doubt that had seized her last night. They must have discussed amongst themselves long after she retired for the night.

"I'm just the go-between—I can't speak for all the Nine Nations, or even for my own," Sid went on, addressing the whole room now, "but I can say this show of strength and solidarity is greater than any I could've expected. I never thought I'd find myself joining another fight, but for the sake of our sisters, our daughters . . . for everyone who's about to be affected by this new law . . . I can promise you all you'll have my help. And when—not if, Aster, but when—Arketta sends its armymen to stop us, there are more than a few of us here who might be able to tell you what to expect from them."

"Thank you, Sidney," Aster said with an exhale, hoping he felt her gratitude from across the room. She looked over to the Lady Ghosts' table, where Aggie seemed to be holding conference with the other Ladies. They were the only ones who had not yet committed.

Aggie turned to Aster a moment later and nodded. "You've persuaded me, Aster, but Priscilla will never agree to something like this—you know that. But I promise to take this back to her and argue on your behalf. She knows we need to take action against McClennon, and if nothing else, we will do what we have always done: write to our sympathizers in the government, raise money to help our women, and borderjump who we can out of Arketta entirely."

"And that is necessary work, work that has saved countless lives, including my own," Aster acknowledged, relieved they were not going to argue against her. "There is more than one way to fight the landmasters . . . but in order for this all to work, we have to at least be agreed on what it is we're fighting for. When my friends and I began this thing, it was just to help other Good Luck Girls—but that's not enough. I know that now. The welcome houses are a symptom. The Reckoning is the disease. They labeled our ancestors criminals, but what was their crime? To be too poor to pay the Empire's taxes. To fight back against its invading armies. To live outside its rigid ideals. And when the Empire fell, the landmasters took its place. Our suffering became their currency. They grew rich off it. And they say it's all justified because we're criminals." Aster swallowed. "Are there dustbloods out there who deserve that distinction? Are there murderers and rapists, people who hurt children, people who are needlessly cruel and take advantage of the weak? Of course there are. But no more than there are among the fairbloods— and among the fairbloods, *those* people are called landmasters, and they are considered great. So it is time for a new Reckoning. These criminals must be brought to justice. They can't give back the lives they've taken, the years they've stolen, or the damage they've done. But they can give back the land. They can give back their wealth. Either they pay with their pockets, or they pay with their lives. The time for bargaining is over. So I ask you all now, and don't hold back—what are your demands?"

There were raucous cheers, and people began to shout out. Derrick, taking notes, hurried to write down every suggestion. Soon they had a complete list, ready to be sent to all the major papers:

TO JERROD MCCLENNON AND THE
LANDMASTERS' GUILD:
  YOU ARE NOT MEN OF STONE AND STEEL,
BUT MEN OF FINE SILK AND STAINED GLASS.
YOUR STRENGTH COMES FROM US, AND YOU
KNOW IT. THESE ARE OUR NEW DEMANDS:
1. YOU WILL CEASE BUSINESS AT ALL WELCOME
HOUSES IMMEDIATELY

*2. YOU WILL FORGIVE ALL OUTSTANDING
DUSTBLOOD DEBTS AND PAY FOR OUR STOLEN
LABOR
3. YOU WILL PROVIDE DUSTBLOODS FULL
CITIZENSHIP AND EQUAL RIGHTS
4. YOU WILL RETURN THE LAND TO THE PEOPLE
5. YOU WILL OUTLAW THE HIRING OF
RAVENERS*

*YOU CALL US LIARS, BUT YOU ARE NOT AS
TRUSTWORTHY AS YOU WOULD HAVE THE
PEOPLE BELIEVE. YOU TOLD THE PUBLIC WE
WERE CAPTURED AND KILLED BY YOUR MEN,
BUT WE ARE STILL HERE, AND WE WILL NOT
GIVE UP SO EASILY. ATONE FOR YOUR CRIMES,
OR BE PUNISHED FOR THEM.*

SIGNED, THE RECKONERS
ASTER
CLEMENTINE
TANSY
MALLOW
RAVEN
VIOLET

CHAPTER TWENTY-ONE

The first landmasters on Derrick's list were Colin and Anthony Harker, twins. Anthony worked in government, while Colin ran the family's agriculture business—everything from Sweet Thistle and sugar cane to cotton and tobacco. They each had several children of their own, Derrick explained, but unlike Derrick himself, they weren't yet old enough to hold any power. They were not Aster's concern.

"You sure we shouldn't round up them kids while we're at it, though?" Mallow asked in a half-hushed tone as they leaned over Derrick's journal. "I mean, we wouldn't actually *do* anything to them, of course, but . . . if we're really trying light a fire under their parents' asses . . ."

"No," Aster said firmly. "Using children is what the landmasters do. We have to show the people that we want a different world. If those children grow up to commit the same crimes, then we'll deal with them then. But not before."

Derrick looked relieved, though he said nothing. "Well, Colin Harker is here in the Scab, in an estate outside Pinecrest. We can go after him anytime. Anthony Harker lives in the capital, but he comes back at the end of every month to meet with his brother."

Tansy was doing the math in her head. "So you're saying if we want to get them both, we'll have to wait . . ."

"Two more weeks," Derrick said.

Aster let out a huff of frustration. They couldn't make a public demand for immediate action and then do nothing for two weeks.

"Isn't there anyone else we can go after in the meantime?" Aster asked.

"Well, the Harkers are the second most powerful landmaster family after my own," Derrick said. "It would be best to take care of them first, if you ask me. But if time is of the essence . . ." He flipped through his journal. "Leonard Sullivan's estate is the closest to our current location. Their family doesn't have much political power—Sullivan's the only son his parents had, so he doesn't have a brother in government—but they are quite wealthy."

Aster's spine stiffened at the sound of that name. *Sullivan.*

The railroad baron Lizzy worked for.

The landmaster Aster's family was indebted to.

"How do we get to him?" she said darkly.

"It'd be better if we lured him out," Derrick replied. "The Sullivan estate is built into a mountainside—it's hard going getting up there, and we'd be at a disadvantage if it came to a fight. But a big enough disaster at one of his camps will force him to come out of hiding and deal with it. We could lay a trap."

"Sam has me going undercover to some of the nearby mining camps this week anyway, to pass out weapons and supplies," Eli jumped in, catching Aster's eye. "You could come with me. We could set up the trap together."

Derrick looked annoyed that Eli had interrupted him. He huffed and pushed his hair out of his eyes. "The two of you alone are hardly going to be enough to take on Leonard Sullivan and his raveners," he said pointedly.

"You think we need you?" Eli asked, flicking his gaze to over to Derrick.

"Leaving aside the fact that, yes, it would seem you *do* need my help even to plan all this, I'll remind you that I studied hand-and-foot combat for six years, so I'm not as useless in the field as you seem to think—"

"Oh, is that so? Did they teach you the foot-in-ass maneuver? Because if not, I'd be glad to demonstrate—"

Their bickering grew unintelligible. Raven rolled her eyes. Tansy hid a snicker. Zee just looked bewildered. Aster and Violet turned to each other, a wordless conversation passing between them. Aster knew this pointless posturing was for her own sake, but she had no time for it anymore.

"Enough!" she barked, and they both fell silent. "Derrick, just . . . tell us which camps we can target."

Derrick sighed and rolled out the map. "So, Sullivan's land includes the following tenant camps and farms—"

"Why are we even talking about this? We already know where we have to go," Eli interrupted, pointing to a mining camp a day's ride away. Shade Hollow. Aster's heart hitched in her chest. It was the camp where she'd grown up.

"Aster," Eli said. "Let's go see your family."

Aster and Clementine rode together, hidden in the back of the wagon full of supplies bound for the tenant mining camp while

Eli drove them down the Bone Road. The rest of their group were camping deep in the woods near Shade Hollow, awaiting Aster's signal to begin the ambush. On one thing, at least, Derrick and Eli had agreed: using dynamite to cause a cave-in during the night was the simplest way to get Sullivan's attention. He would have to be on the scene before sunset the next day.

It would have been safer for Aster and Clementine to wait with the others in the woods—now that Aster had revealed their identity to the public, the whole of the Scab would be hunting for them. But it was important to Aster, getting there a day ahead of the others. It would give her and Clem time to talk to her parents.

If they were still there.

"They've probably been moved on, haven't they?" Clementine asked neutrally, as if she'd read Aster's mind. They were bent almost double underneath the burlap cover thrown over the wagon, both of them dressed in black hallowers' robes. "Mallow and Tansy both tried to write home once we got to Ferron, but the letters got sent back unopened. Their families weren't there anymore."

Aster craned her neck to look up at her sister, raising a brow. It wasn't like Clem to be a pessimist—but then, Aster supposed, maybe her sister was just guarding her heart. This wasn't like most challenges they'd faced. This was personal.

"Yeah, well, you know how it is," Aster said carefully. Her stomach churned with every bump on the road, and she swallowed to steady it. "Families get moved around all the time. Maybe Sullivan needed them at another camp. Or maybe he traded them off with some other landmaster.

Or maybe our folks got themselves into some kind of real trouble, and they were . . ." Aster trailed off.

Executed.

"Well, I very much doubt *that*," said Clementine, and despite the pit in her stomach, Aster knew she was right. Aster's parents had never been the type to step out of line. *Be better than your betters*, that was what her mother had always said. Work their land and respect their laws. If you did as you were told they would treat you more kindly.

We're like dogs to them, Aster thought bitterly. So long as they behaved, so long as they were loyal and obedient and they did the work expected of them and never showed their teeth, they'd be fed and sheltered and maybe even indulged with a patronizing kind of love. And plenty of people, including Aster's parents, had told her to be grateful for that.

But she wasn't an animal. She was a person. And it was time she demanded to be treated like one.

"Aster, you're making that face," Clementine said. "Like you want to hit someone."

"This is just my face, Clem."

"You're hoping our parents *are* there," Clementine went on shrewdly. "Not because you'll be happy to see them, but because you're spoiling for a fight. Aren't you?"

"And what if I am?" Aster asked, more defensively than she'd intended. It was sweltering here underneath the burlap cover, enough to make Aster drip with sweat, and her anger only served to make her skin burn that much hotter. "Nearly ten years since they sold us to the welcome house. You think my resentment's gone away in that time? No. It's full-grown now."

"What would you even say to them, though?"

Aster ground her jaw. Nothing she could say would change the past.

"It's not about what *I* need to say to *them*. It's what *they* need to say to *us*. We deserve an apology. Or at least—at least some acknowledgement that what they did was wrong," Aster explained.

Clementine said nothing, though Aster could read her silence well enough. Clem didn't think their parents were wrong for choosing to sell them; she thought the landmasters were wrong for forcing them into such a cruel decision. That was what they were fighting for—a future where no one would have to sell their daughters off in order for them to survive.

But just because Aster understood that well enough in her head, it didn't change the betrayal she felt in her heart. For all she'd been through, Clementine still didn't truly understand what Aster had experienced. And Aster was grateful for that, beyond words—but it was lonely, not being able to talk to her sister about this.

I wish Violet were here, Aster found herself thinking. Clementine looked up to her, and so Aster had to set a good example for her. But Violet would have understood Aster's anger, even if it wasn't entirely fair. Aster would have been able to speak honestly with her. And then, when the time actually came to face her parents, maybe Aster would be able to do so with something like a clear heart.

The wagon jolted to a stop. Eli rapped twice on backboard. "We're here, friends—habits on."

Aster and Clem glanced at each other before dutifully

donning the headwear that all hallowers wore—a black veil, symbolic of the Veil between the world of the living and the dead, that covered the face. It clung to Aster's cheeks like a cobweb. Then she threw off the burlap cover and hopped out of the back of the wagon, her spine aching as it straightened, dust kicking up at the hem of her robe as she surveyed the camp.

Aster's memories of Shade Hollow were as scarce as the patches of drygrass that dotted the cracked earth. The smell of it came to her first: the acrid scent of coal, then the taste of grit between her teeth. The cabins threatened to cave in on themselves, leaning drunkenly against one another in ramshackle rows. Crude iron wardants stood outside each one like scarecrows, a last line of defense against the dead. Among the living, women hung their laundry to dry, children ripped and roared unsupervised, and men filed in and out of the mouth of the mine up the road like ants on a hill. Yes, this was it . . . this was home. This was the dirt that she and Clementine had drawn in with blackened fingernails. That was the water pump where they had washed the honey from their hands in the summer. But "home" was smaller than Aster remembered, and filthier, too. She felt as if she had stepped into one of Raven's leadpoint drawings, soot smudged across every surface in a thin gray film, even casting a pall over the brutal, beating sunlight.

A single ravener patrolled the area, a long gun slung over his shoulder. There would be more down in the mines, but, for now, they would just have to deal with this one.

"Do you remember where your family lived? What name did they go by?" Eli asked quietly. He too was dressed as a

271

hallower—a Brother and his Sisters come to spread the faith to the people.

"Walker," Aster said, the name strange on her tongue after so many years. "Wilma and Clyde Walker. But I'm . . . I'm not sure which house we lived in."

"All right then, let's ask around," Eli said.

He went first to the ravener, leaving Aster and Clementine behind so the ravener wouldn't sense the magic of their favors. The two men talked in low voices for an uncomfortably long time, and Aster's skin began to itch with anxiety. She knew lying didn't come easily to Eli. What if he couldn't sell their story? Or this ravener ordered them to turn around anyway?

Aster had a revolver hidden underneath her robe . . . just a simple six-shooter, not a voltric pistol. They'd saved those for the rest of the group, still making their way here through the woods. But still, if there was going to be trouble—

Then, finally, Eli turned around and waved them forward. Aster relaxed, but only slightly. Something about being back here put her on edge, threatened to pull her mind apart and push her heart to a gallop.

The ravener disappeared up the hill and left them to go door-to-door, delivering gift baskets that they'd claimed were filled with garlands of grayleaf but were in fact filled with food, medicine, and weapons. At each house they asked after Aster's family, too, but were met each time with shifty eyes or blank stares. Either no one knew where her parents were . . . or no one wanted to tell them.

Fifteen minutes later, though, they knocked on the door of a house with a broken front window and a dirty-faced dog peering out of it. It barked twice, sharply, announcing their presence. An old woman cursed it as she came to the door, holding the mutt back by the scruff of its neck. Dark veins snarled beneath her papery skin, and her blond hair was thin and brittle as dried corn silk.

"Afternoon, ma'am," Eli said.

"I've heard enough sermons in my time," she said shortly.

Aster caught the door before she closed it. "Actually, ma'am, that's not what this is about . . ."

The old woman's milky eyes widened with surprise as they told her of their true work and warned her to keep silent until the time came to strike. No one was going to be forced to join the fight, Clementine reassured her—but regardless, they wanted everyone to have the means to take care of themselves until it was over.

"One last thing," Aster said as the old woman grinningly beheld her gifts. "We're looking for Wilma and Clyde Walker and were told they lived here. Do you know where we could find them?"

The mischievous smile that had spread over the old woman's face faded immediately.

"Wilma and Clyde Walker?" Her voice dropped. "Didn't you hear? Didn't you *see*?"

Something about her tone made Aster's scalp prickle with dread. "See what?"

"You must have come in from the south. If you'd been coming from the north, you would've passed them. They've been out there for four days."

Aster struggled to remain grounded, focusing on her

quavering breaths, on the unbearable heat, on anything other than the old woman's words.

"You mean . . ." Eli said slowly.

"The raveners had them executed—left out in gibbets for the vultures and vengeants. Their daughters were two of those Good Luck Girls, the ones behind the attacks on McClennon. Maybe you've even met them, if you're doing all this on their orders. I reckon you wanted to find Wilma and Clyde to save them from retribution, but old man Sullivan must've seen it coming and got to them first."

Aster's chest grew tight. Sounds suddenly became distant and muffled, colors overbright. She had been prepared to meet her parents, had been prepared to hear that they had been moved along. But she had not been prepared to learn that they were simply . . . gone.

Murdered.

The old woman's dog whined and licked Aster's hand, and the old woman pulled him back gently.

"I'm sorry to be the bearer of bad news, truly," she said. "The Walkers . . . they were good folks."

And the door creaked shut.

Aster swallowed and turned to Clementine, who was trembling, tears standing in her eyes.

"Hey," Aster said softly, touching her shoulder. "This doesn't change anything, hear? We've had to find our way without them for years. We still have each other. You still have me, Clem."

But Clementine shrugged off her hand and walked away, wiping furiously at her eyes from behind her veil.

"This is our fault. We got them killed," she choked.

"Clementine—Grace, please—"

Aster started after her, but Eli touched her elbow.

"Let her go," he said.

Now tears started burning in Aster's eyes, and she blinked them away angrily.

"Of course," Aster said, her voice breaking as Eli followed her back to the wagon. "Of course he murdered them. Of course he took my parents away from me. The landmasters have already taken everything else. Why not this, too."

She climbed into the back of the wagon and curled into herself, grateful now for the veil covering her face. She did not want Eli to see her like this, devastation breaking across her like a storm. He climbed up and sat down next to her, the wagon sagging with his weight. He said nothing for a long time, and his silent, solid presence was reassuring.

"They don't even deserve my grief," Aster said finally, swallowing painfully. "That's the hell of it, Eli. They betrayed us. They abandoned us. And now . . . now I'll never get to make it right with them."

When Eli spoke, his voice was soft as the tulle on her skin. "You can still say what you need to say, Aster. The Veil's not so thick that the dead can't sometimes hear us."

But now, somehow, after all these years of imagining this moment, Aster suddenly found herself without words. She had not ever expected to come back to Shade Hollow, and now, to find it just as she'd left it, but without her family . . .

"It wasn't real, Eli," Aster said, her voice growing thick. "None of it was real. I loved them. I trusted them. And I loved this

275

place, even though . . ." She closed her eyes. "I miss it sometimes. I miss all of it. I miss the girl I was then."

And maybe that was the real loss she was grieving here. The tears were pouring freely down Aster's cheeks now, and she didn't bother to wipe them away anymore.

"Two things can be true at the same time," Eli said. "It can be true that your parents loved you, and it can be true that they hurt you. It can be true that you have good memories of this place, and it can be true that you deserved better. You're allowed to feel whatever it is you're feeling, Aster, and it's okay if it doesn't make sense right now. Your love *was* real, though. It's okay to mourn it."

Aster's mind was a scattered mess. When she'd been a little girl, she'd wanted nothing more than to get away from here. But she'd also missed it once she'd been sold to the welcome house, and built it up in her mind as something precious that had been taken from her. So now, to come back to it with fresh eyes, older eyes, and see how ugly it truly was . . . and to realize how ugly it had always been . . .

"I grew up in a mining camp a lot like this," Eli said quietly. "Before me and Sam ran away. They start the boys working young—soon as you're big enough to hold the tools. It's dangerous work, even for the little ones. Especially for the little ones. But the damnedest thing was . . ." He laughed a little. "I couldn't wait to do it. I looked up to Sam and the other boys in the mines like they were the heroes in a two-copper novel. They looked so tough with their beat-up helmets and their steel-toed boots and their greased-up faces and their picks on their backs. I wanted to be just like them—never mind that half of them would be dead before the age of thirty, and half of those who survived would suffer from dust lung or a crushed leg or some other ailment the landmaster couldn't be bothered to treat. Sam himself was only twelve when he lost the fingers on his left hand to an accident. It was a bad place, Aster. A place where children were sent to suffer and die. And yet there was still some part of me, on that first day, when I got *my* hardhat and boots, that couldn't contain my excitement. And then we went down into the tunnel, the theomite glittering all around us . . . it was like being swallowed by a star." He looked at Aster. "That was real. The love and admiration I had for my brother was real. The excitement I had to start working, and the pride I felt once I did . . . the loyalty and friendship I felt towards all the other boys working with me . . . it was all real, Aster. As real as the pain and the suffering and the hate and the anger and the resentment. Just because you found some joy in a bad situation doesn't mean you're childish or spineless or—or grateful, somehow, to the people who hurt you. It just means you managed to make something beautiful grow where there shouldn't have been any life at all. And that in itself is a beautiful thing."

Aster sniffled quietly, wiping her nose on her sleeve, the words a balm on the burning shame and anger she felt.

Aster let out a shaky breath. "Thank you, Eli," she murmured, letting herself lean against him. He stilled, seemingly surprised, and then, after a moment, wrapped his arm around her shoulder. The heavy weight of it reassured her. She was still tense under his touch—she suspected she always would be— and it was tempting to hate herself for that, or the world, for making her this way. But Eli was right in that two feelings could exist side by side. She could be tense under a man's touch, even if it was gentle . . . and she could be grateful for that touch all the same.

"I'm sorry I brought you here," he said. "I should've known something like this would happen—"

"No, I'm glad you did," Aster said, and she was. At least now she knew. Not knowing would have been, in some ways, worse. "We have to find Clementine, though. She thinks this is our fault. And maybe it is . . . by the dead, this is such a mess."

Eli climbed into the driver's seat. "She went north. She can't have gone far. We'll find her, Aster."

North?

"Oh hell," Aster swore, "she went to see them. We have to stop her."

Eli's face crumpled with horror, and he quickly turned and snapped the reins to start the horse down the road. But before they even reached the edge of Shade Hollow, he stopped at the sight of a posse on horseback blocking their path—three raveners, one mortal man, and . . .

"*Clementine!*" Aster shouted, leaping down onto the road and reaching for her pistol.

"Ah, ah, careful," the man called out. He dismounted, grabbing Clementine by her collar just as the old woman had held her dog. He was short and slender, impeccably well dressed, with bronzed skin, slick black hair, and a thin, twitching moustache. Aster recognized him from Derrick's meticulous description, from the secondhand horror stories she'd heard growing up right here in Shade Hollow.

Leonard Sullivan.

CHAPTER TWENTY-TWO

Aster expected rage, but instead, her first reaction was simple, stunned silence. For all she and her friends talked about landmasters, they still felt more like an abstract threat than men made of flesh and blood. They were like the weather, a force beyond her control, destroying lives without thought or remorse. And Jerrod McClennon had just about lived up to the legend that Aster had built up around him, crackling with charisma and deadly intent every time he entered a room. But to know this weasel of a man had worked her parents to the bone before killing them so cruelly, to see him now with his hands on her sister—

Anger welled up from her stomach.

"You let her go, or I swear I'll—"

"You'll what?" Sullivan said with a chuckle, and the ravener behind him dismounted and pushed up to the front.

Lizzy Greene.

Eli, who had moved to stand beside Aster in a subtly defensive stance, drew a sharp breath. "A lady ravener . . ." he whispered. "Aster, is that—"

"When I saw your little declaration of war in the papers, we figured you might come home to try to get your parents out of harm's way," Sullivan went on. "So I decided to get here first myself, and I sent for Elizabeth, as well. She's been tracking you vermin for some time. My men had orders to report any suspicious behavior to me immediately, and, well . . . you certainly didn't keep us waiting long. A couple of fallen women, though, thieves and murderers no less, donning the sacred robes of hallowers to tell their lie? That's low, even for you."

Aster swallowed back a sick feeling rising in her gullet. They'd planned to lay a trap for Sullivan, and instead, *he* had laid a trap for *them*. She tried to think. Her friends were making their way here in the woods now; all she had to do was signal them. But they weren't expecting her signal until tomorrow at the earliest—what if they were still too far away to help? What if they didn't even see it?

Lizzy started towards them with unhurried steps, drawing the revolver from her belt.

"Eli," Aster said in a harsh whisper. "Grab the flare gun from the back of the wagon—"

"But—"

"Just do it!"

Eli turned and ran for the wagon, and as soon as he did so, Lizzy hit them both with a crushing wave of despair. Aster let out a cry of pain as she fell to her hands and knees, fresh tears springing to her eyes. Eli collapsed against the side of the wagon, barely remaining upright. Lizzy's mouth curved in a grin, her orange eyes bright as the sun above.

"McClennon'll pay me double if I bring you in alive, so do me a favor and don't make any sudden moves," she said. It was

280

the first time Aster had ever heard her speak, and her voice was so much like Zee's, it startled her. Like his, it sounded like it was always on the edge of laughter—but where Zee's laughter was kind, hers was cruel.

Aster fought to regain her feet. "Elizabeth," she choked out. "Lizzy, please, you don't have to do this. Come with us. We can take you to your brother—"

Lizzy's grin shifted to a snarl. "My brother is a traitor and a fool. I have nothing to say to him."

"You're angry. I understand that. I know how it feels—"

"I don't *feel* anything, Lucker."

Aster tried to remember what Raven had taught them about resisting raveners, tried to close her heart to her own feelings. But they were already too near the surface. Guilt for letting her parents die on her behalf. Anguish at the sudden loss of them. And the old, bone-deep betrayal at the thought that they had never loved her and Clementine enough to save them from the welcome house. Lizzy raised her hand to hit her with another heavy psychic blow, and Aster's rib cage seemed to cave in on itself. She fell back to her knees.

"*Aster!*" Clementine cried out, and Aster heard her struggling against Sullivan's grip, only to be silenced with a cuff to the face. Aster's wrath flared up once again, but the frost Lizzy had enveloped her in quickly snuffed it out. Lizzy was almost upon her now, grinning down at her with relish. She raised her boot and kicked Aster square in the chest. Aster fell on her back in the dusty road, the wind knocked out of her, Lizzy's silhouette blocking out the sun.

"Thank you kindly for making this easy for me," Lizzy said,

holstering her gun and reaching for the lasso at her belt. She knelt to bind Aster's hands and feet—

And then a gunshot split the air.

Lizzy swore and stumbled backwards, clutching her shoulder where she'd been shot. Raveners didn't feel pain, but that didn't stop her right arm from going dead at her side. Aster scrambled back, looking around quickly to see who'd fired the gun. Eli? No, he was still reeling from the ravening, only just recovering now that Lizzy's concentration had snapped. Then who—?

"You there! Get back inside!" Sullivan shouted hoarsely.

Aster followed his gaze to the old woman who had told her about her parents.

"No, I don't think so," the woman shouted back. She stood defiantly in the road, walking towards them, her gun steady in her liver-spotted hand. And she wasn't alone. More of the people they'd just armed were stepping outside their homes, weapons raised. They were not the people Aster had planned to use those weapons, not the young men who were currently working down in the mines. These were women, elders, men who were sick and injured. And yet they formed a line between Aster and the raveners. Aster's heart hitched with sudden hope. She climbed to her feet.

"You all best turn the rip around!" Sullivan shouted again at the growing crowd. "I'm not gonna warn you again!"

The two raveners flanking him advanced toward the crowd, drawing their own weapons. Lizzy, still clutching her shoulder to stanch her bleeding, sent out a pulse of fear. But there were too many of them now for her to concentrate her power on any one of them.

"Go on and do as he says. I don't want you all hurt on my behalf," Aster warned.

Another woman shook her head. "We're not doing this for you. We're doing this for us," she said grimly.

"Been breaking my back for that bastard for over sixty years," an old man agreed. "And now he wants to sell my granddaughter to a welcome house? I don't think so."

Aster heard a hiss and a pop from behind her. She whirled around.

Eli had fired the flare gun.

A look of panic crossed Sullivan's face. He pushed his raveners forward. "Beat them down!" he roared.

The other two raveners rushed forward on their hellhorses towards the crowd, billy clubs raised, while Sullivan threw Clementine over the back of his horse and took off in the opposite direction. Aster panicked. She couldn't abandon her sister, but she couldn't abandon these people, either. She would not let anyone else die because of her.

And then Eli was at her side, revolver already in hand. "Go," he said. "I'll protect them."

Aster looked at him and, with no time to express her gratitude, swallowed and nodded, sprinting after the landmaster. Scattered shouts and gunshots rang out behind her as the crowd clashed with the raveners, but she forced herself to push forward. Elizabeth's hellhorse was still standing in the middle of the road, and Aster would need it to have any hope of catching Sullivan. He was no doubt on his way to rally reinforcements of his own, and she couldn't let him. If the law came in and surrounded the camp, they were done.

The hellhorse let out a wet snort in warning the moment Aster grabbed its reins.

"Easy," Aster murmured nervously. It stood head and shoulders higher than a mortal horse, its cordlike muscles rippling beneath its chestnut coat, its rust-colored eyes gleaming like a bird of prey's. Hellhorses were beasts that had been corrupted by the same black magic as raveners. They felt no fear or pain, and they had a predator's instincts. They were not intended to be ridden by normal people.

But Aster had no choice.

Steeling herself, she stepped into the too-high stirrup and swung her other leg up over the saddle. The hellhorse let out a screech, rearing up on its hind legs. Aster's stomach dropped as she almost fell back to earth, the reins tangling around her wrists with a painful bite.

"Whoa!" she shouted, pulling back on the reins sharply. The hellhorse landed so heavily it set Aster's bones shuddering, and she barely had time to recover before it took off at a gallop—first, towards the crowd, and then, only after desperately muscling it around, down the road and after Sullivan.

Aster's hallower's outfit didn't come with spurs, but she didn't even need them. The hellhorse was faster than any other steed she'd ever ridden. The wind tore at her skin. The beat of the hooves threatened to shake her apart. It was like riding a thunderstorm. Soon the little dirt path joined up with the Bone Road, and Aster tore her eyes away from the trees and the cages hanging heavily from their branches. She did not want to see what was left of her parents.

She wanted to avenge them.

It didn't take her long to begin catching up to Sullivan, who threw a desperate glance over his shoulder at her, Clementine still slung over the back of his horse like a sack of grain. Aster drew her revolver to fire at him, but it was impossible to aim while keeping control of the beast below her. Her first shot went wide, and the second nearly clipped Clementine's temple. A punch of fear slammed through her, and she holstered the gun.

"You shoot at me again and I'll drag your sister behind this horse until she's worn to the bone!" Sullivan shouted back at her, his face red with effort.

Clementine began to struggle at the threat, but Sullivan just cuffed her with the butt of his gun. Aster snarled, pushing the hellhorse faster. Sullivan fired back three shots of his own, and Aster ducked to avoid them. But the fourth struck her hellhorse in the chest, causing it to stumble. Aster's stomach dropped as the beast came to a sudden stop, almost throwing her. Then, before she could even begin to calm it, it let out a screech of rage, tossing its head and pawing at the ground like a bull, and charged for Sullivan at full speed.

Ripping hell! Aster thought, terror whirling through her, skull rattling with every pounding step. She struggled for control as they closed the remaining distance to Sullivan and Clem in seconds. Then the hellhorse lunged for them, knocking Sullivan's horse over on its side with a savage kick to the ribs. Sullivan cursed as his leg was crushed beneath the weight of the thrashing animal.

"Clem!" Aster shouted, her voice raw with panic. But Clementine being slung over the back of the horse rather than stuck in its saddle seemed to have saved her—she had been thrown off the horse rather than trapped underneath it, and she was already stirring. The horse itself finally regained its feet and bolted, leaving Sullivan crumpled on the ground. Clementine was wriggling away from him as fast as she could. But Aster's hellhorse seemed determined to trample them both, rearing up to crush them beneath its hooves.

"ENOUGH!" Aster shouted, yanking back on the reins with all her strength. She managed to pull it back at the last moment, twisting the hellhorse away from her sister. It squealed in protest, but Aster grappled with it until at last it relented. Exhausted, her face slick with sweat and her arms shaking with the effort, Aster dismounted and tied the hellhorse up to the trunk of an evergreen before it could renew its anger. For all she knew, it would be strong enough to pull the whole damn tree down—but not before she finished her business here.

Breathing hard, Aster drew her knife.

"Sullivan," she growled, approaching the fallen landmaster. He was sitting up now, but he couldn't seem to stand, his left leg twisted at an unnatural angle, his fine trousers dark with blood. His gun lay in the dirt, well out of reach. He watched Aster approach with eyes wide as a trapped animal's. But Aster knelt next to Clementine first, freeing her from her bonds.

"By the Veil, are you all right?" Clementine whispered as Aster helped her up.

"*I'm* fine. How are *you*?"

"Nothing that won't buff out. I'm more shaken up than anything," Clementine said. "But Sullivan, he—"

"You stay back, now," Sullivan threatened. His confidence

had clearly cracked, but it didn't keep the commanding tone from his voice. "If you know what's good for you you'll just walk away. You're already in enough trouble with the law without adding the murder of a landmaster to your crimes."

"Who said I'm here to murder you?" Aster asked calmly.

"It's what you promised in your little declaration of war in the papers, isn't it?" He wet his lips. "You Luckers want revenge."

"We want justice," Aster corrected, kneeling down to hold the knife to his throat. "But I'll settle for revenge if I have to."

"And what about mercy?" His face was reddening, with anger or shame, Aster couldn't tell. "You think you're so much better than us? You think you're more than the animals we all know you to be? *Prove it.*"

Aster curled her lip and pressed the tip of the blade deeper into his skin. "I do not forgive you."

Sullivan's throat bobbed as he swallowed. His beady black eyes flickered down to the knife, then back up to meet Aster's glare.

"Here's what happens next," she went on softly. "You'll be coming with us, somewhere none of your lawman friends will find you, and we'll keep you prisoner until our demands are met. No one's gonna hurt you—we'll even see to your leg, make sure you're comfortable—but if you ever want to see the sun again, you better hope your puppet authoritant and whoever else is left in the government are willing to change the way things are done."

"And how do I know you won't just kill me as soon as you're out of danger?" he spat.

Clementine knelt next to Aster. "Because unlike you, we don't just throw lives away."

Sullivan shifted his gaze to Clementine. "No," he said slowly. "I think it's because you need me alive. What good am I to you dead? You have nothing to negotiate with."

"So then we're agreed," Aster said with a grim smile. "It's in everyone's best interest for you to come quietly. Clem." She nodded at her sister to grab the ropes on the ground and tie Sullivan up. Sullivan's breathing quickened.

"No . . ." he said, a strange look coming over him. "No, I will never be your prisoner."

And then he thrust himself forward onto Aster's knife, the point of the blade piercing the hollow of his throat. Aster swore, shock and disgust ripping through her as his warm blood rushed forth until her hand was hot and sticky with it. Clementine let out a shriek and fell backwards.

"The dead protect us, what are we supposed to do now?" she sobbed.

"I—I don't know." Aster dropped her knife, her heart thumping erratically, bile rising in her throat. She struggled to keep her mind from tearing away completely. If they left his body here, the law was sure to blame them for his murder—which was, no doubt, exactly what he'd wanted. Not just to deny them a valuable hostage, but to make them look like bloodthirsty killers in the eyes of the public.

But if they took his body with them, made it disappear . . .

"We have to take him back to Red Claw," Aster said, already moving to pick him up and drag him over to the hellhorse. "We won't take credit for his disappearance. Let

288

the law make of it what they will. They won't be able to prove anything."

Clementine looked sick. "And then what? We just . . . leave his body down there forever?"

Aster felt a twinge of uncertainty, but she thought of her parents, and the other people of Shade Hollow, and all the young men and boys Sullivan had sent to suffer underground and the girls he had allowed to be stolen away, and she closed her heart to it.

"He'll have the vengeants to keep him company."

CHAPTER TWENTY-THREE

When Aster and Clementine returned to Shade Hollow with Sullivan's body in tow, they found the rest of their group waiting for them: the others had rushed to Eli's side at the sight of his flare, and together they'd taken out almost all the raveners in the camp—not just the pair Sullivan had brought with him, but the ones overseeing the mines as well. Now the miners and their families alike were celebrating in the streets.

"And Lizzy?" Aster asked her friends, unable to let herself share in their celebration. Zee's sister was not among the fallen raveners. Perhaps she, like Sullivan, had escaped their grasp.

"She tailed it as soon as she realized backup was coming," Eli explained, wiping at his bloodied knuckles with a whiskey-soaked rag. "Just disappeared into the woods. I guess she figured she wasn't in any fit condition to fight, not with her good arm injured like that."

Like Aster, Zee was the only other one who didn't seem to feel like celebrating. "I wanted to go after her," he started, his voice thick, "but . . ." Zee looked over his shoulder to the people now dancing, laughing, firing shots into the sky. "I was needed here."

"You could still follow her, Zee, now that it's over," Eli said. "I know these woods well enough. I can get everybody back."

Zee shook his head. "No, it's too dangerous. *She's* too dangerous, even now—she could still make me see terrible things, feel terrible things. I probably just need to . . . let her go. At least McClennon won't want to send her after us again for some time, not until she's back in fighting form." Zee smiled weakly, looking up at Aster. "And at least we're free of Sullivan, right?"

Aster returned the smile, but inside she felt hollowed out, brittle, like a field after a fire. She'd lost something precious today. The people of Shade Hollow had promised to give her parents a proper burial, but still . . . they should never have been killed at all. It wasn't enough that Sullivan himself was dead now, too. Justice had not been done.

But she didn't want to let her own misgivings take this victory away from her friends, and she couldn't blame them for their high spirits—they didn't think there had been much love lost between Aster and Clementine and their parents. Hell, neither had Aster, for that matter. Even Clementine, who had certainly taken it harder than her, had now turned all her attention to comforting Zee, and they both seemed to be lifted temporarily by the happiness of those around them, as they so easily were. And so Aster kept forcing a smile as they made their way back to Red Claw through the gold-painted forest, covering their tracks as they went in case the law—or Elizabeth—tried to follow them.

291

"I still can't believe the old man died for his pride! Saves us the trouble of killing him, at least," Mallow was saying. The woods hummed with the drone of insects, and the late afternoon sun baked the rugged earth below the horses' hooves. Zee took point, riding with Clem, while Eli carried Sullivan's body and Raven rode the hellhorse. Aster rode with Violet, who had offered to take the reins once she'd heard about everything Aster had been through. It was an unspeakable relief, to let someone else take control in this moment, and she couldn't help leaning forward wearily against Violet, the steady rise and fall of her breathing lulling Aster into a half sleep. This close, she could smell traces of lavender perfume on Violet's neck—because of course Violet had worn perfume to an uprising.

"We weren't *supposed* to kill Sullivan, though," Clementine pointed out, a twinge of worry in her voice. "What if McClennon and them assume we did? Why would they give in to our demands then, if they think we're just going to kill them all anyway?"

"We left no hard evidence. They'll have their suspicions, but nothing more," Aster said, exhausted.

"I don't know, I'm with Mal—I don't really care why it happened, I'm just glad the bastard's gone," Raven said with a laugh. "The folks at Shade Hollow'll keep our secret, and to the rest of the world he'll just . . . disappear, like the dead only know how many of our people have. It serves him right."

"And now that he's out of the way, it'll make it that much easier for his other mining camps to free themselves," Zee added. "The raveners aren't going fight if they're not getting paid."

292

"Not that we couldn't take them if they did. You missed a good scrap, Aster," Mal said.

Tansy let out a long-suffering sigh. "You almost broke your neck."

"But I *didn't*."

Aster forced a chuckle. "Seems like you all did just fine without me."

Violet glanced over her shoulder back at Aster, worry flashing in her eyes.

"Come on, though, Aster, you've hardly told us anything about *your* fight with Sullivan," Mallow pushed. "What did he say when—"

"You all go on ahead," Violet interrupted. "I think our horse sprung a shoe. We'll catch up in a minute."

"You sure? We can wait," Eli said, swinging his own horse around.

"We'll be *fine*," Violet said pointedly.

Eli still looked uncertain, but Raven waved him forward. "Come on, we have to get that body back. Those two can handle themselves."

Aster was too tired to argue, but once the others were gone, she sat up a little straighter and tried to muster her last reserve of willpower. "What the hell, Vi? You know damn well you don't know how to fix a loose shoe. Now *I'm* gonna have to do it."

"There's no loose shoe, you fool," Violet muttered back. "I just wanted to get the others off your back for a minute. You can stop pretending to be happy now."

Aster scoffed. "I'm not pretending. I'm thrilled. We freed

my hometown. I've been dreaming about doing that since I was a little kid."

"Don't bullshit me. That's not how we are with each other." Violet spun around in the saddle so they were facing each other, their knees touching, their calves entangled. The wind twitched at Violet's hair, and she tucked the loose lock away behind the shell of an ear. "Talk to me, Aster."

Aster felt a lump forming in her throat, and she swallowed painfully. "I . . . I thought it would make me feel better, seeing Sullivan dead . . . but instead, I just feel sick."

"Because it doesn't bring them back," Violet said softly.

"No . . ." Aster's words were slow, strained, as the truth forced its way to the surface. "Because he made me do it. First Sullivan took away any choice I had in making things right with my family . . . and then he took away any choice I had in killing him for it. And maybe I would've done it anyway, maybe I would have decided they were worth risking everything for, but . . . now I'll never know. And I am so tired . . ." Her voice cracked, and she let it. "I am so tired of people taking my choice away from me."

She fell forward in Violet's arms, crying softly into the crook of her neck. Violet wrapped her in a strong embrace.

"I just feel so damned helpless, Violet. I let this happen."

"There's nothing helpless about you," Violet said fiercely. "You're the strongest person I know."

"But it's so hard being this way. I have to work at it. And it's wearing me down. I can't do this forever."

Violet pulled back, and her blue eyes shimmered with tears of her own. "Well, you don't have to, hear? You don't have to be strong around me, Dawn. And if the day ever comes that you decide it's too much, you let me know, and I'll take you away from all this."

Aster laughed hollowly. "What, just . . . stop fighting? And what about everyone else?"

"To hell with everyone else." Aster sighed, and Violet pressed on. "I'm serious. Dawn, you've done more good in the past year than most people do in their whole lives—certainly more than me. No one would blame you for walking away."

Aster thought of Sid, who had found ways to keep fighting even after devastating loss. Of Priscilla, who was still fighting even though she was old and gray. She shook her head.

"I can't," she whispered.

"Yes, you can. You've never learned to be selfish, that's your problem. So let me teach you, as someone who knows too well. This world has already taken so much from you, and you've given it so much more—but it does not get to have all of you. You have to save some for yourself."

Aster wiped at her eye with the heel of her hand. "And some for you, too, is that the deal?" She'd become so close to Violet, she could not imagine trying to go back to a time when she hadn't shared everything with her.

Violet smiled, her teeth flashing in the fading sunlight. "Well, yeah. Like I said, I've *always* been selfish . . . but you've helped me learn how to give more of myself to others, too. We can hold each other accountable."

Warmth spread through Aster's chest, and the knot of tension there loosened for the first time that day. She laughed a little, self-consciously, suddenly embarrassed that she had gotten so worked up in the first place.

"Hold on, now, was that a smile?" Violet asked, tilting Aster's chin up. "I thought you were too tough for all that."

"I am." Aster shoved her away. Violet raised an eyebrow, holding her gaze for a heartbeat before turning back around in the saddle.

"All right then. I'll leave you to your brooding," Violet said over her shoulder. "But promise me that you'll try to forgive yourself—not just for Sullivan. For all of it. For being a human being."

"I promise," Aster murmured. She wrapped her arms around Violet's waist and leaned against her as Violet urged their horse forward again. The warmth in her chest seemed to fill her whole body now, her cheeks burning with it.

"Violet," Aster said after a while, her voice almost lost in the chorus of the forest as it slipped into the evening.

"Mm?"

"Thank you."

When Aster and Violet returned to Camp Red Claw, they found Derrick and Eli fighting.

They pushed their way through the crowd that had gathered around the boys in the square outside the meeting hall, the Scorpions egging the boys on as they circled each other with arms raised protectively in front of their faces. Eli was still dressed in his hallower's robes, the loose black sleeves shucked up past his elbows, the dust from the road casting a ghostly pallor over his dark skin. Derrick wore only his trousers, braces

296

cutting into his bare white shoulders, freckles dusting his arms and a chest surprisingly wiry with muscle. He pushed a sheaf of red hair out of his bloodied face as he made a desperate lunge at Eli, his knuckly fist flying towards Eli's chin. Eli swatted it away impatiently and tried to grab him, but Derrick ducked out of the way, hopping on the balls of his feet like a sparrow.

Aster and Violet exchanged a knowing look. Aster heaved a sigh and stepped into the clearing.

"What the rip is going on here?" she demanded. The boys both stopped and looked up at her.

"Aster—?"

"Aster—!"

"CLEAR OUT!" Aster ordered the crowd. The rest of her friends were nowhere to be found among them. Where the hell were they?

"*Aster*," Derrick cried again, running towards her unsteadily. His nose looked broken, a thin trickle of blood dripping down to his lip. *By the Veil*. "Aster, you promised me, you *promised* me—"

"Your little pet landmaster here heard we killed Leonard Sullivan and went rabid," Eli interrupted, rubbing at a cut on his chin.

"Don't you speak for me!" Derrick's voice was harsh and scabbed. As often as he and Eli had butted heads, she'd never seen him like this before, and some part of her shrank away from his anger instinctively. It was the same anger that, in his brother, had almost gotten Clementine killed. Violet stepped forward, straightening up as she did when it came time to assert authority.

"You watch your tone, Derrick," she warned. "Ripping hell, I can't leave you unattended for more than five minutes, can I? Where are the others?"

"They're in their cabins, getting some well-deserved rest," Eli answered for him. "I volunteered to take care of Sullivan's body myself, and I figured I'd get Derrick to help me, since all he does is sit on his ass anyway. Found him lying around in his drawers and scribbling in his notebook. As soon as I told him the old boy was dead, he lit into me. I tried to walk away—this was about as far as I got before I decided I might as well start hitting back."

Derrick's face reddened even further. "I won't apologize for my anger! You promised me no one would be killed!" Then he turned to Aster, his voice cracking. "You all were supposed to be *different*."

Aster's exhaustion beat against her skull, a dull headache that pulsed in time with her heart. It had been a long day, and she had no energy left to try to justify herself to Derrick. But his anger was already slipping off him like an ill-fitting suit, beneath it a raw look of hurt and betrayal that Aster knew all too well.

"Violet, do me a favor and take Eli to the medical ward," Aster said wearily. "I'll talk to Derrick."

"You're all right with him?" Violet asked, looking between them.

Eli sucked his teeth. "She's fine. She's not afraid of the fairblood boy."

Aster felt her face warm with frustration. "Eli, I told you that's not—"

"Come on."

Eli and Violet left them, Violet looking over her shoulder worriedly. But Aster just waved her on.

"I don't need you to babysit me," Derrick muttered under his breath once they were out of sight.

"The hell you don't," Aster shot back. "Clean your face." She tossed him a dustkerchief to stanch his bleeding, and he pressed it to his crooked nose, sitting down in the dirt with a heavy sigh of his own. Aster sat down next to him, still uncomfortable being so near a half-naked man, but less so now that he had crumpled beneath his own upset.

"You weren't kidding when you said you'd studied hand-and-foot combat. You have a mean uppercut," Aster said more gently.

But Derrick wasn't having it. He sniffed, wincing as he did so. "This is no laughing matter, Aster."

Fair enough.

"Let me start by saying none of us killed Leonard Sullivan," Aster tried again. "The bastard threw himself onto my blade when he realized we intended to take him prisoner."

"And you expect me to just believe you?"

Aster squared up. "Yes, actually, I do. And I'm not exactly happy about it, either. I can't even begin to explain how it felt for him to just . . ." She broke off, thought better of it. He could not understand. "Look, I won't mourn a man like him, true, but I do wish it had gone differently."

Derrick continued to sulk in silence, the dustkerchief sopping with blood now, and Aster furrowed her brow as she tried to read his expression.

"Are *you* mourning him, Derrick?" she asked suddenly.

"*No*," he said with disgust, throwing the dustkerchief away. "I was *frightened* of him. Just as I was frightened of my family. Of my brother. But now I am also frightened of *you*."

"But I told you—"

"You didn't mean for it to go that far, I know. That's what they always say."

Aster fell silent. Derrick closed his eyes and took a steadying breath, his ribs standing out underneath his skin like piano keys.

"Why were you so frightened of your brother?" Aster asked quietly. Because she recognized this fear of his, the kind that twisted your every thought into the shape of a monster.

His eyes cracked back open. "Do I really need to answer that question? Do I really have to explain such a thing? To you, of all people?"

"But you're not some Good Luck Girl he could kill without consequence."

"No. True. He could only get away with so much, with me."

Suddenly certain things about Derrick were beginning to make sense in Aster's mind: his skittishness, his insecurity, his disgust for his family, for himself. Was it the abuse that had left him so fragile? Or had his brother simply seen a fragile thing and sought to crush it?

Or both?

"My father did not protect me," Derrick went on. "He recognized my weakness and despised it. Pushed me off on his brother to raise. Then Uncle Jerrod saw how soft I was and took it as a chance to pull and twist me in his own image. I don't know who I am, Aster, only what others have done to me. And I trust you to understand this, better than I ever could." He looked up at her then, his eyes glassy. "So when I see how you are with your sister—with all of the people you call your own—I am filled with so much hope. And longing, because I did not know it could be that way. I have never known a family like this—one built not by blood and power but by love and respect. And I know it's not my place, but I want to be a part of it. I want that more than anything. But not . . ." He took another deep breath, steeling himself. "*Not* if you're going to be just like *them*."

Any other time, if anyone else had accused Aster of being just as bad as a landmaster, she would have reacted with anger. But she understood Derrick now—why he was so afraid to trust others, how easily that trust could be broken. She did not know exactly what he'd suffered, but she knew enough. And so she would be patient with him, as she'd had to learn to be patient with herself.

"Derrick," she said softly, "surely you can see the difference between people like your family and people like us. Between the—the cornered animal lashing out for its survival and the hunter chasing it for sport." She had to speak in metaphors with him; she knew he found that soothing.

He pushed his hair back. "Yes . . . at least, I think I do . . . I just—" His face contorted with frustration as he grasped for words. "I am just so afraid of doing the wrong thing. Of *being* the wrong thing. Of becoming my brother."

"I don't think you could be as cruel as your brother even if you were trying," Aster said. "You feel others' pain too much and too deeply. And maybe, to your family, that made you weak or—or soft, but it's what I admire most about you, Derrick. You say you wish you were a part of *this* family, but as far as I'm concerned, you already are."

"Do you mean that?"

"I do."

For the first time, Derrick smiled, then winced again as his face muscles pulled at his tender bloodied nose.

"I'm . . . I'm sorry for making such a scene," he said, his face reddening now. "That was . . . unlike me."

Aster huffed a laugh. "Honestly, it was good to see you have some fight in you. I'm going to need you to make it right with Eli, though. I can't have you two going after each other every time you're in a room together."

"We both just think the world of you," Derrick said, his voice a little quieter.

Aster glanced down awkwardly. She wasn't sure what to do with that, wasn't sure how to tell him that she loved him less like a sweetheart and more like the big sister he'd never had. She did not want to hurt him when he had shown her true vulnerability for the first time. But Derrick seemed to sense her discomfort, taking her silence for an answer, looking away and clearing his throat.

"Anyway," he chirped, "I've been a proper fool. But I promise I'm going to make it all up to you."

"Oh?" Aster asked, relieved. "And how's that?"

"Well, firstly, I'd like to give you this . . ." Derrick loosened the theomite ring from his third finger, the thin silver band embedded with a square black jewel. It was more delicately

302

crafted than Baxter's ring had been, the metal decorated with a fine filigree.

Aster shook her head. "Derrick, I can't possibly accept this—"

"I'm offering it to you as a friend," he insisted. "Please, I . . . it represents everything I want to shed myself of, and I know you will have more use for it than I ever could. Please."

Aster hesitated, then accepted the ring, sliding it over her thumb, where it fit as if it had been made for her. The metal was still warm. Her chest tightened with tears. She had never expected to experience such tenderness from any man, let alone the son of a landmaster.

"Thank you, Derrick," Aster said softly.

"And secondly—" he continued.

"*Secondly?*" What could possibly top this?

Derrick grinned impishly. "Secondly, I'm going with you to kidnap the Harker brothers."

CHAPTER TWENTY-FOUR

Aster and her friends spent the next few days planning their move on the Harker brothers, twin kings of agriculture. But while they were lying low, plenty of their allies were on the attack. Every day scouts arrived with coded messages written in one of the languages of the Nine, detailing every new victory and defeat. But for all the bad news that came in—failed ambushes, destroyed supplies, Reckoners captured by the law—there was far more good. In Northrock, Cora and her friends had organized their strike, and dustbloods throughout the city had emptied the factories and filled the streets. The first national bank had been burned to the ground, the statues of the landmasters of old had been pulled down, and the capitol building had been seized and turned into the Reckoners' headquarters. It didn't take long for other cities to light up as well, until the whole of the north was burning. Cora wrote to reassure them that though the lawmen had been merciless in their retaliation, they were outnumbered and losing the will to fight.

Best of all, though, was the news that the Reckoners in the north had captured Sylas Cain—one of the heads of the great landmaster families and council member of the Landmasters' Guild, the man whose name had been on seemingly every factory in Northrock's industrial district. With both Cain and Sullivan now out of the picture, they'd taken out a third of the guild's leadership. Camp Red Claw was filled with drinking and music the night of the news.

Meanwhile, the Lady Ghosts had anonymously petitioned Authoritant Lockley, calling on him to take a stand against the landmasters that owned him as surely as any dustblood miner. They'd also rallied support from their wealthy fairblood friends, who traveled to the Scab to form a chain around the welcome houses and prevent brags from walking in. There were not enough of them to protect more than two or three houses a night, and they were fined steeply for their trouble—but unlike the dustbloods on strike, the law was not so quick to beat them, their shadows providing them a layer of protection. Aggie wrote that Priscilla was worried things had gotten out of control and was desperate to rein them back in, but that most of the rest of the Ladies were brimming with more excitement and anticipation than she'd ever seen in all her years of serving there.

Finally, the Scorpions and the Nine worked together to free the families living in the tenant camps, the Nine providing the food while the Scorpions provided the weapons and other supplies. The voltric weapons gave the rebels a fighting chance against the raveners, and the dustblood families themselves took up arms to overwhelm them with numbers. With Sullivan out of the way, it had been only a matter of days before most of his camps had fallen. The papers had reported the landmaster missing by now, and though no blame had been laid, the word

305

on the street was that the Reckoners were responsible, to many dustbloods' delight.

Aster received the updates each day with a mixture of excitement and dread. Excitement, because she would never, even just a year ago, have expected to see this: men fighting for the freedom of Good Luck Girls, fairbloods fighting for the freedom of dustbloods, people hundreds of miles away risking their lives because of her words and actions and those of her friends. Aster had long since coated her heart in armor to avoid disappointment. People could always, *only*, be trusted to disappoint you. But these past few days had split that armor near in two, leaving her vulnerable to tears of relief in the quiet of the night.

But of course, Aster felt dread, too, because she had seen how landmasters responded to dissent and did not want anyone else hurt or killed on her behalf.

The only choice now was to see this through before the landmasters had a chance to strike.

When Aster and her friends finally left for the Harker estate, a week after the failed capture of Leonard Sullivan, it was the largest group she'd ever overseen. With both Derrick and Eli along for the ride, they were nine strong. Attempting to cover the tracks of such a large group traveling through the woods was going to be a nightmare, Zee warned her, but they had no choice. The law was out in full force now, patrolling the Bone Road and guarding the entrance to every deadwalled town. And so they picked their way across the uneven forest floor, doubling back to confuse any pursuers, going out of their way to travel over rocky ground or thread-thin creeks, and dragging branches behind their horses to brush away their tracks.

In the end it took them three days and two nights to reach the shallow valley where the Harker estate lay, and the grueling journey drew their strained nerves near to the breaking point. A starved pair of coyotes was drawn to their cookfire, and Zee suffered a nasty bite to his forearm in the fight to drive them off. Derrick's theomite ring slipped off Aster's sweating hand, and they spent over an hour retracing their steps to find it in a race against the coming night. Sometimes they heard the shouts of angry confrontations between travelers and the law on the Bone Road, and though they deliberated over it every time, they never stopped to get involved. Their current mission was too important.

Derrick alone kept his spirits high, complimenting the Scab's rugged beauty with forced cheer rather than complaining about the blistering heat or the biting flies. He seemed determined to make himself useful at every turn, to prove he was willing to suffer whatever the others were, despite his obvious and growing dread as they neared their destination. But Aster couldn't blame him for that—she felt it, too, fear and anticipation as charged as a bolt of voltricity in her blood. With Sullivan, they'd had a whole camp full of dustbloods to back them up. With the Harkers, they'd be on their own.

"I have eyes on a patrol," Mallow murmured. She had climbed the lower branches of a twisted evergreen, and from there peered down into the valley with a pair of binoculars. Even from the ground, Aster could see the Harkers' mansion from here: a massive whitewashed building with three stories and two wings, sitting in the pool of shadows at the base of the valley like a lantern in the dark. Up here, though, the woods were still rosy with fading sunlight, and Aster wanted to wait until the cover of nightfall to strike.

"Well? How many do you see?" Aster asked Mal.

"I count four raveners circling the perimeter of the estate and two guarding the gate at the deadwall."

Aster fixed an accusatory glare at Derrick. He had shorn his hair and dyed it black in preparation for tonight, and now he was busy fumbling bullets into his handgun. He seemed to feel Aster's eyes on him, looking up sheepishly.

"What?"

"You *said* these bastards wouldn't have much security at the house," Eli rumbled. "You said they'd put all their raveners in their camps to prevent rebellion."

"Not *all*. Most," Derrick corrected. "Listen, given what happened to Sullivan, you can't be surprised they've hired some backup. But it's hardly enough to stop us."

Raven snorted. "Us?" she echoed.

"Yes, *us*," Derrick insisted, finally holstering his gun. "I told you, I'm not hanging back this time. I've been to this estate many times before. I can show you where the back entrance is. Just because I didn't know about the raveners doesn't mean—"

"It's fine, Derrick," Aster said with an impatient sigh. "Just don't forget your dustkerchief. We can't have these bastards recognizing you."

"I've already given up my hair! Let that be enough! *You* all aren't wearing dustkerchiefs," he protested.

"That's because the Harkers already know *we're* after them. But we still need them and the rest of the world to think you're being held prisoner somewhere. We can't take any chances."

308

Derrick mumbled something under his breath, but obediently tied his dustkerchief around the bottom half of his face. The others were beginning to ready themselves, too, loading their weapons and grabbing supplies from the saddlebags. Mal jumped down from her lookout post and landed catlike on all fours.

"So, what's the plan to get around those raveners?" Eli pressed, crossing his arms. His own rangeman's hat cast a shadow over his eyes, but Aster could see the tightness of his jaw well enough.

Aster ticked over the options in her mind. "We'll need to create a distraction," she said after a moment. "Something to draw them away into the woods. That'll give the rest of us a chance to slip down to the house unnoticed. And since you're the one champing at the bit, Eli, I'll let you take the lead on that."

"What, the distraction?"

Aster nodded, handing him the theomite ring. "I want this back, hear? And take Zee with you. The rest of us will go get the Harkers."

Eli dipped his chin. "We better get going, then. Be dark soon."

"Wait, why Zee?" Clementine interrupted, crossing her arms and standing in front of Aster. "You know how he feels about raveners—"

"*Clem*," Zee said through his teeth.

"—and he's still recovering from his run-in with his sister."

"It's fine," Zee insisted, turning to Aster. "I know my way around the woods in the dark better than anyone else. I'll take Eli over to the other side of the estate and start an exposed campfire. The raveners'll see the smoke and come to check it out."

It was clear that Clementine still didn't like it, but she sighed and pressed her forehead to his. "Fine, just . . . be careful, Zee. You don't have the voltric weapons anymore." They had been distributed among the freed camps.

"No," Eli said, strapping his shotgun to his back. "But he'll have me."

Aster caught Eli's eye. *Thank you*, she said silently.

The boys saddled up on the back of Eli's horse and took off. Aster and the rest of the group hiked down to the edge of the forest, waiting anxiously for the ravener patrols to take the bait. It was only another few moments before the sun set and the vengeants' wails started up—distant enough, but still too close for comfort. Without the theomite ring, they only had iron to protect them, and Derrick's hand fell to the lucky horseshoe at his belt without his even seeming to realize it.

"They'll give this area a wide berth. They know there's a dead-wall down there," he whispered.

"You actually believe that, or you just trying to reassure yourself?" Mal muttered.

He didn't answer. Clementine's eyes were closed, her lips moving silently as if in prayer, and Aster reached for her hand and gave it a squeeze.

"He'll be fine," she promised.

She only hoped it wasn't a lie.

They spotted the smoke a moment later, a thin silver ribbon unfurling from the tree line. The raveners caught wind of it instantly, raising the alarm, and the one nearest to it took off into the woods with frightening speed. The others spread out to cover the lost ground.

"*Damn it*," Aster swore under her breath. She'd hoped more of them would take the bait.

"Hey, it's okay," Violet said. "There's a big enough gap between them now for us to slip past, see?"

"Yeah, I guess we'll just have to—"

Then the first gunshots rang out—the staccato *pop-pop-pop* of Zee's six-shooter, and the heavy blast of Eli's shotgun. One of the raveners down below shouted out an order to the others, and all but the two guarding the gate swarmed to join the fight.

"The dead preserve us," Tansy murmured, and Clementine let out a soft cry.

Derrick looked at Aster desperately, his eyes so wide the whites were showing. "Shouldn't we go help them?"

"No," Aster said, though her gut had gone loose at the sounds of a firefight. This had been Zee's own plan. He knew what was at stake tonight. "We have to finish this."

She broke cover from the woods and started down the hill at a low crouch before anyone else could question her, before she could question herself. Her knife was already in her hand. They had to take out the remaining two raveners quietly. They couldn't afford to raise another alarm.

"Mallow—" she began.

"Already on it," Mal said. She held the tip of her own blade between her fingers.

They reached the deadwall and crept alongside the glittering stone, hidden in the shelter of its shadow. Toothy shards of colored glass had been embedded in the top to prevent intruders from climbing it. The guarded gate was the only way past. Mallow took the lead as they silently approached the raveners,

311

who already seemed to be on high alert, their long guns unslung. She paused to take aim, set her jaw.

And sent her knife sailing towards the nearest ravener.

The blade sank into his throat without a sound. He reached for the hilt with inhuman calm, but he was losing blood too quickly to do anything more, and he dropped to the ground. His partner swore and ran over to help him. Aster sprinted out of the shadows, knife raised. She lunged, aiming for his chest—

"I don't ripping think so," the ravener snarled, catching her arm and pushing her back. Aster hit the ground so hard her vision doubled. She gasped as the breath was forced out of her lungs. The ravener loomed over her, greasy hair hanging past his shoulders, eyes flashing in the moonlight. He pressed the muzzle of his rifle to her chest. Her heart beat painfully against it.

"*Who are you with?*" he demanded, drowning her with waves of dread.

Aster swallowed, sick with fear. "I—"

Then a sudden rush of noise and confusion as her friends rushed him.

Violet and Raven grabbed him by the arms and threw him to the ground, pinning him there while he struggled. Mallow pounced on his legs. Tansy cupped her hand over his mouth to keep him from raising the alarm, and Clementine helped Aster back to her feet, clapping her on the back to help her regain her breath.

"Thank you," Aster said shakily, reasserting her grip on her knife. She approached the ravener, wincing as he hit her with another surge of fear, pushing through the nausea of it.

312

"What do you want us to do with him?" Raven asked through her teeth.

"Nothing. I'll finish it," Aster said in a low voice. She knelt beside him, raised the knife. Hesitated.

"Aster, why don't you let me—" Violet started.

Then Aster saw the flash of understanding in the ravener's eyes as he recognized her at last, and she plunged the knife into his chest.

"By the Veil!" Derrick swore.

They all turned as one to face him. He was still hidden in the shadows, pale as a remnant.

Aster freed her knife with a slick squelch. "I thought you were here to help," she growled.

"I am—I just—" He shook his head, seeming to think better of it. "I know the way from here. On me."

Derrick pushed the iron gates open with a grunt of effort, then dashed across the darkened estate towards the Harkers' mansion. The sounds of the firefight in the woods continued from beyond the wall, but it was masked well enough by the vengeants' keening. The dead willing, Aster hoped, they had kept the element of surprise. Her muscles were still jellied from the fight with the ravener, her mind still blurred at its edges, but she forced herself to focus. The night was far from over yet.

"There," Derrick whispered, pointing to a doorway hidden in the shadows. He had led them wide around to the side of the house, avoiding the light from the windows. "That's the servants' entrance. It leads into the kitchens. There'll still be some staff on duty."

"That's fine," Aster said. "We planned for this. Let me do the talking."

She darted for the door at a low crouch and tested the handle. Still unlocked. She motioned silently for the others to follow her, then pushed the door open and snuck into the mansion.

For an instant, Aster was thrown back to the welcome house. Nowhere else had she seen such a lavish kitchen: enough sparkling silver cookware to pay off a dustblood's debt, and more food in the pantry than most families saw in a year. Eli would have gone to glory at the sight, but Aster just felt sick. All this excess, while regular folks starved.

There were two dustblood women on duty, one mopping the floors, one elbows deep in dirty dishwater. It was the first woman who saw them, shock breaking across her face as she let her mop clatter to the ground. The second whirled around and let out a yelp of terror.

"Don't scream," Aster said quickly, holding her hands up. "Look at my face, my favor—do you know who I am?"

"I—I don't—" the first woman stammered.

"You're one of the runaway Good Luck Girls that's been picking off landmasters," the second woman said, her eyes widening. "You're in the papers, all of you. The Reckoners."

"That we are," Aster said with a friendly smile. "And now we've come for the Harker brothers. Where can we find them?"

The women exchanged glances, some unspoken tension filling the space between them.

"They won't be killed," Aster added, recognizing the hesitation in their eyes all too well.

"Won't they? Baxter McClennon was," the first woman said.

"That . . . couldn't be helped," Aster said carefully. "But—"

The second woman shook her head. "Look, I've no love for the Harkers, but if something happens to them and the law thinks we had anything to do with it—"

"Yes, they had the Yanceys' poor boy gibbeted just for praising the Reckoners' work—"

"Hey, hey," Aster whispered, taking a step towards them, gesturing for them to keep their voices down. "Don't you worry about the law coming after you. We've already taken care of it. There's a nearby tenant farming camp that's been freed by the Scorpions—they've seized the road that leads there, they're expecting you. But I need you two to wake the rest of the staff and get them ready to go right now, hear? Because as soon as we're done here, we're burning this ripping place to the ground."

The women exchanged another glance. Aster felt a sudden wrench of doubt in her gut. Maybe they didn't want this. Compared to most dustbloods, they lived well—in a mansion, with clothes on their backs and food in their bellies.

But then, that was what everyone had said about living in the welcome house, too, and it had not made Aster yearn for freedom any less.

"Colin and Anthony are on the second floor, in the two master bedrooms at the end of each corridor," the second woman said at last.

"Give them hell for us," the first woman added.

Aster exhaled, and her grin widened. "We'll try our best," she said, tipping her hat in gratitude.

The women disappeared up the back stairs to wake the other dustbloods. Aster turned around to face her friends.

"All right, we don't have a minute to spare," she said, still thinking of Zee and Eli. "Raven, I want you to stay here and help the staff. Tansy, Mal, I want you to go find the kids and get them to safety—they're not to be harmed, hear? Everyone else, follow me. We're going after the brothers."

They split up. Aster's group went first, with Derrick at her left, Violet at her right, and Clementine covering their backs. The excess that had been on display in the kitchen was even worse upstairs, but now Aster was glad of it. The plush carpeting muffled their footsteps. The heavy furniture provided them with cover. The many windows let plenty of moonlight into the darkened rooms, giving them just enough light to see by. More than once Aster startled at a black shape in the corner of her eye only to discover it was the stuffed and mounted head of a boar or a ram or a twelve-point stag. Every room boasted trophies. These were men who killed without restraint, for no other reason than the pleasure and power of it. The sick feeling in Aster's stomach deepened. They would not hesitate to kill her.

Derrick wiped at the sweat on his forehead as they started up the stairs.

"Keep it together," Clementine whispered harshly from behind them.

"I'm trying," Derrick whispered back, "but these are not going to be easy men to subdue."

"You'll be fine, Derrick," Violet promised. "I've already risked too much for your pretty head. I'm not going to let anything happen to it now."

They reached the second floor, where the corridor split in

two. Sure enough, just as the kitchen staff had promised, light flooded out from underneath the cracks of the doors at the end of each hallway. Aster drew her revolver, her heart climbing her throat. She had no intention of using it, but this would go easier if the landmasters thought she did.

"Should we split up?" Clementine asked. "Take them at the same time?"

"We better," Aster said quietly. She hesitated, trying to decide how best to divide themselves. She wanted Violet at her side—Violet, who had been ready to kill a man just moments ago to spare Aster the ugliness of it. Or Clementine, with her stubborn confidence. But then she looked at Derrick, shivering like a kitten, and knew she could not in good conscience leave him with anyone else. She sighed. "Clem, you and Violet go right. Derrick and I will go left."

Violet caught Aster's eye. "All right, but if there's trouble, you better holler."

"You know I will."

Aster and Derrick set off down their corridor, creeping along the papered wall. Muffled voices rose and fell from behind the door at the end. They sounded like they were having an argument. Aster panicked when the floorboards squeaked underfoot, worried it had given her away, but whoever was on the other side of that door seemed to be rowing too loudly to notice.

"I told you I needed the bedroom this evening, Winnifred!" a deep voice bellowed. "Have one of the serving girls draw you a bath and come back in an hour."

Almost there now.

"I won't be chased out of my own bed, not again, not tonight—" a second voice said shrilly.

"What, you'd rather stay and watch?"

"*Damn* you, Colin. And damn your dirty Lucker bitch—"

Aster slammed the door open.

"On the ground!" she ordered, raising the revolver to point it square at Colin Harker. He was a short, meaty man, swaddled in a forest green robe and house slippers. Next to him, in a nightgown, stood a bony woman who Aster assumed was his wife, Winnifred. And sitting on the bed behind them, dressed only in a silk slip—

"He has a fortuna?" Derrick whispered, sounding shocked.

The dustblood girl looked to be no older than Clementine, with straight black hair that draped over her frightened face like a veil and a gemstone favor that glittered on her golden skin. Aster's vision went white with rage, her chest suddenly so tight it felt ready to burst.

"*On the ground!*" she ordered again when the Harkers remained frozen in stunned silence.

"Y-You're the leader of the Reckoners," Winnifred stammered.

"Damn right," Derrick said in a clear, steady voice. He raised his own revolver. "Now do as she says."

"The children—" she choked out desperately.

"Won't be harmed," Aster promised. She took another step forward, her revolver clicking as she released its safety. "But you two will, if you don't cooperate."

Winnifred began to sink to her knees, but Colin stepped forward, shielding her behind his arm.

"You think you can bully me? In my own house? I'll have my raveners strip the flesh from your bones and hang your skull above the mantle."

"Your raveners are dead," Aster said, hoping it was true.

Colin's jaw tightened, the thick muscles twitching beneath his muttonchops.

"You lie."

A gunshot rang out from the other end of the hall then. A hunting rifle, by the sound of it. Aster and Derrick exchanged a frightened look. Neither Violet nor Clementine had a rifle. It was someone else, shooting at them.

"Should we—" Derrick whispered.

Colin slammed into him. Aster had only taken her eyes off the landmaster for a moment, but he moved with surprising speed, and before she had a chance to react the two men were wrestling on the ground. Derrick kicked and scratched, squirming out of Colin's grip, while Colin pummeled Derrick with heavy fists. Aster trained her gun on him, her blood beating so hard in her head that she saw red, her sweat-slippery finger hovering over the trigger. But she couldn't pull it, not without risking hitting Derrick. She knew she needed to help him, knew she needed to holster her gun and fight Colin Harker with her bare hands, but the idea of getting any closer to him, of putting herself within range of those grasping, hairy hands, of pressing her body up against his, half naked now that his robe had fallen open—

Nausea rolled through her. Her mind was beginning to float away.

No, not now, by the dead, not NOW—

319

Derrick raked his nails down Colin's face, pulling red ribbons of blood from his cheek. Colin let out a roar of pain.

"STOP!" Winnifred shrieked.

Aster whirled around. Winnifred was holding the young fortuna up against her, a penknife to the girl's throat.

"You're here for this little whore, aren't you?" she said venomously. "That's your whole crusade? Free the Good Luck Girls? You'll get no complaint from me. All your kind do is tempt good men to evil."

Aster locked eyes with the girl, who had still not said a word, her face a mask of terror.

"You don't hurt her," Aster warned Winnifred Harker.

"Put your gun down and I won't have to."

Derrick and Colin were still struggling behind Aster. She could hear them. She risked a glance over her shoulder and saw that Colin had now gotten on top of Derrick and wrapped his hands around his neck. Squeezing. Derrick flailed like a fish caught on a line. His dustkerchief still covered most of his face, but what Aster could see of it was turning red.

He's going to kill him.

You have to shoot him, now—

"I SAID PUT IT DOWN!" Winnifred said again, and she pressed the knife against the girl's throat so that a line of blood welled up beneath it. The girl let out a cry of pain and fear.

"*All right!*" Aster cried, immediately dropping her gun and holding her hands up. Her heart had climbed up her throat. She couldn't breathe. In her recklessness, in her ambition, she was going to get this girl killed, and she would never forgive herself for it. "All right, please, just—"

"Aster . . ." Derrick whispered weakly.

He had fumbled his gun out of its holster, but he didn't turn it on Colin Harker. He turned it upwards, to the glittering gasolier that hung above them all. Colin must have seen the weapon from the corner of his eye because he let out a curse, but he didn't move quickly enough.

The sudden crack of a gunshot tore the air in two. The bullet cut through the chain hanging from the ceiling. The gasolier began to fall. Time seemed to slow. Winnifred yelped and jumped clear of danger, abandoning the Good Luck Girl. Aster leapt forward to push the girl out of the way. They crashed into the nightstand with bruising impact, and the gasolier shattered on the ground just behind them in an explosion of glass. The room had been plunged into the same near darkness as the rest of the house, but Aster could just see, in the pale moonlight, Derrick freeing himself of the shocked landmaster's grasp. Colin reached for him again. Derrick shot him once, in the meat of his hand. Colin howled and rolled onto his back, clutching the wound.

"It's done," Derrick panted, standing up, holstering his weapon. He turned to Winnifred, who remained crumpled in the corner. "It's *done*."

Aster stood shakily as well, helping the fortuna girl to her feet.

"Thank you," the girl said quietly, her voice thick with tears.

Aster gave her her jacket to cover herself and held her close.

"You're safe now," she promised. Then she turned to Derrick, not even sure how to begin to express her gratitude. "Listen—"

Violet and Clementine came running into the room from down the hallway.

"What the hell is going on here?" Violet demanded.

Aster let out a laugh of relief. "Here? What was going on over *there*? We heard a gunshot."

"That was me," Violet said. "Anthony was already in bed when we broke in. He tried to get up and grab the rifle over his fireplace, but I got to it first and fired a warning shot. He was docile as you like after that. He's tied up and ready to go."

"*Damn you*," Colin snarled.

"Don't start," Derrick snapped, bending down to hogtie him. Colin struggled, crying out in pain when his injured hand was yanked behind his back, only for Derrick to neatly gag him with a rag.

"This one saved us," Aster said, beaming at Derrick. "We didn't know Colin had a fortuna. Miss—ah—"

"Sapphire," the girl supplied, pulling her long hair away from her face.

"Sapphire here needs to be taken downstairs so Raven can make sure she gets to safety along with all the other staff. And tell them to finish gathering their belongings quickly," Aster added. "As soon as they're done I'm setting fire to this place."

Violet and Clementine nodded, escorting Sapphire gently away.

"You're monsters," Winnifred sobbed from her corner. "All of you. You have no shame, no honor—"

"On the contrary," Aster said wearily, "we're showing you all a great deal more mercy and restraint than you and your friends have ever shown us. Colin and Anthony will be allowed to live, which is more than they deserve. And you, Mrs. Harker, will be allowed to go free, which is more, frankly, than you deserve."

322

"Why?"

"Because you clearly don't care a rip about other women, at least not ones like us."

"No, no," she babbled. "I mean why are you sparing me? What do you people want?"

Aster's mouth hardened. She crouched down on her haunches, so she was at eye level with the fairblood woman, close enough now to smell her perfume.

"I am sparing you because no child deserves to grow up motherless," Aster said, tears burning in her eyes as she thought of her own parents. "And I want you to raise yours to be better than you." She stood then, pointing towards the door. "So go, now. The little ones will already be outside."

Winnifred's eyes were dark and furtive as she looked first at Aster, then at Derrick, then at her husband, trussed up as neatly as the game he hunted. Her face contorted with anger at first, but then, like something collapsing under its own unbearable weight, it was gone, and she simply looked tired, even relieved. She stood, with as much dignity as she could muster, and left them to their work.

"Well done, Aster," Derrick said, crossing his arms as he watched the woman go. Even with the dustkerchief around his face, Aster could sense he was smiling. At his feet, Colin continued to struggle vehemently, his protests almost comprehensible through the gag in his mouth. Aster smiled back at Derrick, sorry she had doubted him.

"Not too bad yourself," she said softly.

CHAPTER TWENTY-FIVE

The rest of the job was pulled off with tense efficiency, although it was still another hour before Aster and her friends turned their backs on the Harker estate, the manor home engulfed in flames behind them, tongues of orange fire licking up hungrily at the night sky. Zee and Eli had fended off the last of the raveners, Raven had seen the dustbloods off safely in a wagon they could ride to the nearby farming camp, and the Harker brothers had been slung over the backs of the horses, ready to be taken back to Camp Red Claw.

The journey home was arduous, made no better by the Harker brothers' making it difficult every chance they got, but everyone's spirits seemed high. Against all odds, they'd finally done it: they'd taken not one, but two powerful landmasters prisoner. And with Sullivan dead and Cain captured by Cora's crew, there were only two men left of the Landmasters' Guild's leadership: Dennis Boyle, prince of the shipping industry, and Jerrod McClennon himself. The Guild was surely losing its influence over Authoritant Lockley and the rest of the Arkettan government, while the Reckoners had surely become impossible for them to ignore. Lockley might give in to their demands any day now. Aster could not wait to hear what news she'd missed in their absence, and the anticipation kept her going through the blistering heat of the days and the bitter cold of the nights.

But once they finally got back to camp, her first job, of course, was to see the Harker brothers safely locked away.

"Take them to the kennels," Aster ordered Eli, while the rest of her friends retreated for some much-needed rest. The Harkers had been blindfolded for the whole of the journey so they wouldn't know where the Scorpion camp was hidden, and Eli guided them carefully on foot towards the long, low building where the camp's dogs were kept. Scorpions and hotfoots alike jeered at the landmasters as they passed.

"My brother's going to have a heartstorm trying to keep everyone from tearing these two apart," Eli muttered out of the side of his mouth. "I'd say he needs to post guards, but they couldn't be trusted, either."

"We'll have to guard them ourselves," Aster agreed, though she hardly blamed anyone who wanted a piece of these bastards. "I'll make sure one of us is with them at all times to see they're not harmed."

"And to see that they don't try to break out, I'd hope," Eli said, raising a brow at her.

Aster snorted through her nose. "Don't worry yourself about that. They're not going anywhere."

They entered the kennels and locked the Harker brothers up in an empty one at the end of the row, at last removing their blindfolds and gags and the binds around their hands. Then Aster sent Eli for food and water—she would not starve her prisoners, whom she needed alive, but neither would she let her guard down around them. It wasn't just them who had to be protected from everyone else. She had to protect everyone else from them as well.

The barks of the dogs in the neighboring kennels echoed through the small space, the racket making Aster's head ring. The Harker brothers considered her with hate.

"You will die for this, Lucker," Colin promised. His face was deeply tanned from traveling, but Aster could still see the red beneath his cheeks well enough.

"Maybe so," she said idly, "but if I do, I'm taking you with me beyond the Veil."

He spat at her. It was not the first time. He had done so whenever they'd taken his gag off to try to feed him on the road. His brother, too. Aster curled her lip in disgust. A pulse of anger beat through her, making spots swim in her vision, but she swallowed it back. These men were at *her* mercy, in *her* power. She would not let them rattle her.

Eli returned with the food—hardtack and salted pork—and a jug of water for them to share. Anthony, who had done nothing but glare with his bloodshot eyes, sat up straighter and sneered.

"We're not eating any more of your shit food," he said.

"Then you'll starve," Eli said bluntly, cracking open the diamond-wire fence door and shoving the tin plates through.

"No one's going to starve," Colin shot back. "The law will find this place and bring it down around your ears by this time tomorrow."

"They've been looking for us for a long time, and they haven't found us yet," Eli said. He'd also brought two pillows and rough blankets, which he tossed into the kennel. "So you'd better make yourselves comfortable."

"How generous," Anthony said dryly.

"It is, actually," Aster said. "Let me tell you how things are going to work, gentlemen. The only way you two get out of here is if Authoritant Lockley and the rest of your friends in the capital meet our demands. So, if you have any information that could help us speed that process along, it's going to be in your best interest to tell us."

"We're not telling you degenerates anything."

"That's fine, too. Then we'll keep rounding up members of your little guild until there's no one left to stop us."

Colin slammed his hand against the bars, making the metal ring out. "What the hell gives you the right?"

"What gave your ancestors the right?" Aster demanded, raising her voice despite herself. "They labeled thousands of people criminals whose crimes were far less than yours. People whose only crimes were to steal bread when they were hungry or to love the wrong person or to fight back against the armies that had come to conquer them. But *you*—you rape and torture and kill. You steal land and lives. And you make yourselves rich as kings while doing it. It's time you pay your dues, Harker. Glory to the Reckoning."

Eli gave an ironic salute.

Colin looked like he was going say something further, but then the sound of someone approaching made them all turn.

Derrick.

What the hell is he doing here? Aster thought, her mind spinning. His partnership with them was still supposed to be a secret.

"Hullo," Derrick said awkwardly when he saw everyone's

eyes on him. He had washed up and changed into a fresh set of dress clothes, and he looked ready to do the Harkers' taxes.

"Go on, now, Red, this is grown folks' business," Eli told him, not unkindly. He had been looking at Derrick differently ever since the Harker job—if Aster didn't know better, she would have called it respect.

"I thought I could be useful," Derrick said. "I know what kind of questions to ask them—"

"Wait a minute, is that Baby *McClennon*?" Colin said incredulously. "Boy, why the hell aren't you locked up like us? What did you tell these bastards to get them to let you out? And what the rip have you done with your hair?"

"More important, why haven't you gone for help, you damned fool—" Anthony started.

Derrick scowled and held up a hand to stop them. "You're asking all the wrong questions," he said shortly. "*What do you expect from us? How can we be helpful to you?* These are the lines of inquiry you ought to follow."

"Derrick," Aster said quietly. "I appreciate your help, but we've got this—"

"Wait a minute," Colin said again. "I see what's going on here now." He pressed himself up against the fence, his knuckles white. "You were never locked up in the first place, were you, you little rat? You've been working with them the whole time."

Derrick's expression betrayed nothing. "Like I said, you shouldn't be concerning yourself with me right now."

"Traitor," Anthony declared. "By the Veil, we should have *known*. We mourned you like the dead, you know. Your mother

328

was inconsolable, and we all felt so sorry for her. To lose both her sons in the space of a year. But your father"—here Anthony sneered unpleasantly again—"your father never shed a tear. He said you were weak to have let yourself be captured in the first place. And you know what, Derrick? Your uncle agreed with him, much as it hurt him to admit it. They blame you for getting yourself caught by a bunch of back-hill Luckers. Imagine their shame when they find out you went with them *willingly*."

"I always knew you weren't worth a copper compared to Baxter, but this—this here is lower than a snake," Colin swore. "Couldn't live up to the expectations put on you so you just decide to help a bunch of dustbloods tear the whole thing down, do you? You fool. You *coward*."

Derrick had grown as red as Aster had ever seen him, wincing as if each word were a lash across his cheek. He opened his mouth to respond, his chin quivering, but Eli beat him to it.

"Mind how you speak to him," Eli said roughly. "Derrick's twice the man either of you will ever be. You all have no idea how much courage he's shown."

Derrick looked at Eli in disbelief. Eli gave him a single nod. Aster was so shocked she just stood with her mouth open as she struggled for words. But then her chest swelled with sudden affection for both of them.

How things have changed, Aster realized, that she could feel so at home with these two young men.

"Courage? How, by hiding down here?" Colin asked, oblivious to the sudden shift in the energy in the room.

"No, by choosing to do the right thing even though it's cost his family and his future," Eli said. "But it would have cost you two *nothing* to do the right thing and meet our demands, and still you refused."

"Actually, it would have cost us a *fortune*," Anthony spat. "It would have cost us the wealth that was left to us by our grandfathers, and that we would leave for our grandchildren. You would rob them of their future because you're too lazy to do the work yourself, and you'd rather just steal it."

Aster snapped out of her brief moment of warmth. "Us? The lazy ones? Us, the thieves—?"

A Scorpion boy came running into the room, panting and out of breath.

"What is it?" Eli asked, brow drawn in concern.

"It's the Lady Ghosts," he said. "The Lady Ghosts—have fallen."

Aster ran to the meeting hall, only to find it in chaos. At least a dozen Lady Ghosts were there, all of them mud-stained and clearly exhausted from traveling underground. Aster scanned the familiar faces looking for Priscilla—she would not believe the Lady Ghosts had fallen until she had heard it from their leader herself—but the old woman was nowhere to be found. Marjorie and Agatha, her second and third in command, were missing, too.

Sam was at the front of the hall, taking down the names of the women when they came up to him. He had pushed his sleeves up past his elbows, and he wiped the sweat from his brow with the back of his bare forearm. He did a double take as he spotted Aster, setting down his pen and striding towards her.

"Aster, thank the dead," he said in an undertone. "Here, come up front with me. They've been asking for you."

Aster held back. "What's going on here?" she asked, her voice thick, as if she were dreaming.

"Something terrible's happened. The Graveyard was discovered by the law. They had only a moment's notice. Most of them were rounded up and at least four women were killed, including Priscilla. These are the only ones who got away."

The words stuck in Aster's throat, and only one managed to escape her lips.

"*How?*"

"We don't know," Sam said quietly. "We think someone must have given them up—one of their fairblood allies who disagreed with the turn our actions have taken, probably. Northrock burning, landmasters disappearing, dustbloods in open revolt . . ."

"But the Ladies didn't even take part in those actions!" Aster protested. "They said specifically that they wanted to keep working within the law."

"You know as well as I do the law doesn't differentiate between the 'good ones' and the 'bad ones,'" Sam said bitterly. "And they *were* still borderjumping girls. That'll be more than enough to justify their capture, as far as the landmasters are concerned."

The weight of the responsibility of her actions pressed on Aster like grave dirt. First she'd gotten her parents killed, and now . . . the Lady Ghosts . . . Priscilla . . .

She suddenly remembered Priscilla's last words to her, spoken in such sadness.

I would wish you all to wander well, but I fear there's only suffering down this path you've chosen. And so, just go with my love.

She could not go up there. She could not speak to them. She had failed these women in every way.

"Aster—where are you going? *Aster!*" Sam called out.

Aster had turned and fled from the hall, tears streaming down her cheeks. She did not know whose comfort she wanted in that moment. She would not burden Clementine. She could not get close to Eli. Violet, perhaps—

Raven, Aster realized. Raven had to be told.

Aster searched for Raven at all of her usual haunts: the kitchens, where she and Tansy sometimes retreated to do some leisurely reading in the warmth and light; Sam and Eli's cabin, where she sometimes disappeared to after supper or a camp meeting; and the shooting range, where Mallow had been helping her better learn her way around a gun. At last, though, Aster found Raven at the cemetery, curled up against a headstone, the end of a leadpoint in her mouth and her sketchbook in hand. The little underground boneyard was a modest affair, and not one Aster had visited often—she didn't like to dwell on all the hotfoots who had died before finding freedom, or the Scorpions who had died trying to help them. But Raven had always claimed she enjoyed the peace and quiet, and found the company of the dead to be a comfort. It was the living she was unsure of.

She looked up from her sketchbook as Aster approached, setting it down and pulling the leadpoint from her mouth.

"Why the long face, boss? Don't tell me the Harker boys broke out already," Raven said with a smirk. Then her smile faded as Aster drew closer and Raven seemed to see how distraught she really was. "By the Veil, I was just kidding. Did they really—?"

Aster shook her head. "It's not them," she said, sitting down beside her friend on the cold ground. She swallowed, her throat swelling with fresh tears. "It's the Lady Ghosts."

Aster told her what had happened. Raven listened, her scowl deepening. Her face remained dry of tears, but Aster knew better than to think that meant she felt no grief. She was just, more than any of them, used to holding her emotions in, only letting them spill out on the pages of her sketchbook.

"Priscilla always knew the law would catch them eventually," Raven muttered, rubbing at a smudge of lead on the pad of her palm. "I reckon it's a testament to the Ladies' strength that they—that *we*—lasted this long."

Aster wiped a tear from her cheek with her thumb. She hadn't thought of it like that.

"This means we have to win, though," she said. "The Good Luck Girls who are still out there, they don't have anyone left to fight for them. If this plan doesn't work . . . we *have* to win, Ray."

"And we *will*," Raven promised. "You just trust me on that."

Aster looked up at her through the film of her tears. She had lost her mother, and she had lost the woman who had been like a mother to her, but she still had, at least, an older sister in Raven. She still had someone looking out for her. Warmth filled Aster's chest at the thought.

"Forgive me," she said, clearing her throat, now a little self conscious. "I'm making this about me when you're the one who knew her longer."

Raven looked away, her jaw working. "Yeah, well . . ." She shrugged a shoulder. "I kind of had a feeling when I left the Graveyard that it was going to be a one-way ticket. I said my goodbyes to Priscilla before I went. I just . . . always thought it would be me who got killed, not her."

Aster felt the threat of fresh tears, and she wiped them away quickly. She curled her knees up to her chest and rested her chin on them, wrapping her arms around her legs, letting out a long, shaky breath.

Raven sighed and turned to face her squarely. "Aster," she began, "sometimes I wonder—it just seems like this is all getting to be too much. I'm worried about you. Is there someone you can . . . you know . . . talk to?"

"I'm talking to you," Aster said, as if it were obvious.

Raven laughed a little. "Well, yeah, this time, because it's about Priscilla. But I know there are other things you wouldn't feel comfortable talking to me about. It's like you're still trying to earn my respect, somehow, so you're afraid of looking like too much of a fool in front of me." She gave her a playful shove. "As if I don't already respect the hell out of you."

Aster felt her cheeks warm. She hadn't realized it was that obvious.

"What about little Eli?" Raven went on. "I know you two are sweet on each other."

"Not as sweet as *you* are on his *brother*," Aster accused, rather than answering a question she'd just as soon avoid. "I've seen your drawings of Sam. All that's missing are some little hearts around his face."

Raven blushed. "He's called on me *once* or *twice*," she

334

admitted. "We're taking it slow, but still, it's been . . . good for me, I suspect, to be with someone who's a little childish. Neither of us got to be children. It's like I'm getting a second chance with him." She turned the focus squarely back on Aster. "And listen, if that's what Eli's been for you, then I'm glad."

"I . . . wouldn't say that," Aster said carefully. Raven arched her brow. "No, really, Ray . . . nothing's happened," Aster insisted. "Every time Eli even gets close to me . . . I keep waiting for the day when it doesn't make me tense up, but . . . I'm starting to think that day's never going to come."

Aster tried to keep the bitterness and shame out of her voice, but it crept through anyway, forcing her tears back to the surface. By the dead, she was having a day.

"He's such a good man," she went on. She couldn't stop, not now that she'd started. "If ever there were a man I could . . . you know . . . you'd think he'd be the one. The way he tried to comfort me when we found out about my parents—but even then, when he held me, I flinched. And maybe that's just the way I am now."

"Aster, you have to give yourself some time," Raven said gently. "It's only been a year since you escaped the welcome house. You're still healing from that. And there's so much else going on besides. Just because you're feeling fragile now doesn't mean there won't come a time when you're ready to do more, or a person you're ready to do it with."

"But what if I'm *never* ready?" Aster asked, giving voice to a fear she'd much rather have kept buried.

"Even so. That doesn't mean you wouldn't be able to have something just as special with someone as you would have otherwise." Raven sighed, leaning back against the gravestone. "I've been at this a little longer than you, Aster, and I've seen it all. I've met women who were able to find much comfort in the arms of a good man. I've met women who found more comfort in continuing their sundown work, but this time under their own power. I've met women who could only stand to be close to other women after the welcome house, and women who couldn't stand to be close to anyone at all. And I've met women who were uneasy around me, because of the kind of woman I am . . . and I had empathy for them, as long as they had empathy for me, too, as another woman and their sister, and one who's felt more conflicted about my body than they ever could. It's taken me *years* to learn to love myself, to not feel betrayed by my own flesh and bones. And I reckon it's going to take you a long while, too. You just have to be patient with the process."

"I'm not a patient person," Aster mumbled. But still, it felt reassuring to hear Raven's words.

"Listen, if you rush it, you're just going to get yourself hurt," she went on. "Trust that Eli will wait for you. And if he won't, he wasn't worth your time anyway. But Aster, as someone who's trying to look out for you, I have to ask—do you actually even *want* something with this boy, or do you just want to prove to yourself that you can do it?"

The words caught in Aster's throat. "I . . . both," she said finally.

"Because if you're in this for the wrong reasons—"

"Raven, I *have* to make this work," she almost pleaded. "This may be my only chance at something real. Because as

336

uncomfortable as I can get around Eli, he's still the only person I've been able to get close to at *all*."

"Come on, now, we both know that's not true," Raven said with a soft snort.

But Aster didn't see any humor in the situation. "Do we? Who else has there been? Derrick? I care for him, truly, but he knows I don't feel any—"

"No, you fool. Violet."

Aster felt a sudden punch of panic in her chest.

"Don't mess with me," she said, her voice soft with warning. "Not today."

"I'm not. I've seen the way you two are with each other. That's what 'something real' looks like."

"You have no idea what you're talking about. You barely even know us." Aster didn't know why she was getting so defensive, where this heat creeping up her neck had come from. She saw the hurt flicker across Raven's face and felt a pang of regret, especially given how Raven had taken her in tonight.

But Raven didn't back down, her brows coming together in defiance. "You're hurt. You're scared. You're lashing out. I get it. But I *do* know you, Aster, much as you may try to hide your truest self away. You spend all your free time drawing people, and pretty soon reading their body language becomes second nature," she said, talking about herself now. "I've seen the way the edges of Zee's eyes crinkle up when his smile's genuine, and the way he shows too many teeth when he's just trying to make your sister laugh. Tansy tends to drop her shoulders and shrink into herself when she's upset, while Mallow tends to puff herself up. Sam touches

337

the stumps of his missing fingers whenever he's unsure of himself; he doesn't even realize he's doing it. And you, Aster—you feel like you have to make yourself strong for everybody *except* for Violet. Your whole body softens up when she's around. Your brow relaxes, your fists unfurl. And trust me when I tell you she's no better. Tucking her hair behind her ear every other minute, tugging at her dress to make sure it's fitting right, checking for your reaction every time she speaks up in the group. That girl looks down on everyone, but she looks up to you."

Even as Raven spoke the words, Aster knew them to be true, but they filled her with a fear she could not even begin to confront. It was as if she were walking over a bottomless black pit.

"How do I know . . ." She swallowed, still on the verge of tears, her throat burning. "How do I know I'm not just turning to a woman because I'm afraid? Of men?"

Raven sighed. "Well, maybe that's played a part. But then again, maybe it hasn't. Maybe those feelings were always there, but you needed to get away from the welcome house before you felt safe enough to acknowledge them. Maybe it's not about women or men or anyone else, but about this *one* person. Or maybe you're right, and you've changed because of the things that've happened to you, and what you're feeling now has grown out of that. It doesn't make the feeling any less real."

It was a conversation that, if she'd ever worked up the courage, Aster might've expected to have with Tansy and Mallow. They loved girls, loved each other, and always had. But Aster knew, though they would have helped her gladly, that she would have been too embarrassed to ask them. They were so much younger than her, but so much more confident in this. And they understood nothing of the sundown work that had so scarred Aster's heart.

No, it was right that it was Raven. Raven, who did not expect Aster to know everything; Raven, who herself knew exactly what it felt like to have these feelings twisted up in something ugly. Aster felt so lucky to have her.

The tears spilled freely now. "I'm sorry," Aster choked out.

Raven laughed gently. "What the hell for?"

"I just am."

"There's nothing to be sorry about." Raven opened her arms for a hug, and Aster curled up into them.

"Please don't tell anyone," Aster whispered with sudden urgency. "About Violet, I mean." She did not like this sudden feeling of vulnerability, as if she were a remnant and now anyone could see through her.

"Of course not."

"They wouldn't believe you anyway. A year ago I was trying to kill her. I may still. She likes to test me."

"Not so fast," Raven said with a chuckle. "We have to finish off these damn landmasters first. For Lady Ghost."

Yes, Aster thought, at last wrung dry of her tears. *For Lady Ghost.*

CHAPTER TWENTY-SIX

The last great landmaster family they had to take down before the McClennons was the Boyle family, but unfortunately, the Boyles were well beyond their reach. They lived south of the Scab, along Arketta's narrow coastline, overseeing the dustbloods that worked in the port cities. The north of Arketta was dense with industry, but the south remained rugged and unfinished, as if the Scab were a sieve through which only the crumbs of the north's riches could fall through. Aster had no contact with the dustbloods who lived there: the railroads had not yet made it that far, the Scorpions' tunnels ran the other way, and to send a coded message by post would take longer than she felt like they now had. The loss of the Lady Ghosts had cut the legs out from under all of them, and the air in the camp was heavy with dread and despair. Aster could only imagine the rest of their allies were feeling the same, maybe wondering if they were next, questioning whether they ought to get out of this while they still could. The Landmasters' Guild was old and powerful and might yet survive the blows they'd dealt it, but the Reckoners were new, their bonds still brittle, and one more loss like this could destroy them.

They had to end this. Now.

The problem was, Derrick didn't know much more about the Boyles than the rest of them. The family's visits to the Scab had been few and far between, and he'd only just met Jonah Boyle, the head of the family and its business, for the first time at the emergency meeting after the Northrock fire. Derrick couldn't tell them anything about where they might find the man, or who he kept company with, or when he might next be in the Scab— only that he was a self-proclaimed man of morals who had refused to drink or gamble with the others and would be difficult to catch off guard.

"At this rate you're more likely to get help from the Harkers than me," Derrick had admitted when Aster pressed him for more information.

And he'd been joking, but Aster took it to heart. The Harker brothers would know more about the Boyles than anyone.

She just had to get them to talk.

Violence—against evil men, yes, but still, men who couldn't fight back. It was an unsavory prospect, and not one Aster was prepared to face alone. But neither was it something she felt comfortable asking of anyone else . . . except, perhaps, Violet. Which was why Aster found herself outside Violet's cabin now, heat creeping up her neck as she worked up the courage to knock on the door.

Pull it together, Aster scolded herself. She was embarrassed that she had let herself be so honest with Raven last night. She had been drunk on her own grief, reckless with her feelings, and even now a soft haze of tender sentiment clung to her like a hangover. She tried, desperately, to clear her head. She wanted to see Violet because Violet was the only one with the stomach for the plan she had in mind. That was all this was.

She knocked on the door.

Tansy answered—she and Mallow shared the cabin with Violet and Raven. Her eyes were reddened, as if she'd been recently crying.

"Oh, Aster," she said, her voice subdued. "We were just talking about the Lady Ghosts."

"That's actually why I'm here," Aster admitted. "Or at least . . . part of the reason . . . is Violet around?"

"Where else would I be?" Violet asked with a heavy sigh from her bed. Aster looked past Tansy, to where Violet sat up on her top bunk. Raven sat below her on the bottom bunk, looking at Aster pointedly, as if she knew what Aster had just been thinking about. Aster glanced away, her cheeks heating.

"Tell me you two have a plan to avenge Priscilla," Mallow pleaded.

"Maybe," Aster said. "But I want to run it by Vi first. Do you—do you have a minute?"

"Always," Violet said, jumping down. Tansy let her pass, looking between them curiously.

"Thanks," Aster muttered, and she motioned for Violet to follow her.

"It's funny," Violet said quietly as they walked through the subdued camp. "It was me who convinced everyone to go chasing after Lady Ghost, and now I'll be the only one of us who never met her."

"Priscilla would be the first to tell you that Lady Ghost was bigger than her," Aster replied. "It wasn't born with her, and it wasn't supposed to die with her, either. But . . ."

". . . but?" Violet pressed when Aster didn't finish.

"But we can't let the landmasters hit us like that again. It'll be the end of the whole fight. So we have to do whatever it takes to beat them now, before they ever get the chance."

"Whatever it takes," Violet echoed, her blue eyes meeting Aster's, understanding slowly rising in them. They'd reached the kennels now, and Aster stopped outside the wide double doors, dismissing the Scorpion who was on guard.

"The Harkers will have information on Jonah Boyle, information it might take us weeks to gather on our own," Aster went on once he'd left. "But if we could just . . . you know . . . pry it out of them . . ."

"With a pair of pliers?" Violet suggested, raising a brow.

Aster looked away, hot with shame. This wasn't who she was. But it was who she had to be.

"If you don't want any part of it—" Aster began.

Violet smirked. "Don't be ridiculous. A man needs torturing, and you thought of me? I can't remember when I last felt so flattered."

"Vi, I'm serious."

"So am I," she said, the smirk fading. She stepped closer, lowering her voice so passersby wouldn't hear them. "Look, I get it. Why you came to me for this. You don't want to stain any of the others' souls. You're not even sure you want to stain your own. But mine is already black and dripping, so what's one blot more? And I'll have you know I agree—you ought to let me do this. We both know I'm bound for hell, Aster. I'd just as well have it be for you."

"No, that's not what I—" Aster's words got lost in the swirling fog of her mind. She suddenly felt feverish, her heart jumping in her chest. "I don't think you're—I'd never *use* you like that, Violet," she finally managed. "I just . . . trust you, that's all. To help me do what needs to be done and not to judge me for it. But it *will* be me who does this, hear?"

"Together, then," Violet insisted, stubborn as always. "I'll play the black hat, and you the white. Now, give me your knife."

Aster hesitated for a moment more, then surrendered the blade. Violet grinned as she took it.

"There, now, that wasn't so hard, was it?" she asked, and she pushed the doors open.

Aster followed her into the kennels, equally flustered and frustrated.

"Look, the way I see it, they're soft men who've led soft lives," Aster whispered, to reassure herself more than anything. "It won't take long for them to break."

"Better start with Anthony, then, if that's your thinking. He's the softer of the two."

They fell into silence as they approached the kennels where the Harker brothers were kept. As Aster had instructed, they'd been given cots, pillows and blankets, a bucket of water for washing up, and a first-aid kit to tend to their cuts and bruises. The empty dishes on the ground were proof that they'd been eating their meals, too. Despite this, though, both men looked haggard and haunted, their hair limp and greasy, their faces grubby and beginning to scruff, their eyes bloodshot and bruised from exhaustion. Aster pushed back a wave of contempt. Less than twenty-four hours of living like most

344

dustbloods did—better, even—and they seemed to have fallen apart completely.

"Well, if it isn't the bitch who seduced Baby McClennon," Colin said nastily when he saw Violet. "The boy's weak. I'm not surprised he was led astray. But Jerrod should have known better than to trust you."

"Jerrod McClennon is a bigger fool than most folks seem to realize," Violet said smoothly. "He couldn't see past the shadow at my feet. The man believes wholeheartedly that fairbloods represent the best of humanity, that we are inherently 'decent' and 'honorable' in a way dustbloods are not. But you know . . . and *I* know . . . that that's never been true, has it? We can be more wicked by half, and we can get away with it, too."

Violet drew the knife.

"What the hell is this?" Anthony asked slowly, backing away from the fence. He turned to Aster. "What the hell is this?"

"I'm going to make this simple, Harker," Aster said. "We need to know where we can find Jonah Boyle, and you're going to tell us."

"Why? So you can drag him down here, too? I don't think so." But Anthony's voice trembled as he spoke, his eyes shining with uncertainty, fixed on the knife. Perhaps he could sense how things had changed since Aster had spoken to them last.

Violet opened the door to his kennel. Its hinges groaned.

"We don't want to hurt you," Aster continued as they approached. "I'll let you and your brother both write down your answers, and if they match, we'll take this no further."

She heard a rattling crash as Colin threw himself against the fencing of his own cage. "This is madness. When I get out of here, I swear I'll—"

"No," Anthony cut him off. "They're bluffing. They need us alive."

"Alive, but not unharmed," Violet corrected.

Anthony paled, but he set his jaw. "Even so. I'm not telling you anything. You may have been able to make a traitor of McClennon's boy, but you'll never make one of me."

"Because you have courage, right?" Violet asked. Anthony began to back himself into a corner, and Violet closed in on him, using the flat of the blade to sweep away the hair that had fallen in his frightened face. "Because you're not a coward? But I'm willing to bet the only people you've ever laid hands on are the ones who couldn't fight back. Men who called you boss. Women at the welcome house. And now, if you have your way, girls as young as thirteen. I don't know, Harker . . . seems pretty cowardly to me."

"I—I never laid hands on anyone—"

Violet curled her lip. "No? So you just paid raveners to do it for you, then. Even worse." She nodded at Aster. "Hold him down."

"But—"

Aster moved quickly, before she could second-guess herself. She buried a punch in the landmaster's gut to knock the wind out of him, then seized him by the shoulders and threw him to the ground. She held his arms down while Violet knelt on his chest, her knee digging into his rib cage. He coughed and swore in protest.

"*Shut up*," Violet hissed, pressing the point of the knife to Anthony's forehead. "The only thing I want to hear you talking about is Jonah Boyle."

"YOU STOP WHATEVER THE HELL YOU'RE DOING,"

346

Colin bellowed from his cage. Aster looked up at Violet, her stomach rolling with doubt, but Violet's focus remained unbroken, her blue eyes locked on Anthony's with frightening intensity. She began to carve a C into his forehead, a jagged, shallow cut.

"Where is Boyle?" Violet demanded.

"I told you, I'm no traitor!"

She carved an O.

"When will he next be in the Scab?"

"Just tell us what you know, Harker," Aster urged. But he only yelled incoherently, his eyes shut against the blood streaming down his face.

"YOU LET HIM GO! YOU LEAVE HIM ALONE!" Colin pleaded, pounding against the wall.

C-O-*W*-

"How many raveners does he employ?"

"*Damn you*," Anthony spat, struggling mightily, chest heaving with panicked breaths. His arms flexed against Aster's grip, and she resisted the revulsion that ran through her, the instinct to let him go. How many times had she been pinned down like this? Her conscience begged her to release him.

Violet started in on the letter *A*. Her lip curled to show her teeth, her delicate hands whitening as they tightened around the hilt of the knife.

"Violet—" Aster whispered.

"RECKONING DAY!" Colin cried suddenly from his kennel. Violet paused, looking up through the black curtain of her hair. "Boyle will be in the Scab for Reckoning Day!"

Anthony opened his bloodied eyes. "Colin, no—"

"The Landmasters' Guild holds a gala every year in Crimson

Glen to celebrate the holiday," Colin continued. "That's where you'll find Boyle. That's where you'll find all of them."

"*All* of them? Why wouldn't Derrick mention something that important?" Aster asked skeptically.

"Because that little whelp probably doesn't know it's still happening—we canceled the event after the Northrock fire out of concern for our safety. But now McClennon's putting it back on and insisting we all attend as a show of strength and solidarity to the public."

Aster and Violet locked eyes. Reckoning Day. It was only a week and a half away. It would take them most of that time just to travel south to Crimson Glen, the Scab's capital. But if they could make it in time for this gala, where all the remaining landmasters would be in one place . . .

Violet fixed her glare back on Anthony. "Is this true?"

He didn't speak, his expression twisted with pain and hate. Aster gritted her teeth and shook him, hard. "*Is this true?*"

"Yes, it's ripping true!" Colin bleated. "It's at the capitol building, at eight o'clock in the evening. Derrick's been every year since he was a baby. He can tell you whatever else you need to know. Now take your damned hands off my brother."

Aster was all too happy to do just that. Violet removed her knee from his chest as well, but she still held the knife on him as they stood and backed out of the kennel. Anthony climbed to his feet, snarling like a cornered animal.

"What did you do to me?" he demanded.

"Nothing a low-brimmed hat won't help to hide," Violet said evenly, locking him back in. "I'll make sure someone brings you one."

348

"You're a snake. A low-down, poisonous, yellow-bellied—"

"And you," Violet cut him off, "are every bit the coward I thought you were. You just be grateful I didn't get to finish writing it all over your face."

A look of horror rose in his eyes as his hands went to his maimed forehead. Aster and Violet left him to his self-pity, striding in step out of the kennels and closing the doors behind them.

"You were right. That didn't take long at all," Violet muttered, handing the knife back to Aster. She took it uneasily, wiping the blood off on her denims before sliding the blade back into her belt. Derrick's ring glinted on her hand, and his words echoed in her ears.

I am just so afraid of doing the wrong thing. Of being *the wrong thing.*

"I . . . need some air," Aster said haltingly.

Violet raised an eyebrow in question—it was rare anyone risked a trip aboveground unless they had to—but she followed Aster up to the surface. There they climbed up to sit on the low roof of one of the abandoned cabins in the ghost town aboveground. For a long time they just soaked up the sun, Aster's gaze straying from the decaying mining camp out to the impenetrable mountain forests beyond and back again. The remnants were out, as always, their translucent forms scarcely visible in the daylight, like the shimmer of the air on a scorching afternoon. After weeks of living here at Camp Red Claw, Aster had come to recognize the dead as well as any other landmark. The little girl drawing water from the well, the one-armed man smoking in front of his dilapidated house, the old woman asleep in her rocking chair. They were as familiar as the families in every tenant camp the Scorpions had freed. Generations without change.

"You don't think we went too far, did we?" Aster asked at last, the splintered shingles hard under her tailbone, the taste of dust bitter on her tongue.

"You must be kidding, right?" Violet snorted. Her legs swung idly in the air. "We barely touched Anthony. We didn't touch Colin at all. I swear you're getting soft on me, Aster."

"I'm getting tired," she sighed, tucking the bloody memories away with all her others. "There's a difference."

"Hey," Violet said. She turned towards Aster and cupped her cheek, the same hands that she had just moments ago used to cut Harker now infinitely gentle. Aster's face warmed, and she could only hope Violet didn't feel the heat under her palm. "We're almost done, hear?" she promised. "With all of this. If what Harker told us is true, we can end the whole thing on Reckoning Day."

"Yeah, but end it *how*? It's going to get much bloodier than this before it's over, Vi, especially if we're going to be fighting all these bastards at once. It's one thing to kill their raveners, most of them stopped being people a long time ago, but if we have to kill *them* . . ." Aster swallowed. "I'm still scared I don't have it in me . . . or worse, that I do."

Violet pulled away, her eyes downcast. She gripped the edge of the roof. "You don't need me to tell you these men deserve whatever hell we bring down on them," Violet murmured. "The dead know that *you* know better than most what they're capable of. But after some of the things I've seen, living with

McClennon . . . after some of the things he put me through . . . I'm not sure I wouldn't feel worse about letting them live."

Aster stilled. "What do you mean, 'after some of the things he put me through'?" she asked, struggling to keep her voice steady.

Violet glanced up at her, then looked away again just as quickly. Her jaw clenched. It was the first time today she seemed uneasy.

"I shouldn't have said anything."

"But now you have," Aster pressed.

"And I'll say no more. There's no point in upsetting you. It's over now."

Aster was already upset, though, acid anger creeping up her throat.

"Those months, after we left you with McClennon but before Derrick convinced him to free you . . . he . . . hurt you?"

She felt like a fool as soon as she said the words. Of course he had. She had always known, deep, at the base of her skull, that Violet would have been made to suffer as McClennon's prisoner. But she had hoped—had convinced herself—that it wasn't true.

Because if it were, she could never forgive herself.

"I thought you said you were able to convince him you regretted your actions," Aster went on. "That he treated you well because you were a fairblood."

Violet let out a hollow laugh that echoed through the empty streets. "I have no doubt he treated me better than any of you might have expected to be treated. But I would never go so far as to say he treated me *well*."

Aster's hands tightened into fists in her lap. "We should never have abandoned you."

"Don't start," Violet said roughly. "It was *my* choice to stay behind. You don't take that away from me."

"But—"

"And you came back for me, as soon as you learned I was alive. I haven't forgotten that. I'll never forget that."

"Anyone else would have done the same," Aster muttered.

"No, they wouldn't have," Violet insisted. "Nobody's ever risked *anything* for me before, let alone everything. Every day I wake up and try to be worthy of you, Aster."

There was a sudden queasiness in Aster's belly as she swallowed Violet's words, but it was a good feeling, a thrill, as if she were in the middle of a somersault. *That girl looks down on everyone, but she looks up to you*, that was what Raven had said about Violet. And Aster had been afraid to believe it, because that would have forced her to face her own growing love for this girl she had once hated. But if she truly had the courage that Violet seemed to see in her . . . if she truly was willing to risk everything for what she believed to be a worthy cause . . .

Aster met Violet's eyes, and for the first time, *she* reached out to *her*, cradling the curve of her neck with an unsteady hand, grazing a thumb along her jawline. Violet's lips parted in surprise. She softened under Aster's touch, her eyes fluttering shut.

"Dawn . . . what are you—"

Aster closed her own eyes and leaned into Violet, their lips meeting hesitantly at first, as if each of them was afraid of hurting the other, and then with more and more urgency. Violet pulled Aster closer, sliding a hand beneath her leather jacket and around the small of her back. Aster slid her tongue past Violet's lips, chasing the taste of her, drinking in her joy.

Aster had pressed her lips to another person's many times before this. But this—this was her first kiss.

After an endless moment, they pulled apart breathlessly, Violet's cheeks flushed pink. Aster was so light-headed she had to lie back on the roof to keep from tipping over the edge. Violet lay next to her, letting out a giddy laugh.

"By the Veil," she swore, her forearm thrown across her forehead. "Where the hell did that come from?"

"I'm only sorry I kept you waiting so long," Aster said. Her lips still tingled, and she pressed her fingers to them wonderingly. It had never felt like this before.

Violet's hand found hers, weaving their fingers together. "It's all right. You were being careful. So was I. After everything we've been through—"

"I know. I'd never want to—"

"Exactly."

They gave up, laughing again, then rolled to face each other, pressing their foreheads together. The sun was warm on their skin, the wind gentle as a caress.

"I'm never going to let them hurt you again, Violet," Aster promised, brushing the hair back from her forehead. "I'm ending this. Whatever it takes."

For the first time she could remember, Aster could see a life for herself beyond the fight, and that gave her more courage to finish it than any amount of fear or anger had ever done. Reckoning Day was less than two weeks away.

They would be ready.

CHAPTER TWENTY-SEVEN

No one in their group had ever been to Crimson Glen besides Derrick. He had been shocked that his uncle was going through with the gala, especially given how much tensions had risen since the Northrock fire. But, much to Aster and Violet's relief, he remembered enough of past galas to help them plan their infiltration of this one. They kept it simple: the local law would be prepared for the worst, so they would give it to them. The Scorpions, the Nine, and the remaining Lady Ghosts would stage a citywide riot, something on the scale of the uprisings led by the Northrock dustbloods. Fires set to buildings, statues pulled to the ground, banks emptied and all their shine returned to the people—nothing could be held back. They had to keep the badges busy.

Meanwhile, in the capitol building, Aster and her team—Tansy, Mallow, Violet, Clementine, Raven, Derrick, and Zee—would already be in place, disguised as servants. Their job was to take the whole party hostage. Derrick had told them the gala always started with a toast—if they could slip a sedative into the champagne, they could subdue everyone at once. After that, no one would be allowed in or out until the landmasters had given in to their demands.

"And if it takes days?" Tansy asked as Aster explained the plan to her friends. "There's only so much food and water in that building. What are we supposed to do if it runs out before they've given in?"

"Then we go hungry," Aster said without pause, looking around the table. "And they go with us."

There were murmurs of surprise at that, but Aster continued before anyone could lose their nerve.

"Think about it. These are men who have never missed a meal in their lives, men who have never known more than a moment's discomfort," she went on. "Look how quickly the Harker brothers were broken. Their friends are no better. If it comes down to a war of attrition, I promise you they will surrender."

"But Aster, if they *don't*—"

"Then they starve," Violet answered. She was leaning back in her chair, her long legs crossed and propped up on the table. This had been her plan, too, hers and Aster's, and they'd stayed up late into the night to come up with it, a frenzied energy passing back and forth between them like a voltric current. Aster still hadn't told anyone about the kiss—not even Raven, not even Clementine—but she felt a half-panicked certainty that everyone would be able to sense what they were to each other. How could anyone miss it? How had *she*?

"I thought we weren't going to let anyone die on our watch," Zee said carefully, drawing Aster's eye away from Violet.

"You don't have to be a part of it," Aster told him, not unkindly. She would not force this on anyone. "None of you

355

do. I can't pretend this isn't likely to be more deadly than anything else we've ever done—not just for them, but for us, too. But we're going to have all the remaining landmasters in one place—the politicians and the businessmen, the old families and the new blood. Jonah Boyle. *Jerrod McClennon*. We have to consider that this might be a real chance, our *last* chance, to cut off the head of this damned rattletail. You want to know where it ends, Zee? It ends *here*."

Things moved quickly after that, as they had to. Aster held a larger meeting with the Scorpions and the rebels of the Nine, and the next days were spent gathering supplies and rallying volunteers to send down to Crimson Glen. A skeleton crew of Scorpions would have to stay behind to take care of the hotfoots, but most of the boys were eager to join the fight. The Nine agreed on the condition that all precaution would be taken to avoid another massacre, and Sid suggested a network of scouts to watch the army forts nearest Crimson Glen and send word ahead if any troops were summoned so the Reckoners could retreat in time. The remaining Lady Ghosts took more convincing—some were still recovering from the tragedy at the Graveyard, while others were uncertain this was something Priscilla would have wanted. But plenty of others were glad for the chance to strike back at those who had hurt them, and they, too, started south to make their final move against the landmasters.

Once everyone else had been safely seen off, it was time at last for Aster and her team to leave. But Sam would not let them go without throwing one last party.

"This is madness," Aster grumbled as Sam personally ladled

a homemade cocktail into her empty glass. They were in the meeting hall one final time, and Sam, Cutter, and Eli had come to see them off. "How are you going to stand there and serve us bootleg punch as if we're not all on our way beyond the Veil?"

"All the more reason to drink up," Sam said brightly.

"What's even *in* this?" Clementine asked, scrunching her nose up at her own glass. The drink was candy apple red and swirling with sediment.

"That's actually a family secret—"

"Nah, you leave me out of it," Eli said with a low chuckle. He had already served them dinner and was now kicked back with his hands laced behind his smooth-shaven head, his wrinkled white apron still loose around his neck.

"I do wish you were coming with us, Eli," Derrick piped up.

Eli raised an eyebrow. "Why? You don't need me to save your skinny ass. I heard how you handled Harker."

Derrick's face reddened. "I—I hardly think I handled much of anything, but I appreciate the sentiment all the same."

"Honest to the dead, though, I wish I was going, too," Eli said, and his gaze flicked over to Aster. "I know you don't need saving, either, but still . . . I feel like a fool, staying back while the rest of you go and risk your lives."

"Eli, please," Zee said before Aster had even opened her mouth to respond. "Everyone knows you're needed here. These families won't last long without their cook. And *I* need you to be Emily's big brother for me until this is over. I'm willing to risk my life for the sake of her future, but only if there's someone I trust looking after her."

"Thank you, that's what I keep telling him," Sam said. He

had finished pouring the drinks and sat down beside Raven, stretching his arm around her. "What makes you think the girls want you tagging along anyway?"

Eli leaned forward, his somber gaze still fixed on Aster. "Don't they?"

Aster felt a flush of heat beneath her collar. He still had that effect on her, apparently, even if her messy feelings had led her to someone else. And she was sure he could sense it, too, just as she could sense that Violet, several seats down, was watching her for her reaction. But if Eli really was to stay at Camp Red Claw, this night might very well be their last together.

She owed him an answer. She only wished she knew how to give it.

"Of course we want you around, you fool," Raven said, coming to Aster's rescue. "Which is exactly why we can't have you throwing your life away to play the hero."

Aster looked at Raven gratefully, and Raven nodded almost imperceptibly. Eli's brow furrowed, his gaze sliding away.

Aster had a hard time focusing the rest of the night, her mind clouded by apprehension. She felt removed from the others as they drank themselves giddy, Mallow challenging the boys to an arm-wrestling contest, Zee starting up some raucous rangeman's drinking song, Derrick sharing exaggerated testaments to his spy work and Violet cheerfully declaring bullshit. This led to everyone recounting their wildest stories from the past year, the tall tales recited like wards of protection against the danger they'd soon face. *Remember when the raveners chased us across the gorge . . . remember when Aster almost missed the train . . . remember when Raven set the gambling hall on fire . . .* They'd survived before, and they would again, that was what they seemed to be telling themselves.

"It's a miracle any of you are still alive," Cutter said with a bewildered laugh.

Zee puffed up his chest. "They had my help."

"That's why it's a miracle."

Zee deflated, and Clementine laughed and ruffled his hair fondly. "Don't worry, Cutter, we'll make sure Zee gets back to camp in one piece."

"Although," Tansy broke in, eyes lit up with excitement, "if we're successful in all this, we won't even need this camp anymore. Dustbloods will be free."

"Well, it won't happen as fast as all that—" Derrick warned.

Mallow yanked the neck of his shirt over his head. "Shut up, we're celebrating."

"What, before we've even won?" Raven asked with a genial laugh.

"Bringing all the dustbloods together like this, and some fairblood friends, too? I'd say we've already won," Clementine said, and they all, even Aster, raised their glasses to that.

Once everyone had drained the last of their drinks they dragged themselves to bed in ones and twos. They had a long journey ahead of them down to Crimson Glen, and they couldn't jeopardize it by staying up any later than they already had. Aster lingered, though, until there was no one left but Eli, who had begun to wipe down the tables, and Violet, who hovered at her side.

"Everything all right?" Violet asked softly. "You've been quiet tonight."

"Just have a lot of my mind," Aster murmured. "But it's nothing for you to worry about. Go on to bed."

Violet slid a hand over her shoulder and gave it a reassuring squeeze before turning to leave the meeting hall. Eli watched her go from the corner of his eye, dunking his dishrag into a bucket of soapy water.

"Nothing for her to worry about," he said once Violet was gone. "What about me?"

Aster sighed, sliding down the bench to be nearer to him. "I never want you to worry on my account, Eli."

"And yet I do." He was no longer looking at her, focused intently on his work. "I see the way you're pulling away from me, and I worry that I've done something to offend you, or worse, to hurt you. I worry that something'll happen to you out there, and I'll never get to make right whatever went wrong between us."

"Nothing's gone wrong between us," Aster said urgently. She reached for his hand, stilling it. "It's always felt right when I'm with you. It still does. I've just . . . been having a hard time figuring out what it is I really want. No man's ever asked that of me before, not until I met you. It's not something I'm used to thinking about."

Eli looked down at their hands. He sat down across from her, his scowl softening. "Of course. I'm sorry. It was just, with you leaving, I thought maybe . . . but I didn't mean to force an answer."

"You're not. And you're right—you deserve to know before I go." Aster took a breath, steadying herself as she found her courage. "I love you, Eli, truly. And I'll never be able to tell you how grateful I am that you showed me I still had that kind of love in me. But if I'm being honest with myself, there's someone else I've loved even longer. I just didn't have the courage to admit it until now."

His brow crinkled, the corner of his mouth twitching, but otherwise his expression remained carefully neutral. "You can't mean Red."

"No. Violet."

Confusion rippled across Eli's face, then stilled into disappointment. He pulled his hand away.

"Violet," he repeated.

"No one's more surprised than me."

"So you're . . ." He seemed to be struggling for words. "You're like Tansy and Mallow, then? You never liked men?"

"No, Violet and I are different from Tansy and Mallow . . . we're different even from each other, probably. I know Violet's always liked men, and still does. Me, I'm not sure I ever liked anybody until I got out of Green Creek. I couldn't let myself feel much of anything in that place. So, like I said, all of *this* . . . it's new to me." Aster felt a twist of shame and embarrassment at that, that she should still be confused about such things when she was grown, but she pushed it down. "And Violet gets that," Aster pressed on. "She knows, better than anyone, what I've been through, because she's been through the same. I don't have to explain myself to her, or apologize, or pretend to be something I'm not. There's just this . . . *trust* between us. And I watched her build it, so I know how sturdy it is."

"That . . . makes sense," Eli conceded. He let out a long

breath, his shoulders relaxing. "I'm only sorry you didn't feel like you could trust me."

"But I did. I *do*," Aster said. "There are things you understand about me that a fairblood like Violet never could. It's been a great comfort for me, being able to talk to you earnestly about those things—as I hope it has been for you. And as I hope we may continue to do."

Eli's mouth curved into a smile for the first time that night. "Well, don't you worry about that. I'm sure we can work something out."

Aster hadn't realized how much she'd needed to hear those words until she did. Her relief spilled out of her in a laugh.

"You know," Eli went on, leaning forward now, "before you and your friends came rambling into our little camp here, I'd just about given up on the fight. My brother's always been a believer, but me . . ." He chuckled, shaking his head. "Well, you remember how I was when you met me. Hiding out in the kitchen, avoiding anyone who might want to 'talk earnestly' with me, staying away from the action, not because I didn't believe in the cause, but because I didn't believe it would ever do much good. And I just want to thank you for proving me wrong. I'm a better man, a happier man, for having met you, Aster, and nothing you've said today changes that."

Aster's eyes burned with tears. Eli stood to finish his work, and, before she could lose her nerve, Aster stood too and went around the table to embrace him. Eli let out an *oof* of surprise as her arms wrapped around his chest. She could feel the heavy thump of his heart against her rib cage. There was no panic in her blood for once, no humming in her skull.

Just the comfort of being near someone she loved. She let go before the moment could be lost.

"I'm praying to the dead we meet again, Eli. But in case we don't—wander well."

Eli smiled again, wider this time, pride in his eyes.

"Give them hell, Aster."

CHAPTER TWENTY-EIGHT

They only just made it to Crimson Glen in time for Reckoning Day.

The capital of the Scab was brimming with activity when Aster and her friends arrived, the city swathed in the shadows cast by the painted red-rock canyon walls. They didn't dare enter by way of the Bone Road, lined as it was with lawmen, so they scaled the deadwall instead, quietly subduing the patrolman on duty before climbing up and over. On the other side of the wall lay the largest city in the Scab that Aster had ever seen, its neat brick streets crisscrossing the red desert floor. Crimson Glen was not so big as Northrock, its buildings not nearly as tall or densely packed, but still, to see so many people and so many lights this deep in the Scab was startling. A carnival had even been set up on the far side of town in celebration of the holiday, the giant fun wheel at the heart of it turning with all the slow, smooth motion of a giant gear keeping the city running.

"It's a shame we aren't just here on holiday," Mallow said in awe. "Honest to the dead, I thought fun wheels were a myth."

"Hell, I thought *carnivals* were a myth," Raven muttered.

"*Focus*," Aster urged. They were wearing dustkerchiefs now, their favors soothed with the ghostweed salve, and they needed to find the safe house their allies had set up for them. The Reckoners who had traveled ahead of them were already in place all over the city, lying in wait until sundown to begin the uprising. But as Aster led them through the streets, keeping her head down to avoid the eyes of drunken revelers, the first punch of real fear sank into her gut. There were more lawmen on duty here than there had been even at McClennon's speech in Northrock, all of them armed with long guns and half of them leading dogs. The Reckoners might have had an advantage with their voltric weapons, but they would be outnumbered two to one. And if they couldn't keep the law busy while Aster and her friends infiltrated the gala . . .

No, you can't think like that, Aster told herself. The Ladies, the Scorpions, and the rebels of the Nine were some of the strongest people she knew, and now that they were all working together, they would be more than a match for these men. She would trust them to get the job done.

Just as they were trusting her.

"Here we are," Aster said in a low voice. They'd reached a saloon called the Crimson Inn. Their contacts were waiting for them in one of the rooms upstairs. It was still at least an hour until sundown, but the bar was already packed with people, mostly dustblood men who had been given the day off and intended to make the most of it. Every few moments the cacophony of their voices was broken by the crack of a pool ball or the shout of a curse. The air was thick with the sickly-sweet smell of smoke and chaw. Fistfuls of straw had been strewn across the worn wooden floor to soak up spilled beer, and it crunched under Aster's boots as she pushed her way through the crowd.

"Why do they even celebrate Reckoning Day?" Derrick muttered. He clung close to Aster, as if the noise might break him like a glass. "The Reckoning has brought dustbloods nothing but suffering."

Aster swallowed. She was too busy concentrating on keeping her mind from melting in this room full of close, sweating bodies to try to explain the complexities of Reckoning Day to Derrick. "It's rare enough the landmasters give us a holiday. What difference does it make to them if we spend it laughing or crying?" she muttered back. "It gives folks a chance to break bread with family and friends. Not many who'd pass up on that."

"I suppose . . . it still feels a bit ghoulish to me . . ."

"Well, then, let me remind you that we're bringing about a new Reckoning tonight, Derrick, and that soon we'll all have real cause to celebrate."

They finally found their way to the stairs, and Aster took them up to the room where the other Reckoners were waiting for them. She knocked on the door, exchanged the watchword, and greeted their allies: a young Lady Ghost and a Scorpion boy.

"Thank the dead," the girl breathed, waving them all inside. A floral favor crept its way up her light brown skin, half hidden behind long black hair. "You're late. We feared the worst."

"We lost time on the road," Zee said apologetically. "Ran into some razor-backed mountain hogs—"

"Never mind that. You're here now. But you don't have a minute to spare. The other servants are due to start arriving in an hour."

"So you were able to make contact with them?" Derrick asked. He had provided the name of the catering company his uncle always used.

"Yes, and we got ahold of some serving uniforms for you," the boy said. He was white-skinned and redheaded, like Derrick himself, but without the shadow. "And the names of the servants you'll be replacing. It's a work-for-hire outfit, so none of the other servants will know each other, or you, for that matter. Same goes for the raveners—they have a list of who's scheduled to work tonight, but they won't know anyone by sight."

"They *will* sense our favors, though," Violet pointed out, crossing her arms. "Have you accounted for that?"

"Actually, I have," said Derrick. He had touched up his black hair dye to cover the red roots, and now he and Violet looked like they could be brother and sister. "Like a deadwall, the capitol building was built with mortar that's been mixed with theomite dust. Many such government buildings were, before deadwalls became commonplace. So its magic should be more than enough to drown out that of your favors."

"Which we'll still have to cover up with the ghostweed and some makeup," Tansy clarified.

Aster then turned to the girl and the boy, clasping each of their arms in turn. "We'd never have been able to do this without you. I can't thank you enough."

"I'm just grateful to be a part of it, honest," the boy said, blushing brightly.

The girl nodded, her grip strong. "You tell those bastards the Ladies sent you."

Aster and the others quickly changed into the servants' uniforms, crisp black-and-white suits and dresses meant to make the wearer blend into the background. It was not lost on Aster that even now, before the biggest fight of their lives, they were going to face the landmasters dressed like their lapdogs. The thought played hell with her confidence, eating away at the edges of it like bile. She would much rather be facing these men with the clothes she'd worn in freedom.

But as long as this got them in the room with Jerrod McClennon, little else mattered.

"I hope I pass for a man," Mallow mumbled. She'd wrapped her chest even more tightly than usual, and she smoothed down the front of her dress shirt fastidiously.

"A boy, more like," Tansy said dryly. "Twelve years old, maybe."

"Fourteen," Mal haggled.

"I promise none of these bastards is gonna look twice at you," Aster cut in, reassuring herself as much as Mallow. "The help is invisible to them."

After they finished getting dressed, they applied the ghostweed salve to their favors and covered them with concealer. This was the part they could not rush. The makeup would have to stand up to hard scrutiny. As many nights as Aster had spent in front of the vanity at the welcome house, there was a certain muscle memory to her movements now, her hand steady as she made careful brushstrokes. But instead of dread in her belly, tonight there was excitement. She would

368

do this ritual one last time, painting her face for the sake of rich men, and then she would cut them down.

Once everyone's disguises were complete, they only had a quarter of an hour left to race to the capitol building. They said their final goodbyes to the Scorpion and Lady Ghost and hurried out the back of the inn.

The streets had changed dramatically in the time they'd been inside.

The sky had deepened to a dusky rust red, and with the setting of the sun had come the first bursts of activity from the Reckoners' uprising. Several Ladies and Scorpions were breaking into the high-end shops—throwing stones through the glass display windows, pulling goods from the store, and passing them out to cheering dustbloods on the street. Others were climbing to the rooftops, shouting at the top of their lungs, listing the landmasters' crimes and the Reckoners' demands. One young man had even stolen a lawman's horse and was riding up and down Main Street, letting out wild whoops of joy, the horse hooves beating a tattoo on the pavement. The chaos of it became inseparable from that of the drunken revelers who spilled out from the bars, joining in the destruction and pushing it to even more dangerous extremes. The sizzle and bang of firecrackers, the smell of smoke. Aster could not tell, as she and her friends bobbed and weaved through the teeming streets, who had come here with the Reckoners, who had rushed to their aid, and who was simply taking advantage of the confusion. It was just a raw release of fury, bright and burning, the heart of an explosion years in the making.

But the law had swarmed the streets, too, of course—lashing

out with their billy clubs, unleashing their hounds, shooting to maim, threatening to kill. Cries of pain rose up through the chanting and cheers. Gunshots rattled off in quick staccatos. Every so often a Scorpion would fire off a crack of voltricity in return, the blue-white light arcing into the advancing dark, the thunder rolling through the canyon.

"These dissenters can't all be ours, can they?" Derrick asked in an undertone. They had all linked arms so they wouldn't lose one another, but they still got jostled roughly as people sprinted past in every direction. Even so, they limited themselves to a brisk walk, though they were losing precious time fighting the crowds—Aster did not want to draw any attention from the law, and she could only hope their servants' uniforms would be enough to ward off any remaining suspicion.

"No, there's too many people out here," Aster replied to Derrick. "I think some of these are just . . . regular folks who've had enough."

"But that's a good sign, isn't it? If they're joining the protest?" Clementine pointed out.

Aster didn't respond. Her lungs were spongy with the damp heat of her own growing panic. She did not want to see these people hurt. She hadn't even infiltrated the gala yet, and already the night was spiraling out of control.

At last, though, they reached the capitol building.

It took up a whole city block to itself, a line of coaches pulling up to its great circle drive under the light of gas lamps. The surrounding lawn, lush with desert flowers and dotted with rock gardens, was lined by an iron fence that barely held back a crush of people—journalists casting about for a story,

Reckoners crying out in protest, common fairblood folks simply hoping for a glimpse of Arketta's royalty as the landmasters rode through the gates, raveners waving them through. The capitol building itself was built of smooth white stone that gleamed like polished bone, and a great gold dome sat atop its roof, the Arkettan flag flapping from its apex. If Aster had not already been to the capitol at Northrock, it would have been the most imposing place she'd ever seen. Even so, it was a shocking sight in the Scab, the sheer size and scope of this place. Unlike a gambling hall or a welcome house, decorated to gaudy excess with riches, there was a brutish simplicity on display here, a power that had long since surpassed the need to impress.

She could not fail.

Aster led her friends around the block to the back of the building, sweating beneath her stiff servants' uniform despite the night chill. This entrance was much quieter and darker than the front. There were no crowds here, and the line of elegant stagecoaches on their way in was replaced by a line of delivery wagons on their way out. A pair of raveners stood at this gate as well, directing traffic. Aster finally broke into a run, motioning for the others to follow her. They were playing the part of servants who were running late. It wouldn't hurt to look a little frenzied.

"Excuse me! Pardon me!" Aster called out to the raveners as she approached the gate, the soles of her shoes slapping against the sidewalk. The nearest ravener immediately raised his gun, and Aster skidded to a stop an arm's length away.

"This entrance's for staff only!" he barked.

"Yes, that's us," Aster said, breathing hard. "We're late."

He lowered his gun halfway, his eyes still narrowed. "I'll ripping say. The guests are already arriving. I ought to turn your sorry asses around."

"And leave McClennon short-staffed on the most important night of the year?" Violet challenged, stepping forward. "I'll be sure to let him know it was you who stopped us, then."

The corner of his mouth twitched, but he relented and holstered his weapon, replacing it with a clipboard.

"Names," he said in a bored voice.

Aster and the others rattled off the names they'd been given. The ravener ticked them off one by one. He didn't press for details, didn't linger on their faces.

Thank the dead—

"Wait a minute," his partner cut in, and Aster's hopes plummeted just as quickly as they'd soared. "This still don't smell right. Why are you little shits so late in the first place?"

Aster and Violet looked at each other out of the corner of their eyes. They had not yet come up with a good answer for that. None of this had been part of the plan. The raveners exchanged a wary glance of their own. The second ravener reached for his gun—

"It was the riots," Violet said with sudden confidence. "There are rioters out front, and on the streets, too. I'm sure you've seen them. They called us traitors, tried to stop us coming in."

"Mm, is that so?"

"You sure you weren't maybe out there with them?" the first ravener demanded.

"Why would we be? Anyone would be lucky to have this

372

work," Clementine jumped in earnestly. "Please, sir, we've been looking forward to tonight all *year.* There's hundreds of folks would give their right arm for just a glimpse of these great men. *We're* getting paid to be in a room with them—if only you would let us."

"All right, ripping hell, don't get weepy on me," the second ravener said, looking disgusted, and he stood aside to let them pass. "Go on, then, and don't let me catch you causing any more trouble."

"Thank you, sir, bless you—"

"Get!"

They scrambled past the raveners, up the path, and into the building, pushing open the heavy wooden double doors. In the corridor beyond, the arched ceilings soared so far above them that their hurried footsteps echoed up and down the tiled floors. They'd endlessly studied the layout of the capitol building in Derrick's notes, but the simple black-and-white blueprint had not made any mention of the enormous vases of cascading Sweet Thistle plants, or of the looming statues of generals with sabers at their sides, or of the life-sized oil paintings of landmasters at their mines. Everyone's voices grew hushed, then went silent, as if they were walking through a graveyard—and perhaps, in a way, they were. This was a holy place to the unholiest of religions. How many dustbloods had died to build this temple? How many had suffered under its shadow? Aster felt like she could hear them crying out from the very stones in the walls, and it made her skin ripple with unease.

Leave this place, the dead pleaded.

Get out.

Go home.

Aster swallowed. It was cooler in here, but her face was still flushed and sweating, her throat still thick.

They passed a few other servants on their way downstairs, but everyone seemed just as intently focused as they themselves were, and nobody stopped them. Aster heard the kitchen before she saw it—the clatter and bang of utensils, the pop and hiss of hot oil. They followed the sounds, rounded the last corner—

And spotted another ravener guarding the kitchen entrance. There were more behind him, overseeing the kitchen staff's work. Aster swore under her breath.

"Just walk with purpose," she muttered to her friends, striding forward. "They have no reason to give us trouble."

And sure enough, the man let them pass. They cut through the hustle and bustle of the kitchen to the table where the champagne was being poured and set on silver platters by four dustblood servants. An unsmiling ravener stood behind them, arms crossed, watching them work.

"All right, let me do the talking," Violet murmured. "We're going to run with the same story as before."

Aster nodded, still struggling to shake the feeling of foreboding that clung to her. Everything was happening so fast—and at the same time, not fast enough.

"You're needed upstairs, trouble with the riots," Violet said to the ravener, her voice ringing with command. "They sent us to fetch you."

"Who the hell is *they?*" the ravener asked acidly.

"Those two raveners at the back gate—the riots have spilled over. We barely made it through ourselves."

He swore under his breath. "We're almost done here. They can wait five minutes."

"Not based on what I just saw," Aster said then. The ravener looked her up and down, and maybe there was something of her mounting paranoia reflected in her eyes, because whatever he saw there seemed to convince him.

"Damned dirty dustbloods," he cursed, and he unholstered his gun and stalked off.

"Where the hell do you think you're going?" the ravener at the door demanded.

"There's some kind of action upstairs. You better come with."

Their voices and footsteps receded. Aster let out a shallow breath.

"We'll have to be quick about this," Tansy said quietly, pulling out small vials of sleeping draught from a secret pocket inside her dress.

"You just tell us what to do," Aster replied. She looked up at the other servants, who had paused in their pouring and plating.

"Is it true about the riots?" one of the asked eagerly. "They giving them hell out there?"

Aster gestured for him to keep his voice down. "True enough," she whispered. "And we've got hell to give in here, too. We're with the Reckoners, understand? So we need you to let us take over this table here."

The servants glanced at each other. "There's not going to be any . . . trouble, is there?" another asked.

"Only if you give us away."

A current of furtive excitement seemed to pass between them, and they scattered to find other work while Aster and the others set about drugging the champagne glasses. They even poured a drop in each of the glasses that had been set aside for the raveners who would be on duty downstairs during the toast.

"You sure this stuff is going to be strong enough?" Raven asked doubtfully.

"I promise. I made it myself," Tansy assured her.

Derrick fidgeted, running a spidery hand through his shorn hair. He alone would remain downstairs until after the toast, barricading the back doors so the raveners could not return— his disguise might have been enough to fool strangers, but the men upstairs would eventually recognize him. And yet, despite this precaution, he seemed more anxious than any of them.

"How much longer is this going to take? You need to get these drinks upstairs. My uncle will be making his speech by now," he whispered urgently.

"Don't get your knickers in a twist, we're almost finished," Mallow hissed. Only one more platter of glasses to go. Aster worked as quickly as she could to empty her vial, her hand shaking, the glass slipping from her sweaty fingers—

There.

"Done," she said, grinning loosely. "Let's go."

Aster and the others balanced the platters on their palms and started upstairs. Aster fought for calm with every step she took, counting her breaths, willing her heart to slow. It would not do to arouse the landmasters' suspicion. But as long as she could just get through this toast—

They entered the ballroom.

The first thing Aster noticed was the vast mural of the mountains that covered the ceiling, the craquelure of the paint spidering across the face of it like the cracked earth of the desert floor. Beneath it, their voices overlapping in soft murmurs, their shadows playing beneath the light of the grand gasoliers, mingled the most powerful men left in Arketta—landmasters great and small, architects of government and titans of industry, their well-dressed wives on their arms like birds of paradise. There, just a stone's throw away, stood Jonah Boyle, warden of the south, and not far beyond him, Henry McClennon, Derrick's father. Jerrod McClennon was already standing at the front of the room, making his opening remarks. And at his side—

Lizzy Greene.

A punch of shock hit Aster in the gut. She'd been shot in her arm. Even with a ravener's healing, there was no way she should have been able to recover in time for this event. McClennon would not deign to look twice at the servants, but Lizzy might. If she recognized their faces in the crowd—

Aster turned to warn everyone, but her friends had gotten swept up into the chaos so quickly she had already lost them. The words curdled in her mouth. Her heart fluttered sickly.

"You there! I didn't get a drink," some woman snapped, tapping Aster on the shoulder.

"Oh—s-sorry, ma'am—" Aster stammered, and she held the platter out to the woman. Soon several of the guests were swarming for a glass, whispering insistently so as not to interrupt McClennon's speech. It was all Aster could do to keep from dropping the platter. All the while she kept her eyes down and her back half turned to the stage so Zee's sister would not see her. She could only hope her friends were doing the same.

"And so now, a toast, to a new era of peace and prosperity in this singular great nation," McClennon finally declared. "Does everyone have a glass?"

The last glasses on Aster's platter were snatched up. The guests all held their drugged drinks high. Aster finally risked a glance up to the stage, peering from behind a marble column. And Lizzy—like everyone else in the room—seemed to be focused only on McClennon. Aster's heart kicked again, this time with hope, her stomach twisting giddily.

They were going to do this. They were going to pull this off.

"Glory to the Reckoning!" McClennon declared, holding up his own glass.

"GLORY TO THE RECKONING!" the room roared in response.

Everyone lifted their drinks to their lips—

Elizabeth's eyes widened with some sudden realization.

"*STOP!*" she cried out, and she knocked the glass from McClennon's hand.

CHAPTER TWENTY-NINE

Shrieks of surprise rippled through the room. But for most of the guests, the warning seemed to come too late—they had swallowed the drugged champagne, and they began to fall to the ground within seconds. The raveners held on a moment longer, but then they, too, crumpled to the floor. Aster couldn't help feeling a brief rush of triumph as she watched them drop, these men and women who thought themselves so powerful as to be invincible. The only people who remained standing were a few panicked guests who hadn't taken a drink in time, the baffled servants, Aster's friends, scattered across the ballroom, and . . .

Jerrod McClennon, his face gone white with rage, his glass shattered at his feet. Elizabeth had put herself in front of him, her ember-orange eyes smoldering with deadly intent.

"It's the Reckoners, see?" she told him. "Dressed as servants. I'd recognize my brother anywhere, even from the back."

"You . . ." McClennon said slowly, his gaze flicking from Aster to each of the others. "*You—*"

Aster swallowed back a rush of panic. She flicked her gaze back to each of her friends, who looked just as stricken as she felt. They were all so far away from each other they might as well all of them have been alone.

"NOBODY MOVE!" McClennon bellowed, finally seeming to find his voice. "You are all to turn yourselves over peacefully! Any of you dustbloods so much as flinch and you'll be shot where you stand. The rest of you"—McClennon gestured to the half dozen or so guests who hadn't fainted—"clear out of here. Go get help."

The landmasters scattered like rats. Lizzy jumped down from the stage, landing on silent feet, her shotgun already in hand as she walked towards Aster. Cries of fear echoed shrilly in the vast space as the ravener approached. Aster tensed, wet her lips, instinctively reaching for a revolver that wasn't there. Her only weapon was the knife hidden in her boot. She could pretend to surrender, get in close—

A sudden blur of movement to Aster's left. She looked to the corner of her eye.

It was Zee, running forward towards his sister, leaping between the bodies on the floor.

Zee—

"No!" Clementine wailed, and now she was running after him.

Aster didn't think, sprinting for her sister. Time seemed to slow and tunnel around her. She passed a fallen ravener, grabbed his gun. Kept running.

Lizzy raised the gun, now training it squarely on Zee—

"*Stop!*" Zee shouted, raising his hands. "Sister, please—stop."

"You don't get to call me that," she shouted back, and Zee barely ducked in time to avoid the blast from her shotgun, covering Clementine protectively. "Not when you left me to die."

380

Aster finally reached Zee, and the others weren't far behind, all of them clustering around him. Aster pointed her stolen revolver at Lizzy's chest. Now they were in a standoff. Over Lizzy's shoulder, Aster could see McClennon watching them carefully.

"We don't want to hurt you, Lizzy," Aster said, her voice shaking, and she meant it. This could not continue.

"If you didn't want to hurt me, you should have killed me in the cradle. It would have been a kindness." Aster felt a twinge of horror and surprise at the anger lacing through her voice. Raveners weren't supposed to feel anger, weren't supposed to feel anything. But then, it took time for a person to be consumed by that dark power completely—and Lizzy hadn't been a ravener for very long.

Maybe confronting her brother was bringing some lost part of her to the surface.

"Elizabeth—" Zee said softly, his voice breaking.

"Every day I lose a little more of myself, and every day I thank the dead for it," Lizzy cut him off. *"This"*—she thumped her chest, as if they would hear the hollow where her heart had once been—"is the only way to move through this wretched world."

"You're right to be angry," Zee tried again, taking a step towards her, hands still raised. "With me, with the world . . . I should have done more to protect you from it. But please, Lizzy, just let me make it right. Put the gun down. Let us help you—"

Zee stretched out his hand towards her, but she let out a sound that was half snarl, half sob, thrusting her gun in his face.

"You can't help me. You can't even help yourself. Look at

381

you, Ezekiel, desperate and dirty and running from the law. What can you offer me that these landmasters can't?" She jerked her head back at McClennon, who still hadn't moved, standing tense and ready on the stage, his beady blue eyes watching them closely. "He's given me shine. He's given me power. He's given me a gun, and the freedom to use it. What have you ever given me other than grief?"

And Aster felt that grief then, a gaping ache in her chest, an unbearable heaviness in her belly, betrayal and bitterness and misery come together as one. Elizabeth sent it all out in a wave—though judging from the broken look on her face, she didn't even realize she was doing it. Hot tears streamed down Aster's cheeks. Mallow let out a choked cry. Even Raven's knees buckled. Elizabeth pressed the muzzle of her gun to Zee's forehead.

"*Answer me!*"

"He loves you!" Clementine cried, pressing herself to Zee's side. "*We* love you. Even now. *Especially* now. You're family, you're ours. We'll always want the best for you, even if we can't always give it. We love you, Elizabeth. And *that* man"—she pointed to McClennon—"doesn't."

"We can take him down, Lizzy," Zee pleaded softly, unflinching in the face of the gun. "It's not too late to fix this. You'll be free, and we can go home."

A pained sort of understanding seemed to flicker across Elizabeth's face. She let out a shuddering breath. Lowered her weapon. Aster held her breath. Their words were working, Elizabeth was finally coming around—

The crack of a gunshot tore through the room. A blossom

of blood flowered across Elizabeth's chest. Her jaw fell open in pain and surprise, her eyes shimmering with unspilled tears, the light behind them fading. Behind her, still on the stage, McClennon stood with a revolver raised level.

"NO!" Zee cried out as if he had been the one shot. He caught his sister in his arms. *"No! Damn you!"*

"Worthless. You're worthless, all of you," McClennon sneered. "My father warned me never to trust a dustblood with real work." He turned the gun on Zee then, but Aster was quicker on the draw, firing two shots in rapid succession, anger searing through her. They hit McClennon in the hand, and he howled in pain, clutching his bloodied fingers to his chest as he fell to the floor.

"You shut the hell up!" Aster snarled, stalking towards him. She climbed the stage, her gun still held high. "You're done, hear? It's *over*. No one's coming for you. All your remaining allies are in this room. All your raveners have been taken out. Our people are burning down this city as we speak. The law will never get past them. So now it's just *you*"—Aster pistol-whipped him across the temple, eliciting another howl—"and *us* until this thing is settled. *No one* leaves this building until you give in to our demands."

McClennon laughed acidly, an ugly sound that turned into a hacking cough as he forced himself up into a sitting position. Blood trickled down his forehead.

"Then we are going to be here a very long time, Lucker," he said, and he spat at her feet.

Aster backed away, disgusted. Behind her, she could hear the sounds of Zee sobbing, and of Clementine trying to comfort him, and Aster's wrath burned white at the edges of her vision.

Her finger slid over the trigger.

Maybe she should just end this now . . .

Rapid footsteps echoed from the far end of the ballroom. Someone else was coming. Aster whirled around.

Derrick.

Aster let out a tense breath. Derrick looked winded from running so hard, but he didn't stop until he was at Zee's side with the others. He looked down at Elizabeth's body, then back up to Aster, his eyes wide.

"Aster?" he asked, a waver in his voice. "I—I heard gunshots. What happened here?"

"Derrick—I—"

"*Derrick,*" McClennon interrupted, letting out another ugly laugh. "That *is* you, isn't it? I almost didn't recognize you. Of course you're here. Of course you're a part of this farce. I should've known."

"It's not a farce, Uncle," Derrick said, his voice grown cold and steely. He climbed up on the stage next to Aster, looking down at McClennon. "It's a Reckoning, and it's long overdue."

"Please. Don't try to pass yourself off as man of substance, Derrick. Everyone can see you're a worthless, whimpering little boy. Your father knew it; that's why he foisted you off on me. Your brother knew it; that's why he beat you like the dog you are. And these dustbloods knew it, too; that's why they were able to turn you so easily. They're cunning beasts, they prey on weakness. I'm sure they had their fill of you."

"I told you to shut the hell up!" Aster snapped at McClennon, raising the butt of her gun to hit him again. He backed away, his good hand held up in defense.

384

"Don't bother, I have nothing more to say to him. This little rat was dead to us already."

Derrick's face had gone white as bone. His mouth twitched, but he didn't speak. He crouched on his knees so he was eye level with his uncle.

"It is you who are weak, Uncle," he said finally, his voice scarcely above a whisper. "And every day I spend away from our wretched family I grow stronger. So just know this: there are many in this room who would not hesitate to take your life, and all of them have more right to the pleasure than me—but I count myself among their number."

It was McClennon's face that paled then, his mask of crass indifference slipping at last. Derrick stood and turned his back on him.

"Where do you need me, Aster?" Derrick asked.

Aster looked out over the ballroom. Clementine was cradling Zee in her arms now. His sobs had quieted, but they still echoed in Aster's ears like a vengeant's wails. The others, though, looked deadlier than Aster had ever seen them, their hardened gazes trained on Elizabeth's body or Jerrod McClennon. Aster could feel the anger moving between them like a living thing, a catamount with its fangs bared and a roar building in its chest.

It was time to put that rage to use.

There were over one hundred members of the Landmasters' Guild asleep at her feet—more than enough leverage to convince Authoritant Lockley to make the Reckoners' demands law. He was a weak man, Derrick had told them again and again. He did the Guild's bidding because he was afraid of them.

Let him see how powerless they really were.

It was time the authoritant stopped fearing his friends and started fearing his people.

They fetched the butcher's twine from the kitchen and tied the landmasters and raveners up like sides of meat. Then they took the raveners downstairs and locked them in a storage room, where they wouldn't be able to use their psychic powers against anyone. The other dustblood servants had all been allowed to leave, of course, so the only ones left in the ballroom now were the landmasters themselves. They came around slowly, shock and confusion seeming to settle in as they took stock of the situation. They looked like completely different people than the well-dressed, elegant socialites they'd been when the night started. Now their clothes were dirty and disheveled, and their looks of cool superiority had been replaced by red-faced rage. They cursed the Reckoners foully, spittle flying from their lips. They promised all manner of bloody revenge. But Aster was numb to it, and her friends seemed to be, too. There was no pleasure in this work, only grim determination. Zee's sister had already died for the sake of this plan. They had to see it through.

"Word from outside is that the Scorpions have managed to form a perimeter around the building. The law's not getting through, at least not tonight," Violet reported, patrolling next to Aster. A woman on the ground donkey-kicked at them with her patent leather shoes as they passed, and Violet jumped back, curling her lip. "*Watch* it, asshole—"

Aster gave a curt nod, ignoring the scuffle. "Good, that's good. Were we able to get our message out?"

"Yeah. The local lawmaster knows we've got the whole Landmasters' Guild hostage here, and that we're not planning to let them go until Authoritant Lockley gives in to our demands. I'm sure he'll send word up the chain."

"All right. Perfect. I'll make an announcement—"

"Aster . . ." Violet touched Aster gently on the shoulder, stopping her. "Look, it's been a long night, and tomorrow's going to be even longer. Why don't you let me take over and you can catch a couple hours of sleep? Zee and Clem took Elizabeth somewhere quiet. You could join them."

Aster shook her head. She was exhausted, yes, sickeningly so, but she could not stop now. She did not want to let her thoughts catch up to her.

"We need you well rested," Violet insisted.

"How the hell is anyone supposed to rest with the way they're carrying on?" Aster asked bitterly. The landmasters' neverending, outraged cries echoed so loudly through the ballroom that Aster could barely hear herself think.

Violet smiled, though there was no humor in it. "We learned to sleep through the vengeants' keening. This isn't half so bad as that."

Well, that was the truth if Aster had ever heard it . . . but still . . .

"Vi, I can't."

Aster strode forward to the stage before Violet could talk her out of it. She clapped her hands for attention.

"Listen up!" Aster shouted over the crowd.

"Lucker scum! You'll pay for this—"

"*Listen up!*" she continued, and they quieted as she began

delivering new information. "The lawmaster's office has been made aware of your situation, and they'll have gotten a voltragram directly to the authoritant himself before the hour's end. I expect a negotiator on the authoritant's behalf sometime early tomorrow. I want you all to think *carefully* about what you'll tell this man when the time comes. If you tell him to agree to our demands, you can all walk out of here by sundown."

"Why would we ever agree to your demands after this?" one man cried out.

"Because if you don't, we'll all of us die here," Aster said roughly. She pointed to Jerrod McClennon, now sitting trussed up next to his brother Henry, a fresh bandage on his injured hand, a scowl on his face. "When my friends and I were guests of Mr. McClennon, he told us that if we wanted to eat, we'd have to work for it. Well, now that you're in our care, the same rules apply—do the hard work of righting the wrongs you've lived by for generations, and then, and *only* then, will you be allowed back into the world."

"We'll never give in to the likes of you," Henry McClennon declared, and the room erupted into noise again. Aster left the stage.

The rest of the night passed with creeping slowness. Tansy and Mallow doled out water, first aid, and limited rations of leftover food to any who would accept it. Raven guarded the raveners downstairs. Violet kept in contact with their allies on the outside. Derrick argued his case to the many lesser landmasters, whom he seemed to think would be more amenable than any of the greats. And Aster circled the room, a hawk on the hunt. Any sign of someone escaping their bonds or making a move, and she would strike them down.

Violet was right—Aster needed to sleep. Her head pounded with every step she took. Her eyes were drying up in their sockets. Midnight crawled into two in the morning, and two crawled to four. Though Aster refused sleep herself, she insisted that the others take their rest. Once Zee and Clementine returned, she sent Tansy and Mallow to go take a couple hours for themselves. Then Violet and Raven, each insisting that Aster take their place, then Derrick, looking defeated after his efforts had yielded poor results. Aster, though, was not yet worried.

"It hasn't even been twelve hours," she told him. "Try them again after they've missed a couple meals."

"But—"

"You've done well, Derrick. You've worked miracles. Get some sleep."

By the time the sun rose in the morning, most of the landmasters had succumbed to sleep as well. Aster sat at the front of the ballroom, watching them toss and turn fitfully on the hard marble floor, listening to them whisper among themselves, no doubt about how much they despised her. Hunger was beginning to claw at Aster's belly, so she knew it would be getting to them by now, too. She let herself eat half of her ration of the food they'd found in the kitchen—fresh fruit, smoked meat, thin slices of bread—but it was scarcely enough to take the edge off. They had to make the limited supply of food last. If everyone here ate only one meal a day, their provisions would still run out before a week had passed.

And now the battle truly begins, Aster thought.

She was just starting to nod off despite her best efforts to remain alert, her chin dipping towards her chest, when Raven burst into the ballroom. At her side was a fairblood man in a dark green suit. He didn't look like a badge, but he had an air of authority to him all the same. Aster climbed to her feet, weary and wary.

"Who's this, Ray?" she called across the room.

"Says he's here on behalf of Authoritant Lockley," Raven answered. "Says he's here to negotiate."

"My name's Mr. Monroe," the man introduced himself. "And you're Aster, are you not? Why don't we find somewhere private we can talk?"

So he could take her out quietly? Not likely.

Aster set her jaw. "Anything you want to say to me you can say in front of my friends," she said. Now that it was morning, they were all here, with the exception of Clementine, who was on ravener duty. One by one they came to Aster's side, tensed and ready.

Monroe spread his hands amicably. "Very well, then, let's talk terms. It's my understanding you want the authoritant to have another look at those demands you all made."

"You tell Lockley he is *not* to give in to a single one of them," McClennon interrupted, and shouts of agreement rose up from the crowd.

"Before we can even begin to discuss it, Authoritant Lockley needs assurance that all of your hostages are alive and unharmed, *and* that they will remain so," Monroe continued over the noise.

"Unharmed?" a woman cried out. "We've been drugged, beaten, and harassed—"

"An exaggeration—" Derrick said quickly.

390

"McClennon's been *shot*," a man yelled.

"Only because he fired first!" Mallow snapped. "And we fixed him up afterwards, too!"

"This is inhumane. This is degrading—"

"This is how it's always been for us!" Aster cut them all off, shouting so loudly she was light-headed from the effort of it. "You're exhausted? You're hungry? Good! You feel powerless? *Good!* You're tired of being treated like animals? You think you deserve better? You want this all to end? Then you *understand*. You all have suffered *one night*, and even so, it's been gentle compared to the suffering you've forced upon your dustblood countrymen. So you tell the authoritant, Mr. Monroe, exactly what I told these fine ladies and gentlemen: their fate is in their own hands. If they agree to change the way things are done here in Arketta, if they give Lockley their blessing to sign the order, then everyone walks free. Until then, no one leaves this building."

If Monroe was at all affected by any of this, he didn't show it, a pleasant, unassuming smile still gracing his face. If anything, it just made Aster even more incensed.

"I can see you feel strongly about this, Aster. I'll tell you what—I'll have my people provide some more provisions to these folks while you and I take our time to work out the details—" he began.

"*No,*" Aster bit back. "They can starve, just as I did when I was a child, just as thousands of dustbloods are doing now."

Her friends nodded in agreement beside her.

"Aster, please," Monroe continued. "This all started because of your, truly, moving concern for women in welcome houses.

Might we not at least discuss letting these women here return to their homes? They are too delicate to be tested like this—"

"And we weren't?" Violet snapped.

Monroe, at last, scowled slightly.

"There's no dealing with these people," Jerrod McClennon huffed. "You have to speak to them in their own language. Tell Lockley to send more lawmen out here and tear this place down if they have to."

"Our friends outside won't hesitate to return whatever fire the law throws at them, and neither will we," Zee warned, his voice rough.

"Then we'll blow you traitors halfway to hell!" Henry McClennon roared.

There were shouts of agreement, and the noise in the room became overwhelming. Monroe whispered something to Raven, who then escorted him out of the ballroom.

"He says he's going to update the authoritant on the situation and that he'll be back soon," Raven reported when she returned.

"All right, good. We better settle in for the day—" Aster began.

Raven shook her head. "*You* need to get some rest, Aster. You look about ready to drop."

"I'm fine—"

"She's right," Tansy interjected. "We can handle them for a few hours. You shouldn't be here, not like this."

Not like this. Was it that obvious then, how little she had left in her? Could they see her swaying on her feet? Could they hear her heart fluttering weakly in her chest? She wet her dry, cracked lips.

"Do you want me to come with you?" Violet offered softly.

Aster shook her head. "No, no, they need you up here. I'll just . . . I'll go lie down," she conceded. "But if anything changes—if *anyone* breaks—I want you to let me know immediately, hear?"

As it turned out, though, nothing changed for three days. Outside, the law made no attempt to breach the capitol building, as ordered by Authoritant Lockley, and the Reckoners held the line, having heard no news from their scouts yet that any troops had been sent to Crimson Glen. Inside, the landmasters grew weaker and more desperate, pleading for extra rations, but any time one or two of them sought to negotiate they were quickly shouted down by the group. Monroe came back each morning to offer concessions lesser than the ones Aster had asked for, and each morning she and her friends turned him away.

Aster herself was growing feral—she could feel it. Hunger twisted her up, both in her body and her mind. Her stomach cramped painfully, daggers stabbing with every breath she took. Her head swam, spots floating in her vision. Her thoughts ricocheted off each other in her skull, disjointed memories colliding to form horrifying waking nightmares. She was back in McClennon's cellar, being tortured by raveners, but this time her mother was there with her, offering Aster up to them. She was back in the Graveyard, but it was Mother Fleur in charge, not Priscilla, and Mother Fleur was berating her in front of all the Lady Ghosts. She was back in the tunnels with Eli, but the vengeants tore them apart and they died in the dark.

Aster's only grim comfort was the knowledge that, for as

much as she was suffering, the landmasters were surely suffering more. She saw them whispering among themselves and knew they were talking about giving in. They had to be. They were used to three meals a day, and it had now been four days with only one meal each. They could not endure this for much longer.

And sure enough, on the afternoon of the fifth day, Derrick came up to Aster to let her know that Jonah Boyle was ready to talk.

Aster snapped her eyes open at the sound of Derrick's voice, startled. She had not meant to fall asleep, but hunger had weakened her. She berated herself, sitting up straighter.

"Boyle?" she repeated foggily.

"Yes." Derrick slowly came into focus. His eyes had sunk deep in their sockets, bruised with exhaustion, and the faintest peach fuzz had fluffed up on his chin. He had always had a gaunt look about him—the sharp cheekbones, the slender jaw—and now the effect was twofold. Unlike the rest of them, he had never gone hungry like this before, but if he suffered, he did so in silence.

"Boyle . . ."

"He wants to talk to you," Derrick pressed. "Here, I'll take you to him."

Derrick helped her up. Aster murmured a thanks but refused to take his arm. She would not let any of these bastards see her weakened.

Jonah Boyle had taken over the southwest corner of the ballroom, and several other landmasters had maneuvered themselves so they were gathered around him, shifting their eyes as Aster approached. Aster did not know what Jonah Boyle had been like on the outside, but in here, he seemed to be a man of quiet strength—tired, clearly, as they all were, but still alert, with his head held high. Aster knew he was the second most powerful man here after McClennon, and she had expected him to behave accordingly, talking over everyone and shouting out orders. Instead, this was the first time in five days that he'd called attention to himself.

"Aster, is it?" Boyle asked. Aster sat down across from him, and he held out his bound hands for Aster to shake one. Aster crossed her arms.

"I don't shake hands with landmasters," she said. "But might be I'll listen to one. Derrick says you want to talk?"

Boyle let out a heavy sigh. "That I do. I've been speaking with some of my colleagues here. They're in a bad way. Kathleen passed out this morning, and she's only just now fully lucid again. And Gregory has a heart condition—he can't go on like this for much longer."

Aster considered the other landmasters, who still wouldn't meet her eyes. "That so?" she asked flatly.

"McClennon has faith the law will bring you all to justice, but I begin to worry it will come too late for some of us . . . and, perhaps, I begin to see some of the truth of your words, as well. And I believe there are many more who would admit the same, if only someone else were to go first."

Aster looked at Derrick in surprise. She had thought if anyone were to break, it would be because they wanted to end their ordeal, not because they had taken any of her words to heart.

"And you're . . . offering to be that person?" Derrick asked.

"It must be me. I'm the only one who might be considered

a match for the McClennon brothers. Jerrod in particular . . . he holds a lot of sway over this crowd, you understand. And he clearly would rather risk some of us dying than give up his power. But most of the people here don't yet have that kind of power, as much as they may aspire to it. And soon enough they must realize that what power they *do* have . . . is not a fair trade for their lives. I'll make a speech saying as much, tomorrow morning when the negotiator returns, and I'll do my best to plead your case."

"Why not now?" Aster asked, unable to keep the edge of desperation from her voice.

"Because we cannot give people too much time to think. If I speak now, McClennon will just scare anyone I win over back into submission by tomorrow. It must be when Mr. Monroe comes back, and not a moment before."

Aster knew he was speaking the truth. She glanced at Derrick, and they separated themselves from the group so they could talk privately.

"Well? Do we take him up on his offer?" Derrick asked, excitement cutting through the fatigue in his voice.

Aster was more reserved. "I don't know, it seems too good to be true," she muttered. "What's he really up to?"

"I don't know that he's 'up to' anything. Boyle has always considered himself to be a righteous man. My uncle hates him for it, but as far as we're concerned, he's one of the good ones."

"There are no good landmasters, Derrick," Aster said wearily. "Any halfway decent person would leave the life behind . . . like you did."

"Well, that's what he's offering to do, too, isn't it? By agreeing to our terms? He'd be giving up his power—and convincing others to do the same."

Aster glanced across the ballroom, to where the McClennons sat in their own corner, surrounded by desperate, lesser landmasters who'd crawled over to them like they were a raft in a storm.

"And do you think they'd be convinced?" she asked.

Derrick hesitated. "Well, I don't know how many of them will have genuinely come around like Boyle has, but I have no doubt he was right that most of them would be willing to give in anyway—they don't want to die here."

Aster still had trouble believing Boyle himself had come around. She chewed her lip, trying to think of all the ways he might be manipulating her.

Derrick sighed, seeming to read her silence. "Why should it be so surprising that someone was persuaded by your passionate words? Why else say them, otherwise?"

"I guess I'm just . . . not used to it . . ." she admitted. "Not from the likes of him."

"These people know, in their heart of hearts, that what we do is wrong. It's no wonder, in the face of death, that some should want to absolve themselves—or, at the very least, that they should want to delay their judgment a little longer. This was always the plan, Aster. Do not fault it for working so well."

He was right. This was only what they'd always hoped for. If she accepted Boyle's offer, this whole thing could be over by tomorrow.

And then, oh mercy, they could go home. Aster tried to imagine it. *Home.* And the picture that floated up in her mind then was not Shade Hollow, not Green Creek, not any place in the Scab. Not any place at all. It was Violet's face, the two of them lying side by side in the sun, their hands tangled together, their steady breaths in sync. At ease, at rest. Finally done with the fighting. Finally free to live.

Aster's stomach twisted then with a want more powerful than any hunger she'd ever endured.

"All right," she said softly, gripping Derrick's shoulder and meeting his eyes. "All right, let's tell him we're agreed."

When the sun rose on the sixth day, Aster barely had the strength to rise with it. But even so, excitement sparked in her empty belly. She saw her anticipation reflected in the eyes of her friends—she'd told them about Boyle's decision, and, like Derrick, they had all agreed it was the inevitable end of this gambit. Of course the landmasters had blinked first—why was she surprised? Even Zee, still hollowed out from the loss of his sister, had managed a smile at the news.

"Stay strong, brothers and sisters!" McClennon shouted as Aster started her morning patrol. In the beginning, some of the landmasters had refused food and water on principle, but now no one turned it down, and McClennon never had. It was no doubt the only reason he still had the energy for his preaching. He only ever showed optimism in these sermons, never mentioning that he'd had to kill his head ravener or that he'd been shot twice himself. Perhaps he sought to keep the others' spirits up, but, more likely, he sought to keep himself from looking weak. "Trust our deliverance is coming!" he went on. "Today! I can feel it! These vile traitors will get what's coming to them."

"By the dead, I can't wait to see the look on this bastard's face when all his own people turn on him," Violet sighed, patrolling at Aster's side. Her hair had long since fallen out of its careful braided bun, her face gone gaunt with exhaustion. It hurt Aster's heart to see her this way, to see everyone she loved so diminished. They had come here of their own free will, yes, but still . . . she felt responsible for them. The relief she felt, knowing she was finally getting them out of here, was almost enough to make Aster forget her own suffering.

Aster let their fingers brush together. "I know. We're almost out of here, Vi," she promised.

Not ten minutes later, the ballroom doors opened, and Monroe strode through, Raven at his side. Raven's face looked drawn, washed out, as if she'd seen a remnant. Something about her expression made Aster's gut clench with sudden dread.

She's just exhausted . . . we're all exhausted—

She locked eyes with Aster, shook her head once.

Jonah Boyle stood and cleared his throat. "Mr. Monroe—if I may say a few words—"

"*These negotiations are closed!*" Monroe announced. "Authoritant Lockley has sent the army. There are two thousand armymen outside the city. The Reckoners have twenty-four hours to turn themselves in."

CHAPTER THIRTY

There are two thousand armymen outside the city.

Outside the city.

The words echoed in Aster's mind like damnation. What had happened to the Reckoners' scouts? Where had been the warning? Someone, somewhere, must have been captured or killed by the law. That was the only explanation. A full regiment of armymen took time to travel in the Scab; they should have known about this days ago, when there would still have been time to fight their way out. But now—now—

It's over.

The raveners, they could handle. The law, they could fend off.

But the Arkettan armed forces—

"HOW THE HELL ELSE DID YOU THINK THIS WAS GONNA END, LUCKERS?" McClennon jeered. He had not stopped laughing since Monroe delivered the news, a hideous, hacking sound that set Aster's skin crawling. "JUST WHO THE HELL DID YOU THINK YOU WERE? I TOLD YOU THAT YOU WERE GONNA GET WHAT'S COMING TO YOU. I TOLD YOU—"

"Aster, what do we do?" Tansy asked, her face broken by fear.

After speaking privately to Monroe, Aster had gathered all her friends backstage so they could discuss what to do next. But Aster felt as if she'd been thrown into the ocean with stones tied around her feet: there were no good options, only the panicked thrashing of the damned.

She should have known their good luck had been too good to be true.

"What choice do we have? We have to let everyone go," Clementine whispered. The thick, bloodred stage curtains would muffle their conversation, but even so, they could not risk being overheard. "You said he said they'll let us live if we let everyone go—"

"You really believe that?" Raven cut her off.

"If they're going to kill us anyway, we might as well go down fighting," Mallow said. She stabbed the tip of her knife into the warped wooden floor, a declaration of war.

"They won't want fighting," Derrick reminded her. "They won't want to risk the hostages' lives. We still have that critical advantage. This is a show of force, yes, but ultimately, nothing's changed."

"*Everything's* changed," Zee argued. "Our people on the outside don't stand a chance against the army's numbers, and their weapons are just as advanced as ours. The Reckoners will be massacred. We can't risk our allies' lives in the hopes the army's bluffing."

"And what about us?" Violet asked quietly. She glanced at Aster. "Are *we* bluffing?"

Aster's tongue felt like it was stuck to the roof of her mouth. She pried it free.

"About what?" she managed.

"About hurting the hostages—killing them, even—if the army tries to force entry."

The circle fell quiet. Aster could hear the blood pushing sluggishly through her veins. Every heartbeat was an effort. She could not seem to form thoughts, let alone words.

"If we kill any of the landmasters, whatever amnesty Lockley's offering goes up in smoke," Tansy said finally. "Maybe it's an empty promise anyway, but . . . right now, it's all we have."

"So what, they let us live?" Raven shot back. "What's the point, if they send us to a prison camp? If they still get to pass their awful laws? I'd rather die than let that happen—and I will, if I have to."

"If we turn ourselves in, we may be able to convince them to let the rest of the Reckoners go," Aster said at last. Her voice felt thick and halting, as if she were talking in her sleep. "We're the ones they want. We're the ones who started all this. As long as they capture us, they'll be able to spin this as a victory, and they'll be glad to have avoided a prolonged and costly fight with our people—even if it's one they'd be sure to win."

"Aster's right. We have no other choice but to turn ourselves in. For our allies' sakes," Tansy urged. She looked around the circle. "We'll survive this, we will. And we'll find a way to keep fighting, just like we always have. We may have lost this battle, but that doesn't mean we give up on the war. No—we settle in."

They all fell quiet again. It was a cruel thought, "settling in." For more suffering, for more loss, for more failure. It was not what any of them deserved. Aster's chest felt like it was caving in on itself, grief and anger threatening to crush her. Raven was right: she would rather die.

But that would not be the brave thing to do.

"All right," Aster whispered, wiping away the wetness at her eyes.

Mallow looked around, panicked. "All right, what? We're handing ourselves over? Right now?"

"No, not now, please, let's at least take all the time we have. I just mean . . . all right. I'll do it."

She stood to leave before any of the others could see her break down any further, their murmurs of dismay chasing her. The ancient floorboards creaked with every step she took.

"Everyone, just—go back to your posts for now. We'll talk more later," Violet said finally, and Aster heard hurried footsteps as Violet ran after her. She made it as far as an old grand piano upstage before Violet caught her.

"Aster . . ." Violet's hand slid over her shoulder. The gentleness of her touch was Aster's undoing. A wrenching sob forced its way past her lips. Hot tears spilled down her cheeks. Violet pulled her into an embrace, and Aster melted into it.

"I should have seen this coming, Violet. The Nine warned us—Sid *warned* us—"

"And still they joined us in this fight, because they know, as we all do, that the landmasters need to be stopped. And by bringing everyone together, you've gotten us closer than anyone ever has, Aster. This is good work we've done."

Aster did not think so. Things were worse than they'd ever been.

"It's like Tansy said . . ." Violet went on, ". . . we'll keep fighting. We always find a way."

Aster sighed, her breath shuddering. "I am so tired, Violet."

"I know."

Violet held her for a moment longer, then stepped back, still gripping Aster's shoulders. "What do you need from me?"

Aster searched for an answer, but she couldn't seem to think clearly anymore. Her head felt too heavy for her, pounding with every heartbeat. Her empty stomach clenched in agony. And beyond the curtains, in the ballroom, McClennon was still crowing victory. He had never stopped.

"I'LL BUILD A WELCOME HOUSE IN YOUR NAME, LUCKERS! DON'T YOU WORRY! I'LL MAKE SURE YOU'RE NEVER FORGOTTEN!"

The sound of his cackling raised Aster's hackles.

That was the greatest injustice of them all, wasn't it? That Jerrod McClennon should walk away from all of this. That he should prosper, even, from it. It would only strengthen his campaign against dustbloods. He did not deserve such freedom, this man who had taken welcome houses nationwide and lowered the working age to thirteen, who had tortured Violet for months and offered her up to his nephew like a piece of meat. Elizabeth had sold her soul for him, and he had shot her in the back as soon as she ceased to be useful. He did not deserve freedom. He did not deserve even to live.

Aster could perhaps endure whatever suffering lay in store for her, but not if McClennon was there to bear witness.

She wet her lips, meeting Violet's eyes. *We both know I'm bound for hell*, she'd said. *I'd just as well have it be for you.*

Perhaps they could go together.

"Violet . . ." Aster said slowly. "I need you to help me kill McClennon."

They asked Derrick to get his uncle alone for them.

"Are you certain, Aster?" Derrick whispered. "I meant what I said when I told my uncle I'd see him dead, but that was before the army showed up on our doorstep. Now I wonder if this might not only make things worse."

"Worse for the three of us, maybe. But not for anyone else. They won't be a part of it. I can't risk their amnesty," Aster explained.

"They'll be blamed anyway."

"Not if we play this right," Violet assured him. "None of us will be blamed."

Derrick was quiet for a long time, seeming to turn their words over in his mind.

"It's just . . ." he said finally, ". . . it's just that there is the easy thing, and there is the right thing. It seems to me that the easy thing is to try to kill my uncle now, and likely die in the attempt and so spare ourselves much suffering . . . but the right thing is to go peacefully with the others, as we promised them we would, and save this fight for another day, when we're sure we can win."

Aster felt the sudden heat of frustration, partially because she knew Derrick was right. But that didn't necessarily mean they were wrong.

"We're never going to be sure," Aster said. "And we may never get this close to him again. If we accomplish nothing else after all this, let's at least be able to say we ended this man's reign of terror."

"And that's why you're doing it?" Derrick asked shrewdly. "This isn't just some sort of . . . elaborate . . . suicide mission?"

"No, Derrick. I do not intend to die for Jerrod McClennon."

He exhaled and nodded. "Very well . . . what's your plan?"

"All we need from you is to convince your uncle that you've come around," Violet said. "Tell him whatever he needs to hear—that you never meant things to get this far, or that you've been a double agent this whole time, or that you only did all this as some sort of twisted way to get his attention and prove yourself because you actually look up to him. *Whatever.* Beg him, if you have to. And make sure you're seen doing it. Then you're to bring him down to the auction room—this time tell him that's where we're keeping his raveners, and you want to let them out."

The auction room: the place where, at the dawn of the Reckoning, thousands of dustbloods had been brought from the government's prison camps and sold to enterprising landmasters as private labor. There were few enough dustbloods left in the government's care now, and the space had become more ceremonial than anything in recent years.

Even so, it seemed a fitting place for McClennon to face a reckoning of his own.

Derrick had begun to sweat. "He will not believe me."

"*Make* him believe you," Aster said. "You can do this, Derrick. You are more than a match for him. You always have been. And when we're done, we'll all of us be free of him."

"Yes . . ." Derrick nodded slowly. "Yes, we'll be free of him."

"Can we count on you?" Violet asked.

He looked back and forth between them, red webbing the whites of his eyes, but the blue of them bright with anticipation all the same. "Always."

They clasped arms and parted ways.

Aster and Violet hurried through the hallways. If the ballroom was the heart of the capitol building, the auction room was its stomach, where people were broken down and fed to the rest of the Scab. It was a dark, circular room, with ascending rings of benches and a raised dais at its center: the auction block.

"I don't like this, Aster . . . I feel like I'm walking through the Veil," Violet murmured, her shoulders hunched inward like a child's in the cold. "These aren't even my dead, and I can feel them calling to me."

"The dead belong to all of us," Aster said softly, remembering what Eli had once told her. "And your heart is nearer to theirs than you may think. We were auctioned, too, after all, on our Lucky Nights. The practice of buying and selling people like animals . . . it started in places like this." Aster's face screwed up with sudden regret. "I only wish we could have ended it here, too."

"We're ending one of the longest legacies of it with McClennon. Let that be enough for now."

They sat together in the front row of seats before the auction block. Aster pulled her knife from her boot and set it on her lap. Baxter McClennon's knife, once. There was a certain symmetry to that that pleased her—it would be their own blade that killed them.

And yet, as many times as she'd imagined this moment—as sure as she was that this man deserved to die—her stomach churned at the thought of plunging the knife into his chest.

"I can do it, you know . . . if you want . . ." Violet offered haltingly. The sound of her own voice in the large, empty space seemed to spook her. "I can be your shadow, Aster. Let me be the one who stays in the dark."

407

"No, this time it has to be me," Aster said. "I could never ask this of someone else, not even you. But . . . thank you, Violet. I mean it. Not just for today . . . for everything."

"It's not enough. I was going to take you away from all this. I promised."

Aster's throat swelled painfully as she thought of her dream, already fading, of the two of them free one day. Somewhere, anywhere. Ferron, maybe, with Clementine and all the others, far beyond the reach of the evil memories that plagued them. For one brief, euphoric moment, she'd actually allowed herself to believe.

"It's just enough that we're together," Aster said finally.

Their fingers intertwined.

The minutes passed with agonizing slowness. As the time neared half an hour, Aster began to feel a worm of worry.

"What the hell is taking Derrick so long?" she muttered.

"It hasn't even been thirty minutes. Give him some time. You know how that boy likes to talk."

But Aster's dread only grew as the hour mark approached. She could not even tell how much of it was her own and how much had simply seeped into her bones from this evil place. Spots swam in her vision and formed twisted faces. Her skin prickled with phantom sensations. A rabbit-like panic was beginning to take ahold of her.

"We should go," she said finally. "Something's gone wrong—"

Derrick entered the room, his uncle at his side. His left eye had been blackened, but he caught Aster's gaze and nodded at her.

Aster felt the fog of her mind clear. She sat up straight, gripped the hilt of her knife.

"Where are the raveners?" McClennon asked. Despite the punishment of the past three days, he still walked with strong, confident strides. He stopped when he spotted Aster and Violet. Confusion clouded his face. "What are *they* doing here?"

"Keep walking, Uncle," Derrick said coldly.

Aster and Violet stood.

"No," McClennon said, stepping backwards. "Turn around. This is a trap, son."

"Yes, and it's me who's laid it." Derrick shoved him between the shoulder blades. McClennon whirled around to face him, realization and rage rising in his cold blue eyes.

"Derrick, I swear to the dead, if you don't—"

"Your prejudice has always been your weakness, Uncle," Derrick interrupted. "You believed me when I begged your forgiveness because it fit your idea of how a man like me should be: weak-willed, cowardly, running at the first sign of real trouble. But I told you before, I am stronger now than I've ever been. You *should* have believed me then."

McClennon swung a fist at Derrick with his one good hand. Derrick ducked it, then drove into his uncle with his shoulder and knocked him to the ground. McClennon grunted and cursed. They tussled. McClennon managed to roll Derrick over. He grabbed a fistful of Derrick's hair and slammed his skull against the marble floor—

Aster and Violet sprinted forward. Grabbed McClennon, dragged him away. He thrashed like a wild boar. He was weakened by hunger and exhaustion—but then, so were they.

Aster's head spun sickly as she tried to keep hold of him.

"You ripping rat!" McClennon swore. *"When your father finds out what you've done, he'll kill you himself!"*

"No one's going to find out," Violet said calmly. They had reached the auction block, and now Violet held him from behind, her arms locked under his armpits and around his shoulders, while Aster stood in front of him, the knife at his chest. "We're going to make it look like Elizabeth was the one who killed you."

His eyes were wild, his lips flecked with spittle. "Elizabeth— who the hell is *Elizabeth*—"

Anger welled up in Aster's throat. She curled her lip. "Your head ravener. The dustblood woman you shot in the back. She had a name, you pig."

"But why—"

"She was still in there," Aster said, her voice raw. "She might even have turned against you. Now we'll never know. But we *can* finish the job for her."

For the first time, something like fear flickered across McClennon's face. He stopped struggling, locked eyes with Aster.

"No . . . no, the law will be able to tell it's a setup. Her body's five days gone now—"

Aster cut him off with a sharp laugh. "Even Good Luck Girls know that raveners' bodies don't decay like ours, McClennon, what kind of fools do you take us for? The law won't be able to tell shit. And you, being the fool *you* are, still haven't told anyone that you already killed Elizabeth, have you? Too proud to admit you lost her loyalty."

McClennon's strained silence was answer enough. He wet his lips.

"What is it you want from me, then?" he asked in a lower voice. "You want me to tell Lockley to stand down, is that it? You want to scare me into accepting your demands?"

"We know better than to try that," Violet said into his ear. "You told us yourself: men like you don't yield."

"If we leave you alive, you'd only undo everything we've already done. Maybe we'll never get to see our perfect future realized . . ." Aster pressed the point of the blade until it drew blood. "But neither will you."

McClennon's chest heaved. "You think you can kill me? With the Arkettan army outside these doors? If anything happens to me, they'll shoot down every single one of you, no matter what lies you tell them."

"Even if they do, this fight doesn't die with us," Violet promised. "There are thousands of people who believe in the Reckoners' cause now. They won't stop until they've won."

McClennon cackled, a sound on the edge of hysteria. "I don't care how many thousands of traitors you've turned. We've got boots on the ground now. You really think a bunch of scared, desperate dustbloods is going to be enough to stop the army? The *army*?"

That laughter again. Aster would cut it out of him if it was the last thing she did. She looked to Violet and found her brow arched in a question. Aster answered it with the arc of her blade.

"Glory to the Reckoning," she whispered, and she drove the knife into McClennon's heart.

It was no small task, setting up a convincing scene in which

411

Elizabeth and McClennon had killed each other. It took them most of the rest of the day. Once they were finished, they went about the much more difficult work of telling the others what they'd done.

"Zee," Aster said once she had finally finished, "Elizabeth was your sister. If you don't want her to be a part of this—"

"No, I—it's okay." He swallowed, shock written over his face just as it was on the others'. "After what he did to her . . . he deserves to have died by her hand, even if only in the story we tell. Let it be a lesson to anyone else who would try to use raveners to do their dirty work."

"I was the last one seen with my uncle, so there will no doubt be those who still suspect foul play, even if I did my damnedest to convince everyone I was trying to make amends," Derrick admitted.

"You convinced me," Mallow muttered. "Sorry for giving you that shiner."

Derrick laughed a little, touching his black eye gingerly. "It's all right. It only makes our story that much more believable. I'll make an announcement to the landmasters tonight, telling them there's been a terrible accident with my uncle, that we went to free the raveners but his head ravener went rogue. Even if they doubt us, they shouldn't be able to prove anything. Our amnesty is secure."

"So that's the plan still?" Clementine asked. "To offer ourselves up, even though McClennon's dead?"

"That's the plan," Aster said. A sort of calm had come over her as she spoke. She would not call it peace—there could be no peace, where they were going—but more like the last glow of warmth a man felt before he froze to death. She would savor these last few moments before the end.

There was no longer any need to ration the food, so that night they helped themselves to the last of it. But unlike the many meals they'd shared in the meeting hall at Camp Red Claw or around a campfire on the trail, this one was somber. They sat on the floor backstage, chewing in silence, listening to the excited chatter of the landmasters just beyond the curtain. Even with news of Jerrod McClennon's death, most of them seemed to be celebrating: tomorrow they would be free, and any one of them might take the newly empty throne.

It was all too much. As soon as she finished eating, Aster slipped away with Violet further backstage, no longer caring who saw them together. They could waste no more time with pretense. There was no place now for fear. They found a quiet, dark corner and curled into each other.

Would she have done anything differently, if she had known it would end this way? Aster could not even begin to answer that question. Her friends—her *family*—had been free, and she had led them back into bondage on the wild promise that they might be able to spread that freedom to others. The prison camps would be worse than the welcome house by tenfold, with all of the cruelty and none of the sick riches.

But at least, Aster thought, they would be together. At least they would have their memories of a time when they had answered to no one. And thinking of these memories, Aster fell asleep to the soft promise of Violet's heartbeat.

Aster had not meant to sleep through the night. Clementine should have woken both of them when it was their turn to

413

take watch. Instead, Clementine and the others must have decided to let them sleep, because when she finally did wake them up, it was already morning.

"Morning?" Aster echoed groggily, her back stiff from hours of lying on the wooden floor.

Clementine nodded. Her face was scarcely visible in the shadows, but Aster knew it well enough to see the fear there.

"Yes, Dawn, it's—it's . . . it's time," Clementine managed.

Time to surrender themselves to the law, time to abandon their freedom and future. Time to face their Reckoning.

Aster woke Violet gently, and they joined the others. Tansy, with her quick thinking; Mallow, with her toughness; Raven, with her wisdom; Clementine, with her hope—it had all gotten them further than any of them might have ever dreamed, once. It just wasn't far enough.

Aster swallowed back the frightened tears that rose in her throat.

"All right, Luckers," she told them, her voice steady. "Let's go introduce ourselves."

She parted the curtains and led them back onto the stage.

The landmasters jeered at the sight of them.

"DIRTY LUCKERS!"

"YOU SHOULD'VE STAYED IN YOUR PLACE."

"YOU'RE GONNA ROT IN A PRISON CAMP, THEN YOU'RE GONNA ROT IN HELL."

Zee and Derrick, who had been on watch, fell in silently behind the girls as they strode the length of the ballroom floor, Aster's gaze locked on the doors. She would not look at the landmasters, would not listen to their gleeful hate. She had

414

to remain strong for her friends. She owed them that much, after everything they'd done for one another.

When they reached the ballroom doors, two armymen were waiting on the other side to escort them to their commanding officer. They were dustblood boys, not much older than Aster herself, one with pockmarks scarring his face, the other struggling to grow a moustache. Aster's heart grew heavy at the sight of them. She remembered Sid's lesson in history: ever since the War of the Nine, the Arkettan army had swelled its ranks with young dustblood men desperate to pay off their debts. Bought and sold by the landmasters, sent to do their dying for them. What drove these men to be so loyal to a nation that would never love them back?

The same thing that drove Aster to turn herself over to them now.

Desperation.

"Follow me," the pockmarked boy ordered.

He led them outside. It was a cold, golden morning, the sunlight driving Aster to squint after seven days spent inside the capitol building. She shaded her eyes with her hand and looked out over Crimson Glen.

"Ripping hell," Mallow murmured from behind her. It was the first any of them had spoken since they started this gallows walk, and it was the right reaction. If the city had seemed like an explosion in the making before, now it was the aftermath of one. The capitol building's front lawn was packed with Reckoners camped out in tents, some of them tending to the wounded strewn out in bedrolls, others doling out water, others still cleaning their weapons. They'd boarded up the iron fence to protect themselves from the lawmen's bullets, and several Scorpions patrolled up and down the length of it with voltric rifles.

When they saw the girls, their voices rose up in ragged cheers.

"GLORY TO THE RECKONERS!"

"WE'VE BEEN GIVING THEM HELL FOR YOU, ASTER!"

"YOU TELL THEM WE'LL NEVER SURRENDER!"

Aster had been able to maintain her composure in the face of the landmasters' cruelty, but met with such overwhelming love and courage, she finally broke, choking up with tears.

"You were right, Aster," Raven said, her own voice thick. "We have to do this—for them."

Violet took Aster's hand, the warmth and strength of her grip steadying Aster's nerves.

The Reckoners guarding the front gates let them pass with their escorts, and on the other side stood another camp entirely: hundreds of armymen in Arketta gray, stretching down the street in both directions, some on foot, some on horseback, some perched on the rooftops with rifles at their shoulders. At the head of them stood an old armyman with dark brown skin and salt-and-pepper hair. His mouth was a hard line, and, like most of the men here, he had no shadow at his feet. There were four red stripes on his sleeve.

The commanding officer.

The armyman escorts saluted. Aster stood straighter. Her friends circled around her.

"Are you the outlaw known as Aster, former Good Luck Girl of Green Creek, leader of the Reckoners, and fugitive of the state?" the officer asked, his voice low and rumbling.

Aster swallowed and nodded. "A pleasure," she said, and the others identified themselves as well. *Clementine. Violet. Tansy. Mallow. Raven. Derrick. Zee.*

"I've heard a lot about you girls—and boys," the officer said once they finished. "Demanding to close the welcome houses, demanding to end the Reckoning entirely . . . take this lesson from an old armyman: it doesn't matter how hard you try to fight, how clever you think you are, you'll never win a battle if you don't have the numbers. And you, Aster, didn't have the numbers." Aster felt a flash of her old anger at his words, then confusion as the old man slowly smiled, the wrinkles crinkling his face. "But now . . ." he continued, stepping back, to gesture to the men behind him, ". . . now, maybe you do."

Understanding slowly swept over Aster. She looked at her friends. Derrick's brow was furrowed in uncertainty, Tansy's lips parted in sudden realization.

"You mean . . . ?" Clementine started.

You really think a bunch of scared, desperate dustbloods are going to be enough to stop the army? McClennon had asked, cackling.

But thanks to the landmasters' own fear, the army *was* a bunch of scared, desperate dustbloods. They hadn't joined because they believed in the Reckoning. The Reckoning had left them no choice but to join.

Now they were making another choice. Now they would fight for a new Reckoning. And now, at last, the burden of that fight would no longer be Aster's to bear.

Aster's heart swelled warm and bright as the rising sun. The officer turned back to face her.

"Glory to the Reckoning."

EPILOGUE

ONE YEAR LATER

Eli stood outside the house he and Sam had built with their own hands, shading his eyes from the afternoon sun as he watched Derrick's coach ease up the mountain road. Inside the coach, Aster and Violet sat across from Derrick himself, who ran nervous fingers through his ginger hair. When he spoke in front of a crowd as the youngest legislant in Arkettan history, it was with all the confidence of a man who had ventured beyond the Veil and lived to tell the tale. But when it came time for a reunion with old friends, he apparently could not stop shaking like a small dog.

Aster and Violet exchanged a knowing glance.

"This isn't going to be some room full of politicians you have to cozy up to, you know," Violet said with a smirk, her hand resting easy on Aster's knee. "Everyone here has already decided they like you."

"They liked me *before* I joined the transitional government," Derrick groused. "Now we find out whether or not they think I've been doing a good job."

"Bold of you to assume anyone's been thinking of you at all—"

Aster elbowed Violet in the ribs, cutting her off. "Nobody's going to lay all the blame at your feet, Derrick, any more than they'll lay all the credit," Aster promised him. "We all know you're just one of hundreds doing the work."

Which was true—the transitional government had not yet held an election to replace Authoritant Lockley, but dustbloods of all kinds had joined the new courts and congress, from former miners and factory workers to leaders of the Nine to Good Luck Girls who had left the welcome houses behind forever.

Aster, though, was not among this new class, as much as Derrick, and many others, had implored her. Instead, she had accepted Violet's offer, made so long ago, to take her away from all this. They had joined Clementine and the others in their new life in Ferron. And what a life it was turning out to be: a homestead of their own in the slumbering country beyond Steelway, where they could ride into town on fine afternoons to watch Mallow try to coach her helpless batball team or to see Raven's latest selection of sketches at the artists' marketplace. None of them, Aster supposed, were living the lives that were expected of proper women. But there was no wrong way to be a woman. She knew that now.

Aster looked back out the window of the coach. Sam had ambled out to join his brother on the porch, a longneck bottle of root brew in one hand, the other draped on Raven's shoulder. After months of exchanging letters, they were at each others' sides again. Zee soon followed, his little sister balanced on his narrow shoulders. And then, finally, Tansy, Mallow, Raven and

Clementine spilled out of the doorway, their grins splitting their faces as they waved the coach down.

"Hell, are we the last ones to arrive?" Aster asked, a smile ghosting at her own lips.

"Fashionably late," Violet corrected.

Derrick gestured to the driver to stop, then smoothed the front of his shirt one final time before stepping outside and holding the door open for them. Aster stepped out after him, her boots hitting the hot, hardpacked earth, her throat catching at the fine, dry silt in the air, her skin prickling under the whispering mountain wind. It murmured her name, murmured the names of those she loved.

It told her she was home.

Acknowledgements

Every time I finish a writing project I am convinced it was the hardest thing I've ever done, but finishing *The Sisters of Reckoning* was, truly, the hardest thing I've ever done, and this book never would have been completed without the generous love and support of my family, friends, and colleagues.

First of all, I would like to thank the entire Tor Team—I could not ask for a better home for this series. Thank you so much to my editors, Melissa Frain and Ali Fisher, for your constant thoughtfulness and insight and your much-needed encouragement during the ordeal that was 2020, and to Kristin Temple, assistant editor, for keeping the whole machine running so flawlessly. Thank you also to Saraciea Fennell, Lauren Levite, Isa Caban, and Anthony Parisi and the rest of the marketing and publicity team for being the best an author could hope to work with, and for making my debut with *The Good Luck Girls* nothing short of a dream come true. Finally, thanks to Melanie Sanders for your infinite patience as a copyeditor—sorry I used the word "just" 400 times.

The Sisters of Reckoning also owes a great deal to the hard work of my authenticity readers, Jess Wall and Jordan Merica, and the support of my critique partners, Kristina Forest and Maya Motayne. I cannot thank you all enough for the time you spent with this book, and for helping me write the best version of it.

Finally, I'd like to thank Brent Taylor, my wonderful agent, for advocating so tirelessly for this series, and to Lynn Weingarten and Marianna Baer of Dovetail for sponsoring it.

And, to my family: Thank you so, so much for helping me survive such a difficult year and seeing me through to the end of this book. *The Sisters of Reckoning* is about the importance of family—the family we're born to, the family we choose—and I feel incredibly fortunate to call you mine.

Charlotte Nicole Davis

Charlotte Davis is a recent graduate of The New School's Writing for Children MFA program and is currently working as an editorial assistant at Bloomsbury USA Children's Books. She grew up in Kansas City, which was once the Wild West but today is mostly just fro-yo shops. She now lives in a little apartment in Brooklyn.

Charlotte says: 'I didn't want to tell a story about racism, necessarily—there's plenty of that on the news—but a story about a black girl and her sister finding freedom? Young women of all types getting into good trouble? Underdogs coming together to stand up against the rich and powerful? That sounded like exactly what the doctor ordered.'

HOT KEY
BOOKS

Thank you for choosing a Hot Key book.

If you want to know more about our authors and what we publish, you can find us online.

You can start at our website

www.hotkeybooks.com

And you can also find us on:

We hope to see you soon!